A FATHER'S LOVE

FAITH AND FAMILY

Jean DeFreese Moore

ISBN: 978-1-958920-90-9 (Paperback)
       978-1-958920-91-6 (Ebook)

Parenthesis indicate a personalization of the scripture by the character.

Contents

To my granddaughter, Jayde, who inspired the story. Thanks to my Lord and Savior Jesus Christ, who finished the story.

We also have joy with our troubles, because we know that these troubles produce patience. And patience produces character and character produces hope. And this hope will never disappoint us, because God poured out his love to fill our hearts. He gave us his love through the Holy Spirit, whom God has given to us.

—Romans 5:3–5 (NCV)

Chapter 1

The moon rose above the treetops as a man, bundled against the cold, struggled to make it up the steep slope. He was carrying three dead fox and two coons, along with several traps and a rifle. Two old dogs trailed behind. He had a knitted scarf wrapped around his face so only his eyes were exposed to the night air and the cold wind. His left eye drooped just a little, and his fingers were numb where they hung out the holes in the tips of his gloves.

As he rounded an outcropping on the side of the hill, one of the dogs started to bay. Travis turned around to see both dogs on alert. They took off, bounding up the hill beside them. Travis dropped the skins and traps and ran after them.

It wasn't long before the dogs treed. Their baying changed to more frantic barks, snarls, and growls as they jumped on the trunk of the tree, looking up. Travis looked in the direction of the dogs' focus. There sat a cougar on a low limb. The cat was silently watching the dogs while on guard.

Travis never took his eyes from the cat. He reached down and untied the leather strap on his knife's sheath without looking. The gun powder had been in the long rifle for hours, and it was wet out here in the snow. He may have to use his knife on the cat if his gun didn't fire correctly. The cat needed to be killed quickly to protect the dogs and himself.

The cougar changed his stare as Travis moved around another tree to line up his shot. The cat was now looking at Travis, the dogs still barking and jumping. Molly was making it to within inches of the cat. She was an aggressive hunter, Travis's favorite dog, and his ever-present hunting companion.

Travis quickly lined his shot up and fired. The cat jerked off the limb and hit the ground. The dogs were instantly on top of it. The cougar was injured and wasn't able to stand, but it was still thrashing and fighting the dogs. Travis grabbed his hunting knife and pulled one of the dogs off with his free hand while yelling at them both to get off. The cat was still focused on Molly, who remained in the battle. Travis jammed his foot onto the cat's neck, pinning it to the ground. He quickly plunged the knife into the cat's throat just as the cat grabbed at Travis's leg with its big paws. Travis pulled the knife up, and the cat went limp.

The hunter stood up, let out a long breath, and wiped his knife off on the cougar's fur. He sheathed the knife and turned around. Shaking his head, he looked at the dogs and then at the cougar. He had too much to carry already. Picking up his gun, he called the dogs and left the way he had come.

The temperature was still dropping. The house wasn't far; he'd come back for the cat in the morning. Neither the skin nor the meat would go to waste.

*****

Travis was used to being out in the cold, the wind, and the snow. He spent most days out in this weather alone. He liked the solitude. He was happy with only the dogs for company.

He had been raised here in the mountains of Western Virginia where the nearest neighbor was an hour's walk. He knew his parents only a short time and had been raised by his grandparents.

Zebulon and Cora were good people. Zeb worked hard and never failed to provide enough for his family. Cora was a marvel around the small house. She could cook anything and make it taste like a feast. In her younger days, she had worked alongside Zeb clearing the land for farming and helping to build the cabin, then the house. They raised enough on the small farm to keep themselves and the animals going from one year to the next. They would always have a little extra to share with neighbors and even some to put back for hard times. She cared for her family and the animals and still found time to educate the children. They may live alone on this mountain, but they would not be ignorant. She clung to the scripture in Proverbs:

> My son, if you accept my words and store up my commands within you, turning your ear to wisdom and applying your heart to understanding—indeed, if you call out for insight and cry out for understanding, and if you look for it as for silver and search for it as for hidden treasure, then you will understand the fear of the Lord and find the knowledge of God. For the Lord gives wisdom; from his mouth come knowledge and understanding. [1]

Cora made sure her family understood. Her children would know the Lord, and they would be educated, too. They would read. They would talk correctly. Cora wanted her children to talk like the people in the towns where she had lived just before she had married Zeb. If her children ever left the mountain, she didn't want people making fun of them. People had made fun of Zeb, but Cora had fallen in love with him anyway.

There had been others on the mountain that seemed to have no sense at all. That was not going to be Cora's family! She had grown up in the mountains until she reached the age of ten, when her mother died, and her father sent her to live with his sister near Charlottesville. She saw the differences in the people, and she was not going to let her family be looked down upon by anyone!

Cora and Zeb had produced six children in all, but they were gone now. Only two had made it to adulthood. They didn't know where the oldest boy was; he had left years ago. Travis's dad was buried with the three girls who died of the fever the same winter

---

1   Proverbs 2:1–6.

the snow was so heavy, it caused the roof of the barn to collapse. The baby boy was next to them too, along with Travis's mother.

Cora had a way with plants. She could make anything grow, even in the hardest soil. She also knew all the wild herbs, roots, and mosses. She understood the medical uses and the home remedies. She had learned from her aunt.

Cora was the closest thing to a doctor on the entire mountain, and Zeb, well, Zeb knew the Bible from front to back. Cora had taught him how to read after they got married. The Bible had been the only book in the house. He had been so proud when he learned to read. He made it his habit to read every evening after supper. Now they were getting older, and Travis had learned Scripture and doctorin' from them, and he was good at both.

But Cora never taught Travis how to read. Maybe she had just run out of energy by the time he was old enough. Or maybe she just didn't think it was worth the effort. She had worked hard to teach five children, only to see most of them buried. She had silently wondered if her effort had been wasted.

There hadn't been many people around when Travis was growing up, he'd probably met less than fifty people his entire life. Never been around more than twenty at one time, and that was once a month, in good weather, when everyone on the mountain would meet for "church." Few of them understood the Scripture when it was read, and even fewer could read. Zeb would usually read the Scripture at these meetings and then explain what he read, at least the way he understood it.

The circuit preacher had stopped coming years ago, which didn't really matter since he only showed up about three or four times a year. He never came during the winter when the snow was knee-deep on his horse. That only left about six or seven months, and two of those they were cut off from the nearest towns by the spring floods.

The people on the mountain didn't trust outsiders. They would listen to the preacher but weren't friendly. The preacher didn't know if this congregation understood his message or not. Most wouldn't talk to him. Zeb had explained to the parson that he wasn't there on the mountain enough for the people to know if he was telling the truth or not. They wanted to see how he lived. They wanted to know if his actions matched his words. After that, the preacher tried to stay longer each visit so he could get to know some of the people, but usually ended up visiting at Travis's grandparents' house alone. When he stopped coming, the news from the outside stopped coming too.

Chapter 2

One spring after the snow melted and the flooded creeks slowed, Cora's goats got loose. Travis went to look for them. He had tracked them for two full days when he saw Ruth. She was the prettiest thing he had ever laid eyes on. She was small but not frail. Her stunning raven hair was blowing in her face when he first spotted her from across a meadow. She was dressed in a blue-and-yellow plaid dress, not straight with no shape like the mountain women wore but gathered at the waist with enough fabric that it blew in the wind. She was chopping wood beside a small barn.

Charm is deceptive, and beauty is fleeting; but a woman who fears the Lord is to be praised,[2] came to his mind. Papaw had told him when it was time to take a bride, he would know it. He told Travis to make sure she feared the Lord. Did she fear the Lord? Was she like the woman in Proverbs 31? He wanted to know; he wanted to meet her.

It had been three days since Travis left home. This was the farthest he had ever traveled from home alone, and he had no desire to go back now. His grandparents would be worried, but at this point, Travis didn't care. Maybe he could trade some wood-chopping for a meal. He'd try.

Travis announced himself from a distance so he wouldn't startle her. When he did, her father came out of the barn. He was friendly but cautious. Yes, he would exchange a meal for some labor. Travis wanted to impress, so he worked hard while keeping an eye on the girl as she did her chores.

---

2   Proverbs 31:30.

If he could figure out how to stay a while, he would. He'd get to know this beautiful thing. Offering to help her father get ready for planting was a start. Travis worked hard and slept in the barn. The meals were meager, but they satisfied.

Travis still didn't know how he talked her daddy into letting him marry her, but he did. They packed Ruth's few belongings, she said goodbye to her family, and they headed home, back to Travis's grandparents' house.

Zeb had begun to believe Travis was gone. That's the way it happened: someone would leave home and just never come back. But one afternoon, he spotted Travis coming a distance away, with a woman. He watched and waited. The woman had a sack in her hand, and Travis had another one slung over his left shoulder, his rifle over his right. Zeb grinned. He was a little upset that Travis had been gone so long, but he let it go. He was happy to have his grandson back and happy he had found a wife. Nobody had to tell him; he just knew.

When they got close, Zeb yelled at Travis, "Where ya been? Thought ya weren' comin' back. Did ya find ya ga'ma's goats?" He was joking, trying not to fuss at the boy or run to hug him; he didn't know which he wanted to do.

Zeb knew where the goats were. He had found them about a week after they went missing. They were near the creek, grazing on the tender new grass grown after the flood.

Zeb was glad his grandson was back. Zeb loved that boy. He understood that Travis had now taken on the responsibilities of a man, and he would consider him a man from now on. He didn't need to parent him anymore.

Travis had brought Ruth back to Zeb and Cora's house two months after he left. She fit into the small family like she had been there all along. Travis would make up the work he'd missed, and he did it happily with his newfound love by his side. She worked hard too, with a joyful spirit. They were a match in every way.

Ruth enjoyed listening to Travis sing as he worked. It made the long days easier. She'd never met a man so inwardly happy or so gentle.

Travis was fast to pick up new ideas and could quickly figure out the best way to accomplish what he wanted. His mind was sharp, and his spirit was grateful for all he was given. There was no point in fussing about what couldn't be changed. *Do everything without grumbling or arguing, so that you may become blameless and pure, "children of God without fault in a warped and crooked generation."* [3] No matter how many things went wrong, he held his anger in check and kept his words gentle. She had caught a prince, and she knew it.

Travis was barely a hand's width taller than Ruth and had a small frame, but years of hard labor and outdoor life had left him physically strong. His short curly brown hair was cut often. He didn't like it in his face or on his neck. Like most of the other men on the mountain, he wore a beard year-round, but his was short and scraggly. He didn't like it in his way either. Even though he was young, he had a weathered face, and his left eye drooped sometimes, the result of a childhood injury.

Travis and Ruth lived with Zeb and Cora a few months until the children started coming. Stuck in the small house that first winter, Travis began to make plans for their own home. They could continue to live with Zeb and Cora, but Ruth had always dreamed of a place of her own. Travis intended on fulfilling that dream. He picked out a spot and started their cabin the next spring. It was a little over half a mile from Travis's grandparents' home and a little higher on the mountain, pushed up into the rocks. It was far enough away for some privacy but close enough to visit regularly.

It took him all summer to get the one-room cabin ready, and they moved in just before the first snowfall. They cleared land the next summer, and by the time their daughter was two years old, their garden was established, and the barn had been built.

Cora died suddenly during the spring of 1858, the same year Ruth added a second son to the family, and Travis finished the house.

---

3   Philippians 2:14–15a.

Chapter 3

Travis had been out in the cold all day. He ran every trap he had and made several trips back to the house. It had been a fruitful day; the traps had been full. He would have several days' work skinning the animals. When he cured the pelts, and Zeb took them for sale, he would make good money.

Earlier when he passed the Lockwood place, he had seen the oldest boy outside digging through the deep snow, looking for sticks. He had rags tied to his feet and a tattered blanket over his shoulders. The snow and ice were sticking to his feet and pants legs in balls.

Travis knew the Lockwood children had lost their father a few months ago, just after the fall planting. It was a shame too, he was a caring father and a loving husband.

Travis tried to help when he could. He had plowed the garden after the fall harvest. He'd taken them venison a couple of times. He had also shot a turkey a few weeks back and had taken it to them too.

Before the snow fell, he'd taken the eight-year-old boy fishing to make sure he knew how. Recently Travis had taken him ice fishing and taught him how to do it safely. They would go hunting together in the spring, and Travis would teach him to shoot too. Travis would also teach him to trap. The boy would have to be stronger, though, before he could open the traps to set them or to release the animals. The oldest boy was expected to step up and start providing for his mother and younger brothers and sister.

Now as Travis entered his own house, he saw the warm fire waiting for him, and he thought again of the Lockwoods. It was freezing outside; would they be warm tonight?

Supper was ready and being put on the table. Travis took off his coat and hung it on the chair beside the fireplace. It was wet and needed to dry off.

The family ate venison stew Ruth and their daughter, Sarah, had made; their stomachs were full, and the food was warm. There may be cold spots in the house where the chilling air seeped in through the cracks in the walls, but they sat in a room heated by a nice fire. They weren't freezing.

Travis was still thinking of the Lockwoods. "Ruthie, I 'ave ta go back out tanight. I don' think the Lockwoods 'ave any firewood. It's too cold far the little ones. I'm gonna get Papaw's sled an' load some up far 'em."

"Why don't you take 'em a ham or some deer meat? I don't imagine they've had much meat this winter." Ruth injected as she helped him put his coat back on. Travis nodded, his left eye was drooping a little, and he had a crooked smile on his face. She kissed him quickly and turned back to her work.

Travis set out again through the deep snow, with his rifle over his shoulder, heading down the steep trail to his grandfather's place. There was no moon. The gray clouds hung low on the mountain. The trail was black, and the trees left no shadows in the dark. He'd left the dogs at home; it was too cold to bring them out. He heard a wolf howl close by and repositioned the gun under his arm with his fingers near the trigger.

As Travis was about to open the barn door, he had a thought that he should check on his grandfather, so he turned around and walked to the house. The porch had been scraped clean of snow.

He stepped up, stomping the loose snow off his boots. Opening the door, he found his grandfather sitting in front of the fire, working on some leather.

His grandfather turned to look at him. "Hey, boy, what's ya doin' out tanight?"

"Papaw, I'm gonna take the sled over ta the Lockwoods, take 'em some firewood."

"Travis, wait." Travis stood by the door and waited as he watched Zeb put a knot in a strap of leather and stand up.

"'Ere, take these too. I've been workin' on 'em since 'fore da snow fell. I just this minute finished."

He handed Travis four pairs of deer skin moccasins in sizes small enough for children.

"Ever' time I see those Lockwood chil'en, they is barefoot. I don' know if I ever seen shoes on 'em," Zeb said.

Travis took the shoes and said, "Ya need anythin' 'fore I load the sled?"

Zeb shook his head no, then asked, "Want some 'elp?" He was reaching for his coat.

"No, there's no reason far us both ta be out in this cold. Ya stay 'ere an' I'll brin' the sled back 'morrow. I's takin' Ida." Ida was the biggest and strongest of the mules. She was also steady and calm; nothing bothered her. She would be able to pull this distance easily in the dark.

Travis left to go to the barn and hooked the big gray mule up to the sled, threw the moccasins in the corner, and headed up the trail. There was a reason God had prompted Travis to see his grandfather. It was to get the shoes. Travis thought, *God's interestin' that way. He'll get ya where ya need ta be at just the right moment.*

The firewood was taken from a pile Travis had spent the last few months cutting. There would need to be more wood cut for his family before the snow melted. It would be frozen and hard to chop, but he couldn't leave those children and their mother to freeze this winter. It took time to load the sled, and Travis was shivering when he finished.

Travis walked to the smokehouse and returned with a deer loin and a ham and threw them onto the pile. Picking up his rifle again, he grabbed the reins and pulled on the mule to start her moving. "Walk on, Ida, we got work ta do tanight ."

It was blacker in the woods among the trees as Travis made his way up the mountain. The area was quiet except for the snow that crunched under Ida's hooves, and the creaking of the sled and harness were the only sound. If it hadn't been so cold, Travis would have enjoyed this walk. The going was slow; snow was almost two feet high. It took longer to get there than he anticipated because of the deep snow and a few downed trees. Travis was able to move one tree, but he had to go around two others, which took even more time. He yelled as he came near the house, "Hello in ta 'ouse!" A small face poked out the darkened door.

"I brought firewood! Where's ya ma?" Travis stopped just in front of the house. He picked up the meat and slung the shoes against the side of the sled to knock the snow off. He handed the shoes and meat to Mrs. Lockwood when she came to the door.

"What's this?" she asked.

"Just some gifts from ya, neighba's. I'll stack the wood on the porch so's ya can get ta it easy." He carried an armload into the cabin and put it beside the fireplace. It would need to thaw before it could be used in a fire.

A few pieces of wood in the fireplace held red embers but put off almost no heat. It would go out soon. Travis put two pieces of wood at the edge to thaw in the little heat that was given off.

After he unloaded the sled, Travis went inside again. He knew the firewood wouldn't have thawed by now, but he would try to light it anyway. The four kids and their mother stood near, huddled in blankets, watching as Travis worked at the hearth. It took some time but one of the pieces finally caught, sizzling and popping in the process. When it lit, he turned. "I'm a gonna go."

Mrs. Lockwood stopped him. "I don't know what to say. I don't know how to thank you for this." There were tears in her eyes.

One of the little ones stepped forward and stuck a foot out. "Look, I 'ave shoes!"

Travis looked at the children's feet. They all had the moccasins on, and they all seemed to fit. Travis smiled. "Ya keep ya toes in there, keep 'em warm. Ya welcome, Mz. Lockwood. Ya 'ave a good night an' just add a little wood at a time. Don' wan' it meltin' and puttin' out that fire." Travis stepped back out into the cold.

On the way back home, he noticed Ida was nervous. He had to take her muzzle several times and tighten his grip on the reins. Something out there in the trees was scaring her, but they made their way back home without seeing anything. Travis unhooked the sled and put Ida in the barn. Taking a blanket, he knocked the ice and snow off her legs, wiped the snow off her back and neck and then covered her with another blanket.

He turned to close the barn door just as a mountain lion screamed nearby. He looked around and saw nothing but black. He was glad he was home. The cat was closer to the house than it needed to be. Traps would need to be set. If that didn't work quickly, he would have to hunt that cat before it started taking the farm animals.

Ruth had been waiting up for him. She took the rifle and leaned it against the wall, then helped him take his coat off. She wrapped a blanket around him. He took his boots off as he sat near the fire to warm himself. Then she handed him a cup of hot coffee and cuddled on his lap, laying her head on his shoulder. "Glad ya home," she said, and he wrapped his arms around her, careful not to spill what was in his cup.

Chapter 4

Zeb lived by himself now and seemed to have adjusted to being alone. But he was never truly alone. *In my distress I called to the Lord; I called out to my God. From his temple he heard my voice; my cry came to his ears.*[4] God was always there, so Zeb talked to God as he worked.

He kept busy with the animals and the garden in summer and with trapping and leatherwork in winter. Zeb hunted and fished, and he obeyed Scripture. *Make it your ambition to lead a quiet life: you should mind your own business and work with your hands.*[5] He had recited the scripture to his children, and to Travis, when they were growing up and when they got too rowdy. Of course, he was alone now. There was nobody to be rowdy, but Zeb still lived a quiet life, and he talked with God. He spent hours sitting by the fire or on his front porch reading God's Word, listening to God.

He ate supper with his family most nights, and he spent time with his great-grandchildren. He played music, sang and told them stories every day, regardless of the weather. He and Travis would hunt and trap together in winter, but Zeb still took all the skins into town alone, just like he'd done Travis's entire life.

Travis never questioned it. He hadn't been to town since he was a boy, when he'd gone with his pa. He didn't like it in town and didn't care if he ever went back.

Ruth had picked up on Zeb's habit of reading the Bible in the evenings, and Travis eagerly listened. He enjoyed the stories in the Old Testament and could see God talking to the faithful ones,

---

4   2 Samuel 22:7.
5   1 Thessalonians 4:11–12.

punishing the unfaithful, and teaching the Israelites. He loved the New Testament that taught him how to live like Jesus. He'd heard Zeb read it all before, but he enjoyed listening to Ruth as she read. Scripture was just more beautiful when Ruth read it. Ruth tried to get Travis to let her teach him to read, but her husband had said, "No, I want ta listen ta ya."

As Zeb got older and slowed down, Travis often took his place teaching the Bible lessons to their neighbors during their Sunday meetings. He couldn't read the Scripture, but he memorized long passages and could recite them word for word.

The neighbors also started coming to him for help with their injuries and ailments. He knew all of Cora's tricks, and he was easily becoming the most respected man in the area.

April 1860, came and went, and the isolated folks on the mountain knew little about the trouble in the rest of the country. When they did hear about the war that had started between the northern states and the southern states, they weren't really concerned, especially Travis. No one from the outside ever came their way, and the few who did come through didn't stay.

This dispute had nothing to do with the mountain people, they didn't own slaves. They didn't believe in hired help either. You did your own work. If you couldn't do it yourself, it didn't get done. If someone was really in need, their neighbors would provide it. This mountain way reminded Travis of the early Christians who took care of one another. If a need was visible, it would be taken care of. This war wasn't their fight.

As more news of battles filtered onto the mountain, most of the young men in the area left to see what the excitement was about. They didn't come back, and no one expected them to. Once someone left the mountain, they were gone. They were never heard from, never seen again.

No one on the mountain saw any soldiers, at least the first year. The second summer, a few troops moved through, but the mountain, with no roads, was hard to travel with equipment and near impossible with the heavy wagons or dragging a cannon. Large groups stayed to the more easily traveled areas. Then things changed. Travis woke one morning, in late October, to the sound of gunfire in the distance. Not much at first, but as the day wore on, the noise continued—closer—and it seemed more guns were being added. He'd never heard cannon fire, but he imagined that's what the noise he was hearing was. Sound carried far in the mountains. Yelling could also be heard. Travis put his family in the house and stood guard most of the morning and well after lunch.

Late afternoon, the noise stopped. Travis couldn't stand the sudden quiet, and he didn't want anybody sneaking up on them when they weren't ready. He wanted to know what was going on, so he set out in the direction of the gunfire.

A mile or so from the house, he ran into the first survivor of the battle. The soldier was cold and disoriented, so Travis built a fire for the stranger to warm himself.

Then the others started coming, first one, then another. One had a bloody arm, and Travis knew he needed to help the boy. It was getting dark, and the cold would get worse, so Travis made the decision to take them home with him. There were some old blankets and straw in the barn. They would be warmer there than outside in the open.

Travis got the soldiers settled, then went back out into the light snow that was falling to look again. By morning, there were fourteen men and boys in the barn. Some had gray uniforms, and some had blue. Travis took care of their wounds, and Ruth fed them. When she watched Travis with the soldiers, she thought of 1 Peter 3:8, *Be like minded, be sympathetic, love one another, be compassionate and humble.* Yes, that was Travis, agreeable and ready to help anyone in need. He never wanted praise for what he did. He just did it because it was the right thing to do.

Most of the snow had melted. The ground was still too warm for it to accumulate. A few patches could be found in the rocks, but the snow that would stay would come soon.

Two days later, Travis ran into a few more men in gray. After a short conversation, Travis led them to his barn to retrieve their men.

When they left, they took their wounded with them, along with a large portion of the food stores and a couple of the animals. Travis didn't think it was a good idea to argue with them about the food. They would be okay. Travis knew how to hunt, and there were some vegetables in the root cellar the soldiers didn't know about. They could make it through the winter if he could get rid of the rest of the soldiers in blue.

The gray-clad soldiers told Travis that a large contingent of the Union Army was camped somewhere to the east on the other side of the mountain. The Southerners were moving away to regroup.

The troops in his barn seemed to be happy there. They weren't thinking about going anywhere, and with the food the Southern troops had taken, there wouldn't be enough to last the winter if the the injured Northerners stayed.

He couldn't care for his family if he were taking care of the soldiers. Going hunting or fishing was out of the question. He wouldn't leave his wife and children alone with the soldiers. It was almost time to start putting traps out. He wouldn't be able to do that either if the soldiers remained. That would mean no money for supplies next spring.

Travis had had enough of the soldiers, both those from the north and the south. They had to go. He wanted them out of his barn and off his mountain before the snow came and kept them there all winter.

God's words kept running through his mind, *Anyone who does not provide for their relatives, and especially for their own household, he has denied the faith and is worse than an unbeliever.*[6] He'd always provided for his family and intended to continue. So he hooked up the wagon and the mules, loaded the wounded soldiers, kissed his family goodbye, and said a prayer for their safety. Then he headed East toward the ford in the river.

The mules pulled them into the Union camp three days later. Another battle was happening further to the East, and wounded were pouring in as he arrived with his own wagonload.

---

6   1 Timothy 5:8.

There were so many injured soldiers, so many needing help. Travis couldn't stop himself. He knew what to do for a lot of those needing aid, so he started working. He cleaned and bandaged those he could. He was good at this; he had seen all sorts of injuries on the mountain. This was no different. He helped some and left others, assuring himself that someone else would take care of them.

As the number of injured coming into camp began to slow, a soldier on a spirited horse pointed a sword at Travis and ordered him to get back in the field. "You get your carcass back out there. We still have injured to bring in."

Travis didn't know what to do. Scripture had said, *If anyone forces you to go one mile, go with them two miles.*[7] He was willing to help. He got on his wagon and headed for the battlefield.

Minie balls buzzed past him and hit his wagon. Cannon balls exploded around him, but he kept moving, kept loading the injured. The soldiers that were fighting were leaving him alone to do his work. Fighting was all around; the injured, dead, and dying were everywhere, but God was protecting him.

Over and over he drove his mules on the fields of blood and returned with wounded until he could find no more. Then he helped bury the dead.

A few days later, Travis was headed West out of camp when another officer stopped the mules. Grabbing the halter of one of the mules roughly, he yelled at Travis, "Where do you think you are going? Get back there and take care of those men!" Travis tried to explain that he wasn't a soldier, he wasn't a part of this army, but the officer wouldn't listen. He was accused of being a coward and trying to run away. He was threatened with being shot if he left camp, so Travis turned his team around and went back to the hospital tents.

God had told him what to do, but he didn't like it. *Let everyone be subject to the governing authorities, for there is no authority except that which God has established. The authorities that exist have been established by God.*[8] It was the first time in his life that he did not

---

7   Matthew 5:41.
8   Romans 13:1.

want to follow God, but it didn't look like God was giving him a choice.

Over the next several days, Travis tried again and again to get someone to listen, but nobody would. He was called stupid mountain man, ignorant mule skinner, and coward. That was the worst one—coward. One of the first scriptures his grandfather had taught him was, *Be strong and courageous. Do not be afraid or terrified because of them, for the Lord your God goes with you; he will never leave you nor forsake you.*[9] There was no reason to be scared. God was there, and God was with his family too.

When Travis's parents had died, his grandfather had taught him,

> For to me, to live is Christ and to die is gain. If I am to go on living in the body, this will mean fruitful labor for me. Yet what shall I choose? I do not know! I am torn between the two: I desire to depart and be with Christ, which is better by far, but it is more necessary for you that I remain in the body. Convinced of this, I know that I will remain, and I will continue with all of you for your progress and joy in faith, so that through my being with you again your boasting in Christ Jesus will abound on account of me.[10]

Ruth and the children were safe. If Travis died, he would be with his parents and with Jesus, and he would be there, waiting for Ruth when she arrived. Yes, it didn't really matter. Live or die, he would live to care for his family when he got back home, or he would be with Jesus.

Travis was just shy of 5'6" in height, with a small frame, and was strong. But he had a gentle nature. He'd lived his whole life isolated in the mountains and had never asked anything of anyone.

He'd hunted and worked the farm since he'd been old enough to walk. He'd faced wild animals, vicious and deadly. There had been floods and fire, and he had survived. He knew snowstorms

---

9 Deuteronomy 31:6.
10 Philippians 1:21–26.

so heavy he couldn't see through it or move in it. Snow so thick all you could do was hunker down and wait it out. He had confidence in his own independent ability to survive, and he understood dependence on God to care for him and to teach him. He'd never backed away from work or anything else in his entire life.

God had told Travis in scripture, *Whatever you do, work at it with all your heart, as working for the Lord, not for human masters, since you know that you will receive an inheritance from the Lord as a reward. It is the Lord Christ you are serving.*[11] He'd done his share and then some. Neither the bloody battlefield nor the possibility of death scared him. This wasn't where he belonged, but this is where God had put him. He would do his job and do it well, but he still didn't like it.

The troops started moving out a week later, and he was ordered to pack hospital equipment and move with them. He tried once more to get someone to listen. He stopped one of the officers. "Sir, I'm not suppos' ta be 'ere, I'm not a soldier, I never signed up ta—" But he didn't get to finish.

"Dang right you're not a soldier! You're the cowardly scum that cleans the body parts out of the surgery tent! You're the slime that pulls those brave men from the battlefield when they fall! You're the coward, too scared to fight, that buries those that die! Don't let me see your face away from your wagon or away from that hospital tent! Do you understand? If I do…you don't want to know what I'm going to do to you!"

Travis was furious, a feeling he didn't like and didn't understand. *In your anger do not sin,*[12] he thought. Then he told himself, "Calm down, God's got this." Yep, Travis knew God was in control, even in this chaos. *For even if you should suffer for what is right, you are blessed. "Do not fear their threats; do not be frightened."*[13] He didn't know what else to do, so he loaded his wagon and moved with the troops.

---

11 Colossians 3:23–24.
12 Ephesians 4:26a.
13 1 Peter 3:14.

Chapter 5

Back on the mountain, Ruth had continued taking care of her family and the farm. She didn't know what had happened to Travis, but she hoped he was okay and would get back to them. Days were long and lonely, full of hard work taking care of the farm alone. The snow came, and that kept them indoors. Food became scarce without Travis hunting and trapping.

Zeb did manage to bring them a little meat now and then. It kept them going, waiting for spring.

An occasional soldier or two would drift to the house from time to time. Some just wanted a meal; some weren't so nice. Sarah was almost ten now and could manage the single-shot pistol with some difficulty. Her mother taught her how to shoot. The pistol and rifle were kept loaded all the time. Ruth began keeping the rifle close to her as she worked.

As spring neared, just as the winter snow began to soften, three strangers watched the movement at the farm from the trees. Ruth was going in and out of the barn, taking care of the animals while her seven-year-old attempted to chop some half-frozen firewood. The five-year-old stood near, holding the few pieces that were cut. "This will be easy," one of the men said as they crept out of the trees to hide behind the house.

One of the men walked up behind the boys and grabbed little Joseph by the shoulder, causing him to drop his sticks. Joshua yelled, "What a' ya doin'?" as another man grabbed at him. He was yelling for his mama as he swung the ax and caught the man on the shin. But it wasn't a strong swing, and the stranger recovered quickly to de-ax Joshua. Ruth came out of the barn, rifle in hand, only to be grabbed roughly and pulled back into the barn.

Sarah missed it all. She was in the far corner of the root cellar and didn't hear anything until the heavy steps and loud laughter moved over her head. The gun was upstairs. Sarah knew her mother would hear the noise and come to help. She also knew not to show herself, so Sarah moved further back into the small cave that joined the cellar. There she hid.

Time passed slowly in the cave. It sounded like they were destroying the house. Sarah kept telling herself not to be afraid. She prayed for God to take care of her. Pans were hitting the floor. It sounded like the table was overturned. *Where was Mama?* More laughter.

Then Sarah smelled the smoke. She thought at first that whoever was upstairs had stoked the fire, but no, there was too much smoke. The house had to be on fire to get this much smoke in the cellar. She covered her mouth and nose as she began to cough, and Scripture came into her mind, *When you pass through the waters, I will be with you; and when you pass through the rivers, they will not sweep over you. When you walk through the fire, you will not be burned; the flames will not set you ablaze. I am the Lord your God, the Holy One of Israel, your Savior.*[14] Her father had taught her that verse when the creek changed its course during a flood, and she thought it would wash their home away. It hadn't. Now she was sure the fire wouldn't burn where she was either.

The noise had stopped. Too scared to move and too scared not to, she started inching her way slowly out into the open cellar. What was she supposed to do?

Just as she decided she needed to get out and started moving toward the ladder, the fire broke through the floor above her, and things started falling. She ran for the ladder, but it was already aflame at the top. She would never make it.

She started moving back toward the cave, but there was so much falling. She tried to avoid the debris and flames. Halfway

---

14   Isaiah 43:2–3.

across the room, a shelf full of supplies fell on her, knocking her to the floor, trapping her beneath its weight. She struggled to get out but couldn't. More of the floor above her fell as she coughed and put a free arm above her head for protection. Then something struck her in the head, and she knew nothing more.

*****

Zeb saw the smoke when he went for more wood the next morning. He gazed at it with wonder, knowing that was not smoke coming from the chimney. It took a moment for the sight of it to make sense in his mind. He dropped the wood, ran inside for his rifle and coat, and started for the house that held the only family he had left.

When he got to the farm, he could tell that this destruction was yesterday's event. How had this happened, and no one had come for help? The house was gone; just a pile of smoldering logs, and a stone chimney remained. Then he saw the boys lying in the snow next to the woodpile. His heart fell. He ran to them. Joshua lay face down in the snow. Zeb dropped to the ground beside them and rolled him over onto his lap. The life had left him; he was dead.

Zeb didn't have to look twice at Joseph to know he was gone too. He ran his hand over Joseph's head. "Where's ya mama, boy?" he asked, knowing the boy wouldn't answer. He slowly got up and looked around where footprints were trampled into the snow. Slush now, just thick frozen mud and big footprints, too big for the family that lived here.

He moved to the barn, hoping and praying he would find the girls. The barn door was open just a crack, and there were footprints there too. Zeb called Ruth's name, then Sarah's. He opened the barn door and froze. There lay Ruth, her clothes torn, her hair twisted and bloodstained. Zeb knew—he just knew—she was gone too, but he bent down to touch her face softly.

Sarah? *Oh no, not sweet little Sarah!* "Sarah! Sarah!" Zeb started to get frantic now, looking for the last of his family. He had to concentrate and ask God to calm him. He was at a loss for words, so he prayed Scripture, *In the morning, Lord, you hear my voice; in the morning I lay my requests before you and wait expectantly. For you are not a God who is pleased with wickedness; with you, evil people are not welcome.*[15] This wickedness did not please God; this evil would not last! He had hope that he would find Sarah.

He searched every corner of the barn and outside near the chicken house. The outhouse. The smokehouse. Calling her over and over and looking to the trees, searching for her, listening. He fell to his knees in the snow praying—praying like he had never prayed before—for Sarah. He stayed there till his legs went numb from the cold.

Pulling himself up, he headed for the still-smoldering house. He looked from the edge of the house all around. There were a few boards he could move, but some were still too hot and some too big. Two logs near the bottom still had embers glowing in them. He felt weak, helpless. He realized he was shivering. Zeb headed slowly back to his house to get warm. He'd come back later and see if he could dig graves in the half-frozen ground.

Zeb got back to his house and collapsed onto his rocking chair by the fireplace. It still gave off a little heat from the fire he had the night before. He hadn't added any fuel this morning. He stared into the fireplace.

Zeb had taken the loss of his offspring better than Cora; death was a part of life as few children survived in these mountains. Cora's death had been harder to take, and the loss and unknown of what had happened to Travis just seemed to invade his thoughts slowly. But Ruth, Joshua, and Joseph, this was ugly. This wasn't natural. This was wrong! Zeb had never felt so lonely, so helpless, so useless, so weak, and so angry, all at the same time.

He couldn't do anything for them now. Nothing but give them a Christian burial. And although Zeb felt little hope of finding her, he still needed to search for Sarah. "Lord, it's just you and me now," he said, then moved past the table and picked up a

---

15   Psalm 5:3–4.

day-old biscuit but kept walking. On the porch, he grabbed a pick and a shovel and headed to the family's graveyard.

Zeb had just finished digging the third grave, each only about two feet deep. The ground was too hard and rocky, too frozen, and he was a tired old man. He could cover the graves with rocks over time. Zeb laid the shovel down and returned to his grandson's farm.

He stood over the two boys, staring at them, thinking about nothing at all. He was numb. It was getting late. He needed to finish before it got dark. Days were getting longer, but with the low-hanging clouds, it would get dark early tonight. He picked up little Joe and began walking past what remained of the house.

Zeb didn't know why he stopped, but he did. He was looking toward the floor of the house where it had fallen in. It was so quiet, standing there alone in the snow. But as he stood there, he began to listen. A faint sound came from under the house. Was there an animal trapped? He hadn't even thought of the animals. Where were they? He looked around. Three goats—he hadn't seen them in the barn. Hadn't seen the chickens or pigs either. The dogs—the dogs were gone.

Zeb hurried to the graveyard, which was closer to his own house, and lay Joseph gently in the smallest hole before returning to the house.

Board by board, at least the ones he could move, he began to clear a path. Then he saw it, deep, at the bottom on the cellar floor, a small dirty hand sticking motionless out of the rubble. Zeb froze. Tears came to his eyes for the first time. "That's it then," he said to himself. He stood there a long while, staring, then turned to get Joshua.

He finished burying the boys and their mother just after dark. He would come back tomorrow for Sarah. He stood over the graves, trying to think of something to say when God again brought Scripture to his heart, *May the God of hope fill you with all joy and peace as you trust in him, so that you may overflow with hope by the power of the Holy Spirit.*[16]

"God, what are you trying to tell me?" he cried aloud. "Are you telling me to hope? I'm burying my children, shouldn't I be saying, 'For dust you are and to dust you will return?'"[17] He chuckled. "I'm arguing with God!" Zeb stopped and raised his arms toward heaven, speaking loudly, "Oh, make me like Jacob that I may have your blessing!"

The temperature was falling fast. Zeb made his way down the dark trail to his house. He had to start another fire. The embers had gone out. Then he sat on his chair and stared blankly into the flames, waiting for nothing—something—numb to the emptiness around him. The only thing running through his mind was the wreckage and little Sarah's hand at the bottom. He couldn't forget that picture, couldn't get it out of his mind.

"Okay, Lord. I understand." The old man got up and began to put on his coat. He wrapped the knitted scarf that Cora had made around his head, mashed his hat on top, lit a lantern, and headed back out into the cold night. He knew from years of walking with God that when something didn't leave his mind, he needed to physically be wherever his thoughts were. It was God talking to him, and he couldn't let it go unanswered.

At the burned-out house of his grandson's family, Zeb began to move the debris, clearing a path to the center where the floor had fallen through. He worked slowly, carefully in the dark. He was numb from the cold. He had half the strength he once had and little energy left, but he got it done.

By morning, he had found a way into the cellar and was moving the timbers that had fallen on top of Sarah. He would get her out, then dig her grave. He had to use all his strength to move a beam that had fallen on the shelf that was on top of Sarah. When he lifted the end, he thought he heard a grunt. Zeb froze. What was that? He swung the end of the log to the side and let it fall.

---

16 Romans 15:13.
17 Genesis 3:19b.

The shelf didn't weigh as much, but it was bulky; it would be just as hard to move.

He was tired, growing weak. He stopped to rest before moving the shelf and reached out to touch Sarah's hand that was exposed. He ran his fingers across the back of her hand, then into the open upraised palm. The palm closed into a weak fist around his finger.

She moved! Sarah was alive! "Don' worry, child, I got ya!" Zebulon rubbed the hand and then pulled away with more energy.

He lifted the shelf and let it fall backward, moved a few smaller items off Sarah, and then gently rolled her over onto her back. Blood seeped through the scabs of a wound on the side of her head, her face was bloody and scratched, and he thought her arm might be broken. He gently moved her arm on top of her body. As he picked her up, her head fell backward. He looked around in the dim light for a way to get her out. Slowly, slowly he made his way up the pile of fallen and burned logs against the corner where the ladder should have been.

Zeb was a small man, smaller than Travis. He had been strong when he was young, but he was now well into his seventies and had lived a hard life. His body was worn out. Only with God's help could he do this without falling. "Please! Lord, please!" His whispered prayer repeated over and over as he made his way down the slippery trail to his own house, carrying his ten-year-old granddaughter. Every few steps his prayer would change. "Thank you, Lord, thank you." Then it returned to, "Please! Lord, please!"

As he reached the steps, his prayer changed again. "Thank ya far savin' my little girl. Heal 'er. Cora's not 'ere, an' I don' know what ta do."

In the house, he laid Sarah on the bed and added wood to the fire to warm the cold house. Zeb got a pan of water, heated it briefly, and started washing the soot and dirt off Sarah's face and washed the dried blood from around the wounds. He tore bandages and did the best he could to remember how Cora and Travis had closed open wounds and dealt with burns in the past.

But as he looked, he found no burns. Zeb prayed a silent thank you to God.

Sarah lay so quiet. Except for an occasional deep shuddering breath that she took, Zeb wouldn't have known that she was alive.

As he washed her, he prayed, "Lord, 'eal my girl. Take care of 'er. Tell me what ta do." When he finished cleaning her, he felt her arm. If it was broken, the bone was still in place. He could see that it was bruised and swollen. He decided to leave it alone for now.

"It up ta ya now, God," he murmured as he pulled a chair to the side of the bed and opened his Bible. It fell to Isaiah 58:8:

> Then your light will break forth like the dawn, and your healing will quickly appear; then your righteousness will go before you, and the glory of the Lord will be you rear guard.

In the morning, she'll be okay in the morning. God was watching over her. Zeb had his assurance.

Chapter 6

Morning came and went, day after day, and Zeb sat with Sarah and waited for her to wake up. Each day, he prepared soup and had it waiting for her. He had God's promise. He tried to get her to drink some water but had little success. After three days, she began to move a little. After five days, she began to open her eyes. She never said anything, even when Zeb talked to her. Finally early in the morning, a week after that horrible day, she called Zeb by name, "Papaw? Papaw, are ya there?"

Zeb dropped the firewood he was moving with a clatter and went to take her hand. "Yes, child, I'm 'ere."

"Papaw, can ya light a lantern? It's so dark in 'ere."

Zeb moved across the small room to grab the already-lit candle and move it to give off light where Sarah was. "Is that better?" he asked as he took her hand again.

"No, Papaw? I don' see any light." And she drifted back to sleep.

The next time she woke up, she was able to eat a few bites. And over the next couple of weeks, she grew stronger, but her eyes didn't get any better. Zeb read to her, and he worked hard to remind them both that they were to be thankful for what the Lord had given them—Sarah's life. Then while he was reading in Psalm, God spoke to him in chapter 104 verses 33 and 34:

> I will sing to the Lord all my life; I will sing praises to my God as long as I live. May my meditation be pleasing to him, as I rejoice in the Lord.

Yes, they would be glad, they would sing, and they would make music. Sarah would learn too, he would teach her to make music.

Sometimes Sarah would get discouraged, and Zeb tried to come up with ways to brighten her days. He played music, he told stories, and he read the Bible to her. Sometimes he would combine his stories with the music and sing the story.

One night at supper, Sarah started crying. She had had a rough day, and she was wishing her father was with her. Zeb was holding her in his arms as she cried when he started a story.

"Ya know. There was once two frogs that ende' up in a barrel a milk. They got put on a wagon 'eaded ta town. They was kickin' an' kickin' ta keep 'emselves on top so they wouldn' drown. They was gettin' tired. One a the frogs said it just wasn' worth the trouble an' 'e quit kickin' an' sank ta the bottom an' drowne'. Even though 'e was tired, an' it was gettin' 'arder an' 'arder ta kick, the ta'ther frog just kept on kickin'. When the wagon got ta town, an' the man opene' the barrel, 'e saw the frog sittin' there at the top a the barrel with a big smile on 'is face. 'E 'ad kicke' so 'ard an' so long that 'e 'ad made butter. Don' ever give up, girl. Ya never know when the door is gonna open or when ya is gonna reach the top."

Sarah was now smiling. Her eyes were still wet, but she wasn't crying anymore. "I love ya stories, Papaw! Can ya tell me 'nother?"

"Tomorrow, baby. It's time ta go ta sleep."

When the sun came out bright, and the snow was almost gone, Zeb took Sarah out on the porch for some fresh air, but she still saw nothing. Her arm healed quickly and so did her head. She could move around the house without much trouble and even ventured into the yard some. She and Zeb never talked about her lack of sight. They both just accepted it as a part of the hard life lived on the mountain.

As Sarah healed and was able to do more for herself, she became brave and adventurous. Where she lacked insight as to what to do, Zeb came up with ideas.

She helped plant the garden, crawling in the dirt on her hands and knees. Zeb made a rope out of vines and ran one end from the edge of the house to the garden and another one around the edge of the garden. Now she could find the garden and work the vegetables anytime without her grandfather's help. She tended it all summer, then harvested the produce and planted the fall crops. He ran another from the other side of the house to the barn. She was able to care for the animals alone now.

She learned to cook without seeing. She navigated the small farm well, falling often but learning in the process. By the time the ropes weathered and broke, she had learned direction and distance and could manage without assistance.

Every day, she spent hours practicing and mastering the mountain instruments that Zeb had in the house. She could now play the three-stringed dulcimer and the lyre. Zeb was teaching her the fiddle. She began to sing as she played and when she worked. Zeb encouraged her singing. Travis had sung when he was at home, and Zeb missed that. He felt Sarah's singing must be what heaven sounded like, and he looked forward to hearing an angelic choir.

The months passed, and the snow fell again. Zeb read the Bible by firelight in the small house. He and Sarah made music and sang, and they prayed for Travis.

Zeb didn't do much hunting or trapping that winter. The traps had gotten too hard to open, and Zeb had gotten too old to handle the large game. He couldn't take the cold weather like he did when he was younger either. He stayed close to the farm and close to Sarah. He was doing the same thing he had done the previous year, shot just enough small game close to the house for the two of them to survive.

Winter passed, and most of the snow had melted. The days were still cool, but the sun was shining.

Chapter 7

To the southeast, 225 miles, Travis sat against a tree, waiting to find out if the fighting was finally over. There were rumors Confederate General Lee and Union General Grant were meeting. The battle at Petersburg had ended just a few days ago, and there was no talk of moving on. Travis waited like everyone else to find out if this bloody war would end soon.

Travis was tired. Sitting there, staring off in the direction of the mountains, he thought of his beautiful Ruth, the children, and Papaw. It seemed like that's all he thought about, and he wondered when he could go home. He still talked to God, but not as much as he had in the past. Remembering Scripture that he had been taught as a child, Travis knew that *Hope deferred makes the heart sick, but a longing fulfilled is a tree of life.*[18] He was heartsick. He needed that tree of life. He was hopeful, but he had seen so much death and suffering. He wondered if this would be how he would live the rest of his life.

He sat by himself, away from the other soldiers and away from the hospital tents. Travis still didn't like being around these people, even though he had gotten used to them. Most of those he worked with didn't like him, didn't understand that just because Travis was uneducated and came from the mountains, he was still an intelligent man. They treated him like the slaves they said they were liberating. He had a sharp mind, but most saw him as stupid, ignorant.

---

18   Proverbs 13:12.

There was one doctor, though, who saw Travis's potential. This field hospital surgeon would call for Travis sometimes, taking him away from the more manual chores to be with him for surgeries and to care for his more important patients. It caused resentment among some of the other orderlies and even some of the nurses, who also saw Travis as uncultured and simple. They would often retaliate, when he returned, giving him the most dirty and meaningless chores. Travis didn't care, he did what he was told, whatever it was.

He had given up and let people think what they wanted, be it the physician who pushed him to develop more skills or the other orderlies and nurses who resented Travis's gift of healing. There was no sense in wasting energy trying to convince someone of something they didn't want to believe. It didn't matter any way; he didn't want to be friends with most of them. They were lying and dishonest. Mean, short-tempered. Few showed any real compassion for anyone. Few cared what happened to anyone except themselves. And all Travis wanted to do was go home.

Travis heard the celebration from a distance and guessed the reason. "Thank you, Lord," he whispered. There was hope after all.

Within a week, Travis heard that President Lincoln had been shot. When the news came, he was taking care of a blinded soldier. It seemed to upset the soldier, who made a comment about Southerners who wouldn't quit fighting. Travis was afraid the war might start up again. While he didn't care what happened to himself, he still needed to care for his family. He began praying again for peace, but he also prayed for Mr. Lincoln's family and their sadness.

Travis thought, *Where, O death is your victory? Where, O death is your sting?*[19] What good came from this killing? What reason did the man have for doing it? *The righteous perish and no one takes it to heart; the devout are taken away, and no one understands that the righteous are taken away to be spared from evil. Those who walk uprightly enter into peace; they find rest as they lie in death.*[20]

---

19   1 Corinthians 15:55.

20   Isaiah 57:1–2.

Yes, death is sometimes better, but usually not for the people left behind.

*****

Two months later, Travis was permitted to go home. He was discharged, although he had never enlisted, and he was paid accordingly. He had saved almost every cent he had been paid the last year and a half and intended on making improvements to the farm with it. Things that he had seen while traveling with the troops had caught his eye. He marveled at them; tools he never knew existed. Right now, though, all he wanted to do was get home.

Travis had been moved from the field hospital to a hospital in Washington, DC. His wagon had been taken by the army, and his mules were gone. One had died on the battlefield, and the other had gotten sick and died six months ago. He'd seen the steam trains but didn't want to get on one of those noisy dirty beasts, packed with angry and hate-filled people. Trains didn't go close to his home anyway, so he started walking.

Travis was traveling through an area that was sympathetic to the South, and he was wearing a northern uniform. The area had been devastated by the war. He wasn't received well. A few people cussed at him and chased him off, threatening to shoot him. Every few days, he would find someone in a house that was willing to share a little food. Most people he came across were in as much need as he was. Occasionally he found someone in a wagon headed the same way he was who was willing to give him a ride. He was thankful for whatever help he received.

Two weeks after he left Washington, he trudged up another mountain, slowly at first. He was so tired, so hungry. Then as he thought of his cozy home and his beautiful Ruth, he gained some energy. He moved faster still as he recognized the area. He passed his grandfather's house, eyeing it from a distance and continued with excitement to his own farm.

He stopped suddenly when the barn came into view. Something was wrong. It was in such disrepair. Moving cautiously past the outbuildings, he saw the burned-out house. He walked slowly around what remained, quickly glanced into the barn, and took off running for Zeb's place.

As his grandfather's farm came into view again, he started yelling, "Papaw! Ruth!" But he didn't yell more than twice when he caught sight of Sarah standing up from the chair on the porch where she was churning. Sarah was listening. Travis was still running toward her. He changed his goal. He was no longer calling for those unseen; he was calling his beloved daughter. She was closer now. She was looking his way, but she didn't wave; she wasn't coming to him, did she not recognize him?

"Sarah! Sarah!" he called to her again and saw her hands go to her mouth in surprise. She turned as he came up on the porch, and she reached for him. It was the most wonderful hug he had ever known. Oh, how he missed her! He held her, and they both allowed the tears to roll down their faces onto the other. Travis finally asked, "Where's your mother, girl?"

Travis sat silent and stunned as Zeb finished telling him about his family. His daughter sat beside him on the steps, holding his hand in hers, her head resting on his shoulder. Their backs were to Zeb, and he could feel his grandson's suffering. Telling him was like living through it again, all the emotions returning. He and Sarah had not spoken of it once since he found her in the cellar of the destroyed house. She just seemed to know that everyone else was gone. This was the first time she had heard the details.

Zeb stood up, patted Travis on the shoulder, then leaned over and kissed Sarah on top of the head. He returned to his rocking chair and sat, silently praying for his grandson.

When Zeb spoke again, he repeated scripture he had taught Travis when his parents had died, "For to me, 'To live is Christ and to die is gain.' If I am to go on living in the body, this will mean fruitful labor for me. Yet what shall I choose? I do not know! I am torn between the two: I desire to depart and be with Christ, which is better by far, but it is more necessary for you that I remain in the body."[21]

"She's with Cora an' ya folks and' the babies. We will rejoice far Christ cometh an' will make all things new," Zeb said. "Right now, it is necessary that ya stay with Sarah."

As they sat quietly on the porch, the shadows grew long. Zeb got up and patted Sarah on the shoulder as he quietly said, "Come on, baby. Let's get supper ready."

Travis remained alone on the steps. He was feeling the alone too. He felt abandoned. His hope for almost two years had been to get back to Ruth, but she had been gone for a long time. She had not been here waiting for him. His mind wasn't working. He didn't know what to do. Leaving the steps, Travis walked toward the cemetery.

At the graves, he stood, staring at the three newest piles of rocks. He collapsed to his knees, no thoughts in his head, just emptiness. He was weak. He didn't know how long he had been here. Not long, or maybe forever. He was thinking how nice it would be to just lie down and stay there until he saw Ruth. But the sound of his daughter's voice pulled him back to reality.

"Papa? Papa? Where are ya?"

He heard Sarah call for him again. Travis realized it was close to dark, the trees were casting long shadows. He needed to be with Sarah. Pulling himself up, he felt totally defeated. His body felt heavy, like he might drop at any moment. It was hard to move. He walked slowly toward the house. As the porch came into view, he saw Sarah standing at the edge of the porch, her arm wrapped around the corner column. She was in the same spot she had been standing when he first saw her this afternoon as he returned home.

His heart sank further as he thought of what Sarah had been through. He didn't know it was possible to feel this bad. She had endured everything that had happened alone. The attack, the fire, the destruction. Trapped alone in the cellar. Neither he nor her

---

21   Philippians 1:21–24.

mother had been there while she was recovering from her injuries. She was just a little girl, how had she survived?

He started running. As he stepped onto the porch, he grabbed her, wrapping his arms around her and holding her tight, resting his head on top of hers. "I'm so sorry, baby! I didn' mean to leave ya! I was tryin' to protect ya, but I failed."

"Ya home now, Papa, that's all that matters," she replied as she pulled him toward the door.

Travis had been so hungry just this morning, but now he sat at the table as the others ate but ate nothing himself. He remained at the table as the others cleaned up, leaving his plate on the table in front of him.

Zeb took his Bible to the front porch and sat down. Travis still sat at the table, but he could hear his grandfather reading, just like he had done Travis's entire life, like nothing had changed. Travis listened, but he didn't understand the words his grandfather was saying. Sarah came up behind Travis and put her arms around his neck, hugging him, standing there, holding him. He held onto her arms.

It seemed like no time had passed when Zeb told Sarah it was time to get ready for bed.

"Papa, would you come hear my prayers? Would you come lie down with me like you used to when I was little?"

Travis obeyed without hearing. When Sarah was asleep, he got up and went outside to sit on the porch. It was a long night. The longest Travis had ever known. He tried to pray, but no words came. He felt like crying, but there were no tears. He stared into the dark trees, numb, feeling abandoned and defeated.

The next morning, Travis ate a few bites of breakfast, then lay down and stared at the wall until he fell asleep.

It was after dark when he woke up, but he didn't stay up long. He was too tired. He slept most of the next three days, eating little and saying nothing.

Sarah was concerned something was wrong with her father, but her great-grandfather told her that he was okay and to be patient.

The first morning he sat with them at breakfast, he listened to his grandfather pray. When his grandfather was finished Travis added, "My flesh and my heart may fail, but God is the strength of my heart and my portion forever.[22] Blessed are those who mourn, for they will be comforted."[23]

He ate what was put in front of him and slowly walked out the door to begin his work.

Life turned a new normal after that day. The three went about their chores quietly, each knowing their own job and the others' pain. When Travis caught sight of Sarah working, he would stop and watch. She had an amazing spirit, and her skill at performing tasks was truly a blessing from God.

Travis wondered what kind of life she would have and thought of the soldiers who had been injured and blinded. She seemed to be taking her blindness much better than most of them. But it had been well over a year since she was injured. He had seen the injured soldiers as they realized their lack of sight. He was also thinking of what the doctors had said to the soldiers who had been blinded, how they were treated medically, and what he saw some of them being taught. He would figure this out in his head over time. God would tell him what to do to help her.

One thing he knew, God had done this to show his power. Jesus had been asked the question, *"Rabbi who sinned, this man or his parents, that he was born blind?" "Neither this man nor his parents sinned," said Jesus, "but this happened so that the works of God might be displayed in him."* [24]

If there was anything good about what had happened to Sarah, this was it—people would see God through her. But people wouldn't see her or God if they stayed on this mountain.

This sin belonged to another man. Travis would have to figure out a way to forgive him, but he wasn't ready to do that yet. Until he did, he would take his anger out on the woodpile.

---

22   Psalm 73:26.
23   Matthew 5:4.
24   John 9:2b–3.

Chapter 8

Late September 1865, and the weather was cooling off. The summer crops were in, and the fall crops almost ready to harvest. Sarah and Travis were at breakfast alone. Zeb had died quietly in his sleep several weeks earlier, and they had buried him alongside Cora.

"Sarah, get things ready. Tomorrow we're goin' inta town," was all Travis had to say. Sarah, like her mother and her grandmother, never questioned what the men said; she just obeyed. She trusted her father to do what was right and to take care of her. Even if she hadn't trusted her father, she would have still obeyed. One of the Ten Commandments told her, *Honor your father and your mother, so that you may live long in the land the Lord your God is giving you.*[25]

She loved God and didn't want to disappoint him, just like she loved her father and didn't want to disappoint him either.

She was excited too. She'd never been to town. She'd never been anywhere, never met anyone except her family and a few distant neighbors. During the war, she'd stayed hidden when soldiers came to the house. Her mother had told her about Richmond. Ruth had been there only once and had talked to Sarah about one day having adventures in the city. It was time, Sarah thought, to have her adventure.

It took four days to get to Charlestown with Zeb's two-wheel cart and only one old mule. That was all they had left. Travis had loaded the cart with the few furs Zeb had collected the last two years. He had never been to Charlestown, but after being in several

---

25   Exodus 20:12.

cities with the troops, he figured he could handle a town this size. He stopped twice, asking directions to where he could sell the pelts. He didn't get as much as he thought he should for them, but he didn't want to argue with the man. He just wanted to get paid and do what he really came here for—take Sarah to a doctor.

Dr. Brandon Davidson looked at Sarah and asked questions, but before he was finished, he was interrupted by a black man who came looking for some medicine. There was sickness at the camp outside town where the former slaves lived.

The townspeople didn't want to go near the camp. This doctor and just a few others entered the camp and traded with the people who lived there. They weren't wanted here, not because of their race or that they had been slaves but because they were outsiders. These were mountain people living in a mountain town. You didn't ask someone else to do your work for you. You took care of yourself and your own. The government had built the camp and put these people here. The government was providing food for them. They weren't working, this was not the mountain way. But there was no work, and there was nowhere else for these former slaves to go.

When sickness started spreading, only a few people were willing to help them. Travis listened as the doctor and the big man talked. The doctor seemed at a loss as to what to try next, so he gave the man something that would make the sick person sleep and hoped for the best. Travis sympathized with both the big man and the doctor.

It had been the same with Travis and the troops. He knew how the doctor felt, what it was like to have someone in front of you who needed help, and you didn't know what to do for them. He also knew how the slaves felt. Few had wanted him with the soldiers. He had been forced, like the slaves, to do labor no one else would do. He understood, too, how these men felt, unable to care for their families and unwanted by others. Except when the war ended, Travis had somewhere to go. These people didn't.

Before the doctor spoke again Travis asked, "Doc, have they tried the black cumin, flax, neem, or willow? Anise, garlic, or mint?"

"I don't know. I certainly haven't given them any of that. It's not medicine. It won't heal them."

"But the tea will bring the fever down, and eucalyptus will help them breathe easier. I've seen it work, put them in a sweat lodge."

The doctor listened but didn't respond, then returned to Sarah. When he was finished, he told Sarah her blindness was probably permanent. He told Travis about a school in Philadelphia that taught blind people how to deal with their daily needs. They would teach her how to sew, cook, and get to the market. He said that the school was the best place for Sarah.

Travis wasn't listening. He was thinking about the sick. He knew what to do; he couldn't leave these people with no help. Didn't anyone have compassion anymore? Scripture said, *For I was hungry and you gave me something to eat, I was thirsty and you gave me something to drink, I was a stranger and you invited me in, I needed clothes and you clothed me, I was sick and you looked after me, I was in prison and you came to visit me.*[26]

Travis had needed help at the troop's hospital, but no one had cared for him. He knew what it felt like to be abandoned, suffering without help. At the very least, he needed to try.

"Doc, Sarah knows how ta do all them thin's. Can she stay 'ere with ya while I take care a some more business?" Travis asked. "It might be 'morrow when I get back." After a little more discussion, Sarah was taken to the doctor's house and introduced to his wife. Travis had already left.

Travis didn't make it back the next day nor the day after. In fact, it was six days before he returned. In that time, Sarah had found her way around the kitchen and cooked several meals. She had found work to do: weeding the garden behind the house, washing the family's clothes, hanging them to dry, and neatly folding them. The doctor's wife was impressed and so was the doctor.

Sarah had come across an old fiddle in a chest in the room she shared with the little girls, ages four and seven, and had entertained the family and some neighbors the last few nights. Sarah had

---

26   Mathew 25:35–36.

missed having other children around. She had never known what it was like to have someone new to talk to, but she liked it. She also found she enjoyed playing and singing for an audience. She had never known the scorn or rejection of others, so there was no reason to be anxious when she sang.

Travis returned with the big black man he had met in the doctor's office. The man reported to the doctor that his family was better, and so were many who were sick. Travis had come and looked at his family. He'd taken a couple of men with him into the mountains and returned with roots, flowers, leaves, and moss, which he taught some of the women how to use. The men had built a sweat lodge and had put the sickest inside, off and on for several hours. They had given the "medicine" to everyone who would take it, and most of them showed improvement within a day or two. There were a few new cases, but as the people saw that the new medicine was working, everyone was willing to give it to their family members.

The doctor didn't want to believe that this concoction worked. He left with Travis's new friend to go to the camp and see for himself. Travis went to collect his daughter and started home.

Sarah and Travis had been traveling a couple of hours when a rider came up behind them fast. He slowed when he got alongside the cart. The rider looked at Travis walking beside the mule.

"Are ya Travis? Doc Brandon wants ya ta come back ta town. He said he needs ta know more about what ya gave those people. He also said he had something else ta tell Sarah. Are ya Sarah?" the man asked, looking at the girl in the cart.

Travis stopped the cart, thought a minute, then turned the cart around. They headed back to Charlestown.

At the doctor's office, Dr. Brandon Davidson asked all kinds of questions about how Travis learned what to do and how often he had used these plants. He asked about other plants and the sweat lodge and what Travis knew about them. Travis was still wearing the blue uniform. It was the only clothes he had. The doctor asked where Travis had served during the war and learned what Travis had done at the hospitals. Yes, Dr. Davidson had also served in the

Union Army Medical Corp, but he had been stationed at Jefferson Barracks in St. Louis.

Dr. Davidson asked where to find the plants and how to know what they looked like. Travis finally told him he would have to see the plants to know what they looked like. They grew in the mountains.

At supper that night, Dr. Davidson told them about a doctor in Chicago who was working with blindness. He'd had some success with treatments and surgeries. Travis asked Dr. Davidson to contact this doctor in Chicago and find out if he would see Sarah. The next morning, Travis and Sarah left again, headed home. Dr. Brandon had directions to their mountain and said he was going to visit to learn more about the plants.

Two weeks later, the doctor showed up at the farm, just like he said he would.

Travis showed him the dried plants and oils stored in the cellar, left over from when Cora used them. Some were still usable. Then Travis took him out onto the mountain to show him where to find and how to collect the plants. He also showed him some plants that were similar but were poisonous. At the house, he taught the doctor how to dry some, how to make oil from some, how to mix and make the tea and elixir. He also taught the doctor what to use the different plants for and when they were dangerous.

Doc Brandon wrote it all down. He wished he had brought someone to learn with him. He was afraid he wouldn't be able to remember it all. Travis had learned this over a lifetime, but the doctor was trying to learn it in just a few days. No, it would take more than a few days. Doc Brandon began to go back and sketch the plants to better identify them. This would take weeks or maybe months. Travis told him he needed to be gone soon, otherwise once it snowed; he wouldn't be able to get off the mountain.

When the doctor left, Travis gave him everything in the cellar: the oils, dried herbs, and the roots. He and Sarah wouldn't need them anymore. Travis had already begun silently making plans to take Sarah north. He had not heard back from the doctor in

Chicago, but that didn't matter. If there was a chance to help Sarah, they were going.

Chapter 9

The winter was mild that year, and Travis had plenty of opportunity to trap. By spring, he had more pelts than usual. After the spring floods started to recede, Travis loaded everything of value in the cart, closed up the house, turned a few of the animals loose, and tied some to the back of the cart. He loaded the chickens in boxes and put them with the valuables. Then he went to tell Ruth goodbye.

"Ruthie, I won't be talkin' ta ya 'gain till I see ya face-ta-face. God 'as a plan for Sarah, an' we 'ave ta follow it. 'E told me, 'For I know the plans I have for you,' declares the Lord, 'plans to prosper you and not to harm you, plans to give you hope and a future.'[27] I don't know what 'e 'as planned, but whatever plan 'e 'as, it's a good one. She's gonna be fine."

They headed north. When they got to Morgantown, they sold everything they could: chickens, goats, household items, Cora's handmade quilts, and even the tools that had belonged to Zeb. As they continued to move north, the rest of the items were sold. At Pittsburgh, Travis sold Zeb's mule and cart. They ate their first meal in a restaurant, replenished some of their supplies, and bought train tickets to Chicago.

The train ride was long, smelly, and noisy. Sarah clung to her father's arm most of the way. She was wearing a dress Dr. Davidson's wife had given her. It didn't fit right and hadn't been washed since they left home. She also wore a pair of moccasins her father had

---

27   Jeremiah 29:11.

made for her out of deer hide. Her hair was flowing loose and hadn't been brushed in days.

Travis had on Zeb's good shirt, which was too small, and the same pants he had left Washington in. His beard was long and messy. Travis wasn't going to waste money on getting cleaned up just to ride a train. He was saving his money for the doctor.

Sarah heard a few comments about the trash that they were letting on the train, but she didn't realize the comments were about them. Travis did, though. He did his best to avoid people and stay to themselves. He didn't want any trouble.

In Chicago, it took some time to find the hospital where the doctor doing the eye research was located, but the second afternoon, it was found. Walking into the lobby, Travis asked for the doctor. No, he wasn't available. No, the orderly didn't know when he would be able to see Sarah.

On the porch, Travis told Sarah that if it was going to take time to see this doctor, he would need to find a job to support them. They also needed to find a place to stay. He stacked their things in the corner and told Sarah to stay there, on the porch of the hospital, and he would be back to get her before dark.

So there she sat, alone, with nothing to do. City sounds and smells were all around her. She didn't know what these were; she didn't know how to handle them. She was scared sitting there alone. Picking up the sack she carried Zeb's dulcimer in, she took it out and began to play. She thought this might calm her and give her something to do while she waited. When Travis returned three hours later, she was still playing. Patients, nurses, orderlies, and even a few doctors lined the porch, enjoying her music. She knew people were there, but she was unaware of how many or that they were focused on her.

Travis walked up and put his arm around her. She jumped, not expecting him at that moment.

"Let's go, we need ta find a place ta stay the night," he said as he began picking up the sacks in which they carried their few belongings.

"Are you looking for a place to stay?" The question came from a young man who had obviously been a soldier at one time.

"Yeah."

"My sister takes in boarders. You want me to show you where she lives? It's not far."

"That would be good, thanks."

Two blocks to the left and three blocks north, they came to the house. The young man left them at the gate of the white picket fence in front of a large two-story house. He walked away with, "Hope she's got something for you."

Sarah hoped so too. The noises in the city scared her, but she wasn't going to tell her pa that. He had told her too often not to be afraid. He had also taught her scripture early in life that served her now. She had been reciting it to herself all day. *Surely God is my salvation; I will trust and not be afraid.*[28]

And, *The Lord is with me; I will not be afraid.*[29]

No, she was not alone, God was with her. But she sure wished she could feel him or hear his voice.

Travis hoped for a room too and a meal. He knew Sarah was hungry; she hadn't eaten much during the train ride or over the last few days. He didn't think she'd had anything to eat since early this morning when they each had a slice of deer leather from their pack. There wasn't much left. He was hungry too, but he'd make it. He'd been hungry before. His concern was for Sarah.

The lady at the house said she didn't have a room, but after watching Sarah clinging to her father, she did offer them a couple of blankets on the back porch and a meal. As they ate, Travis told the woman that they had been traveling for weeks. He asked if Sarah could get a bath. If they looked more like the city people, maybe it would be easier to get in to see the doctor. Tomorrow Travis would find a bathhouse for himself.

The next morning, Mrs. Weatherford gave them both breakfast. And seeing how much better Sarah looked, told them that she had a room Sarah could sleep in, but just Sarah. She would share with

---

28   Isaiah 12:2a.
29   Psalm 118:6a.

another young lady and didn't need to sleep on the porch anymore. Sarah didn't like sleeping away from her father, but he told her he was still with her, right outside on the porch.

Sarah had on a dress that Travis had bought her in Pittsburgh. It was the only store-bought dress she had ever had. Mrs. Weatherford helped Sarah braid her hair, which made her look even more like the city people.

Travis carried the same three sacks they traveled with. He walked with Sarah to the hospital, and after the orderly looked them over good, the answer came again. No, the doctor could not see her. So she sat on the porch again while Travis looked for work.

After some time, Sarah got out Zeb's old fiddle and began to play. About midday, one of the nurses brought Sarah some bread, cheese, and water. She placed a bowl on the floor at Sarah's feet. Sarah had nothing else to do, so that afternoon, she played some more. As she played, she occasionally heard a noise, like someone dropping something against a pan near her. She heard the noise again, sometimes two or three times close together. She listened but couldn't quite make it out.

Late that afternoon, Travis came to collect his daughter and their meager belongings and walked back to the boarding house. No work today. Everywhere he asked about work, the people looked at him like he was nobody, the same way the troops had looked at him in the beginning. He realized what the people were thinking; some of them even voiced their thoughts, "Dirty ignorant mountain man."

He had a bath that morning, had a haircut, and trimmed his beard, but he wore the same clothes he had been wearing for weeks, the only clothes he had. He also wore a pistol on his hip; he realized that he hadn't seen many wearing a gun in the city. Several people looked at him and the gun and saw outlaw, but he wasn't. He'd always carried a gun. The mountains were dangerous and so was everywhere he went during the war. No, he wouldn't take off his gun.

The third day, they were again told no at the hospital. A nurse came to them on the porch and handed Travis some coins. "Your daughter made this money yesterday playing her fiddle. She left it in the bowl."

Travis looked at it. He couldn't count it, wasn't sure exactly how much it was, but he did know that it was enough to pay for another night at the boarding house. The nurse also told Sarah she could sit in the lobby and asked her if she knew how to play a piano. Sarah said no, but she would like to see it.

The woman took her to the piano against the wall of the lobby, and Sarah sat on the bench. She ran her hands across the keys, the case, and the legs. Travis set the bags near her and told her he would be back. Then he left. Sarah played with the keys on the piano, touching one key at a time and listening to its sound. Every so often, someone would stop and show her something about the piano or play a few chords for her. By midafternoon, she was picking out simple little tunes that she knew, listening for the right sounds. Someone was always in the room listening, and more and more people stopped to watch. But Sarah wasn't listening for the people; she was enthralled with this new instrument.

The next morning, as they entered the hospital, an orderly was waiting for them. A patient upstairs had asked to meet the young woman who had been playing the instruments. He had heard the music over the last few days and had taken great comfort in it.

Upstairs on the second floor, next to the balcony over the front porch, a middle-aged man lay on the last bed next to the window. He introduced himself as Joseph Martin. He was a friendly talkative man. He complimented Sarah on her music and asked where she learned to play. Over the next hour, he learned why Sarah was at the hospital, the problems she was having seeing the doctor, and the trouble Travis was having finding work. Travis was comfortable with him from the start.

Joseph Martin shared with them that he was the head of a large music school and thought Sarah would do well at this school. He asked that Sarah sit with him today while Travis looked for work. Sarah liked the jovial man.

Later that day, he insisted his doctor get the eye specialist to look at Sarah.

That evening, Sarah was examined. She found this doctor friendly and engaging. The doctor found her amazing. To have been blind just over two years and having no training, she was amazingly mobile and able to do more than many who had been sightless their entire life. He discovered a slight hope that she might be able to regain some sight.

Returning Sarah to Joseph, the doctor found Travis sitting there too. He told them what he discovered and explained the therapy would take months—maybe years—to accomplish the most he hoped for. He also told them the cost of the treatment. Travis and Sarah left to return to the boarding house. Travis had no idea how he would pay for this. He still had his severance pay from the army that he hadn't touched yet, but he wasn't making any money either.

A new day came, and Sarah joined Joseph again. This time, when Travis returned, Joseph had been discharged and had taken Sarah with him. The ward nurse gave Travis the address where he could find Sarah. It was well after dark when he finally found the large house in an upscale neighborhood. Travis knocked on the door as the family was sitting down for supper. He was invited to eat with them. Sarah's father still had not found work.

Sarah spent the next few days with the Martins and began her treatment at the hospital. Travis confided in Joseph about their lack of money and told him they wouldn't be in Chicago long unless he found some work.

The following day, Joseph Martin made a proposal.

"Listen, Travis, Sarah needs to be in school. She can't spend all day every day at the hospital alone. Let her stay with us. We have extra room and plenty of food. You go wherever you need to get work. I can give her a scholarship to attend music school." Travis looked perplexed. He wasn't sure what a scholarship was. Joseph saw his confusion.

"What I mean is, I won't charge Sarah any money for going to school. She can work for her school by playing music at parties. I have a lot of rich friends, and I'm sure I can get them to hire her when they need someone. She'll meet people, and they will love her. I'll make sure she learns other things too, like how to read, write, and do arithmetic. I'm not trying to take her away from you. You can visit anytime, come get her anytime. But she is so gifted at music. Please consider giving her this opportunity. I'll make sure she's taken care of, just like she was my own daughter."

Travis thought this was a good man. They had talked. Travis knew he believed and trusted God. The Martins had several children of their own, and all were polite and friendly. Sarah liked them all. It would be a good place for his daughter to live.

Mr. Martin had given them food and provided for Sarah while Travis looked for work. Now Joseph was offering a new life for Sarah, a life that would change her direction, allow her to prosper. He was practicing his faith the way God told people to. *Suppose a brother or a sister is without clothing and daily food. If one of you says to them, 'Go in peace; keep warm and well fed,' but does nothing about their physical needs, what good is it? In the same way, faith by itself, if it is not accompanied by action, is dead.*[30]

He wasn't offering charity either. Joseph hadn't offered to pay the doctor. Travis would still have to do that, and Sarah would work for her schooling. It was only fair. *The one who is unwilling to work will not eat.*[31] Travis and Sarah knew that scripture well. They could maintain their self-respect and not be a burden on anyone.

Travis lay awake all night, thinking about Joseph's offer and praying. This man was doing what God wanted him to do. He was showing his faith through what he did. He'd seen during the time that they had known this man that he could be trusted. This was what needed to be done. He'd made up his mind.

The next morning, he had Sarah pack up her few belongings, and they moved her out of the boarding house. He left Sarah at the Martin's house and went out into the city looking for work. When he came back that evening, he still had not found employment, but he had paid the doctor every cent he had.

Travis also brought Sarah a gift—a small blond puppy. Sarah named him Sam. Then Travis told Sarah he had to leave the city

---

30   James 2:15–17.
31   2 Thessalonians 3:10b.

to find work and that he was leaving her there with the Martins. As she stood with tears rolling down her face, Travis prayed for her, kissed her forehead, told her that he loved her, and left her in God's care. It was the best he could do for her, giving her a different life, a future without him.

As he walked away in the darkness, Travis said a prayer of blessing for the house. He knew from Scripture that *When you host a banquet, invite the poor, the crippled, the lame, and the blind, and you will be blessed. Although they cannot repay you, you will be repaid at the resurrection of the righteous.*[32] Yes, Joseph Martin would be repaid in the hereafter, but Travis wanted that house to be blessed while his daughter was living there too.

---

32   Luke 14:13.

Chapter 10

Travis started walking west out of the city. Two days later, he got a short job driving a team on a farm, tilling the soil after the summer harvest and through the fall planting. He made enough to buy a mule and an old saddle. The mule was named Bessie.

He continued west working when he could, hunting and fishing for food. Snow fell, and he found an isolated trapper's cabin abandoned in the woods. Inside he found a few old traps, so he cleaned them up, repaired what he could, and spent the rest of the winter trapping. That spring, he moved on. He spent the minimum amount of money and saved all he could. He would send it to the doctor in Chicago to make sure Sarah's treatment continued.

He was finding it hard to walk with God right now. He'd lost his wife, both of his sons, and the man who had loved and raised him. His home was gone, and he couldn't be with Sarah.

Travis had forgiven the men who had attacked his family, most days anyway. But he had taken the blame on himself. If he had not taken care of the soldiers, if he had not brought them into his barn, if he had not taken them to the Union camp, things would have been different. He would have been home and could have protected his family. He could have stopped what happened.

Now he felt guilty for what had happened to his family and for abandoning his daughter in Chicago. He knew what was happening now was a part of God's plan to prosper Sarah, but he still felt bad.

Travis kept reminding himself, *And we know that in all things God works for the good of those who love him, who are called according to his purpose.*[33] Travis tried, he really tried. He talked to God but heard no reply. He tried to sing praises but couldn't think of words; he recalled God's words that were hidden in his heart, but he felt no peace.

It was different here in the flatland than it had been in the mountains. The days were uncertain, more uncertain than when he had seen death all around him during the war. On his mountain, he took care of his family and his farm. With the soldiers, he knew what his job was. He knew what to do. Here there was no direction, nothing urgent that needed to be done—except make money, which seemed to be almost impossible to do.

Sarah was busy now with her new life. Everything was new to her: the city, the people, and her loneliness. She had never felt lonely on the mountain, but here with people all around, she was. She went through her days without complaining, just like her father taught her, just like when she was at Zeb's farm. She did what she needed to do, what she was supposed to do, and she prayed for her father.

Sarah learned quickly, though, and began to get accustomed to the city. She began to enjoy parts of her new life, like the music and meeting new people.

The treatments were long and sometimes hard, but she never complained. The doctor was nice to her and told her often to hope for the best and to be patient.

Sam grew and Sarah took him everywhere with her, training him to walk when she walked and sit when she needed him to, and stay where she put him. When she put her arm around him during the night, she thought of her father. Sam would let her know when someone was approaching her and gave her a sense of security, a feeling of protection when she felt vulnerable.

She never heard from Travis, and she didn't expect to. After all, he never learned to read or write.

---

33 Romans 8:28.

Travis continued west and south, then north again. He worked when he could, trapped in season, hunted, and lived off the land. When he made money, he sent it to Chicago.

*****

Two years went by. In Nebraska Territory, Travis came upon an injured man. He had been shot and was in bad shape. He needed the bullet removed. There wasn't a doctor or even a town anywhere near. The man had a federal marshal's badge. Travis knew he had to help the man, so he took out his knife and laid the blade in the fire. Travis had never removed a bullet before, but he had seen it done.

Travis prayed, "Guide my hands, Lord, let my eyes see what I need to see. Protect this man when I make a mistake."

Three days later, Travis helped the marshal onto his horse. The marshal rode a chestnut saddle horse that stood seventeen hands at the withers and what had to be a custom saddle with sheepskin lining. Travis thought it was beautiful, great craftsmanship. Papaw had been skilled. He could have done this. But Travis didn't see any reason to own one.

Travis climbed onto Bess and headed south toward Kansas. The blood loss had made the marshal weak, so they had to move slowly, stopping often. They talked only when they needed to. Travis did what the marshal asked, which wasn't much. The marshal accepted Travis's help without question or comment, grateful for the care he was getting.

Marshal Mark Forester was a big man, well over six feet. He dwarfed Travis. He had sandy-brown hair mixed with some gray and had a few days' stubble on his face. His hair was combed straight back and hung down over his collar in the back. His gun hung low on his hip, the way gunfighters wore their guns. The carved leather on the belt and holster had to be a custom job too.

A few days later, as they skirted the edge of a small lake, the marshal reined in his horse and stopped. When Travis noticed, he made a small circle on Bess and came to a stop beside the marshal.

"What's wrong?"

"Look over there, just below the tree line," Mark whispered. There sat a man low to the ground, tending a small fire. "That's my prisoner, Will Cramer. I was escorting him to the federal prison in Lansing when he got loose. I'd been chasing him for four days when somebody shot me. Keep watch. Someone else might be close by." They moved away from the lake, up the hill, into the forest cover and dismounted. There they sat and watched. It wasn't long before another rider appeared, smaller, carrying a sack which he dropped on the ground beside the fire.

Will opened the sack and stuck in his arm, pulling out a fat chicken. Sound carried far over the lake. "Uuooooo! Would yo' look at dat! Yo' dun good, boy." He wasn't worried about being heard or seen. He thought he had gotten away clean. He thought the marshal would be dead by now, and he would have been if it hadn't been for Travis. Now Travis watched the pair from his hidden lair. He didn't know why this man was headed to prison, didn't know what he'd done, but he knew this was the type of man who had visited his farm so many years ago. And he seethed inside.

"Would there be a reward for this guy?" Travis looked at Mark, who didn't answer. "If we wait till dark, we can sneak over there and put a gun to their heads."

"Maybe," was all the marshal said. So they waited and they watched.

The shadows grew long as the pair waited. Mark had fallen asleep and felt better after he woke up. They shared the last of the jerky.

Travis started to doze when he heard rustling nearby. He jerked around but saw no one in the shadows. Turning back, the marshal was gone. The men across the lake had a nice fire which lit the small clearing where they lay. Then Travis saw movement at the edge of the clearing. It was the marshal. The moon was up and full. Travis must have slept longer than he intended.

There was no way Travis could join Forester before he reached the men. All he could do was lift his rifle and point the sight toward the fire. Forester was able to get next to the smaller man, the gun pointed at his back, when Travis saw the man jump.

Instantly the larger man was on his feet, swinging his gun in the direction of the commotion. But he didn't stay on his feet. A shot rang out across the water, and the man went down. Travis moved his sight toward the other man who gave up easily, without realizing the danger from the other side of the lake.

As the two men moved out of sight, Travis moved away from the water and up the hill. He would meet them somewhere in between. A quarter of a mile took him over a small stream that emptied into the lake. There on the ground sat the marshal against a tree, gun loosely held on his prisoner. If the captured man had had any experience, he would have gotten away easily. Travis took the prisoner as the marshal's hand and gun fell to the leafy ground. Travis tied the prisoner up, helped the marshal back to camp, and then went to salvage what he could from the dead man's campsite and bury the body.

The next morning, as Travis was saddling the horses and Bess, he asked the marshal, "What were ya doin' all by ya'self last night? Ya tryin' ta be a hero?"

Mark appreciated Travis's stepping up and handling the situation the night before. Mark hadn't known Travis's ability. He hadn't wanted to put him in danger, but Travis had handled himself well. There had been no hesitation as to what he had needed to do. Mark liked Travis. He was handy to have around too.

Mark grinned. "What were you worried about? I knew you would back me up. Besides you shot Cramer. There's a reward, you know, dead or alive." Travis smiled back.

Chapter 11

When they rode into Harris, the marshal locked up his prisoner, then collapsed on a cot.

"Doc is three doors down, on the other side," was all he said as he dropped his hat on the floor.

As the doctor looked at the marshal's injuries, he asked, "Mark, who took the bullet out?"

"Travis." Mark pointed toward his desk where Travis sat.

"Well, he did a good job. It's still bleeding, but with all the riding you've done, I'm surprised you're still alive."

Dr. Jessie Cooper looked at Travis, who was leaning back in the office chair with his feet propped up on the desk, a coffee cup in his hand. He looked Travis over long and hard. He didn't look like someone you could trust to clean his nails right, much less clean a wound this well.

His clothes were dirty, faded, and torn in places. They had a few old patches as well. With his feet on the desk, Doc could tell that his left boot had a hole in the sole, and the right one would have a hole before long. They were Union Army boots. Doc had never seen a hat like that, deep in the crown and a wide floppy brim hanging over one eye open and one eye squinting like the sun was in his face. The hat was torn too. The faded band looked like a twisted woman's scarf, frayed on the edges and knotted together so it wouldn't flap in the wind. Travis hadn't shaved in weeks, and it had been even longer since his last bath.

Jessie gathered his things to leave, still talking to Mark.

Travis liked the marshal. He didn't ask questions, and he didn't talk much. He had respected Travis and listened to his advice. He was smart and seemed steadfast and honest. The doctor talked to Mark, but he wasn't talking to Travis. Travis liked that too. He just might stay a while.

*****

Mark was recovering quickly, but he wasn't ready for this particular Saturday night. He had heard that the cowboys were getting more and more rowdy without anyone around to stop their antics. Mark knew he would have to let them know he was back by asserting his authority with them.

He hadn't seen Travis for a couple of days, the man seemed to stay to himself. But the marshal knew Travis was still in town. Mark thought he would find Travis and have him walk with him tonight. Maybe they could get a drink together.

Mark found Travis behind the livery stable with a small fire and a couple of fish. He stood there talking and let Travis finish his meal, then invited him to see the town.

At the Buckskin Saloon, they stood at the bar. The room was full, there wasn't an empty chair in the place. Mark had bought Travis a drink, and Travis held it in his hand. He took a sip, now and then, not really wanting it. Some ranch hands in the corner were getting loud, and Mark was watching them.

"I'm going to have to take care of that before the night's over," he said to Travis. The marshal waited a few minutes and finished his drink as the men got louder and louder. Mark moved in the direction of the disturbance.

Travis watched curiously, he'd seldom been in a bar and was suspicious of any rambunctious activity.

He saw the marshal talking to two cowboys. Mark separated the two and pointed one toward the bar, giving him a shove. The other didn't seem to be able to stand steady. Mark turned around to say something to an older man at the table when the man standing took a swing at Mark. Travis was instantly on alert. Mark had managed to avoid the swing, and the cowboy hit the floor. Mark helped him up. He sat the man on a chair, finished talking with the older man, and turned around, walking back toward Travis.

The drunk jumped up and ran at Mark, knocking him into a table. Mark turned around and grabbed the man's arm, twisting it and forcing the man facedown onto another table.

The man the marshal had pushed toward the bar stood a few feet from Travis. He began to pull his pistol from his holster. Travis saw it from the corner of his eye and used the butt of his rifle to punch the man in the stomach. The man folded, his gun hitting the wood floor, making a racket as it hit and drawing attention from everyone in the room. The room went quiet. Everyone looked at Travis who stood there like nothing had happened.

"Boys!" Mark said loudly, "meet my new deputy."

*****

They were sitting around the table, drinking beer—Marshal Mark Forrester, the gunsmith Jake Monroe, Jeb Mitchem, the owner of Mitchem's Mercantile, and Travis. Travis never bought his own drink. He would just sit down with everyone else and stayed there until someone passed him a mug. If they didn't pass him one, that was okay too. He didn't drink much anyway, never touched the stuff on the mountain, or during the war, and had just learned to stomach it since being here in Harris.

Travis had been here six years and was well known in town and the surrounding area as a hard worker. But Jeb and a few others considered him a mooch. Travis accepted free drinks from others but never bought a round for anyone else or even himself.

Travis worked at the livery stable and slept there many nights. Sometimes he helped out on a few of the smaller farms, especially the ones without men. He worked at the gun shop when he had time and there was extra work. Mostly he served as deputy marshal. He was friendly but talked very little, most of the time, and never seemed to have any money.

Sometimes Travis would start talking, telling a story that made no sense to anyone, or he would get into an argument with the old doctor, Jessie Cooper, about nothing of importance.

Occasionally he would look at people with just one eye open. The other sagged some, making him look a little sinister. Mrs. Mitchem told her husband that Travis's squinting eye made some people uncomfortable, especially the women. Once Dr. Cooper had asked Travis about his eye. Travis joked that he had run into a tree. Doc got frustrated with him and called him clumsy but didn't believe him. Jessie had a short fuse, and he got upset easily. All he wanted was a straight answer.

Dr. Cooper had tried to talk Travis into learning how to read, but Travis had flat refused. When Travis recited Scripture in his head, he heard Ruthie's voice. That was all he had left of her, and he didn't want to mess it up. Travis avoided Jessie after that.

People reported that Travis would talk to himself when no one else was around, like he was talking to another person. Sometimes Travis would disappear for hours and turn up with a silly grin on his face and no explanation. To Mark, Travis seemed to be a happy person, a little quirky perhaps; but to many other people, he was just plain strange.

The conversation was dull when the boy brought the telegram in. He handed it to Travis and stood waiting while Travis stared at the piece of paper. The boy held out his hand.

"Oh, here!" the storekeeper said with frustration as he put a coin in the messenger's hand.

The boy turned with a thanks and walked away.

Then knowing Travis couldn't read, Jeb added with a snicker, "Well, what does it say?"

The gunsmith was a little more understanding. Giving Jeb a scornful look, he took the telegram from Travis and read,

ARRIVING BY TRAIN 11:00 A.M. MONDAY
STOP HOPE TO SEE YOU STOP SARAH

Travis was sitting with the chair turned backward in his typical way, straddling the seat and leaning forward on the back of the chair. His eyes never moved from the table, didn't say anything, then knocked the chair over as he got up and walked from the room without picking it up. It was Thursday. For the next three days, nobody saw Travis. He simply disappeared.

Sunday evening, the gunsmith found Travis leaning on a fence near the stable, staring at an open field, slowly eating some corn bread. Jake liked Travis and considered him a friend. Travis would joke with him, but they never talked seriously about anything except business.

"So who's Sarah? An old girlfriend?" Jake was joking, trying to make conversation with a man he had a hard time talking to.

Travis looked him in the face. "My daughter," he said. Then he walked away. He just wanted to be alone with his thoughts.

Chapter 12

On Monday, those who had been at the table with Travis when he received the telegram and Mrs. Mitchem walked over to the train station. They had been told Travis was there, and, yep, there he sat, on a bench facing the tracks. It was early; heavy clouds hung low over the open land. The sun was hidden from view. It would rain soon. Mark was sure of it.

The train wasn't due for hours. Travis just sat there. Mark decided to join him, so he walked over and sat beside his deputy. For a while, neither of them said anything. Travis didn't realize his friend was there until the marshal finally spoke.

"Travis? You never told me you had a daughter."

Travis turned his head to look at Mark. "No, I didn'."

"Where's she been?"

"Chicago." Travis had turned back and was looking at the tracks again.

"Is that where her mother is?"

"'Er mother's dead."

"Oh. I'm sorry." The marshal was truly sorry. His own wife had died just a few years before, and Travis had been there for him. Mark had no idea Travis had ever been married or had any children. "How long has it been since you've seen Sarah?"

"Long time. Couple a years 'fore I came 'ere. Do I 'ave ta answer any more questions?" Travis asked, looking at his friend again. "I really don' wanna talk right now."

"Just one more. Do I get to meet her?"

"Sure." Travis nodded.

The marshal would respect his wishes, no more questions. Travis had always been a private person. Mark really didn't know anything about his deputy before the time they met. Except that he had served in a Union medical unit during the war. Mark had found that out when he asked where Travis had learned how to remove a bullet.

Travis had been a good friend, a dependable deputy, and he looked like he needed a friend right now. They sat together in silence.

All Travis could think about was Sarah. Was she angry with him for leaving her? How did she find him? Why was she coming here? Would she be so changed by the city they would have nothing in common? What would he say to her? Would she be able to see? Was she still blind? Had the treatment worked? He felt guilty for abandoning her—twice now—and he felt responsible for her mother's and brothers' deaths and Sarah's injury. Travis was ashamed for not seeing his daughter these past eight years. How would she feel about him? He loved her so much! Had he done the right thing leaving her in Chicago? He kept telling himself it had been the right thing to do, but it sure didn't feel like it!

Travis had tried to talk to God about these unsettling feelings, but he had not received peace in his heart. He knew that, *In the same way, the Spirit helps us in our weakness. We do not know what we ought to pray for, but the Spirit himself intercedes for us through wordless groans.*[34] Too many thoughts had run through his head. Travis was relying on the Holy Spirit to pray for him and bring him peace when he welcomed his daughter.

The train was over an hour late. The rain had come and gone, leaving wet slippery boardwalks and puddles in the streets. Clouds still covered the sun, but they were blowing out toward the east.

Travis didn't move when the train came in. Mark, however, decided to give him some space and time alone to reunite with his daughter, so he got up and left. Travis sat on the bench while four men and two women got off. One woman had a child with

---

34   Romans 8:26.

her. Then the conductor got off and sat two suitcases down on the platform and turned, waiting for someone else.

There she was. A beautiful young woman with a large blond dog on a leash. He would know her anywhere; she looked just like her mother. Just over five feet tall with coal-black hair pulled back with strands hanging loose around her face. She wore a tailored ankle length dark-green split riding skirt, brown boots, white tailored blouse, and brown vest trimmed in green and gold with a simple brown wide-brimmed hat on top of that raven hair. Travis thought she was the most beautiful woman he had ever seen.

He got up and walked toward her. "Sarah?" he asked softly.

She turned in his direction with a smile and put her hand out. "Papa?" He gently took her hand, and she pulled herself into his arms and embraced. "I've missed you so much, Papa!"

There was no anger in her voice, no hesitation, nothing that led Travis to think that she felt anything but love for him. He let himself relax a bit and breathed a sigh of relief. A single tear rolled into his whiskers as they embraced.

Mark Forester had joined Jake Monroe and Mr. and Mrs. Mitchem. They had left when it started raining and returned after the rain stopped, when they heard the train whistle in the distance. It was still overcast, and it could rain again. Now they watched from across the alley.

"She's beautiful," Mrs. Mitchem said softly.

Her husband added, "I never would have believed it."

Travis and Sarah both turned as he picked up her bags, placing one under his left arm and taking the other in the same hand. His right arm was taken by Sarah, who was holding on to it tightly. They walked around the corner of the depot and across the alley, stopping in front of the onlookers.

"Sarah, these are my friends, Mz. Mitchem, Marshal Forester, Jake Monroe, an' Jeb Mitchem."

Sarah's whole face was smiling, but she gave a clear "Good morning, nice to meet you." They continued past with Sarah hugging her father's arm, obviously wanting only him, the dog trailing beside her.

They all gave a greeting, but Travis had already guided Sarah past, not waiting for their reply. They walked arm in arm, leaving the four to watch in astonishment.

Mr. Mitchem repeated, "I never would have believed it. Travis has a daughter! And she is beautiful and cultured. How did that happen?"

Travis didn't know what to do or what to say. He was so happy that his daughter was with him, but he didn't know why she was here. Did she plan on staying? Why did she come? How did she find him? He had so many questions, but one thing he wouldn't ask— could she see? He could already tell she couldn't.

They walked on to Mrs. Granger's Boarding House. Travis had arranged for Sarah to stay there while she was in town. He carried her things to her room, set her bags on the floor in front of the window, and just stood there. Sarah turned, never letting go of Travis. She stared at him as if she could see him, but he knew she couldn't. Then she reached up, grabbed his neck, and gave him the biggest hug, the way she used to when she was a child. He closed his eyes, so comfortable in her embrace yet still a little uneasy. She held on to him.

"I want you to know I have loved you always," she began as she whispered in his ear.

*****

The sun was just peeking over the horizon. It was a clear cool morning. The marshal was doing his rounds. This was normally Travis's job, but Mark was doing it while Sarah was here. Across the street stood the boarding house where Sarah was staying. He glanced over and saw Sarah huddled in a blanket on the porch swing, the dog's head lying on her lap. He stopped and looked at her for a minute, wondering why she was there so early.

Mark had seen her with Travis yesterday. They were leaving town on Bess. Sarah was straddling the mule behind her father. She was holding on to him with one arm and holding fishing poles in the other, Travis holding on to a picnic basket.

Mark was glad Sarah had come. He was glad to know that Travis had family. Travis had always been content and happy, but he could never seem to sit still. He always had to be doing something. Mark had seen Travis several times since Sarah had arrived. He just seemed more settled, less restless.

It was obvious to everyone how much Travis loved Sarah. Mark could tell just by the way Travis looked at her and cared for her. His love was returned too. Sarah was always holding onto her father, either hugging his arm or holding his hand. Mark thought they were cute together.

Mark hadn't had a chance to talk with Sarah yet. This was his opportunity to do more than just say hello.

Crossing the street, he headed over to say good morning. As he passed through the swinging gate, it squeaked. Sarah turned and looked at him. He walked up the steps as she said, "Good morning."

"Good morning, Sarah, what are you doing out here in the cold?" He leaned down to scratch the dog's head.

"Waiting on Papa. He said he'd be here early. It's so peaceful and quiet out here, not like in Chicago. Early morning is the only time it's peaceful in Chicago. Even then it's not quiet." She laughed.

"May I join you?" he asked.

"Of course." And Sarah slid over to the side of the porch swing.

"Are you enjoying your visit?" Mark asked as he sat down beside her.

"Yes, I love being with Papa." Laughing again, she continued, "He took me fishing yesterday. I haven't been fishing since I was a little girl. I'm so happy Papa likes it here and that he has so many nice friends. That's something we didn't have in the mountains— friends. We were extremely isolated there."

Mark had just learned something about her and her father. They had lived in mountains. Mark had always suspected this but had never asked, and Travis didn't talk about his past.

This was his opportunity to learn more about Travis. He thought he'd take advantage of it. He could be inquisitive when he wanted to be.

She kept looking at the porch and to the gate. She never once looked at the marshal. He began to wonder, was she shy or looking for her father or was something wrong? She had the blanket around her and up over her head and face some. They couldn't see each other clearly because of the blanket, and she didn't seem to mind.

"Sarah, can I ask you something personal?" She nodded. "Why were you living in Chicago without your father? Why did you leave the mountains?"

She smiled and, for the first time, turned to look at him. He looked into her eyes, and the realization hit him. There was something wrong! His face fell as she spoke.

"He took me there to see an eye specialist to find out if he could help me regain some sight, but Papa couldn't find work in Chicago. So I went to school and lived with some very nice people who took me in, and he left to find work. The doctor was really expensive. I don't know how he managed to pay all these years."

She smiled a sly smile, like she knew something no one else did. It reminded him of Travis and the way he sometimes smiled. "I knew where he was because the doctor knew where the money came from, the town, I mean. All I had to do was ask the telegraph man. He'd been sending the money from Saline. When I contacted the telegraph operator there, he told me the deputy from Harris was sending it. So I knew where Papa was and what he was doing."

The marshal sat stunned as she talked. Two days of seeing her around town with Travis, and he never realized she was blind. Then the blanket fell back, and he saw the tiny scars on the side of her face, unnoticeable unless you were close to her. "What happened to you?" he asked softly.

"Some renegades came to the farm while Papa was away. They killed Mama and my two little brothers and burned the house down. I was in the cellar. I didn't hear them until it was too late."

"That's awful! What did you do?"

"Papa's grandfather found me a few days later. He carried me home and took care of me. He's the one who first taught me music. Then I studied in Chicago. Every time I play, I think of him. He was such a sweet old man. I don't know how he did everything he did, he was so old and frail." And she went quiet. He guessed she was thinking about this man who had meant so much to her.

"Where was your father?"

"He had taken some injured soldiers to the Union camp. They had forced him to stay and work at the hospital. They thought he was part of the field hospital, I guess. Anyway it was the end of the war before he came home. Almost two years. That must have been a shock. After being conscripted into the army during war and having to be around all that death. And then to come home to find it gone and most of his family dead and me like this. Then Papaw died just a few weeks later. I think he was just waiting on Papa to get home before he let go so I wouldn't be alone." She laughed as she spoke again, "Papa doesn't talk about it, does he?"

It was more of a statement than a question. She spoke with such quiet assurance. Mark changed his opinion of her. She wasn't shy at all. He thought she must be very confident of herself to speak so frankly to a total stranger.

She was still talking. "Once he talks to God about something, he's through talking. He just doesn't see any point in rehashing it with anyone else. If there's something really serious he wants to talk to God about, he'll go off by himself. He doesn't come back till it's settled, and he has an answer."

She stopped to take a deep breath, then continued, this time questioning her father's friend. "Is Papa really doing as well as he says? Nobody makes fun of him, do they? Because he can't read or anything?"

"He's well respected around here. He's a hard worker." The marshal knew he was not telling the whole truth. There were those who talked about him behind his back, even some of his friends. While he was likeable, there were unexplained behaviors that bothered some people. He wouldn't try to learn to read, even got sullen when someone suggested it. Travis talked to himself, and he told stories that nobody understood. They just didn't make sense. And he never had any money, even if it was the day after he got paid.

Mark understood now, about the money anyway. He was sending it all to Sarah, doing without himself and bumming drinks, food, and whatever else he needed from anyone who was kind enough to give it to him. He nodded to himself. Yes, he understood Travis better now, and he liked him all the more. All that he had gone through, all he had done for Sarah, and without a word to anyone. There was no anger or animosity in Travis. That was unusual in a man who had been through so much tragedy.

The dog started wagging his tail, and the marshal looked up to see Travis coming down the road.

Chapter 13

Three days after Sarah arrived, they stood on the platform at the train station again. Travis was anxiously quiet, but Sarah talked on and on. As the train pulled in, a tall slender young man in a gray suit stepped off, eyed the gathering of people briefly, then moved straight to Sarah. Thomas Stewart took her left hand, held it between both of his, and kissed her fingertips.

Arrangements were made quickly, and that Sunday afternoon, after the church service, Thomas and Sarah were married. Travis gave his daughter away and stood with his new son-in-law as witness. He also fulfilled Sarah's wish for a wedding present, that he would sing at her wedding.

It was a new song to Travis. Sarah had taught it to him on Friday, and he learned fast. He was always a quick study with songs; it came from years around his musically gifted grandfather. Travis knew that's where Sarah's gift had come from too, from his grandfather and from God.

Travis kept his musical gift to himself; he'd shared it with his family and would keep it that way. He had played the banjo, but it had been destroyed with the house. He hadn't touched one since.

Travis had tried singing at the field hospital, and most of the patients seemed to like it. But there were a few nurses and doctors who called it disruptive. So, Travis sang at night when no one else was around. The few patients who lay awake listening had commented on the peace it brought into their suffering. Since the war ended, he had only sung with Sarah and to his Lord. He knew God liked it. He told him so in Psalm. *Shout for joy to the Lord, all the earth. Worship the Lord with gladness; come before him with joyful songs.*[35]

Quiet snickers could be heard throughout the church as Travis stood to please his daughter. He was wearing the only set of clothes he owned but looked a little cleaner than usual. His hair was cut, his beard trimmed, and he had removed his hat—a rarity. Then his clear strong voice rang out through the small church. There was no music, but he sang right on key.

Sarah heard a few quivers in her father's voice. It was such a slight sound she knew others wouldn't have noticed, but Sarah had a trained ear. She knew it was caused by nervousness, yet it was the same voice she loved from her childhood. The voice that had given her strength and had let her know that she was loved.

Mark listened and smiled. He had been able to finish his conversation with Sarah the morning after it started. He had also spent time with Thomas, who had been staying at the hotel. He learned more about all three of them. He had never thought of Travis as a mystery, but there was so much more to his friend than what showed on the surface.

Hearing this song, and that Sarah had just taught it to him, Mark realized just how sharp Travis's mind was. He also knew Sarah's confidence had been inherited from her father, who was obviously sure of himself too.

When Travis finished, the preacher stood again but waited before speaking. He watched the small group that had stayed to witness the union. Some faces showed astonishment. A few of the gentler women had tears in their eyes. The song had been tender and heartfelt. Not many people at the church were familiar with the song, but it had been sung with such meaning. They wouldn't soon forget it.

The preacher looked at Travis. He was in church almost every Sunday but never stayed around afterward to visit. Now the preacher thought, he would have to get to know Travis better.

---

[35]   Psalm 100:1–2

The preacher began, "Beloved, we are gathered here today to witness the union of these two young people, Thomas Stewart and Sarah Britt. Sarah asked her father to sing as a wedding present because she loved his singing as a child. She asked me to read scripture that reminds her of her father's and mother's relationship. She tells me her mother has been gone for many years, but her father still exemplifies this scripture:

> Love is patient, love is kind. It does not envy, it does not boast, it is not proud. It does not dishonor others, it is not self-seeking, it is not easily angered, it keeps no record of wrongs. Love does not delight in evil but rejoices with the truth. It always protects, always trusts, always hopes, always perseveres. Love never fails.[36]

Sarah hopes that she can live up to the heritage she has been given and that she and Thomas will one day have children who say this of them."

After the brief ceremony, the few who knew Travis well went to Mrs. Granger's, who offered her front porch and lawn for a party to celebrate the marriage. It was a beautiful clear spring day with a slight breeze. They could not have asked for better weather.

Sarah and Thomas shared their plans for their new life together as the others shared sausage, fresh homemade rolls, potato salad, and pound cake.

Thomas had grown up near St. Louis, the son of a minister. He had just received his medical doctor's license. He had done his residency at the hospital where Sarah had received treatment, but they had met at a party where Sarah sang. Thomas would be joining his elderly uncle's practice in Denver and taking over when the man retired in a few years.

Sarah would be teaching music at a new conservatory being built by Mr. Martin. Sarah thought he was forming this school just for her, but she couldn't be sure.

---

36   1 Corinthians 13:4–8.

*****

The next morning, they had breakfast at the hotel. Travis was quietly watching his daughter and new son-in-law. They would be happy together.

Later standing at the railway station, as they saw the train in the distance, Travis called the newly married couple to him. He put his arms around them and pulled them close so that he was between them, and his mouth was near their ears. He then prayed softly so only they, and God, could hear. He prayed for their happiness together, for their health, for their jobs, for their safety, their children, and their walk with God. He prayed their home would be blessed and their marriage happy and filled with love. He prayed that when hardships and trials came, they would trust God and remain strong. He told them to "Seek first God's kingdom and his righteousness, and all these things will be given to you as well."[37]

Then he told them again, just to make sure they understood, to put God first, and everything else would fall into place.

When he was finished, he kissed them both on the cheek and released them just as the train came to a stop. He stood with them a few more minutes, hugged Sarah one last time, slapped Thomas on the shoulder, and turned and walked away. He would remember them being here with him, not leaving him here alone, looking down the track as they left.

Now they were gone, one week after Sarah had come back into his life. Sarah was taken care of now. His job was finished. Sarah's father wasn't sure what to do except go back to his previous life, but he knew things would never be the same.

*****

The days that followed were long and quiet. Travis did his usual job and a few other things the marshal asked of him. He took care

---

37   Matthew 6:33.

of a few horses at the livery stable and went fishing. He also helped Jake at the gun shop and spent an afternoon helping at the Cole farm. But he was unusually quiet, even for Travis, not talking or visiting as he worked. The joking and stories were missing too.

Travis was finally at peace with Sarah's visit. They had enjoyed being with each other, and he had liked Thomas. That funny smile that he and his daughter shared stayed on his face now. He had thought a lot about her since she left. Travis was praying for her and thanking God for their reunion when Jessie saw him.

Dr. Cooper had just gotten back into town after being gone more than a week. He had missed Sarah, Thomas, and the wedding. As he took his buggy to the livery, he saw Travis talking to God. He stopped to watch. There was Travis, walking around doing his work, talking to himself. Dr. Cooper couldn't hear what he was saying, but he looked ridiculous.

Doc shook his head and spoke out loud to no one. "Travis is truly nutty, talking to himself like that. Hasn't got a lick of sense."

Chapter 14

On Thursday, Travis was walking past the mercantile. There was a sudden pop, and something hit him in the side, knocking him from the porch. He fell almost four feet onto the street, hitting the hitching rail as he fell. He lay there a few seconds, trying to catch his breath and grasp what had happened. Then he tried to sit up. Sharp pain grabbed him, and he fell back to the ground. Others rushed to him as he opened his eyes, then closed them again.

When he looked up the next time, the storekeeper was kneeling over him, pressing an apron into his painful side. "Get Doc, go get Doc!" he yelled at others standing nearby and then turned back to look at the man on the ground. "Lie still, Travis, just lie still."

The marshal arrived quickly. He helped Jeb Mitchem get Travis up, and they headed to the doctor's office. Travis grunted and moaned a few times as he stumbled forward. The further they went, the more the men on each side had to hold him up and carry his weight. By the time they reached their destination, Travis was almost unconscious. The office was empty, the doctor nowhere to be found. Mark worked to stop the bleeding. "What happened?" he asked Mitchem.

"We'd left my son in the store alone. I was upstairs. Jon thought he would check out the new pistol I ordered for Burton. He was loading it when...he knows better than to touch those guns! I'm so sorry! I'll go find Doc."

Almost an hour later, they returned together. The doctor got to work, sending Mitchem to get his wife so she could assist him. They had been married forty-five years, and Jessie's wife had helped often with emergencies. He would need her help today.

When Jessie finally came onto the porch to talk to Mark and Jeb, he said, "I think he'll be okay, but the bullet went deep. He's lost a lot of blood. Broke a couple of ribs too. He's in a lot of pain, and it's going to take a while to heal."

Jeb mumbled something about someone paying and walked away. Anger showed on his face. Travis wouldn't be the only one to suffer. Jeb's son would suffer too.

Doc watched Jeb leave, then turned back to Mark, "I don't want to move him right now, but when I change the bandages later, I want you to see something. He's been beaten, Mark, a long time ago. It still looks bad. It hasn't healed right. Did you know about this?"

Concern showed on Mark's face. He shook his head no and replied, "Travis has never said anything."

That night, Mark sat with his friend as he slept. Travis's dark face was now as pale as the fresh sheets he lay on. He seemed to be having trouble breathing, and it worried the marshal. Doc had said the broken ribs and the tight bandages would make it hard for him to breathe. Mark watched as Travis lay so still, struggling for each breath.

For some reason, a conversation he and Travis had some months back came to his mind. Travis had told him not to worry so much and had quoted the Bible, "Do not be anxious about anything, but in every situation, by prayer and petition, with thanksgiving, present your request to God."[38] He couldn't remember the last time he had prayed, but now he spoke a prayer for Travis's healing and thanked God for their friendship. When he finished, he watched Travis sleeping again and was soon dozing himself.

*****

The morning sunlight was coming in the window, filling the room with light.

---

38   Philippians 4:6.

Mark had been awake long enough to make a fresh pot of coffee. He was standing in the doorway, gazing into the street, having his second cup, when he heard Travis stir.

Looking into the room, Mark saw that Travis was awake. Weakly, almost inaudibly, Travis said a few words. Mark barely heard him and didn't understand what he said. He moved closer as he called for the doctor.

"Jessie, Jessie! Come in here! He's awake."

Dr. Cooper was sleeping in the next room, but he came quickly when Mark called.

As soon as Jessie saw his patient, he knew Travis was in trouble. Travis was awake, lying there, struggling for breath, but Jessie could tell he had no strength to continue fighting. Doc asked Mark for assistance, and together they gently helped the deputy sit up. Travis would be able to breathe easier sitting up. Doc knew it hurt to move, but Travis didn't make a sound. Leaning on Mark's strong shoulder, Travis didn't have the strength to help himself sit either. His friend was holding him up. Travis's shirt was off, and Mark could clearly see the ugly scars on his back that the bandages didn't cover. Holding him, Mark could also feel something under the skin.

The marshal watched the doctor as he took this opportunity to look at their friend's scarred back again. Jessie was shaking his head and mumbling to himself as he ran a finger across a nasty scar on Travis's shoulder. Dr. Cooper looked at Mark and said, "This has got to hurt."

Travis was breathing easier now. Sitting up helped. Forester thought he had fallen asleep. He prayed again, silently this time, begging God to ease his friend's pain and to help him breathe.

Mark held Travis there for quite a while. Then Jessie helped lay Travis down again. Travis lay quiet now, no longer making the noise with each breath.

Then the doctor inspected the injured man's left eye. "You know, Mark, Travis may have been telling the truth about running into a tree. There's scarring here, too."

*****

As the days went by, and Travis's strength began to return, he sat on his own more and more. As the pain decreased, Travis needed less help. It was easier to breathe sitting up but also more tiring. The old doctor would help him back and forth from the bed to the chair several times a day.

Travis still avoided talking to Jessie. The doctor asked too many questions and wouldn't leave the subject of reading alone. Jessie needed to mind his own business.

Dr. Cooper never heard a sound out of Travis and thought he was probably the quietest patient he had ever had.

One morning, as Jessie helped Travis to the cushioned chair near the bed, he tried to get Travis to talk.

"What happened to your back?" No reply. "Travis, what happened to your back?"

"I was whipped."

"By who?" No reply. Travis always frustrated the doctor. "Travis! Answer my question!"

"One a the officers...durin' the war."

"Stop making me drag this from you, blast it! Tell me what happened! What were you whipped with? Why were you whipped?"

Travis didn't like to talk about it. It was a part of his past he tried to forget. But it was also a part that he was reminded of almost everyday. He took as deep a breath as he could and let it out in several short spurts, then took another. He hadn't told anyone outside of the few people who had cared for him right after it happened, not even Papaw or Sarah. But he saw no way of avoiding this conversation.

Travis focused on the floor. "Maybe 'e thought I wasn' doin' my job. Maybe 'e thought I was tryin' ta run 'way. I don' know. It was the middle a the night. I went ta get an injured soldier somethin' ta eat, an' 'e caught me 'way from the hospital tents. I'd 'ad trouble with 'im 'fore. I don' know what 'e 'it me with... fence... telegraph cable... some kind a heavy wire."

"Did a doctor take care of you?" Jessie asked.

"No, an orderly bandaged it that night. One a the nurses looked at it a few days later, but she said I didn' need ta bother a doctor with it."

Dr. Cooper was furious! He'd been beaten for no reason! How could staff at a hospital not care for their own people! He felt the anger in every part of his body as it tensed. He wanted to lash out at something, someone, but there was no one to attack. Travis's pain was all that held his tongue. He knew blowing up now wouldn't help either of them. Jessie took a few moments to calm himself. He stared at Travis and then softened his tone, "It hurts, doesn't it?"

Travis closed his eyes, hoping Jessie would take the hint and leave him alone. He didn't want to admit there was pain, hadn't even admitted it to himself. But he would now. He pressed his mouth tightly together and nodded slightly.

Jessie spoke to his friend softly, "When you get stronger, I'll look at it again. There's something under the skin. I'll see if I can get it out. It shouldn't hurt as much when it heals, but whatever is there... it won't let it heal. There's still some drainage going on, maybe infection. When I get it cleaned out, well, that should help too."

Travis nodded again, his eyes still closed. Someone was showing him compassion, someone cared. It had been a long time since he had felt that. Maybe Doc wasn't as callous as he had seemed.

"And, Travis, when did you run into that tree?"

Travis smiled. "When I was little. Scared Mama ta death, couldn' open my eye far almost two years."

Chapter 15

Dr. Cooper had moved Travis to the chair. He was sitting comfortably by the window, watching some chickens peck the ground. Jessie was in the next room reading when a man rushed in, calling for the doctor. He would have to leave, an emergency at a ranch outside town. Dr. Cooper told Travis to stay in the chair until someone could help him back into bed, and he left.

Travis sat alone for the first time in days, maybe weeks. He had lost track of time. He liked being alone. He smiled and began to sing softly. He didn't have the breath or energy to do much. His words were broken, the tune clumsy, a song he was making up as he went. God would hear the beauty, Travis knew that. When he finished, he was breathing hard.

A woman's voice spoke, "That was beautiful, Travis!" He looked toward the door to see Mrs. Cooper.

"How long 'ave ya been standin' there?" He wished he had known she was close. He wasn't happy with her hearing his worship.

"Travis, you are such a wonderful singer." She smiled. "You should be proud of your talent. Why don't you ever sing for people?"

Travis shook his head. "Nope, ain't gonna 'appen."

"Travis, this is something you can be proud of. Show it off!"

"There was once two geese sittin' by a pond. They was talkin'. It was almost winter," Travis began his story slowly.

Oh no, Mrs. Cooper thought to herself. *Here comes one of his stories.* She hadn't been around Travis enough to hear any of his tales, but she had heard the gossip.

Travis was still talking. "They thought they'd fly south. A frog sittin' near 'em 'eard an' said 'e wanted ta go with 'em. The geese said, 'ya can't fly.'

"The frog thought an' thought. Then 'e came up with an idea. The geese could carry a stick between 'em with their claws, an' the frog would 'old on. The geese told 'im 'e wasn' strong enough an' 'is feet were too little ta do that. The frog told 'em 'e would 'old on with 'is mouth. So away they flew, the geese 'olding the stick an' the frog hangin' on between 'em. When they flew over a town, the frog 'eard someone say, 'Look at that frog flyin' between those geese. I wonder who came up with that idea?' The frog said, 'I did.'" And Travis drew the word out long, and his voice faded to nothing with the last sound.

He watched the doctor's wife with that stupid grin on his face.

She knew how much Travis frustrated her husband. Jessie would come home raving about Travis and his stupid stories. This was the first time she had heard one, and she understood her husband's annoyance. She had given him a compliment, and he had responded with this! She stared at him with a sour expression. "What's the point?"

He started laughing. "Pride goes before a fall. Well, ta say it correct, 'Pride goes before destruction, a haughty spirit before a fall.'"[39]

He laughed some more, holding his side. It hurt to laugh.

She thought for a moment and smiled. "Your stories aren't pointless, are they?"

"No, they're not. But if ya don' ask why I told it, I'm not gonna tell ya."

Now she was laughing. "Oh, Travis! I understand now. You're using parables, like Jesus did!"

"Yep," replied Travis with a smile. "'Is disciples 'ad ta ask 'im ta explain 'is stories too."

She gave him a soft hug and said, "Let me go get you a cup of coffee."

---

39   Proverbs 16:18.

When Mrs. Cooper returned, she handed Travis the cup and sat on the edge of his bed. Her face showed some question. "You love God, don't you?"

"Of course I do. 'E takes care a me an' loves me."

"How can you say that after what happened to you? You're suffering, and there's no reason for it! You didn't do anything wrong to deserve this!"

"Ya is wrong." Travis's face was now serious. "I've done plenty a thin's wrong. I've done thin's I'm ashamed a, thin's I wish I could take back. I deserve much worse. There was only one man who ever lived who did nothin' wrong an' 'e volunteered ta suffer an' take my punishment. When I stand before God on Judgment Day, 'e's not gonna see me like this, a dirty sinful man. 'E's gonna see me clean as fresh snow! Jesus will be standin' with me an' 'e's gonna tell 'is Father I'm the one 'e died far. 'E took my punishment so my debt is paid, I can get in ta 'eaven."

"But, Travis, if he's taking care of you, why did this happen to you?"

"'Cause a sin."

He said it so simply. She thought it couldn't possibly be that easy.

He saw her confusion and continued, "'He causes his sun to rise on the evil and the good, and sends rain on the righteous and the unrighteous.'[40] Good men and bad men suffer the same. Jon did something his father told 'im not ta do. 'E should have been punished far that, not far shootin' me. That was an accident, the result of 'is sin. The sin was disobeyin' 'is father."

She was still looking at him a little confused. "You are an amazing man, Travis, you make it sound so simple."

"It is simple, Jon sinned, an' I forgave 'im. I sinned, an' God forgave me. Johnny's father punished 'im. Jesus took my punishment. I was the one who disobeyed my 'eavenly Father, Jesus did nothin' wrong. But 'e suffered an' died instead a me. God forgave me 'cause Jesus took my punishment, all 'cause 'e wanted to 'elp me. 'E wanted

---

40   Matthew 5:45b.

me ta be with God. Anyone can 'ave that. They just 'ave ta believe that God will forgive 'em, 'ave faith in Jesus ta save them from the punishment they deserve. 'For God so loved the world that he gave his one and only Son, that whoever believes in him will not perish but have everlasting life.'[41] After ya accept 'is forgiveness, 'e takes care a ever'thin' else. All ya 'ave ta do is follow 'im, do what 'e wants."

"But we can't do everything God wants!" Mrs. Cooper said.

Travis replied, "That's why Jesus died an' rose from the dead. We can't possibly do ever'thin' right. So Jesus took the punishment far what we do wrong. Then God brought 'im back ta life so 'e could 'elp us understand."

"Understand what?" she asked.

"What ta do, how ta live, that we is forgiven if we ask, that we'll go ta live with 'im. Death ain't the end, it's a new beginnin' if ya know Him. Jesus said, 'My Father's house has many rooms; if that were not so, would I have told you that I am going there to prepare a place for you? And if I go and prepare a place for you, I will come back and take you to be with me that you also may be where I am.'[42] Jesus is alive, an' 'e 'as a place saved far me!

"How can you love somebody that you can't see?" she asked.

"I love Sarah, an' I ain't seen 'er far years. I'll probably never see 'er 'gain, but I still love 'er. I still love my father, an' 'e's been gone since I was little. I've never seen my 'eavenly Father, but I will one day. I love 'im too. An' 'e loves me so much 'e made me 'is child. 'The Spirit you received does not make you slaves, so that you live in fear again; rather, the Spirit you received brought about your adoption to sonship. And by him we cry, "Abba, Father." The Spirit himself testifies with our spirit that we are God's children. Now if we are children, then we are heirs—heirs of God and co-heirs with Christ, if indeed we share in his sufferings in order that we may also share in his glory.'[43] That spirit that 'e sent ta live in my 'eart 'elps me do what God wants. It 'elps me 'ear God talkin'.

---

41   John 3:16.
42   John 14:2–3.
43   Romans 8:15–17.

God adopted me, I'm 'is son, and my Father loves me. I'll take the sufferin''e sends, an' I'll look forward ta 'is glory that I'll see later."

Mrs. Cooper could tell Travis was getting tired. His speech was slowing, and his breathing was faster. His eyes were not as bright as when she had come in. She'd let him rest and revisit this conversation at a later time.

She would need to think about what he said. Mrs. Cooper thought she had understood. She had listened to the preacher and thought she believed. But now, the doctor's wife saw forgiveness lived out in Travis. She hoped she would have a chance to visit with him again soon.

"I'll let you finish your coffee while I go find someone to help you back into bed. You are an amazing man, Travis."

"No, Mz. Cooper, I 'ave an amazin' God!"

Chapter 16

"I'm going to let you sit here by yourself, but I want you to remember if you do too much, it's going to set you back. The pain's going to return." Doc kept scolding Travis. He thought Travis was trying to do too much too fast. Jessie would let him sit on the front porch if he sat still, no moving around.

The street was busy, people going about their everyday chores. Wagons rolled down the street, kicking up dust, and some of the cowboys who came through stirred up larger dust clouds when they refused to slow the horses down to a walk. It looked like it might rain later in the day; that would help with the dust.

Dr. Cooper saw his wife coming and waited for her beside his patient. Mrs. Cooper normally had a bit of a grumpy disposition, but she had seemed more satisfied lately. That made Jessie happy. When she stepped onto the porch, she happily said, "Good morning," just before she reached down and gave Travis a peck on the forehead. He smiled his crooked smile, and Doc wondered what those two had been up to. Mrs. Cooper took her husband by the arm as she led him into the clinic, telling him what she was going to bring them for lunch.

The marshal was headed to his office when he spotted Travis sitting alone on the porch of the doctor's clinic. The marshal hadn't been by to check on his deputy in quite a while. He walked over to talk.

Mark's prayer for Travis several weeks earlier had made an impact on him. He had gotten his wife's Bible out of the drawer and started reading it. Mark had been going to church on Sundays because his wife had wanted him to, but now he was actually listening to the preacher. There had been a change in his life. Mark Forester was at peace.

Mark was standing on the ground, leaning on the banister. His arms were folded across each other on the top rail, and his chin was resting on his arms. He heard someone yell Travis's name behind him. Travis smiled. Mark turned around to see the widow of Angus Cole and her three young ones coming toward them. Little Luke was running ahead, arms out, headed for Travis, yelling his name, "Trabis! Trabis!"

Mark tried to maneuver around some bushes to intercept but missed as Luke ran past him and up the steps, flinging himself at Travis. Travis caught him with a grunt. Travis held onto five-year-old Luke tightly, but Mark could see on his face that he was uncomfortable. Brenda Cole came running to pull her youngest off.

"I'm so sorry. I had no idea he would do that."

"That's okay," Travis said, but his smile was gone, and he was trying to catch his breath.

"They just wanted to say hi. They've missed you, I'm so sorry. Are you okay?"

"Yeah, I will be in a minute. Come 'ere, kids." Keeping the rocking chair arm between them, he gave each of the children a brief squeeze and kiss on the head. His face showed strain, but he spoke gently to each child. Then he said, "I'll see y'all back at the farm in a couple a weeks. Okay?"

The girl, who the marshal thought to be about eight or nine, asked Travis, "Did you get hurt bad?"

Travis spoke tenderly, "Yes, I did. But I'm gettin' better. Go on with ya mama now." He looked at Brenda, his eyes pleading for her to remove the children. She mouthed the words *I'm sorry* to him again so the children couldn't hear this time. She gathered her chicks, pushing them toward the street. Mark watched them curiously. Travis's eyes were now telling her it was okay, and he gave her a nod. Brenda Cole smiled, and Travis smiled back.

Mark smiled too. He could read this unspoken communication easily. Was there love here?

Doc came out to see what the noise was, but it was all over. He got there in time to hear Mark ask Travis if he was okay.

"What happened?" Dr. Cooper growled before Travis could answer Mark.

Travis was still watching Brenda and her children move away down the street. "Nothin', I just 'ad some visitors." Jessie looked in the direction of Travis's gaze and saw the Coles.

"You don't need to be around little children right now, Travis!" He gnarled.

Scripture ran through Travis's head most of the time, he recited a verse without thinking about who was around to hear. "Let the little children come to me, and do not hinder them, for the kingdom of God belongs to such as these. Truly I tell you, anyone who will not receive the kingdom of God like a little child will never enter it."[44] He kept his eyes on the children and their mother.

Doc looked at him like he was nuts, but Mrs. Cooper stepped in front of her husband and came to Travis. She spoke for everyone to hear. "It's so simple a child can understand!" She cupped his cheek with the palm of her hand and smiled at him. Then she winked, turned, and kissed her husband, then walked down the steps and out into the street.

Doc stood there confused for a minute. Then he asked, "Mark, do you know what's going on?"

Mark nodded his head and smiled but left without explaining anything to Jessie.

*****

The next week, Travis lay on the doctor's table again. His ribs had healed, but it still hurt to breathe deeply or when he moved too fast or too much. He couldn't remember what it was like without the pain in his back. It had been what, ten or twelve years since he'd been beaten. He couldn't remember. That was another life, another time.

---

44   Mark 10:14b-15.

Doc was talking about nothing, looking at Travis's back and getting his instruments ready. He pulled a towel out and spread it across Travis as he was saying, "You know, you really should have told me about this years ago. I could have done something then, and you wouldn't have been in all this pain."

Travis rolled his eyes. "Doc, will ya just shut up an' cut."

Jessie huffed, put the knife to Travis's skin and said, "Here goes." He made the first incision. Travis gripped the sides of the table, closed his eyes, and gritted his teeth hard.

*****

Three days later, Jessie and Mark walked Travis to Mrs. Granger's Boarding House. It had been almost six weeks since he'd been shot, and he now looked and felt more like himself.

Travis had regained most of his strength; however, he still got tired easily and slept more than usual. The bandages on his back didn't need to be changed as often as before. The wounds had scabbed over nicely. The bandage around his ribs had come off and Travis could now see the scar left by the bullet and the fading purple bruising at his ribs. Travis was breathing a little heavy after the long walk, but as long as he didn't do too much, he would be okay.

Jessie was giving him instructions on what he was and was not allowed to do. Travis nodded his head every so often, but he wasn't paying much attention. Jessie worried too much.

Travis would stay in the same room Sarah had stayed in at the boarding house until he was back to his old self. He was ready to do something. He was bored and tired of just lying around.

As soon as his friends left him alone, he would sneak off and go fishing. The creek wasn't far. He could take it slow getting there, fish, take a nap, and walk back before dark. He had to go past the livery stable to get there. He would pick up his pole then.

Chapter 17

Mark watched Travis from a distance as he left the livery stable on Bess. This was not the first time. Doc had told him to stay off "that mule" for now, but Mark knew Travis had ridden a few times during the last week.

Travis was making his rounds of the farms he had frequented before. There was really no distance to it. They were all near town. Travis would stop at each to talk and rest. He usually made it to a farm near suppertime. In the past, he'd also gone early in the morning and shared breakfast. He hadn't started doing farmwork yet, but Jon Mitchem was helping. When Travis was ready, he would ease his way back into plowing. Jon could ease his way out.

Travis seemed to have a bond with three farmers. His relationship with the older couple was friendly and helpful, and they appreciated his company as much as they did his doing some of the harder chores. They showed their thanks with food and treated Travis like he was their own grandson. Mrs. Smith had made him a new coat and given it to him at Christmas two years ago.

Mr. and Mrs. Smith had visited Travis every Sunday after church while he was laid up at Doc Cooper's. Mark had walked in once while they were there and had seen them praying for him.

Brenda Cole appreciated whatever he did, including playing with the children. The children needed a man around, sometimes more than she did. It was good for the boys to be around him, to learn from him. He enjoyed the Cole children. He had watched them grow up. The boys were now five and eight, and they had an older sister, nine.

Travis had known the family for years. He and Angus had become friends just after Travis arrived in town, but the children's father had died four years ago. Travis had been at the farm helping with the harvest when his friend was involved in an accident. Travis had tried to save him. He had remained calm and focused throughout the entire ordeal, first trying to help his friend, then supporting the family immediately afterward and in the days that followed. He still had a good relationship with the family. Travis had assured Mark there was no love interest with Brenda, but Mark wasn't convinced.

Mrs. Nelson was alone except for an elderly man who worked for her. Travis wasn't needed there as much, but he checked on them regularly. He helped when he saw a need.

After the shooting, Mrs. Nelson had asked everyone she saw how Travis was doing. Jessie had assured her several times that he was making progress. Mark had told her repeatedly that Travis would be okay. Mrs. Mitchem had gone on and on about what a good man Travis was. Mrs. Nelson told the storekeeper's wife that she had known that for years. Travis had always been a good man. Mrs. Mitchem had just needed to open her eyes to see it.

Both the widows, the old couple, and the other small farmers appreciated that Travis kept an eye on them and on their farms. It made them feel important to the town.

Travis would help when he saw trouble coming between the farmers and the local ranchers. Most of the trouble was caused by ranch hands that looked down on the farmers. The ranch owners, managers, and foremen all knew and respected Travis. They had learned through experience that Travis was honest. The marshal's deputy would search out and tell the truth. When Travis intervened in a dispute, it would usually result in a positive outcome for the farmers.

Occasionally he'd run off some drifter that was hanging around or who had set up a squatters' camp on the farmer's land. All the farmers had fed Travis at some point, and none of them felt like he took more than he had earned.

Mrs. Cole and Mrs. Nelson had also offered some of their husband's clothes when they noticed his were getting worn. Travis's relationship with the farmers worked out well for everybody. Travis got free meals and an occasional shirt; the people he helped got a strong man who knew his way around farmwork.

Travis could hear Ruthie's voice reading, "Religion that God our Father accepts as pure and faultless is this; to look after orphans and widows in their distress and to keep oneself from being polluted by the world."[45] That's what he was doing, taking care of the widows, the fatherless, and the elderly. Travis liked the work on the farms, and he enjoyed helping where he could. He hoped he was keeping himself from being polluted but wasn't exactly sure what that was.

Travis had walked the early morning and evening rounds with the marshal for almost two weeks now. He was moving around and enjoying freedom from pain. Well, almost. There was still a twinge at his side, and his shoulder still pulled quite a bit where the doctor had to dig deep to fix his old injury. But they were both getting better.

Travis was ready to get back to work. He had already helped Jake at the gun shop. The deputy had also sat at the jail a couple of times after Mark had locked up some rowdy drunks. Mark had stayed at the jail at night and until Travis had gotten there the next morning. Travis just had to sit in the office and wait for the sleeping cowboys to wake up sober. When the cowhands were awake and calm, Travis would let them out.

Mark was looking forward to the help his deputy would give when he returned. This was a job that required physical and mental strength and long hours. Daily they had to deal with the ranch hands that came into town. These cowboys always got drunk. They had to be handled in a way that kept fistfights and gunplay to a minimum.

---

45   James 1:27.

Mark knew Travis could handle the psychological play that went on, but he wanted to make sure Travis was physically ready, just in case there was trouble.

Mark didn't worry about Travis using his gun. The deputy didn't use his weapon very often, but when he did, he seldom missed.

Nobody would ever call him fast, but Travis held his own.

The deputy usually carried his rifle in the evenings but was fairly accurate with his pistol when he needed to use it. It never rattled Travis either when someone else drew a gun on him. He just didn't seem to be shaken.

If the deputy was close enough, he'd use the butt of his rifle to knock a gun out of a cowboy's hand as fast as the cowboy could get the gun from his holster. They usually couldn't use that hand for several days afterward. No one talked about this. It was embarrassing to the cowboys to be beaten by the stupid little mountain man.

All the ranch foremen had warned their men about messing with either of the lawmen in town, but there were always a few that had to learn on their own.

The marshal had asked his deputy if he was up to riding over to Summersville with him, just to keep him company. Mark pretended to adjust his saddle, but he was really watching Travis mount Bess, gauging if Travis was ready for this long ride. They could take it slow if they needed to. They were in no hurry.

Now Mark noticed that Travis was protecting his right side, holding his arm close to his body. Was he protecting his ribs or his shoulder? Travis was mounting slowly, carefully, straining some to get on the big mule, but when he was on the saddle, Mark thought he looked relaxed. That was good. He'd be okay.

They had never talked much when they rode together. When they did talk, it was usually Travis rambling on about something stupid, trying to prove he was the bumbling idiot that Mark knew he wasn't. Mark let him have his fun. He watched Travis act this way in town and left him alone to entertain their friends who would laugh at him. The marshal had watched, knowing that it was all an act. At some point early in their friendship, he had realized that Travis did this on purpose. Travis knew others were laughing at him. Forester thought it was entertaining for Travis to make the others believe he was something he wasn't.

But with all his joking, Travis did make his friends happy.

People would see him coming and start smiling. When he left, they would still be smiling.

It may have taken years, but after being forced to spend time together in recent weeks, Jessie Cooper and Travis had formed a mutual respect for each other. They still weren't what you would call friendly, but they weren't going at each other all the time either.

Jeb had quit belittling Travis too. In fact, Jeb Mitchem had been unusually quiet since the shooting. The storekeeper had always been a testy and sarcastic person with everyone. But he had criticized Travis constantly and had tried to embarrass Travis by asking him to read whatever was available. He would make snarky comments that Travis ignored. Mark got irritated with Jeb, but Travis had told the marshal to leave Jeb alone. Travis had quoted scripture, *Do not answer a fool according to his folly, or you yourself will be just like him.*[46]

Recalling a verse in the Bible he had read the previous night, Mark knew the Bible was true.

> For it is God's will that by doing good you should silence
> the ignorant talk of foolish people.[47]

Travis had never responded to the storekeeper, and now Jeb was silent. The owner of the mercantile couldn't find anything to criticize Travis for, not without opening the door for criticism of his own foolish son.

Mark remembered how Travis had taken care of him those first weeks they'd known each other on the trail after he'd been shot. The marshal also remembered the time that his wife had been sick and the night his wife died.

---

46 Proverbs 26:4.
47 1 Peter 2:15.

They had been married thirty-four years and raised five children. The children were now scattered across the country from Boston to San Francisco. The last had left home just a few months before his wife got sick. She died three months later.

The deputy had taken on more responsibility at the marshal's office as her illness got worse, leaving Mark more time to spend with his wife. Travis had also done some of the chores at the marshal's house. He had cut firewood and repaired the roof when it was damaged during a storm. Mark hadn't known it needed repair until he heard noise on the roof and had gone outside to see about the disturbance. Mark had found the ladder against the side of the house with Travis, tools, and supplies on the roof. He had repaired the roof quickly and disappeared without a word.

Mark had been alone with his wife the night she died. He had come out of the house to find Travis sitting on the front steps, waiting. It seemed like Travis knew what had happened before he was told. Travis had remained close to Mark during that time. He had been there when Mark had felt like talking and had listened sympathetically.

Mark didn't know how his deputy managed to be with him so much and still take care of the business in the marshal's office. But Travis had done it. Mark had suspected Jake had read for Travis during this time, but he had never asked. He just knew that Travis had handled things, and there had been no complaints.

Mark had always felt he knew Travis well. Now he knew Travis much better. He was a capable deputy, smart, confident, and trustworthy, even if others saw him as a clown. But other people knew him better now too.

Mark had never heard any of the farmers make fun of Travis, although some ranch hands and some who lived in town had.

But no one had made fun of him since Sarah's visit or since the wedding, and not since the shooting. The Mitchem boy had come to apologize. Travis had mercifully accepted while suffering persistent pain. Travis had shown his true self during that time of difficulty, and Mrs. Mitchem made sure everybody heard about it.

Chapter 18

The deputy had awakened on the second day after the shooting to find twelve-year-old Johnny Mitchem sitting beside his bed. Weak and barely able to open his eyes, he asked softly, "What are ya doin' 'ere, Johnny?"

Travis was the only one who called him Johnny; others just called him Jon, except for his mother who called him by his real name, Jonathan.

"I...I want to say I'm sorry." Jon looked down, and his words trailed off to nothing.

"Sorry far what?" Travis asked as he tried to focus his eyes on his visitor.

Johnny looked at Travis's face; tears had started to roll down his. "Sorry I shot you." Then the words came faster. "I didn't mean to. It was an accident."

Travis had to think about this. Johnny shot him! Was that what happened to him? Travis stared at Jon, then squeezed his eyes shut for a moment to get control of his thoughts. Opening his eyes, Travis stretched his hand over to the boy and placed it on Jon's knee. "It's okay. I know ya didn' mean ta. Go on 'ome. All is forgiven."

How could he not forgive Johnny for something he didn't mean to do when Christ had forgiven him for all the wrong things he had done? Didn't God command it? *Be kind and compassionate to one another, forgiving each other, just as in Christ God forgave you.*[48]

---

48   Ephesians 4:32.

"I can't. Pa told me to sit with you. He said I needed to see the pain I had caused."

Travis was having more and more trouble breathing. He didn't want Johnny to see him struggling. It wasn't right. He told the boy to get the doctor, then to run home and fetch his father. They needed to talk.

Johnny left, and the doctor came in. He helped Travis sit up for a bit. When he was breathing easier, Jessie gave him some broth. Then Travis lay back on his pillow and closed his eyes again.

It wasn't long before Johnny was back with his father and his mother, who was crying. Jessie stopped them at the door.

"Listen, Travis isn't strong enough for this conversation, and if he hadn't requested it, I wouldn't let it happen. I let Jon sit with him because you asked me to, Jeb. I didn't think Travis would wake up. I sure didn't think Jon would tell him what happened. You take it easy on him. I don't want him upset."

Doc woke Travis gently and slowly, giving him time to be awake before they talked. Travis was looking at Doc with only one eye. The other one wasn't open far enough to see anything. Doc realized that he only squinted that eye when he was tired, like the muscles weren't strong enough to keep the eye open. "Jon's back with his parents. You ready?"

The family came to Travis's bedside. Doc stayed close by. Jessie had played this conversation out in his head and saw Travis getting upset. He saw Mrs. Mitchem arguing with Travis about punishing Jon. But it didn't happen that way.

Travis called Jon to his side and reassured him that everything would be okay. He patiently listened as Jon's mother apologized over and over and promised to bring supper when Travis was up to it. Then Travis asked to speak to Jeb Mitchem alone.

Travis's voice was close to a whisper now. It sounded strained, and Jeb had to listen closely to hear and understand him. "I know what ya's tryin' ta do far the boy, but I don' need 'im sittin' 'ere watchin' me suffer."

As if to make his point, he stopped to struggle to breathe for a moment, then pressed on. "If ya want 'im ta know...what 'e's done...

send 'im out ta... the Smith's farm... an' let 'im 'elp the old man... with 'is chores. Let 'im go over ta... widow Nelson's an'...'elp there... an' Brenda Cole's. Ya can let 'im take Bess... She needs ta be ridden an' taken care a too."

There was another break in his voice as he stopped to control a wave of pain.

Jessie sat down next to Travis and put his hand on Travis's shoulder, interrupting, "That's enough. Travis, you need to rest."

"No... let me finish," Travis continued, his eye closed, his voice weaker still. "Johnny can learn what takin' care a others is 'bout...an' there's no need for 'em...ta do without... from my not bein' there... when 'e can just take my place."

He stopped, struggling to take as deep a breath as he could, and continued. "'E'll 'ave ta explain ta 'em... why 'e's there an' I'm not. That will be punishment 'nough." He didn't wait for Mitchem to agree; he just rolled his head over a little and stopped talking. Now he was finished.

Mitchem had accepted Travis's words and immediately told Jon what he would be doing the next several weeks after school, in addition to his chores at home and at the store.

Doc Cooper heard it all and approved. Travis was a good man, and he had remained calm and in control, something Jessie had not expected. At this moment, the doctor realized Travis was smarter than he acted. He had forgiven the one who hurt him, eased the mother's worries, and arranged needed help for the old couple and the widows, all in one short conversation.

Mrs. Mitchem was grateful for the gentle way Travis had handled it. She hated what Jonathan had done, but she had also been scared for her son. There would be consequences for his actions, however, she didn't want her son to suffer. Now her heart had been put at ease. She realized too, after her worry left, that she hadn't really known Travis.

At the wedding, Travis's daughter had said that he was a loving man. Mrs. Mitchem had never realized it, never looked past Travis's appearance and his strange behavior. She wouldn't have forgiven Travis that quickly if he had accidently shot her boy.

Travis forgave so graciously without asking anything for himself in return. Now Mrs. Mitchem saw him as something more than the dirty sidekick that the marshal tolerated. She was thankful for his gentle caring spirit.

Chapter 19

About thirty minutes outside of town, the marshal decided it was time to get things in the open. "Well, are you going to say anything?"

Travis questioned him, "Like what?"

"You spent a week with your daughter that you haven't seen in years. You gave her in marriage to someone you didn't know. You watched them leave for Denver. All in a week. Then you got shot by a kid. C'mon, Travis! You've got to have something to say about all that."

There were a few moments of silence. Then Travis spoke, "I love my little girl. I'm 'appy she still loves me after all I did. But...I still don' know if what I did was right."

"Travis! 'Trust in the Lord with all your heart and lean not on your own understanding; in all your ways submit to him, and he will make your paths straight.'[49] Do you believe that?"

"I've tried ta. I've told myself over an' over ta trust the Lord, an' I can usually do it, but I still 'ave some doubts when it comes ta Sarah."

"Well, doubt no more. God is faithful! 'He who began a good work in you,' and in Sarah, 'will carry it on to completion.'[50]

She knows everything you did was for her good. She knows how you sacrificed for her. And the treatment was worth it."

He looked at Travis riding beside him. Now Mark had a silly grin on his face. He knew something Travis didn't know.

---

49   Proverbs 3:5–6.
50   Philippians 1:6.

Travis continued, "We never talked 'bout 'er blindness. I don' know if that doctor 'elped 'er or not. I was scared ta ask. I didn' wan' ta know the treatments didn' work."

"They helped." Mark was still watching Travis.

Now Travis was looking at him. "She still can't see. I could tell the day she got off the train."

"But she now sees light and dark. She can't see in the shadows or at night, but she can see objects close to her in the light, and she sees colors. She can't see in the dark, but in the sunlight, in bright light, things aren't clear, she can't see details, but she has some vision."

"How do ya know?" Travis asked as he turned back to stare at the road ahead.

"Because we talked about it. She told me." The marshal could see Travis was still trying to understand, so he continued.

"She said it's like being in a dark room at night, and she opens the curtains and lets the moonlight in, but there's fog in the room. It's still dark and hazy, but depending on how bright the moon is or where the shadows fall, that's where she can see." Travis was breathing heavy now, his forehead in furrows, his chest heaving with gulps of air, chewing on his bottom lip. He was still watching the road.

Travis asked, "So ya mean the day we went fishing—"

Mark interrupted, "She saw you, not clearly but she saw you."

"An' the afternoon at the weddin'?" Travis was stunned by what Mark was telling him. He was a little confused, this news was so sudden. Travis had been convinced that Sarah still saw nothing. He was trying hard to understand.

"I'm sure she saw everyone at Mrs. Granger's house. I think she probably saw you when you sang too."

Moisture was in Travis's eyes, but then a smile spread across his face.

Mark turned back to watch the road, a smile on his face too. They rode on in silence.

Almost an hour passed without a word. Travis started his low mumbling that he often did. Mark had never actually heard him do it, but he'd been told about it. Seldom did Travis do it when he knew there were others around, but he was comfortable with his friend.

The marshal would understand.

Mark listened closely and realized Travis was praying. When the mumbling stopped, Forester heard him softly singing. And with each clop of the mule's hoof the tune grew stronger until Mark could make out every word of the song. Travis's beautiful rich voice was praising God.

He sang for quite a while when he suddenly started coughing. Coughing and then gagging. Bess stopped as the coughing continued. Mark stopped, watching Travis curiously. Travis started laughing with the coughing. "I think I swallowed a bug!" Travis made a few more noises, trying to clear out his throat. "God sure 'as a sense a humor, don''e." He kicked Bess to start moving again. Mark couldn't help but laugh too. One more cough, and Travis started singing softly again. Finishing the song, his voice went silent.

Just past the ferry, Travis commented, "I think I'll go find us a campin' spot down there." He pointed to the riverbank. "I'll catch us some fish an' have supper ready when ya get back."

"Oh, no you don't!" Mark replied. "Not tonight! We're sleeping in a bed tonight, and I've got my mouth set on those pork chops the hotel restaurant serves."

Travis was too good of a man to hide and isolate himself. Mark would make sure it didn't happen anymore. The marshal was through letting his deputy avoid people. Over the last several weeks, the people in Harris had gotten to know Travis well. There would be no more pretending.

They arrived at the hotel, and Mark checked them in. Travis confessed he had never stayed in a hotel before. Mark headed to their rooms. It was more to make sure Travis found his way; Mark really didn't need to go himself.

Mark had thought about how quickly Travis had learned the song Sarah had taught him. He thought Travis should be able to learn to read quickly if he would just try. He'd decided to start teaching Travis numbers, letters, and common written words. Mark would do it in a way that Travis wouldn't even know he was learning. He'd teach his deputy how to write his name too. Mark would tell him he had to learn for the job.

Mark was walking down the hall, pointing to the doors and reading the room numbers out loud, "Five, six, and seven. There you are. Number seven." Mark pointed to the number. "That's your room. I'm across the hall in number eight." He pointed to his door.

"Why don't you go rest. When I get finished with the sheriff, I'll come back and get you. We'll go get those pork chops."

It was almost two hours before Mark returned. He knocked on Travis's door, but there was no answer. He tried turning the knob, and the door opened. Inside he found Travis stretched out on the bed, sound asleep. "In peace I will lie down and sleep, for you alone, Lord, make me dwell in safety,"[51] the marshal whispered.

Mark smiled. Scripture had begun coming into his own head throughout the day too, the way it seemed it come to Travis randomly. Now the marshal understood why Travis would start smiling for no reason and where the scriptures he quoted came from. The Spirit was guiding his actions. He would let Travis sleep.

The marshal went downstairs with a grin on his face and ate his pork chops alone, then took a tray up to Travis. He was still asleep. Mark left it on the table beside the bed and stepped out the room's door to the outside onto the porch that ran the length of the second floor of the hotel.

Mark listened to the noise on the street below. He was sitting on the banister and leaning over to watch the people moving around. Then he spotted a rocking chair in the far corner and pulled it near the open doorway. He stopped to look into the room again and to thank God, one more time, for sparing his friend.

As he sat there rocking, Mark found himself humming. He thought about going to get his wife's Bible out of his saddlebags to read, then decided not to. He'd do that later. Right now, it would be nice to sit here, pray, and watch the moon rise.

---

51   Psalm 4:8.

Chapter 20

Travis stood there, watching the cloud move off to the east, then it turned north. His eyes grew wide as he realized the Cole farm was in the path of the tornado. It would take too long to get Bess. He grabbed the first saddled horse he saw and took off.

The deputy headed through town too fast, but he managed to avoid people and debris. Mark saw him and stopped for a moment while helping a trapped man from under a collapsed porch. Then he returned to the rescue effort. Jessie looked up to see who was leaving town. This person had some nerve running off instead of staying to help free the trapped. He saw only Travis's back, and he scowled.

Travis could still see the storm in the distance. He was headed toward it, but it was moving too fast, he didn't have to worry about catching it. Rain was still coming down, but it was beginning to slack off.

As Travis got to the Cole farm, he saw the collapsed roof of the barn, and then he saw the children. He said a silent "Thank you, Lord, far keepin' the chil'en safe."

All three of them were standing in front of the house in the drizzling rain and wind. One of the boys had a cut on his face; blood was running down his cheek onto his neck. Mary was crying as she yelled Travis's name. She was jumping up and down, pointing toward the barn. Travis jumped off the horse before it stopped and just let it go free.

"Are you okay?" Travis asked the children as he leaned over to take a closer look at Cleve's cheek. Travis took the kerchief off his neck, folded it, and placed it on the cut. He took the boy's hand

and put it on top to hold the kerchief in place without speaking. He was listening to Mary.

Eleven-year-old Mary was clinging to his shoulder now. "Mama. Mama's in the barn!" she cried.

Travis looked toward the barn again. The walls were still up, but the barn was leaning. The roof was gone.

"Ya'll stay 'ere," he told the children as he moved toward the barn.

When he got to the door, he had to yank hard to open it. A beam fell out the door, almost hitting Travis. He jumped back.

"Brenda! Brenda! Can you hear me?" There was no answer. Travis pulled a board out of his way, then another. Something shifted and several boards fell. "Brenda! Brenda!" Moving to the other side of the barn, Travis used a fallen board to pry part of the siding loose. He squeezed inside, out of sight of the children. They could hear him moving around, throwing things, or was that something falling? He was still calling their mother.

Travis thought about his daughter. She had been buried in the cellar of their home when it had collapsed during a fire. She had not been found for two days. She could have died. This would not happen to Brenda. He would find her tonight.

"Brenda! Brenda!"

Travis stopped. This wasn't working. He needed to get this debris out of the barn. He moved back through the hole he had made and pulled a few more boards off to make a bigger hole, then went back inside. As he entered the barn again, he spoke a prayer, asking God to help him find the children's mother and to let her be alive.

He began clearing the barn floor. He was appearing occasionally, moving some of the debris he had thrown outside away from the opening. He needed to get this rubbish cleared so he could see what was on the floor. He didn't want to overlook Brenda who might be under something.

He went back to Mary and told her to get fresh water and put it on the stove to heat. He looked at Cleve again. The cut was still oozing blood.

"When the water gets good an' hot, ya put some in a bowl. Let it cool until ya can put ya hands in it an' then wash Cleve's cut. If it's still bleedin', ya get a clean rag an' kind a pinch it 'gether so it'll stop."

He showed her how to pinch the skin on his own hand. "Hold it that way till it stops bleedin'. Make sure ya keep the pan full a water, an' keep it hot. Find me some extra rags too." He was anticipating Brenda being injured. He turned to go back into the barn.

It was dark in parts of the big barn, even with the roof missing. The setting sun was casting long shadows inside. It would continue to get darker as the sun set. Near dusk, he came out again and asked the children to get him a lantern.

The children did as they were asked. Then they got a blanket and huddled on the porch, waiting to see their mother emerge from the destroyed structure.

Just after dark, Travis pulled the cow out of the opening and slapped her on the rump, setting her free. A few minutes later, he brought a limping horse out. He realized it had stopped raining, but he was already soaked.

He worked into the night alone. There was no point in sending for help. It was too dark now, there was no moon, and there was too much damage in town. People would be concentrating their effort there.

Every so often, Travis would call Brenda's name again. A couple hours after nightfall, he called her name and she answered. Her voice was soft and distant.

"Keep talkin', Brenda. I'll follow ya voice."

Her voice was low, but she kept calling. Now that he knew where to look, he would be able to find her. Yes! There! He found her! She was buried under debris, but he saw her. He started moving boards, tools, and hay. Shoot! he thought, everythin' in the barn ended up in one spot. He was working carefully. The barn wasn't stable. It would creek and moan every time the wind blew. It could collapse at any moment.

About an hour later, he helped her up. They crawled over what remained on the barn floor and out the hole that Travis had made. Brenda was safe.

Travis pulled her into his arms and held her for a long moment, then took a step back to look at her, his hands on her shoulders. He asked, "Are ya okay?"

"I don't know, I hurt all over." She began to cry. "Where are the children?"

"They're okay. They're at the house. C'mon, let's go look at ya." And they headed around the barn to the house.

The boys were asleep, but Mary was still awake. She was sitting on the porch and saw her mother and Travis as they rounded the barn in the dark. She jumped up and ran to hug her mother.

"Mary!" her mother called as her daughter neared. Brenda put her arms out to hug Mary but stopped suddenly and gave a low moan of pain.

"What is it?" Travis asked as he turned to look at her. Mary stopped too, just short of her mother. Mary didn't want to hug her mother if it was going to hurt her.

"My arm. It's hard to move."

"Let's get inside an' take a look." Travis put his arm around her gently and escorted her inside.

When the lamps were lit, Travis looked her over from the top of her head to the tips of her toes. Everywhere that she said hurt, he checked out. She had several small cuts and even more large bruising. There was a knot on her head, and she said her head hurt. Travis didn't find any broken bones, but her shoulder was bruised badly. It was hurting too. Her foot looked a little swollen.

Travis washed the cuts and wrapped a bandage around a cut on her leg. Then Travis asked Mary to help her mother clean up and get her into bed.

The rest of the night, Travis sat with Brenda. In the morning, he surveyed the damage to the house, outbuildings, fields, and fences. The house would be a fast and easy fix. There was a small amount of damage. A few fences needed repair. That would be easy too.

An old oak tree was down on one of the fences. Travis thought, *There's the firewood for next winter.* He wouldn't have to haul it far.

Two of the fields were flooded, but most of the crops looked okay. They had lost part of one field and all of another. It would be a lean year, but they would make it.

The barn, however, would have to come down and be rebuilt. He went back inside and sat with Brenda again, holding her hand and talking to her, telling her of the damage, explaining what he would need to do.

Luke ran in to tell them the marshal was coming.

Standing on the porch, Travis talked to Mark, telling him about Brenda and the damage. Mark never got off his horse. He told Travis he was glad no one was seriously injured.

The marshal said he had to get back to town but was checking everyone in the tornado's path. He had already checked on Mr. Smith, who was now living alone since his wife had died, and Mrs. Nelson. Both had little damage and were safe. When Mark left, Travis went back into the house to help Mary prepare some food.

Late that afternoon, Travis went back into town. He found Mark, who was working to clear debris from a side street. Travis joined him without speaking.

Mark looked at his deputy but said nothing. Travis had changed since he had been shot. He wasn't joking around as much. He wasn't telling stories as often either. People weren't laughing at him like they had before. Without the joking, Travis was quieter around other people, but he had begun to talk to Mark more. Their friendship had grown.

As they worked, Mark asked, "Travis, why don't you marry that woman. You've been playing house for years. We all know you love each other, and those children may as well call you Dad. They were so young when their father died. You're the only man they've known. Stop pretending."

Travis froze and stared at Mark. Mark had used that phrase on him before, "stop pretending." Was Mark right? Did he really love Brenda? Yes, he knew he loved the children, but he still thought of

Brenda as Angus's wife, even though his friend had been dead for six years. He continued thinking about this as he went back to work.

Two years ago, Mark had told Travis that pretending was okay if you were a child playing, but to pretend in life was living a lie. He had been living a lie, acting irresponsible when he wasn't, showing people he was a stupid mountain man instead of letting them know who he really was.

Was he pretending now? Was he pretending he didn't love Brenda when he truly did? He needed to think about this, to pray about it. Travis worked long into the night. His body was tired, but he wasn't sleepy. His head was spinning with thoughts of Brenda, and then of Ruth.

The next day, when Travis rode out to the Coles, he saw Brenda sitting on the porch. He stared at her as he got off Bess and walked up the steps.

Brenda was a handsome woman, but nothing like the beauty Ruth had been. Ruth had always worn her coal-black hair tied loose at her neck or braided down her back. Brenda had dull brown hair. It was nothing to look at. That's probably why she always wore it up on her head. But wearing her hair that way made her long beautiful neck that much more beautiful.

Ruth had been shorter than Travis, and he had felt tall next to her, but Brenda and he were the same height. If they stood next to each other, he could look straight into her large brown eyes. Her smile was contagious, though, it could brighten even a sunny day.

There was something about her that was mesmerizing; Travis didn't know what it was. She wasn't well versed in Scripture nor was she confident in what she did. She always needed reassurance, and she cried over everything. She was physically strong, a hard worker but seemed inwardly delicate, like she needed to be cared for.

Travis realized Mark had been right. He did love Brenda. How could that have happened? He couldn't forget Ruth. What was he going to do?

Travis sat down beside Brenda, asking her how she felt. She replied that she was sore and wasn't moving around very well. She still had a headache.

Travis knew it would be several days before she would be able to do much work. They sat together silently and were comfortable together with the silence. Then he got up to do some chores before he started tearing down what remained of the barn.

Chapter 21

Mark spotted Travis sitting at the edge of the graveyard next to the church. He stopped and got off his horse.

"Travis, what are you doing here?" he asked as he got closer to his deputy.

Travis turned to look at his friend. "I think ya was right. I do love Brenda. But 'ow do I let go a Ruth? I can't be with Brenda an' still 'ave Ruth with me too. I know the Bible says ta 'Forget the former things; do not dwell on the past. See, I am doing a new thing! Now it springs up; do you not perceive it?'[52]

"I can see what God's doin', brin' me an' Brenda together. I've been blind ta it far a long time, but I understand it now." Travis turned back to look at the graves.

There was a break in his words, then Travis added, "I couldn' go ta where Ruth is buried, so I came 'ere—ta talk ta God."

Mark felt for Travis. He understood. He still loved his Martha too. Even after all these years, he still felt like she was with him. Mark hadn't thought of being with another woman. When he was away from home, it felt like Martha would be there waiting for him. The only time he felt the loneliness was when he was at home. Then Martha was everywhere. Sometimes it felt like she had just stepped outside for a few minutes, and other times the house was just empty.

He sat down beside Travis. Mark wasn't sure what to say, so he sat quietly.

---

52   Isaiah 43:18–19a.

Scripture came to the marshal's mind, *Praise be to the God and Father of our Lord Jesus Christ, the Father of compassion and the God of all comfort, who comforts us in all our troubles, so that we can comfort those in any trouble with the comfort we ourselves receive from God. For just as we share abundantly in the sufferings of Christ, so also our comfort abounds through Christ.*[53]

Mark silently prayed, *Lord, I know you want me to comfort him, but how? I don't understand his pain. His family died so violently, and you know how he blames himself. Take his feelings of guilt away, he's not to blame, you know that.*

They sat silently a few minutes. Then Mark asked, "Are you lonely, Travis?"

"No. Not really. God blessed me with friends. But sometimes I would like ta 'ave someone ta share with. Someone ta wake up beside. Ta eat supper with. An' when I let myself think 'bout it, I do miss Ruth an' the chil'en. But..." He stopped and laughed at himself. "It sure sounds like I'm lonely, don' it? 'Yet I am not alone, for the father is with me.'"[54]

Travis sat silent for a moment, and then added, "Maybe I'm just still grievin'. But I know God's with me, an' he keeps me 'appy. I do 'ave joy in my life." Travis looked at Mark a moment, then turned back to look at the graves.

Mark said, "You've never told me anything about Ruth. Have you talked to anyone about her?"

"Just God. When I got home that day, I found the house burned. I ran scared ta my g'an'father's, an' there was my beautiful Sarah, standin' on the porch. I thought everythin' was okay. I ran ta hug 'er. Then I found out she was blind...and Ruth..."

Mark looked at Travis when he paused. He was chewing on his bottom lip again.

"Ruth, Joshua...an' little Joseph were gone," Travis said. And he stopped to rub his lip where he had been chewing. Then Travis continued his story.

---

53   2 Corinthians 1:3–5.
54   John 16:32b.

"I had been so hungry that mornin'. I'd been walkin' far more 'an two weeks, just livin' off a what I could find, what people would give me. Then that night, I 'ad food put in front a me, an' I couldn' eat. Couldn' stand ta look at it. Papaw sat on the porch, readin', just like 'e'd done my whole life, like nothin' 'ad 'appene'.

"I was so tired, but I couldn' sleep. I sat on the front porch all night, tryin' ta pray but couldn'. But the next day, I started sleepin'. Sarah said I slept far three days. When I got up, there was nothin' ta do but start workin', so I did. I 'ad ta take care a Sarah."

"I'm glad you're telling me this," Mark said sympathetically. "Have you told Brenda anything?"

Travis shook his head. "No."

"Don't you think it's time? 'There's a time for everything,' Travis. 'A season for every activity under the heavens: a time to be born and a time to die.'"[55] Mark paused to look at Travis.

He continued slowly, "'A time to plant and a time to uproot, a time to kill and a time to heal, a time to tear down and a time to build, a time to weep and a time to laugh, a time to mourn and' then there's 'a time to dance.'[56] You know that scripture don't you?"

"Yeah," Travis said somberly, continuing the Scripture. "A time to scatter stones and a time to gather them, a time to embrace and a time to refrain from embracing, a time to search and a time to give up, a time to keep and a time to throw away, a time to tear and a time to mend, a time to be silent and a time to speak, a time to..." Travis stopped. "Love,"[57] he said softly. "I do love Brenda."

"Then go talk to her. You've talked to God, now talk to Brenda. Have you told her anything about your past? Did she meet Sarah?"

Travis shook his head. No, he had never told her anything. All she knew was that Travis had a daughter who was blind, that she had visited two years ago. They had never talked about Sarah or what had happened to her. Brenda didn't know about the two boys either, or what had happened during the war. Travis had never spoken of Ruth or their farm in the mountains or Papaw.

---

55   Ecclesiastes 3:1–2a.
56   Ecclesiastes 3:2b–4.
57   Ecclesiastes 3:5–8a.

He would have to let her see his scars also and tell her about that. He couldn't hide them from her if he was going to make her his wife.

Scripture came to Travis. *The godly give good advice to their friends.*[58] Mark was giving good advice. It would be a hard conversation, maybe several hard conversations.

He had known Brenda's husband. They talked about him all the time. They had talked about him a lot right after he died. But talking about Ruth with the woman he now loved, that needed to be done too.

"Thanks," Travis said quietly as he got up. He had been sitting there talking to God, waiting for God to tell him what to do. God had now spoken to him through Mark. Travis prayed sadly, "Thank you, Lord, far usin' my friend ta get your message ta me. Now help me through this. I need to talk to Brenda."

He'd talk with Brenda. He didn't know how to start or what to say, but he'd talk. God would give him words when the time was right.

Mark smiled as Travis walked off. Travis had talked, but he still hadn't said anything about Ruth.

---

58   Proverbs 12:26a (NLT).

Chapter 22

It was a small wedding in Brenda's parlor, just Brenda, Travis, the children, Mark, and the preacher. Jake, Mr. Smith, and Mrs. Nelson were there too.

Everyone was in favor of this marriage, including the children. Luke didn't remember his father at all. Cleve had just a few memories of him. Mary had a few more, but they were fading as she got older. They were all happy to get Travis as a father.

None of the children could remember a time when Travis wasn't around. He had always been there, and they all loved him, even when their father was alive.

Travis had held Luke when he was just a few days old. Sometimes Travis would show up at their house and wouldn't do anything but sit, sing, and rock the baby. He sang softly, barely loud enough for anyone to hear him. It had a calming effect on everyone in the room.

Mary and Cleve had always wanted their turn too. Mary had been three years old when Travis had started coming around. Cleve had just turned two. All of them would have their turn as Travis would rock and sing. Mary always fell asleep in his arms. Even now, as old as she was, Mary would sometimes sit on his lap and fall asleep.

The children were ready for him to be their father. They had come to Travis just before the ceremony and asked if they could call him Daddy now. He had agreed happily. He was ready to be their father. He loved them as much as he had loved his own children.

Travis remembered the scriptures, *Children are a heritage from the Lord, offspring a reward from him.*[59] *Blessed is the man whose quiver is full of them!*[60]

God was blessing Travis with more children.

The ceremony had ended, and the congratulations had been said. Everyone was enjoying themselves, visiting and telling stories. Travis sat listening with that crooked smile on his face as Mr. Smith told of his marriage to his "bride." He had always called her his bride.

Travis was happy. But as he watched the children, his thoughts began to wander.

He thought back to Sarah, Joshua, and Joseph. They had been younger than these children when he had last seen them, before he left home and got caught up in the war. His children had been so happy and had their whole lives ahead of them when he had driven off in that wagon.

He had been right. He was still grieving. He had never gotten over the pain of their loss. Not completely anyway. He hadn't gotten past the guilt either. He blamed himself for what had happened to them. For what had happened to his wife and to Sarah, his beautiful Sarah. He hoped he would be able to hide his feelings about them. He didn't want his guilt to affect this family.

This should be a happy day, and he kept a smile on his face, but he was feeling sad inside. There were lots of old memories running through his head. He wanted to stop them, but they were persistent.

As Travis had arrived at his grandfather's house, he had seen Sarah standing up from a chair on the porch. She hadn't run to him or waved. He should have realized something was wrong, but he had been so glad to see her, so excited to be home. She had hugged his neck, and they had held each other a long time before he found out she was blind, and her mother and brothers were gone.

---

59   Psalm 127:3a (ESV).
60   Psalm 127:5a (ESV).

All his hopes for a year and a half had been shattered when his grandfather told him what happened. His prayers had been useless. He had prayed for them, but they had already died.

He was sitting on Zeb's porch with his grandfather and his daughter, and then they had left him sitting there, alone. Travis remembered mindlessly leaving the steps and walking toward the cemetery.

At the graves, he had stood there, staring at the three newest piles of rocks. Then he had collapsed to his knees. He had thought it would be nice to just lie down and stay there until he saw Ruth.

But the sound of his daughter's voice pulled him back to reality.

Travis closed his eyes and silently prayed, *Oh, God! Take these memories from me!* Even now he could hear Sarah's voice calling him, *"Papa! Papa! Supper's ready."* He remembered pulling himself up from the ground, how hard it had been to move.

He was having trouble keeping the smile on his face. He didn't want anyone to see the tears he was wiping away. Why were these thoughts coming to him now?

He had walked back to the house, not knowing how Sarah had lived through all that had happened, but he was thankful she had survived.

Travis was feeling defeated again. Not today, Lord. Not now. The smile left his face. He closed his eyes tightly for a moment, trying to get control of his emotions.

He had grabbed Sarah in his arms and held her tight, resting his head on top of hers. He apologized to her, admitting his failure. "I'm so sorry, baby! I didn' mean ta leave ya! I was tryin' ta protect ya, but I failed."

Travis leaned over and put his head in his hands, wanting the memories to end. He slid his hands down his face to stop on his mouth, leaning on his hands, looking at the floor.

Mark was watching Travis. What was wrong with him? He looked miserable.

Then Travis remembered how thankful he had been for the words his daughter had spoken to him, *"Ya 'ome now, Papa. That's all that matters."*

You're home now. You're home now! Travis sat up and smiled again. He gave a big sigh. God was letting him know he was home. He could give the past away and just love his new family! "Thank you, Father." He said softly, looking up. Then he turned his attention back to the group.

Mark was still watching Travis. He looked better now. Mark thought about his friend. Travis was a simple man, but he was also complicated. Just when you think you understand him, he throws something new into the mix, and you realize you don't know him at all. Mark prayed silently for Travis and for his new family.

Travis turned to look at the children again. They were being given a second chance with a father, like he was being given a second chance with a family. He vowed to himself, he would not fail them like he had failed his first family.

Chapter 23

The wedding had taken place three months ago, and tonight was one of the few evenings Travis got to stay home. It felt strange. It was raining outside, and the whole family was in the house together. This may be the first time this had happened. They usually worked till supper, and then Travis would leave for town, or he would go back outside to catch up on some chores. The children would be in bed when he came back inside. Sunday evenings, the children were usually playing outside. Sometimes he was with them, but they were seldom inside the house together.

He watched his family. Brenda was sewing. All the children had Brenda's large dark eyes. Cleve had blond hair and looked more like his father than either of the others, tall and skinny. The cut on his cheek had healed, but it had left a mark.

Luke looked more like his mother, with brown hair. He was slim too but wasn't as skinny as Cleve. The boys were playing checkers together.

Mary didn't look like her brothers. She was smaller, she wouldn't be very tall. She had blond streaks in her brown hair, her hair wasn't the color of her mother's or her father's hair. Her face was more rounded than the boys' faces and her lips fuller. She was slender but was reaching an age when she would stop looking like a child. She sat at her mother's feet, learning how to knit. She looked like she was getting frustrated. Travis laughed silently. She was cute when she got mad. She tried so hard to control her anger, to not let anyone know she was upset. But she was seldom successful.

They had been to church that morning, like they had done for years. Travis always stood in the back of the church when Angus was alive, and since his death, Travis had made an effort to sit with the children. Angus had always prayed before meals. Since his death, Travis had prayed when he ate with them. But Travis had never seen Brenda or the children reading the Bible. Travis knew they needed to learn Scripture.

Travis remembered Deuteronomy 11:19, *Teach (God's laws) to your children, talking about them when you sit at home and when you walk along the road, when you lie down and when you get up.* He was now their father. It was his responsibility to teach them God's Word.

"Mary, do ya know where a Bible is?" he asked.

"Sure, it's in the chest by the door," she said.

"Would ya fetch it an' read ta me?" Travis didn't like asking this. He hated admitting that he couldn't read. But he also knew this was another step that needed to be taken to fully let go of Ruth. It was sad, though. She had been with him through so much, not in body but in spirit.

Mary came back into the room carrying the big family Bible and put it on the table. Travis lit another lantern and set it beside the Bible, then sat down himself.

"Where do I start?" Mary asked.

Travis answered, "'Ow 'bout the book a John."

Mary fumbled a few pages, and Travis could tell she had no idea where to find it. He knew John was nearer to the back but couldn't help her locate it. He couldn't read.

"Why don' we find it together?" Travis suggested. He smiled at Mary as he moved beside her. "Start here, what does this say?" And he pointed to a word at the top of the page. She told him what it said, and he turned a few pages and found a different word. He asked the same question.

As he and Mary were looking at the Bible, the boys joined them, looking at the Bible upside down from the other side of the table.

This exchange went on several times, and finally Mary said, "John. We found it!"

"Great. Start 'ere." And Travis pointed to the beginning. Mary read,

> "'In the beginning was the Word, and the Word was with God, and the Word was God. He was with God in the beginning. Through him all things were made; without him nothing was made that has been made. In him was life, and that life was the light of all mankind. The light shines in the darkness, but the darkness has not understood it.'[61]

I don't understand, what is that talking about?"

"Jesus," Travis said. "It's talkin' 'bout Jesus. Read it 'gain an' put Jesus's name where the word 'word' is."

"'In the beginning was the' Jesus—no wait. 'In the beginning was' Jesus, and Jesus 'was with God, and' Jesus 'was God.'" She looked at her new father and smiled. "Jesus 'was with God in the beginning. Through' Jesus, 'all things were made; without,' Jesus, 'nothing was made that has been made. In' Jesus, 'was life, and that life was the light of men.' What's the light of men?"

Travis thought for a moment. "Jesus, it means Jesus is the one who shows us thin's. 'E's the one who 'elps us understand thin's. He opens our eyes, like lightin' a candle in the dark."

She smiled and nodded, then continued reading. "'The light,' Jesus, 'shines in the darkness, and the darkness has not understood it.' That means you can't understand Jesus if you don't see him, right? Have you seen him?"

Travis laughed. "Sort a. It means if ya don' trust Jesus an' believe Jesus is who 'e says 'e is, ya won' understand when 'e talks to ya or when ya read the Bible."

"But we learn about Jesus at church, why didn't I understand what I just read?"

---

61   John 1:1–5.

"Learnin' 'bout Jesus an' knowin' Jesus is two diffe'ent thin's. Ya knew 'bout the marshal 'fore ya met 'im. Ya 'ad seen Mark, an' I told ya 'e was my friend, but ya didn' know the marshal until ya met. Then after ya 'ad been 'round Mark some, ya knew 'im better. 'E became ya friend.

"It works the same way. Ya know 'bout Jesus now, but after we read some a the Bible, an' after we pray 'gether some more, ya will get ta know Jesus as ya friend. Then ya will understand more a the Bible, an' ya can 'ear 'im talk ta ya some."

Luke asked, "Does he talk to you?"

"I 'ear Jesus all the time."

Cleve added, "Daddy used to, you know, my other daddy. He used to say prayers with us at night, before we went to bed."

"Would ya like me ta do that with ya?" Travis asked. "Sometimes we will 'ave ta do it at breakfast 'cause I won' be 'ere when ya go ta bed, is that okay?"

Both the boys nodded their heads. Travis looked at Mary who was staring at the Bible.

"Mary?" Travis was leaning over to put himself in Mary's field of vision, making faces at her. She didn't seem to be paying attention. The boys smiled. Luke put a hand over his mouth to muffle his laughter.

"I guess," Mary said sadly. "But it won't be like our real daddy." She looked at Travis. "'Cause you're not our real daddy, no matter how much we want you to be."

Chapter 24

Travis was sitting on a bench in front of Jake's shop. It was almost center of the activity in the evenings, and Travis could keep an eye on several problem areas.

He was thinking about what Mary had said, that he wasn't really their father. He felt like their father. He knew she loved him, and she had said she wanted him to be their real father. He didn't know how much more of a father he could be to them. Travis didn't know what to do to help Mary feel like his child. The worst part of the conversation had been that he knew she was right. He wasn't their true father.

Jake locked the door to his store and turned around to see Travis.

"Evening, Travis," Jake said.

Travis was deep in thought. He didn't hear Jake or answer.

Jake leaned over to Travis and spoke louder, "Travis? Hello?"

"Oh! Sorry. Hey, Jake," Travis said automatically, he still wasn't paying attention.

Jake sat down beside Travis. "Anything going on this evening?" he asked.

Travis didn't answer. Okay, Jake thought. It's one of those days that Travis isn't going to talk. There was no point in hanging around if there wasn't going to be conversation. Jake got up and walked down the street.

It wasn't long before Jake ran into Mark. They talked a few minutes, then Jake told Mark he had seen Travis outside his store. Jake commented that "Travis isn't talking again," and walked away laughing. Jake had never had a complete and serious conversation with Travis. He didn't know why he thought today would be any different.

It was still early. Mark walked in the direction of Jake's shop. When he got close, he saw Travis sitting on the bench, staring at the street.

Mark thought marriage had been good for Travis. He looked better than he had in the past. Brenda had gotten him some new clothes. Travis wasn't wearing shirts or pants with holes or patches anymore. And his clothes now fit him, they weren't hand-me-downs from bigger men. Mark thought she was probably making him take baths in the washtub instead of the river. His beard stayed trimmed neatly now. You could also see the gray beginning to show in his beard. Travis looked more distinguished, less like a wild man. Mark laughed to himself. The right woman will do that to a man.

There was a lot of noise coming from the Foresquare Saloon just down the street. As Mark got close to Travis, Mark said, "Come on, Travis. Let's go in there"—pointing to the Foresquare—"looks like we may have to oversee things."

Travis got up without saying a word and went with Mark. They stood at the bar near the door. It was a location where they could see the entire room, a good vantage point to spot trouble that was brewing.

Mark ordered two mugs. He knew Travis wouldn't order one for himself. It had been years since Travis had sent money to Sarah, but he still acted like he didn't have any.

Mark was watching a card game on the far side of the room. Travis had his eye on a stranger in the corner.

"What's wrong?" Mark asked.

"Don' know. Can't figure out if I know that guy from somewhere or if..." Travis let his voice trail off.

"I don't mean here. What's bothering you?" Mark and Travis had become close the last two years. They had not talked as much the first few years they had known each other. But as Mark had begun to learn Scripture and had begun to follow the Holy Spirit's leading, their relationship had changed. Mark had become a more caring and outgoing person. Travis had opened up to him.

"Just somethin' Mary said yesterday. She said that no matter how much she wanted it, I would never really be 'er father. I mean, I know I'm not 'er real father, but 'e's dead. I'm the closest thin' she's got. I feel like she's my own daughter, but she still don' feel that way 'bout me."

"Give her time, Travis. You haven't been married to her mother for long."

"I know. But a all the chil'en, I thought she would be the one ta accept me the easiest."

Just then, one of the men at the poker table stood up and started yelling. Mark turned and began moving in that direction. Another man at the table stood up and threw a punch at the first man, catching him in the jaw, knocking him to the floor.

"That's enough!" Mark said as he grabbed the second man by the arm. Mark put out his other hand to help the first man up. The man that had been hit was rubbing his chin, and Mark could see in the man's eyes that he was angry. Mark talked to both the men and to everyone else at the table.

It looked like Mark had stopped this before it got very far. Travis turned back to look at the man in the corner again. Travis knew this guy, but he didn't know how.

The rest of the night continued the same way. Mark would stop a fight, and then it was Travis's turn to stop one. Then it was Mark's turn again. At one point, they were both working different areas of the room at the same time.

Mark suggested there might be a full moon, but they went outside and checked. It was a quarter moon. They had a good laugh together.

Late into the night, they were called to the Buckskin Saloon. As they were leaving the Foresquare, Travis looked over at the stranger and suddenly realized who he was—Andrew Webber.

It took both the lawmen to breakup an all-out brawl at the Buckskin. Mark went to the jail to lock up three cowboys, and Travis took two more to Dr. Cooper's.

Travis had gotten punched in the eye but wasn't feeling it.

Anytime he had to swing hard with his right arm, his shoulder would hurt. That deep pain took over all others. It wasn't like before Jessie had cut into it. It didn't hurt all the time, but it could get to be piercing at times. When it started, it would hurt for several hours, sometimes days.

Jessie had to sew up a cut on one man's head, and then he put a bandage on the other cowboy's busted hand. "You're both lucky no bones were broken." Jessie was talking to the two cowboys. "Stupid thing to do, you would think you two would know better. Go on, get out of here." Dr. Cooper flung his hand, indicating the doorway.

Travis started moving toward the door too.

"Not you, Travis. Come here and let me look at that eye."

"Aww, Doc. I'm okay."

"I said come here!"

Travis walked over and stood in front of the doctor. Jessie pointed to the table, and Travis grudgingly slid onto it. Dr. Cooper was talking about nothing of importance again, which always annoyed Travis, but tonight it was unbearable. There was just no point in rambling on and on about nothing.

Then Jessie said, "You need to take care of this eye." Doc had made a poultice and was pressing it against Travis's eye. "You wouldn't want to have two eyes you can't see out of."

"I can see fine out a the other eye!" Travis was irritated now.

Doc bellowed, "When it's open! What's been wrong with you lately anyway? Every time I see you, you look like you're going to drop. You're a married man now, get some rest!" And Jessie slapped Travis on the shoulder. Travis winced. He immediately hoped Jessie hadn't seen him. He would have to be more careful, harden himself to the pain like he had done years ago. Travis took the poultice and slid off the table. He started for the door again.

"Stop!" Too late, Jessie saw it. "What's wrong with your shoulder?"

"Nothin'."

"Don't lie to me, Travis."

"Just 'urts a little sometimes after I've been in a fight." Travis was trying to downplay what had happened. He wanted to get away from Jessie.

Jessie was pointing to his table again and expected Travis to comply.

"Not now, Doc. I got thin's ta do." Travis turned and walked out the door.

There were a few more minor altercations that night, and both Mark and Travis were glad when the saloons shut down at midnight. They walked the street together, making sure everyone was gone. Mark said he'd stay at the jail and told Travis to go on home.

*****

It was a peaceful Sunday morning. The choir sang well—a familiar song—and the sermon was interesting. The preacher tried to talk Travis into singing with the choir again, but again Travis had refused.

Sometimes during a congregational hymn, people around Travis would stop singing so they could listen to him. Travis never acknowledged that this was happening but just kept singing until the end of the song. Brenda and the children noticed it, though, and so did Mark and everyone else in the church, including the preacher. But no one mentioned it to Travis.

Mark and Travis saw each other, but they didn't have much to say. Everything seemed fine, except for Travis's black eye.

That afternoon, Mark rode out to see Travis. Brenda visited for a while on the front porch, then left to prepare supper. She invited Mark to stay.

When she was gone, Mark said, "Jessie told me you were having trouble with your shoulder, but you wouldn't let him look at it. What's going on?"

Travis rolled his eyes. "Nothin' an' I told 'im so. It 'urts sometimes when I 'ave ta fight. That's the only time. It's nothin'. Sometimes old injuries will just 'urt, ya know that."

Yes, Mark knew that. He nodded his head. Sometimes they did. His leg would hurt in cold weather where he had broken it when he was younger.

"So you're okay? It's not something Jessie needs to take a look at? It's not going to get in the way?"

"No. I'm fine."

"He also said you weren't getting enough rest. What's with that?"

"That old sawbones needs ta take care a 'is own self!" Travis stood up, walked to the edge of the porch, and turned around, looking to Mark. He was beginning to get upset. "How does 'e know how much rest I'm gettin'?"

"Well, according to Jessie, the more tired you are, the more your eye droops. He said the muscles are weak around your eye, and when you get tired, they can't keep your eye open."

The marshal was watching Travis. His eye was sagging some, and Mark could tell Travis was getting upset. Something was wrong. Travis never got angry. He never lost his composure. Travis was glaring straight at Mark, but he wasn't talking.

"Okay, I'm going to tell Jessie you're fine. I'll tell him not to worry about you," Mark said, standing up. "Travis, you let me know if you need a break. I'm going to say bye to Brenda and let her know I can't stay. I want to get home and go to bed early myself." And Mark got up and went into the house.

Travis walked toward the corral. He stood at the rail with his back toward the house. When Mark came out to get on his horse, he stopped to watch his deputy. Travis was standing at the rail, holding his right shoulder with his left hand, rubbing it.

Yes, something was wrong. Mark would have to stay close to him to find out what it was. Travis wasn't going to tell him.

*****

For the next two weeks, Mark left Travis alone when there was nothing going on in town, but he stayed close when there was activity. He didn't ask Travis to do anything other than his usual routine. Mark would let Travis rest if he would.

When they were together, everything seemed normal. Travis didn't get upset. He didn't seem to be in any pain. His eye squinted some, but Mark had seen it worse. His deputy was quiet though. Mark wondered if he had crossed that invisible line of being intrusive. Had he asked Travis too many personal questions? Had he pushed too hard?

Another busy Saturday night, and Mark and Travis stood at the Buckskin bar. They had managed to stay in the same place for almost an hour and had surveyed all the occupants of the room. There was no one unusual, no one they hadn't seen before. Their conversation was casual. Mark had forgotten about Jessie's comments and Travis's anger.

Then the door swung open, and the stranger walked in. Both the marshal and his deputy saw him as he entered.

"I need some air," Travis said and walked out the door.

Mark looked at the stranger again as he sat against the far wall. It was the same man that had been at the Foresquare two weeks ago. The man Travis thought he might know but couldn't place.

Mark walked over to introduce himself. The man identified himself as Major Andrew Webber, retired. He seemed crude and cocky. Mark didn't like him from the start. He was working for the T-Bar Ranch as security. That was another way of saying a gunfighter. Trouble was coming.

The T-Bar was only one of several large outfits in Kansas owned by Ted Meadows. Ted lived just south of the state line, in Oklahoma Territory. Some of the other T-Bar ranches had recently been involved in range wars, but there had been no trouble around Harris. Mark wanted to keep it that way.

Mark walked outside and found Travis around the corner, leaning on a porch column, bumping the heel of his boot against the edge of the porch, looking down the street. Travis stopped bumping when Mark stepped close.

"I just introduced myself to that stranger you thought you knew," Mark began. "He said his name was—"

Travis interrupted, "I know, Andy Webber."

"You remembered. Good, you know him then. That will help. Tell me about him, where did you know him?"

"'E's the Union officer"—Travis gave a big sigh—"that beat me." The deputy stood looking whipped, staring into the dark.

"Aww, Travis! I'm sorry. When did you figure it out?"

"The night I first saw 'im. Just before the big fight."

Just then, a cowboy came flying out the Buckskin door onto the street. He got up and ran back inside. Mark and Travis followed.

Chapter 25

Trouble started sooner than Mark wanted. He had sent a message to Ted Meadows about Webber and had told Meadows he wouldn't tolerate trouble around Harris. Mark had not gotten a response. Camden's outfit lost some cattle when they stampeded and got tangled in a barbed wire fence. No one seemed to know how the stampede started.

That same day, the Beaver Canyon Ranch had two men brought in to Dr. Cooper's. Cowboys passing through the area on open range had found them. No one knew what happened here either, including the injured men. They had been ambushed while looking for strays.

All the ranches were now on high alert. They were working together, trying to figure out what had happened and trying to protect themselves. All except the T-Bar. The men at the T-Bar had isolated themselves. They weren't in town on Saturday night, and none came into Harris for supplies. This was unusual.

Travis had been quiet too. He hadn't talked about Webber or the incident during the war. Mark didn't know any more than he had known two years ago when Jessie had discovered the scars. The only new information had been the officer's name.

Travis was still doing his job well, and they hadn't seen Andrew Webber in town anymore either.

One of the farmers came into the marshal's office and told Mark that he had found some fences down. He had repaired them, but a few days later, they had been torn down again. The marshal sent his deputy to check on all the farmers. Travis reported that most of them had experienced the same problem, including himself.

131

That's the way it started, with a fence down and stray cattle crossing the line. Some of the boundary fences were barbed wire, put up by the ranchers. The farmers used wood or log fencing. When fencing was destroyed, the ranchers could claim the farmer had damaged the fence and was stealing cattle. Travis had warned all the farmers to be careful, to keep repairing their own fences, to stay away from the wire fencing, and to report any more problems.

Barbed wire was easy to cut. No one needed to see a farmer at a wire fence. That was too dangerous. The cattlemen could easily accuse a farmer of destroying the fence.

A cattleman's cut fence needed to be reported to the rancher, preferably by Travis or Mark. But this was hard too. It took time to report to the marshal and get someone out to the ranch.

*****

Travis was sitting at the table, cleaning his rifle, when Mary came to him. She told her father that her mom was taking a nap and that she had gone to bed early the last few nights. Travis was in town most evenings and had been in the fields plowing during the day, he hadn't seen his wife much the last few days. Mary knew he wouldn't have known this.

Mary ended with, "Do you think she's getting sick?"

"I don' know. I'll check on 'er. Thanks far lettin' me know, Mary. Can ya fix supper for ya self an' the boys? Save some far ya mom, in case she wants somethin' later. Let 'er sleep." She nodded and he told her, "Good girl, thanks."

When Travis finished putting his rifle back together, he put on his gun belt and looked in on his wife. She was still sleeping, so Travis left for town. He'd talk with her tomorrow.

It was Thursday night, and there would be a little activity at the saloons. The weekend started for some of the cowboys on Thursday, more men came to town on Friday. By Saturday, Travis sometimes felt like there were so many men in town the ranches should be empty.

Travis had to stay in town that night, at the jail. When he got home the next morning, he found Brenda sitting at the table alone. The children were outside doing chores. They would leave for school shortly. Travis got a cup of coffee and sat down with her.

"Are ya all right?" he asked.

"Just sleepy. I woke up during the night, and you weren't there. I was worried. It kept me awake."

"Ya know I 'ave ta stay at the jail sometimes when there's a prisoner," he replied.

"I know, and I thought that was probably the reason, but I was still worried," Brenda said.

"I can take care of myself," Travis told her.

"I know," she replied.

Travis asked, "But ya still worry?"

"I'm sorry. I don't know what's wrong with me." She looked like she might cry.

"'So do not fear, for I am with you; do not be dismayed, for I am your God. I will strengthen you and help you; I will uphold you with my righteous right hand.'[62] That's God talkin' ta ya, my love." Travis put his hand on her face, turning her face to look at him. "Ya can trust him ta take care a me. Don' worry."

She nodded her head. Travis repeated himself, "I'm gonna be okay. God's takin' care a me. Ya knew this was my job when we got married. It didn' bother ya then, did it?"

"No. And I'm proud of you, the job doesn't bother me. I like knowing that you can handle people and problems and things. I know you're good at your job. I do trust you. I don't know why I was so scared last night." She started to cry.

He pulled his chair closer to her and reached over to take her hand.

"When you lie down, you will not be afraid; when you lie down, your sleep will be sweet. Have no fear of sudden disaster of the ruin that overtakes the wicked, for the Lord will be at your

---

62   Isaiah 41:10.

side and will keep your foot from being snared.'[63] Do ya know that scripture?" Travis asked.

Brenda shook her head, and her husband added, "Ya will, I'll teach it ta ya. An' when ya learn it, ya will trust it as God's spoken word ta ya."

Travis smiled at her, then surprised her with his next question. "Are ya havin' a baby?" Travis had remembered that Ruth had always slept more and was always tired during the first months of all three of her pregnancies. She had also gotten emotional. He had never seen Ruth cry except when she was carrying a child.

Brenda jerked her head around to stare at her husband. Slowly she replied, "I don't think so." There was a pause. "I don't know, maybe." Travis put his arm around her and pulled her to him. He held her there until one of the children came running in.

Cleve blurted out! "There's some cows in the cornfield!"

Travis jumped up and took the boy by the shoulders, looking into his eyes. "Ya go fetch ya brother an' ya sister an' get ta school right now! Leave now! Hurry! When ya get ta town, stop an' tell Mark we 'ave cows in the field. If ya don' see 'im, tell Jake or Mr. Mitchem or Dr. Cooper ta tell 'im. Do ya understand?"

"But it's not time yet. We don't have our lunches ready. We need to get our books."

Travis softened his tone some, but his voice still sounded the urgency. "It's okay, me or ya mom will brin''em later. Now go! Run!"

Travis turned to his wife. "Ya stay in the house. Don' look out the windows. I don' care what ya 'ear. Can ya do that?"

She started to shake her head no but stopped. "What's happening?"

"Promise me, Brenda! Promise me!"

"Okay. I'll stay here. I won't look out the windows."

He took her in his arms and held her, then kissed her passionately. He turned to pick up his rifle and opened the door. He stopped on the porch to see that the children were on their way. They were down the road. Cleve was running ahead of the other

---

63   Proverbs 3:24–26.

two. He had heard the urgency in his father's voice. Travis watched until Cleve was out of sight, then started slowly for the field.

When Travis cleared earshot of the house, he started praying out loud, "Protect me, Father. 'The righteous person may have many troubles, but the Lord delivers him from them all.'[64]

Thank you, Lord, for your protection. 'God, (you are my) refuge and strength, an ever-present help in trouble.[65] Deliver me from my enemies, O God; be my fortress against those who are attacking me.'[66]

Travis had passed the barn and was in the field now. He stopped and surveyed the land. The tender young plants, less than a foot tall, and six cows, he didn't see anything else. He approached slowly. "Keep me safe, Lord, from the hands of the wicked; protect me from the violent, who devise ways to trip my feet."[67]

"Well. Well. Well." The voice that Travis had not heard for a very long time came from behind him. "So. It's the little mountain preacher."

He would always remember Major Webber's voice. He had heard it as he lay bleeding on the ground. That memory had never left him. Webber must have been hiding behind the barn.

"Did you think I didn't see you in town wearing that badge? Think you're big stuff in town, don't you? I'm surprised you left your mountain, little man. Different out here in cattle country, isn't it?"

He had his horse moving and was turning tight circles around Travis. "Nothing to say?" He stopped behind Travis. "Turn around here and look at your old commander."

Travis turned around slowly and looked into the eyes of the man that had caused him so much pain.

"You know. I don't think I finished that night. You didn't learn your lesson. You didn't stay where you belong, on that mountain of yours." Webber was talking slowly, deliberately. "Now here you are

---

64 Psalm 34:19.
65 Psalm 46:1.
66 Psalm 59:1.
67 Psalm 140:4.

with my cattle. Did you get hungry? Couldn't grow enough food, so you thought you'd butcher a few cows and share with the other sodbusters?"

Webber had his hand on the whip that was hanging from his saddle horn.

Travis was not going to stand by and be whipped again. "Ya on my land now, Webber. I know what ya doin'. Take ya cows an' get off my land."

"A little bossy for a thief." He snapped the whip sharply.

Travis had his hand on the trigger. Would he be able to raise the rifle and fire before the whip caught him? He wished he was faster.

It was now a standoff. Who would move first? Then Webber suddenly kicked his horse, making it jump forward, knocking Travis to the ground. Travis fell backward, but he held onto his rifle. Webber was moving. Travis rolled over, trying to get a look at where his enemy was. Then the whip snapped just above his head. Travis rolled again—faster this time—to his left, freeing his right hand to use the rifle. As he rolled, he fired. The horse was right on top of Travis. The blast spooked the horse, and it fell on its side, throwing the rider off.

Travis jumped to his feet, but Webber was just as fast. He was up and slinging the whip in Travis's direction. The tip caught Travis on the neck, stinging and gushing blood. Travis fired, nicking Webber's forearm. The whip came at Travis again, wrapping itself around Travis's right arm and the rifle.

"*Hold it!*" The command came from behind Travis. It was Mark.

Webber was instantly on the offensive. "This thief was stealing our cattle!" He pulled the whip hard to release Travis, and it cut into Travis's arm. "Just look at that." Webber pointed to the cows. "Has them right here! You see them!"

"Take your cows and get off this land, Webber," the marshal commanded. "I don't want to see you on this land again."

"Okay, I'll leave," Webber said innocently. Then his tone changed. It was now menacing. "But you mark my words, little preacher." Webber was looking hard at Travis. "We're not finished."

Webber got on his horse and drove the cows casually through the middle of the cornfield.

Mark sat on his horse a long time, watching Webber cross the ridge. Then he stepped to the ground. "How bad are you hurt?" he asked Travis, eyeing the blood on his neck and shirt. Then the marshal saw blood on Travis's arm too.

Travis stood there, looking at the cornfield. They had just lost about of third of the crop.

"I'll live," he replied, then turned and started walking slowly back to the house. Mark followed.

Chapter 26

In the kitchen, Brenda had done as she was told. She stayed sitting at the table, but she was still crying. She had been scared for Travis when he left, and she had heard the rifle shots. She had also heard Mark's horse go past the house at a full run. She knew something serious was happening.

When Travis walked into the kitchen, she gasped at the blood and ran to him. Travis held her with his good arm and assured her that he was all right. Then he let go of his wife and sat down at the table.

Mark asked Brenda to get him some rags, bandages, and water. He looked at Travis's neck and held a cloth to it. It was still bleeding. Travis took the cloth and held it against the wound while Mark wrapped his arm. It was still bleeding too.

"These are nasty cuts to come from a whip. You really ought to let Jessie look at this. You know what happened last time." Mark said.

Travis nodded. "I know. I'll go later." He kept his eyes on Brenda. He didn't want her to be scared. He didn't want a repeat of last night every time he left the house. But he couldn't stay with her constantly. She had to trust God to overcome her fear. He would help her learn to trust God, but not right now.

"Fix the chil'en's lunches, please, Brenda. I'll take 'em in ta town with me. Can ya get their books too?"

When the blood stopped running down his neck, Travis put on a clean shirt and threw the one he took off in the fireplace. The whip had cut into it in three places, and it was covered with blood. It was ruined.

Travis told Brenda not to leave the house any more than she had to. He didn't want Webber coming back and seeing her. He held her face to force her to look at him and said, "We're going ta be okay. Do ya understand? God's takin' care a us. He'll protect us. But ya 'ave ta do what I say. Understand?"

She nodded, but she didn't look like she believed him.

The town heard what happened quickly. By the time Travis left the doctor's office, everyone seemed to know.

Travis took the children their books and lunches. He wanted them to see him, to know that he was okay. Travis told them he would be back to get them after school and that they were to stay together and not to leave town without him.

Cleve had been shaken by the morning's events, and all three were concerned about their father's injuries. Travis told Cleve how proud he was of him, taking the message to Mark as fast as he had. He thanked him for doing it.

Before Mary went back to class, she hugged her father tightly. "Daddy, I love you," she told him.

That afternoon, another farmer's field was destroyed by a herd of cows. The cowboys said the herd had "stampeded and we couldn't stop it."

But the farmer said the stampede was "awfully quiet." When he saw the cows, they were being herded in a circle over his wheat field.

Other ranchers came into town to meet with Mark and Travis. They assured the lawmen that they were not involved with what was happening, and they were just as concerned as the marshal was. As they were leaving, the owner of one of the smaller ranches stopped to talk to Travis.

"I'm sorry this happened. I want to apologize on behalf of all of us here"—he indicated the group with a sweep of his hand—"and let you know we don't want any harm to come to anyone. We've always gotten along well with you farmers, and we'd like to keep it that way."

Travis nodded. He didn't feel like talking, didn't want a long conversation.

When school let out, Travis was there, waiting for his children. They walked home together, leading Bess.

That night, the deputy didn't go into town, and Travis was the one who went to bed early. When he lay down, just wanting to sleep, Mary stuck her head in the door. "Do you want me to read to you tonight, Daddy?"

No, Travis didn't want to read. All he wanted to do was lay there and stop the pain in his neck and shoulder. But he said, "Ya can come read far a little while. That'd be nice, Mary."

They had been reading in Psalm. Mary started where they had left off, in chapter 34. When she finished verse 22, Travis asked her to stop. "Go back a few verses. Read 'gain where it starts, 'The righteous.'"

> The righteous cry out, and the Lord hears them; he delivers them from all their troubles. The Lord is close to the brokenhearted and saves those who are crushed in spirit. The righteous person may have many troubles, but the Lord delivers him from them all; he protects all his bones, not one of them will be broken. Evil will slay the wicked; the foes of the righteous will be condemned. The Lord will rescue his servants; no one who takes refuge in him will be condemned.[68]

Mary stopped when she finished verse 22 again. She looked at her father.

"Thank ya, Mary," he said, gave a small grin, and closed his eyes.

"Is God talking to you right now, Daddy?" Travis nodded his head. "He's talking to me too. He took care of you today, didn't he? And he's going to continue, isn't he?"

She set the book down and kissed him on the cheek. He smiled his crooked smile and again said, "Thank ya, Mary."

When she left the room, Travis said, "Thank ya, Jesus," and went to sleep.

---

68 Psalm 34:17–22.

*****

Every day it seemed like one of the farmers had trouble of some kind. They all had fences down, some had herds of cattle run over their crops, some had strays on their land, and some were confronted by cowboys, but no one saw Webber. Travis silently hoped that Webber was gone. But he knew Webber too well. The gunman was still around somewhere.

In town, everything continued as usual. The cowboys came into town at the end of the week, but there weren't as many, and they didn't get as rowdy.

Travis had taken his children to and from school for about a week. Other farmers' children reported encounters with a man they didn't know. This man was asking questions about the deputy's children. Then the man was gone, none of the children saw him again.

After another few weeks of not seeing Webber, Travis started letting his children walk alone again. He was cautious, though. He would stand on the porch in the mornings and watch them until they were out of sight. He prayed for their protection as he watched them go each day.

They had been told that when they got to town, they were to stop at the gun shop and say good morning to Jake. Jake knew what was going on, he was there to make sure the children arrived in town safely. Travis had asked Jake to let him know if there was a problem.

In the afternoon, Jake would take a break when he saw the children. His shop would be closed, and he would walk them part of the way home. Travis had not asked him to do this. But Jake was concerned for their safety too. He knew what kind of trouble Webber could cause. He'd seen this type of intimidation before.

Brenda would wait for them to come home, watching for them from the porch. Travis did his work but would come in from the fields in early afternoon. Until everyone in his family was safe at home, he wouldn't go back.

Travis was happy when school ended, and he knew everyone in his family was safe at home.

A herd of T-Bar cows had stampeded across the only sheep ranch in the area, destroying grazing and fences, scattering the sheep. A few of the ranchers had helped repair the barriers, but there had been strays. None of the cattlemen had any patience with the sheep. The shepherds were trying to find and retrieve all their animals but were losing them as the cattlemen shot the sheep when they strayed onto the rancher's land.

This had always been a delicate area. The cattlemen disliked the sheep. The ranchers felt the sheep destroyed the land, making it unusable by the cattle. The shepherds tried hard to keep their animals on their own land and had been successful as long as the fences remained intact. Tension increased on both sides with every report of a sheep being shot.

Cattlemen were beginning to argue too. They couldn't agree on how to stop this from escalating. There had been altercations between ranch hands on the open range that had resulted in injuries.

Cattle herds had been mingled when multiple strays had wandered into other ranchers' herds. On one occasion, a small herd had stampeded into a larger herd and caused major problems and damage to property. One cowboy had died.

Mark and Travis were talking with everyone, trying to calm temperaments and appease all involved. They were breaking up fights every night and had even stopped some gunplay on the street.

They were both tired. This was now a constant source of uncertainty. Travis was spending more time in his role as deputy and was getting little work done on his own farm.

Suddenly things begin to settle down. No more stray cows, no more stampeding herds, no more fences destroyed.

It had been four months since Travis and Webber had the confrontation in Travis's field. Travis had let his guard down without Webber around, but he was still concerned. Webber had said it wasn't finished.

Summer was coming to an end. Most of the crops had been harvested, and fall crops were being planted. School would start soon.

Travis had stayed in town and was late leaving that morning. It had been a long night. There had been unusual activity all night, and Travis was tired.

Next to the road, Travis saw a man sitting on the ground behind a cluster of trees. As Travis neared, he strained to see who the man was. His face was turned away, he wasn't moving. There wasn't a horse in sight.

Travis slowed to ask the man if he needed help. As he turned Bess off the road, and neared the trees, the man jumped up and ran at Travis. Travis now recognized Webber, but the deputy's rifle was in the scabbard on his saddle. He reached for it, but the whip was already in the air.

Travis turned Bess as he heard the whip snap. Bess stumbled. Travis held on, but he could tell Bess was having trouble staying on her feet.

Travis got off his mule, rifle in hand. He looked at the mule's back leg. There was a gash, blood running down the leg. He turned to face Webber. "I told you we weren't finished." Webber snickered.

Travis slapped Bess on the rump, and she limped off.

This is it! Travis thought. He softly prayed, "God 'elp me!"

Webber responded with, "God can't help you now," and he raised the whip again. Travis raised his rifle, but the whip was faster. It caught the rifle just as Travis pulled the trigger, and it fired as it left Travis's hand, the bullet hitting nothing but air.

Travis ran at Webber. The whip caught Travis on the leg, stinging and making him stumble. He was closer now, too close for the whip to be used. Travis tackled him midsection, and they rolled to the ground together. Webber got in a few good punches, cutting the deputy's lip. Then the gunslinger managed to get an arm around Travis's neck, but Travis elbowed him hard in the gut, knocking him off. Travis turned quickly to punch Webber in the nose. Blood started running onto the lip of Travis's opponent.

Webber backed up, smiled, and licked his bloody lip, then snapped his whip again. Travis put his left arm up to protect his face, and the whip wrapped itself around his arm, cutting into the skin. Travis grabbed the part of the whip that was in front of him with his left hand. There were barbs embedded in the leather! They were cutting into Travis's hand, but he wasn't going to let go. He pulled hard, and Webber came flying to him. More punches were thrown, then Travis hit Webber under the chin, sending him backward.

Travis held onto the whip tightly. Webber would have to let go at some point. Travis wasn't going to.

The gunman hit the ground and pulled back on the whip, making it taut as Travis was pulled forward, digging his boots into the dirt, the barbs pulling at his hand. Webber jumped up and reached for his gun with his left hand, then let go of the whip, and Travis fell backward. As he hit the ground, Travis reached for his pistol, drew, and fired.

Webber had made a fatal mistake. He had reached for his gun with his left hand. The front sight hung on carving in the fancy holster and slowed his draw. Travis didn't see this, but Webber felt it. Travis's bullet hit Webber in the shoulder as Travis fired again. Two hits!

The gunfighter had also underestimated Travis's ability.

Webber was on the ground, and his pistol was now pointed directly at Travis. They both fired at the same time, and both hit their mark. Webber was gone this time, but Travis was on the ground too.

Everything was now calm.

Travis opened his eyes. He was lying on his back, looking up at the sky. It was over. "Thank ya, Lord!" Travis said.

Travis looked over at his right arm. The bullet had gone through and through. It had missed the bone. It was a clean wound and would heal quickly.

Travis shook the whip off his left arm, and the barbs hung in his sleeve and pulled at his skin. There was blood running down both arms and in the palm of his left hand. He laughed to himself.

"Well, I won' be doin' any work far a while. I'll get that rest Jessie wanted me ta get."

Struggling to get up, Travis smiled his crooked smile—he was alive!

He was having trouble moving his right arm. Travis knew that he wouldn't be able to move it much longer, the muscles would weaken soon. He strained to get his pistol to his holster. He tried using his left hand to pick up Webber's gun, but the cuts stung as Travis gripped the gunman's pistol to put it in his belt. He limped over to retrieve his own rifle. It had been slung into the road by the whip. He clutched it with his left hand and hardened himself to the pain that holding it caused.

Travis looked toward town. It wasn't far, maybe half a mile, so he started walking.

As he neared town, he met Mark coming toward him. The marshal had heard the gunshots and was coming to investigate. Mark slid off his horse, but Travis kept walking. Travis was afraid if he stopped, he would never get moving again.

"Major Andrew Webber will not be botherin' anybody 'gain," Travis said slowly, not looking at the marshal. He kept his eyes straight ahead on the road as he walked.

Mark looked at Travis. He was dragging. Both arms were covered in blood. The left side of his face was swelling, and it had a few cuts. His eye was swollen shut, and he was limping some. Mark wasn't sure if Travis could even get on a horse. The marshal thought he had better just stay with Travis and let him walk.

Travis walked into town, right down the middle of Main Street. Mark stayed beside him. People stopped and watched, but nobody came to ask what happened, nobody offered to help.

Jake saw them as they passed his shop. He locked up quickly and caught up with Mark, taking the reins of his horse. Jake stopped as they neared the doctor's office, watching Travis and Mark continue.

Travis stumbled on the steps, and Mark caught him. The injured man straightened up and pulled away. "I've made it this far,

"I'm gonna finish," he slurred without looking at Mark. His lip and jaw were swollen, making it hard to talk.

Jessie turned as the door opened, and he watched as Travis hobbled in and slid onto the exam table to lie down. The wounded man closed his eyes and waited, rifle still in his left hand, left leg hanging off the table.

Mark pulled the gunman's pistol out of Travis's belt and reached out to take the rifle, which was covered in blood. But Travis didn't let go. Mark looked at the hand holding the gun. It was swollen. The marshal wrapped his fingertips around Travis's bloody fingers and gently pulled. His deputy's fingers scarcely moved, and Travis took in a few gasping breaths as Mark pried the gun from his deputy's rigid hand.

Jake was waiting for Mark outside Jessie's office. He took Travis's gun to his shop to clean. Just as he was opening the door, Jake looked up to see Bess limping slowly down the street. Jake caught her, taking her to the livery stable to care for her leg. He wasn't sure if anyone would be able to ride her again.

Jake returned to his shop to clean Travis's rifle. Then he walked back to the doctor's clinic to return it to Travis.

Jessie looked at Jake as he entered the clinic but said nothing. Jake nodded to Jessie, then spotted Travis in the next room. He was bandaged, lying on the bed with his eyes closed. Jake sat down with his friend and waited.

Mark had gone out to get Webber's body and had taken it to the T-Bar Ranch. When he told the cowboys that Travis had outdrawn the gunfighter, no one spoke. Mark knew that would make an impression on them. They would respect Travis more, but it would also leave Travis open to challengers. Any want-to-be gunman would now be seeking out Travis to see if he was faster than the deputy. Both of the lawmen would need to be more watchful.

Mark had also stopped to tell Brenda what had happened. She had heard the shots and had already had a good cry. Travis had not made it home, and she knew in her heart that the first shot she heard had come from Travis's rifle. She had prepared herself for the worst, so she was relieved when the first words out of Mark's mouth were, "Travis is okay. He's hurt, but it's not serious."

Early that afternoon, Travis opened his right eye. Both Mark and Jake were sitting across the room, talking quietly.

"Jake," Travis said, not moving. "Would ya take me 'ome?"

"Sure. I'll get Doc's buggy," he responded as he got up to leave.

Mark helped Travis into the buggy beside Jake. The deputy had both arms bandaged; one was in a sling, and the other was wrapped from his elbow to his fingertips. His pant leg was ripped, and a bandage could be seen beneath it.

As Travis sat down, Jessie began giving instructions.

"I don't want you doing anything, Travis. Nothing, do you understand me? Lie in bed and sit on the porch. That's it, nothing else."

Travis had to laugh at Jessie. He couldn't do anything anyway. He couldn't lift his right arm, and his left hand wouldn't move. Travis's eye, jaw, and lip were swollen. He probably wouldn't be eating much for the next few days either.

Jessie yelled from the doorway as they drove off, "What are you laughing at?"

As they passed the spot where he and Webber had fought, Travis looked toward the trees.

"Stop. Please," Travis asked. "Look over there by that tree that's leanin'. Would ya get me the whip?"

Jake got out of the buggy. He looked at Travis as he walked in front of the horse. His whole face looked swollen, how had he even seen that? His eyes didn't look like they were open. Jake had to get close before he saw it in the grass. He started to pick it up but dropped it when he felt the sharp sting. He took it by the handle and was careful this time as he coiled it in his hand. He laid it at Travis's feet.

"Sorry," Travis said as Jake put the finger that had been stabbed in his mouth.

"It's okay," Jake replied.

Jake looked at the whip again as he climbed into the buggy. So this is what Webber had used on Travis. Jake wondered why Travis would want it, but he didn't ask out loud.

Travis knew what Jake was thinking. "I'm not leavin' it there far somebody ta find. I don' want anyone else ta get 'urt by it."

Jake nodded and understood. Today he wasn't interested in holding a conversation with Travis. He just wanted his friend to feel better. But here Travis sat, injured and in pain, and he was thinking about protecting other people.

When they got to the farm, Jake helped Travis out of the buggy. Travis made it as far as the bench on the porch. He sat down heavily, pulling Brenda down with him. He leaned on her as she softly felt of his disfigured face. Travis closed his eyes and smiled. Her touch was healing. It felt good to be with her. He'd sit here in the sun for a little while; then he'd ask Brenda to help him into bed.

He opened his eyes and watched Jake leave, then looked down at the small bulge in his wife's stomach and smiled. He was alive and would be here for the birth of his child.

"Thank you, Lord." His silent prayer of thanksgiving continued.

He looked at the children standing in the yard, watching him. He felt their love too, and he smiled at them. Then he laid his head against his wife and closed his eyes.

No one seemed to know who wanted to start the range war. When word came from Ted Meadows, it had said he had not hired Webber. The ranch manager found the letter of introduction that Webber had presented to him, and it was signed by Meadows. At first glance, the handwriting looked the same, but on closer inspection and when compared to other letters, there were some inconsistencies. No one could say for sure if it was his signature or not.

The local cattlemen's association sent a few cowboys out to Travis's farm to help while Travis recovered. They only thought they worked hard on the ranch. Travis pushed them steadily—just for the fun of it. Every day they left drained but with more respect for the farmers. By the time Travis started working again, the farm was in the best condition he had ever seen it.

The T-Bar sent Travis a horse to replace Bess. When the foreman saw Travis on the horse with his old saddle, Travis was sent a new saddle too. Bess was retired to the small pasture behind the barn.

The T-Bar fired several of the ranch hands. There was no place for those who wanted trouble or for those that had befriended Webber.

Chapter 27

Travis sat rocking the baby, singing softly. Little Angus was just a few months old, and the house had gotten used to the diapers and crying. Twelve-year-old Mary wanted to do everything for him, except change and wash the messy diapers, but there were some things only his mother could do. Brenda was willing to let Mary do as much she was able. Travis, however, wouldn't let her do it all. He wanted time with his son too.

Eleven-year-old Cleve wasn't too excited about his new baby brother. "It's just a baby," he had said.

Luke was now eight years old, and he was more reserved. He didn't want to have anything to do with Angus. When Travis was holding his new son, Luke would find reason after reason to get his father to put Angus down. Brenda had told Travis that this was normal, all the youngest in a family were jealous when a new baby came into the house. Mark had confirmed what Brenda said.

Travis wasn't sure, though. His children on the mountain had never been jealous of one another. He didn't think it was natural, regardless of what Brenda and Mark said.

Luke had not been doing as well in school as he had done in the past. His problems had started just before Angus was born. Travis was concerned, but he didn't know what to do. He couldn't help him with his studies. Luke had never been a strong student like Mary or Cleve, but he had enjoyed school, until recently.

Now he was getting into trouble. Luke's teacher had spoken to Travis about it on the street. Travis had told Brenda about their conversation, and he had spoken to Luke. Mary had begun helping her younger brother with his homework, but no one was seeing a change in his behavior or in his grades.

Luke had quit walking home with Mary and Cleve. He would play along the road and would stop to look at almost anything. Cleve had told him to stay with them, but Luke lagged further and further behind each day. He always made it home not too long after Mary and Cleve, so their father had told them not to worry about Luke. He knew his way home.

Luke had also been slacking on his chores at home. He would do them slowly so that he wouldn't have time to finish before school. In the evenings, he would start a chore but not finish before he moved on to the next. Someone would have to check behind him daily. This was causing conflict between Luke and Cleve. Luke's older brother was usually the one to discover the unfinished job.

Cleve was a good kid. He would finish whatever needed to be finished and move on to his next chore, but tension was building between the two.

Travis had stayed at the jail that night and was late getting home. He had passed the children on his way, as they were going to school. Travis had stopped to give them a hug and told them he would see them that afternoon. He planned on being home when they got out of school.

But Travis would be busy plowing this afternoon. He had gotten behind when it had rained for two weeks straight. They needed the rain, though. The hot summer was coming. Travis didn't want to have to deal with another dry well.

Travis wasn't sure how much he would see the children tonight. He needed to spend more time with them, but he had too much to do.

It was nearing the end of the school year and near planting season. He would spend time with the children when the planting was finished.

The fear of the Lord is the beginning of knowledge, but fools despise wisdom and instruction [69] came to Travis's mind as he thought of his

---

69   Proverbs 1:7.

son while riding home a few weeks later. He thought, either Luke wasn't understanding the scripture—Travis stopped his horse at the creek so the horse could get a drink—or he was choosing to disobey.

Travis had been having the children read Scripture almost daily. Luke was hearing and learning it, but it wasn't sticking. His heart didn't understand what was being read.

"Father, is 'e bein' disobedient? Or does 'e not understand?" Travis asked out loud.

Another scripture came into his thoughts, *Folly is bound up in the heart of a child, but the rod of discipline drives it far away.*[70] "No, Lord, please, there's got ta be a better way! Show me what ta do ta change my son's heart. I don' want ta whip him!" Travis didn't think he would be able to spank his son. "Please, Father, find 'nother way."

Then Travis remembered the verse in Ephesians, *Father's do not exasperate your children; instead, bring them up in the training and instruction of the Lord.*[71]

"That's what I'm tryin' ta do. Am I doin' somethin' that's causin' rebellion, or is this just childish behavior?" Travis asked his Lord. He started moving the horse again. The spirit spoke, *If any of you lacks wisdom, let him ask God who gives generously to all without finding fault, and it will be given to him.*[72]

Travis was already having a conversation with God. He'd continue following the Spirit's leading. "Lord, give me wisdom in correctin' Luke."

And again, God spoke to him, *All your children will be taught by the Lord, and great will be their peace.*[73]

Travis smiled. "I'll 'old ya ta that promise, Lord." He gave his horse a kick to speed up.

God responded, *Let us hold fast the confession of our hope without wavering, for he who promised is faithful.*[74]

"Thank ya, Lord," Travis answered.

70	Proverbs 22:15.
71	Ephesians 6:4.
72	James 1:5.
73	Isaiah 54:14.
74	Hebrews 10:23 (ESV).

Travis tried to see the children when they first came home from school, but today that hadn't happened. Travis was busy in the field; he wasn't paying attention to the time. It had been a few days since Travis's conversation with God about Luke.

Cleve came to get him as supper neared.

As they carried tools to the barn, Travis asked Cleve, "How was school today?"

"I had a good day, made a good grade on my arithmetic test. I moved to the next level in spelling."

"Great! Ya do good in school. I'm proud a ya." Travis gave Cleve a squeeze of the shoulders.

"But Luke got in bad trouble. He hit Lizzie Butler. Then he yelled something ugly at the teacher."

Travis was silent, he hadn't thought about Luke's problems all day.

"Daddy, did you hear me?" Cleve asked.

Travis responded, "Yes, I was just thinkin'. Who's Lizzie Butler, I don't remember that name?"

Cleve explained, "She's new. They just moved here from Oklahoma. Her dad's the new range foreman at Treadway's."

Travis nodded and gave a sigh. A new foreman. Any time there was new management at one of the ranches, his authority in town would be challenged. He'd have to prove himself again.

They got the tools to the barn and Cleve put them away while Travis washed up.

At supper, Travis asked Mary how her day had gone. Mary started talking about something one of the other girls had told her and how her best friend had given her a ribbon for her hair and how Michael Frost had sat with her at lunch. Then she looked at Luke and said, "But Luke got his hand spanked."

Everyone turned to look at Luke. He didn't look ashamed or saddened. He looked defiant.

"Luke!" Brenda said as she looked up from feeding little Angus.

"Do ya wanna tell us 'bout it?" Travis asked.

"Not really." Luke went back to his meal.

Travis changed his tone. "Let me put it 'nother way then. Tell us what 'appene'."

Luke glared at Mary. "Lizzie said she would bet me that her daddy could beat you up. She said you were nothing but a stupid mountain man that couldn't read or write, and her daddy said he didn't know how you got the job as deputy. So I hit her."

Travis sat there, looking at him sadly. He had heard all this before and he just ignored these comments. Now Luke was dealing with Travis's failures. "Is that why ya got ya 'and spanked?"

Luke glared at Mary again. Why did she have to tell? "No, I had to apologize and got sent to the corner."

"So why did ya get ya 'and spanked?"

"Because I called the teacher a name when she said Lizzie was right about you being ill...illit—"

"Illiterate." Cleve injected.

Travis looked at Cleve and shook his head slightly. The other children knew not to speak when Travis was talking to one particular child.

"Illiterate! That's it!" Luke said.

Travis looked at Brenda. Brenda said, "It means you can't read or write."

Travis nodded his head. "Well, it's true. I can't read much, an' I can't write more than my name. Does that mean I'm stupid?"

Luke looked at him. "No, you're not stupid. But Lizzie said you were."

"Luke, I've 'ad ta deal with people thinkin' that my whole life. In the book of James, it says, 'Who is wise and understanding among you? Let them show it by their good life, by deeds done in the humility that comes from wisdom.'[75]

"I try ta live in a good way, an' I think God gives me wisdom ta do that.

"Proverbs says, 'Fools find no pleasure in understanding but delight in airing their own opinions.'[76] If someone says somethin' that ya know isn't true, just ignore it. I know it's 'ard, but we wanna live as Jesus did, not like those in the darkness that don' understand the truth God gives us."

---

75   James 3:13.
76   Proverbs 18:2.

Luke looked down. "Yes, sir."

Travis looked at Brenda to see if she wanted to add anything. She nodded her head to Travis. He had done well. She went back to feeding Angus.

Travis held Angus and sang to him as Brenda and Mary cleaned the kitchen after supper. Then Mary read a few scripture passages. Luke sat staring at Travis. Travis knew Luke was looking at him, but he didn't know what else to do or what else to say. He hoped Luke was just thinking about what had been said, letting it sink in.

When the kitchen was clean, and the scripture had been read, Travis handed the sleeping baby to Brenda, and he left for town.

Chapter 28

A week later, Travis was plowing a field when Cleve came running to him. It was in the middle of the day, and Cleve should have been in school. Travis stopped the plow. "What's wrong?"

Cleve was out of breath, and his words were coming fast. "Luke and the teacher had an argument. The teacher was hitting Luke with her switch across the back, Luke was crying. Mary was yelling stop and the teacher threatened to hit Mary too. So I ran out of the school and found the marshal. He went back with me and got Luke and took him to Dr. Cooper's. The teacher told me and Mary to get out, so we came home. Mary's with Mama."

Travis dropped the lines and left the horse in the field as he and Cleve ran to the house.

Mary was still crying in her mother's arms. When she saw her father, she pulled away from her mother and ran to him. "She kept hitting him and hitting him!" She cried as her father took her in his arms. Travis looked at Brenda who was also crying.

Travis held Mary as he said, "I'll go in ta town an' find Luke." He began to pull away.

Cleve said, "I'll saddle your horse." And Cleve left.

Travis looked into his wife's eyes. He knew what Brenda was thinking, he was thinking the same thing. Neither of them wanted their son's back scarred.

He went to her, and they held each other for a moment. Travis put his hand on Brenda's face as he looked into her eyes again.

"I'll go get 'im. 'E'll be okay." His voice was a whisper. He turned and walked outside to find Cleve almost finished buckling the cinch.

As Travis was mounting, he looked up and saw the marshal coming toward the house, Luke behind him on the horse.

Travis dropped back to the ground and waited. As the marshal came to a stop beside him, Luke's father reached up, helped his son down, and held him tight. Travis was trying hard to hold back the tears that came to his eyes.

Mark started talking first. "Jessie says he's okay. He may have a few bruises, and he's a little scratched up, but the skin's not broken very bad. It won't leave scars."

Travis's body relaxed with a big sigh, and the tears came freely.

"Thank ya, Lord." He dropped his face over Luke's head, still holding him.

Mark continued, "They're calling a meeting of the school board tonight. They will want some of the older children there to tell what happened. Can you bring Mary and Cleve?"

Travis nodded.

"It scared most of the kids." Mark added, "She could get fired."

Travis nodded his head again. Right now, he didn't care what happened to that teacher. All that mattered was his son was safe at home.

In the house, no one spoke. Mary and Cleve were looking at Travis, waiting for him to start. Luke was sitting beside his mother, leaning on her, his eyes on the floor, her arm around him.

Travis stood at the window a long time, looking out. When he turned around, he had a look on his face the children had never seen before. They weren't sure what to make of it.

"I don' know what 'appene', and I'm not gonna ask right now, but I will later," he began. "What I wanna know now is, Luke, are ya okay?"

He waited for Luke to answer, but the answer came slowly. "Yes, sir. I guess."

"I know it hurt. I also know ya was scared. But it's over now. I promise all a ya that nothin' like this will 'appen with that teacher 'gain." Travis stopped and looked at each face, then continued, "But right now, we 'ave ta decide what we're gonna do. Are we gonna 'old a grudge 'gainst Ms. Spurgeon or are we gonna forgive 'er?"

Brenda's face looked shocked. "Forgive her? Travis!"

Travis gave his wife a look of caution. "Just 'cause we forgive 'er don' mean we're gonna be friends. Forgivin' don' mean trustin' 'er. But unforgiveness will grow. It's bitter an' stays with ya. While Jesus was hangin' on the cross, 'e said, 'Father, forgive them, for they know not what they do.'[77] Miss Spurgeon didn' know what she was doin' either. I'm sure she's already regrettin' what she did. She let 'erself get upset. She lost 'er self-control. Now, Luke, tell me why she was upset."

Luke looked at his father, and his words again came slowly. "I called her a fool. I told her that she wasn't trying to understand, and she wouldn't know the truth if it was sitting in front of her because all she wanted to do was push her own belief on the rest of us. I told her she was lying."

Travis stood silently a moment. The expression on his face didn't change. Yes, that would make anyone angry. "What started the argument?"

"Peewee couldn't answer her history question, and she called him ignorant. That means stupid. Peewee's not stupid, it just takes him a little while to figure things out, and he's really quiet. He hardly ever says anything."

Travis looked to Cleve who nodded. Travis nodded to Luke. "Okay. So ya was protectin' ya friend."

"He's not my friend. He doesn't have any friends. He's just a kid at school."

"Okay. What ya did was right, Luke, tryin' ta protect this boy, but the way ya did it was wrong. Do ya understand? Ya don't talk ta ya teacher like that, even if she's wrong, it's disrespectful." Travis turned to his other children. "Mary, Cleve, can ya come with me tonight an' tell the people on the school board what 'appene'?"

They both nodded. "Yes, sir," Cleve said.

"Cleve, would you go unhook the plow horse an' put her 'way? Luke, I'd like ta see ya in the bedroom."

Luke looked at his mama. They were never called to the bedroom.

---

77   Luke 23:34.

"Go on, you're fine," she said as she gave him a little shove.

In the bedroom, Travis sat on the bed to remove Luke's shirt. Travis turned his son around to look at his back. There were several small cuts, some light bruising, and a few red welts. Travis touched an area and asked if it hurt. Luke said just a little. Travis turned him around to face him and hugged him again, holding him longer than necessary.

Travis recited scripture to his son, "'Defend the weak and the fatherless; uphold the cause of the poor and the oppressed. Rescue the weak and the needy; deliver them from the hand of the wicked.'[78]

"Ya did good, son, I'm proud of ya. We're just gonna 'ave ta come up with a better way ta do it," Travis said sadly.

Then Travis released the boy and started unbuttoning his own shirt. Luke looked puzzled, wondering what his father was doing.

When Travis pulled the shirt down off his shoulders, he stood up and turned around. Luke gasped. "Daddy! What happened?"

Luke reached out and touched his father's scarred back softly.

Travis spoke, "Do ya remember the man I killed on the road back near the first a school?"

"Yes, sir."

"Do you remember how my arm was cut, an' how 'e had cut my neck a few months before that?"

"Yes, sir."

"Well, during the war, 'e was one a the officers over me. 'E didn' care what 'appene' ta anyone, an' 'e took out 'is anger on me." Travis pulled his shirt back up and started to button it again. He turned around and sat back down on the bed, looking into his son's eyes.

"I had ta forgive 'im, or it would 'ave eaten me up. I would 'ave gotten angry just like 'im. Ya saw what 'e was still doin' ta people, tryin' ta start 'nother war between the ranchers an' the farmers. It was all 'cause a 'is hatred, an' 'e didn' even know what 'e was mad at."

Travis watched Luke. He hoped he was getting through to him. "Ya don' want ta be like 'im, do ya?"

---

78   Psalm 82:3–4.

"No, sir! I sure don't."

"So can ya find it in ya heart ta forgive ya teacher?"

"Yes, sir, I'll try."

"Ya gonna find that ya is gonna 'ave ta forgive 'er today, an' 'gain 'morrow an' 'gain the next day. Ya gonna 'ave ta forgive 'er ever' time ya look at 'er. Ever' time she speaks ta ya. Can ya do that?"

"I'll try."

"And if ya 'ave problems doin' it, would ya come ta me and let me 'elp ya?"

"Yes, sir." Luke flung himself at his father, and they held each other. Travis felt he had his son back.

*****

Travis, Mary, and Cleve arrived at the school just before the meeting started. The room was crowded, but someone had saved them places near the front. "After all," he told Travis, "it was your kid that caused all this."

The chairman began by asking the teacher what happened.

"Well, I was teaching history, and I asked a child a question. He wouldn't answer me. I was trying to get him to talk when Luke Cole called me a fool. He said I was trying to push my opinion on the children and that I didn't understand anything, that I was telling a lie. So I spanked him for being disruptive in the class and disrespectful to me. Then his sister started yelling at me to stop, so I told her I would whip her too if she continued to be disrespectful. That's when Cleve Cole ran out of the room. I finished the spanking, and the marshal came in and took the Cole children with him."

The chairman thanked her and asked her to sit down. Then he asked if anyone had a different story. Travis stood up slowly.

"Yes, Travis."

"The story my chil'en told me is a little diff'ent."

"Okay, let's hear from, which one?"

Cleve stood up. "When she was trying to get Peewee to talk, she was calling him names and telling him he was stupid. She was

160

telling the whole class that he couldn't learn anything. Nobody's going to answer a question when you're treated like that. And she wasn't spanking my brother. She was beating him across the back with a switch. And we didn't leave with the marshal, she told me and Mary to leave."

"Thank you. Are there any other witnesses?"

Four children stood up. "Do any of you have a different story?"

"No."

"No, sir."

"I saw what Cleve saw."

"Cleve said the truth."

The chairman continued, "Okay, thank you children. Dr. Cooper, are you here?"

His voice came from the back. "Yes, I'm here." And he walked forward.

The chairman asked, "I understand you examined the Cole boy. What did you find?"

"I found marks on his back that could have come from a switch. Several marks on top of one another. Some were bleeding. There was also bruising," Dr. Cooper reported.

The chairman then called on the marshal.

Mark spoke, "Cleve came to my office saying that Miss Spurgeon was beating his brother and threatening to beat his sister. I went to the school, and as I got near the door, I heard children crying. When I walked into the room, I found Miss Spurgeon standing over Luke with this in her hand." Mark produced a thin four-foot branch. The bark had not been cleaned, and there were rough knots and points where smaller limbs had been broken off.

"Luke was on the floor crying. Several of the other children were crying too. A few were hiding their faces. I took this out of her hand and took Luke to Dr. Cooper's office."

"Thank you. Are there any other comments before we consult with one another to determine what is to be done, if anything." He waited a moment then added, "Okay, let us talk this over, and we will return." The five-man council stood up and left the room.

A few that remained in the room started talking quietly. The longer the council deliberated, the more talking took place.

When the council came back into the room, everyone quieted quickly.

"After hearing the witnesses and discussing this among ourselves, we find that Miss Spurgeon has not conducted herself as she was expected to do. While we understand that the Cole child was disrespectful, we cannot condone the manner in which punishment was given. Are there any comments before we deliver our decision?"

There was silence in the room. Travis slowly stood again.

"Yes, Travis."

"Gentlemen. Miss Spurgeon," Travis began by looking at the people he was addressing. "I would like ta offer my apology, an' that a my son Luke, far the disrespect 'e gave ta Miss Spurgeon." Travis nodded toward the teacher. "I realize Luke 'and led the situation poorly, an' 'e an' I 'ave discussed it. I don' believe 'e will be disrespectful ta this degree 'gain. And I don' think Miss Spurgeon 'as 'ad any trouble like this in the past. This would be the first time."

Travis was talking slowly, carefully. Mark had never heard Travis talk this much in front of anyone, except himself, and he had never seen him so proper.

"I would like ta ask the council ta show mercy on 'er an' give 'er 'nother chance."

"It was your children involved. Your child hurt. Why would you want to show her mercy?" The question came from a woman in the audience.

Travis turned to look at the small crowd of parents. "'Cause we all deserve a second chance. We all make mistakes. Jesus was asked 'bout stonin' a woman who sinned. He said, 'Let any one of you who is without sin be the first to throw a stone at her.'"[79]

Travis took a deep breath. He was still choosing his words carefully.

---

79   John 8:7.

"Our chil'en will tell us what 'appens in class. There's no secret what goes on in this room. I'm willin' ta give 'er a chance with my chil'en, provided she makes a few changes."

Travis looked at the people in the room. Then he turned back to the council. "That's all I 'ave ta say. Thank ya." And he sat down. His children were sitting on either side of him, and he reached over and took their hands, like he was drawing strength from them.

The room was quiet. The chairman asked, "Are there any other comments?" There was more silence. Then he spoke again, "I believe the council should discuss this again." They leaned together and talked quietly in front of the crowd.

"Okay," the chairman said when he sat back up. "Here's what we're going to do. We will finish out the last few days of school with another adult in the classroom to watch. Before school starts back in the fall, we are going to set some rules of behavior and discipline for both the students and the teacher. We will appoint a committee to do this, and you will be informed of these rules before school starts next fall."

The chairman turned to face the teacher. "Miss Spurgeon, would you please stay."

Then turning to face the classroom again, he said, "This meeting is adjourned."

Some liked this idea, some didn't. Travis didn't care what people thought. It wasn't his idea. It came from Jesus. The teacher would have a chance to redeem herself. Travis had said his peace, and everyone knew how he felt, even his children.

On the way home, Travis talked with his two older children about forgiveness, and they agreed to give Miss Spurgeon another chance. They had always thought she was a good teacher and knew Luke had been challenging lately.

Luke had just gone to bed when the other children returned home. Mary and Cleve stopped to tell their mother what had happened.

Travis went into the room Luke shared with Cleve.

Luke was still awake, so Travis sat down on the edge of his bed to tell him about the meeting. Then he prayed with his son, ending with, "Let us follow the Lord our God and revere him. 'Keep his commands and obey him; serve him and hold fast to him.'[80] 'Create in (us) a pure heart, O God, and renew a steadfast spirit within (us).'[81] Keep your servant(s) also from willful sins; may they not rule over (us). Then (we) will be blameless, innocent of great transgression.'"[82]

The father kissed his son and left him to sleep.

80   Deuteronomy 13:4b.
81   Psalm 51:10.
82   Psalm 19:13.

Chapter 29

All Mary wanted that morning was a little quiet so she could read the new book her father had gotten her. Well, it was new to her. Her father had bought it from a traveling salesman who told him it had only been read once. Travis had laughed when he told her that, even her uneducated father could tell the pages were worn out.

Two-year-old Angus wouldn't leave her alone, and ten-year-old Luke was nothing if not a pest. Her baby sister had been crying all day. Mama had said she was getting her first tooth.

Mary had asked her mother if she could go out behind the hayfield, to the aspen grove that grew beside the creek, to read. Her mother had granted permission, provided she was back before her father returned from town. He had just left the farm, so she would have a few hours to read.

She took The *Adventures of Tom Sawyer* and headed through the field. When she got to the trees, she looked back at her home and smiled. She was happy. She had a great family, if she excluded her brother Luke. Her parents were wonderful people who loved their five children. They weren't rich, but they didn't need anything. They had enough food, clean clothes, and a warm house in winter. Her father would bring her books from time to time, and she loved to read.

She had just turned fifteen years old and was in her last year of school, the eighth grade. That's as far as school went in Harris. She didn't know what she wanted to do next year. Her father had told her that was okay. She had all year to figure it out.

Mary made herself comfortable under the aspen trees where the fall leaves were just beginning to turn colors. She was soon journeying down the Mississippi with Tom.

She heard a noise behind her and knew it was Luke. He wouldn't leave her alone. She would ignore him. There was more noise.

"Go away, Luke. Mama said I could come here to get away from you. She's not going to be happy if she finds out you followed me."

She looked up to see three Indian braves. She jumped up! Backed up a few steps and bumped into—someone! She looked around to see another Indian put his arms out and throw a blanket over her head. She screamed! And screamed! But the blanket was muffling the sound.

Cleve heard something. He wasn't sure what it was. He stopped the horse and listened. Turning around, he looked down the hill in the direction his sister had gone. He saw them. Indians! Was that Indians? And they had Mary!

"No!" he yelled as he dropped the reins and jumped to the ground. He started running toward them. He had no idea what he would do when he got there, but they were carrying Mary away.

By the time he made it out of the field and to the trees, they were gone. He saw them riding northwest, Mary thrown facedown over one of the horses in front of an Indian, the blanket still over her head. Mary's new book was lying on the ground.

Cleve picked up the book and started running back through the field. When he got to the hay rake, he unhooked it from the horse quickly. He could ride the horse, harness and all. He kicked the horse and was running the old mare as he passed the house.

Brenda looked out the window and saw her oldest son leaving the farm. She ran outside. Where was he going?

She called Cleve's brother. "Luke! Luke! Come here!"

"Yes, ma'am?"

"Where's Cleve going?" she asked as she pointed to his brother, already far down the road.

"I don't know."

"Go get Mary, would you? She's reading her book at the aspen grove."

"Yes, ma'am." And Luke headed toward the field.

A short time later, Luke came back to the house. His mother was still standing on the porch.

"Mama, I couldn't find Mary, but her book was lying on the ground next to the rake." He handed the book to his mother.

Brenda was now scared. Cleve had never left the farm without telling her what he was doing, and Mary had disappeared.

The baby started crying, but Brenda was ignoring the sound.

"Mama? Naomi's crying." Luke wasn't getting a response from his mother, so he walked into the house and picked up his baby sister. He brought her outside. The baby was still crying, and now so was his mother.

In town, Cleve slowed down to look for his father's horse. Not at the marshal's office, not at Dr. Cooper's, not at the gunsmith's, not at the mercantile. He didn't see it at the livery stable either. Cleve turned around and went back to the marshal's office. He slid off the plow horse and ran inside.

"Marshal, where's Daddy?"

Mark answered without looking up, "I haven't seen him, why?" When the marshal did look at Cleve, he could tell something wasn't right. He started to get out of his chair. "What's wrong, Cleve?"

"Indians took Mary! I saw them! Four of them!"

"You're sure?"

The boy's face showed the displeasure that the marshal was questioning what he said, and he repeated himself distinctly, "I saw them!"

He was excited, and now his words came faster. "I was in the hayfield. She was reading at the aspen grove by the creek, the book Daddy brought home yesterday. I heard her scream, and they had a blanket over her, carrying her off! I ran down there, but they were riding off with her!"

"Okay, go get Jake and get to the livery and get us some horses saddled. I'm going to get Dr. Cooper to do something for me, and I'll be right there." Mark was thinking and talking as he was moving. What needed to be done first? They both headed in different directions.

Mark asked Dr. Cooper to send telegrams to the surrounding cavalry forts asking about Indian activity. He then asked Jessie to see if he could find Travis.

Dr. Cooper sent the telegrams. Coming back through town, he spotted Travis's horse at Judge Barker's house. Knocking on the door, Mrs. Barker answered.

"I'm looking for Travis, is he here?"

Just then, Travis stuck his head around the corner.

"What?"

Jessie told Travis what Mark had told him, and Travis took off headed home. He cut across the open land, a shortcut for a short distance. It would take him straight through his own turnip field. Travis wasn't worried about trampling the tender young plants, his only thought was Mary.

Dr. Cooper stood with Judge and Mrs. Barker and watched him go. "I'm going out there," the judge said.

"I'm coming with you," added Jessie.

When Mark, Cleve, and Jake got to the farm, Travis had already talked to his wife and Luke. They didn't know anything. Travis was holding Brenda when he saw the others coming down the road toward them.

Travis was impatient, and he questioned Cleve before he got off his horse. Cleve told him what happened. Travis stood there, looking at the aspen trees. He started nodding his head. He would have to go after them.

He looked over at Luke, who was sitting on the ground with Angus and Naomi, then at Brenda. He would have to leave his family alone. This was unsettling, but if he rode now, he might catch them.

Mark was talking, but Travis wasn't listening. "Travis, did you hear me?"

Travis looked at Mark. "I said I've sent a message to Fort Wallace and Fort Harker. I should get a response soon. We'll get a group together and be ready to leave as soon as I hear back from the forts."

"I can't wait." Travis moved toward the house to gather supplies. Mark followed him, trying to talk him into waiting. But Travis wasn't responding to him.

Inside Travis grabbed a blanket, his jacket, extra bullets for his rifle and pistol, his canteen, and a few biscuits from the table. He walked out the door. He filled his canteen at the water trough instead of taking time to draw water from the well. He went to the barn and came back with his saddlebags, slinging them across the back of his horse and tying the blanket in place. Then he turned to Brenda.

"I'll get 'er back." He gave his wife a swift hug and a kiss on the cheek. Then he moved to his children.

Travis kissed the top of Luke's head. "Luke, 'elp ya mama, would ya?" And then he patted his son on the shoulder. He gave each of the little ones a kiss, moving to Cleve.

"Son, I know I can depend on ya. Take care a thin's far me. There's 'nother rifle in the tack room." He stood there and looked at his oldest son for a moment, gave him a hug, then looked at the others again. Travis mounted his horse and rode toward the aspens.

Everyone stood at the farm, watching Travis as he moved away. They watched him get off his horse beside the trees and look at the ground. He knelt down, touching the ground a few times. Then he walked his horse out of sight over the small rise. A few minutes later, Travis was seen riding northwest.

They were still watching him in the distance when Judge Barker and Dr. Cooper arrived.

"Mark, we got a response from Fort Harker," Jessie was saying. "They were moving Cheyenne from the North to the Cheyenne-Arapaho Reservation in Oklahoma. Somewhere along the line, a few braves disappeared. The commander at the fort thinks they are headed north, back to Montana."

"Jake," Mark said, turning to his friend. "I've got to go with Travis. Can you take care of things? Just do what you can."

The response came. "Sure. Go with him."

"Judge, can you help too?"

"I'll take care of what I can," the judge replied.

Mark got on his horse and headed in the direction Travis had gone.

While the others were talking, Cleve went to the barn and got the rifle out of the tack room. He walked past the group as they watched and went into the house. The rifle was set on the table as Cleve got the ammo out of the box. Then he loaded the rifle. He would protect his family and would now carry a rifle with him wherever he went, like his daddy did.

Chapter 30

Mark caught up with Travis three hours later as Travis was looking at a patch of hard rocky ground. Travis was studying the pattern of the dirt. He didn't look up, but he knew it was Mark.

"They were here, but they didn't go into the grasslands. They want us to think they did but...it looks like they turned around and went this way." Travis was leading his horse to the right. A few minutes later, Travis said, "There! Got them." And he mounted and started moving again. Mark followed.

As night fell, they stopped to make camp. Mark said, "How far ahead of us do you think they are?"

"Not far, but I can't follow what I can't see. If they stop far the night, we should be able ta catch 'em 'morrow. If they keep movin'...I just don' know."

Travis was up before the sun the next morning, and as soon as he could see the ground, he was moving. Mark followed him.

Mark could follow a man's trail when the man wasn't trying to hide, but apparently Travis's ability was far better than his own.

Mark was constantly amazed at the new things he discovered about his deputy. They had known each other for twelve years, and this was the first time he had seen Travis track.

Mark knew Travis could follow a trail. Travis had led a hunting party a few years ago after some wolf attacks at a couple of farms. Three groups had gone out. Two hunting parties of ranchers and a group of farmers, led by Travis. After just two days, the farmers had returned to town with several gray wolves. Those with Travis talked of his skill.

Travis had also hunted a rogue mountain lion soon after he arrived in Harris. He had gone alone and returned unscathed. He had told Mark that mountain lions were easy to track but had laughed that a good dog would have been helpful. Mark still didn't know if that was the truth or if Travis was joking.

Mark had hunted with Travis, but he had never witnessed Travis track, until now. Every time Mark had gone after an outlaw, he had left Travis to take care of things in town. Now Mark thought that may have been a mistake.

Travis was spotting signs that Mark would never have realized were made by men.

Mark tried talking to Travis as they rode, but Travis wouldn't respond. Mark didn't know if he was concentrating on following the trail or if he was just being moody again. Either way, Travis wasn't talking, so Mark just followed.

Travis was praying. He was praying hard. He was ignoring Mark because he was listening for God. Travis didn't mumble when he prayed anymore. He had gotten interrupted too often with wisecracks. Now he either spoke silently to God, or he spoke out loud when he was alone.

Travis never noticed that other people saw him praying out loud, or that they were listening. These people still gossiped about him talking to himself, but it didn't seem to bother people as much as it had in the past.

Today Travis wanted an undisturbed conversation with his Lord. In late afternoon, Travis slowed, raised his rifle, and fired. Mark didn't know what Travis was shooting at. There was no point in asking, Travis hadn't said a word, or even looked Mark's way, for hours. Mark waited to see what Travis had shot. The marshal knew his deputy had hit where he was aiming. He seldom missed.

Travis turned in the direction he had shot and moved the horse forward as Mark followed. Then Travis stopped. He got off his horse and picked up a fuzzy gray rabbit. He held it up by the back legs for Mark to see and said, "Supper." Travis climbed back on his horse and started moving again.

Just after dark, they stopped. Travis skinned the rabbit while Mark built a fire. As the rabbit was roasting, Mark asked, "What do you think? Can we catch them?"

"I'm gonna. I'm not leavin' Mary with 'em. I'll find 'em."

Mark questioned Travis more. "Are you still seeing the trail?"

"No, I lost it just 'fore I saw the rabbit. I'll pick it up 'gain, though," Travis replied. He sounded confident.

Mark offered some advice. "We need to find a town and contact the fort. Find out what they know about where the Indians are. Let them know where we are."

"They've been movin' steady north-northwest," Travis said with certainty. "They're not gonna change direction yet. If they're headed ta Montana, they'll keep goin' until they hit the Dakota Black Hills."

"Have you been in the Dakota territory?"

"Once. Winter's comin'. It's gonna get bad there." Travis shook his head, not liking the thought of winter in the Dakotas.

"Travis, we need supplies," Mark injected. "We should be close to Fort Hays."

"No, I'm not stoppin'."

"Travis, we need guidance. We could be headed the wrong way?"

"No, I'm not stoppin'!" Travis was adamant.

"I'm not going to do this, Travis. I'm not just riding with the hope we'll run into them. We need eyes. We need a plan."

Travis's eyes were focused hard on Mark. Mark couldn't tell what Travis was thinking. Travis had that look on his face. The look that told Mark his deputy was serious.

Travis responded calmly, "Ya do what ya want ta do. I didn' ask ya ta come. Go back ta Harris, take care a the town. I'm gonna find Mary."

Travis reached down and took the rabbit, ripped a chunk of meat off, and walked into the darkness to pray. God would tell him where to find Mary. He didn't need the soldiers, or Mark, interfering.

Travis knew how the soldiers treated the Indians. He didn't want or need that problem as he searched for Mary. Indians were just people, like himself. They had families and homes. But this one bunch of Indians was wicked, maybe desperate. Travis could deal with this better alone.

Travis had grown up near an isolated family of mixed-race Indians. The full-blood Tutelo father had taken Travis with him as he taught his own sons the way of the forest.

As a teenager, Travis had gone with this Indian, attending a few meetings with the neighboring Cherokee and Shawnee tribes. The knowledge he had gained from knowing those Indians would help him deal with any Indian he came in contact with.

Anyway, it would be easier to live off the land if he was alone. He wouldn't have to worry about taking care of someone else, and he could travel faster. He wouldn't be noticed as much either if he was alone.

As Travis left camp, he recited scripture, "Now this I know: The Lord gives victory to his anointed. He answers him from his heavenly sanctuary with the victorious power of his right hand. Some trust in chariots and some in horses, but we trust in the name of the Lord our God."[83]

The marshal didn't hear him.

Mark was almost asleep when Travis came back into camp that night. The deputy added wood to the small fire and lay down, staring up at the stars. Mark rolled over to look at his friend.

Travis was a good friend. Mark hated arguing with him. Travis had always made wise, calculated, and prayerful decisions. Mark thought Travis must not be thinking straight right now. The marshal felt sad and discouraged as he fell asleep.

The next morning, Mark woke to the sound of Travis saddling his horse. It was still dark. There was no sign of the sun rising. The marshal started to slowly pull himself off the ground. But he turned quickly as he heard Travis ride off. Mark had not wanted it to end like this. He didn't think Travis would be so impetuous.

But as Mark rode that morning, he thought about Travis and realized that Travis had told him what to do. He had told the

---

83   Psalm 20:6–7.

marshal to go back to Harris. Travis hadn't said it as an option or even a suggestion. He had given Mark a command. It was the same no-non-sense tone of voice his deputy used when he was dealing with hoodlums in town.

Mark realized that Travis had made a deliberate decision, and he had probably prayed about it too. Travis had started this journey alone, without asking or waiting for assistance, and that's the way he wanted it.

Fort Hays was found about midmorning. Mark met with the commander and reported that Travis was trailing the rebel Indians who had taken his daughter. They were headed for the Dakota territories. The commander would pass the information along in that direction. Mark asked that the forts and towns in that direction be notified and that any help Travis needed be given to him. The marshal would personally fund any expenses incurred, no questions asked.

That afternoon, Mark headed back to Harris.

Chapter 31

At the farm, Brenda was barely able to take care of the children. Travis had been her strength since her first husband had died. As the days passed, she thought of what Travis had done and what he had taught her.

Angus had brought this dirty little man home with him and had invited him to eat with the family. Brenda hadn't liked it. But as the stranger and her husband talked, Travis had let the children crawl into his lap. The children liked him, and he had been comfortable and playful with them. Over the weeks that followed, he began helping around the farm and would sometimes sleep in the barn.

When it was time for Luke to be born, Travis had taken Mary and Cleve camping. Brenda still hadn't liked him, but she had been forced to trust her husband's judgment. Over the next few years, she had learned to trust Travis too. He never asked for anything but gave generously of himself.

Travis had been helping with the harvest the day Angus had the accident. He had tried to save her husband but had failed. When Travis realized Angus was dying, he had stayed with Angus and prayed with him till he was gone.

Brenda had collapsed in Travis's arms and cried into the night. When Brenda couldn't do it, Travis had taken care of the children. He had explained to five-year-old Mary and four-year-old Cleve that their father had gone to stay with Jesus, and he would be waiting for them to join him when they got older. He had cared for Luke, who was just about to have his first birthday. He even changed and washed a few diapers.

Travis had taken care of the farm, the harvest, the funeral arrangements, the children, and her. He had recited that scripture to her so much that she said it to herself in her sleep and had hated it.

> For to me, to live is Christ and to die is gain. If I am to go on living in the body, this will mean fruitful labor for me. Yet what shall I choose? I do not know! I am torn between the two: I desire to depart and be with Christ, which is better by far; but it is more necessary for you that I remain in the body. Convinced of this, I know that I will remain, and I will continue with all of you for your progress and joy in the faith, so that through my being with you again your boasting in Christ Jesus will abound on account of me.[84]

Travis had told her that it was necessary for her to take care of her children, and he had been right.

Angus and Brenda had married when she was seventeen. She had moved from her father's home to her husband's, and she had never learned to deal with problems herself. Angus had taken care of her, and she had relied on him for everything.

She knew Angus was a strong Christian, and that was what had attracted him and Travis to each other. She had been a young Christian and hadn't understood the bond these two had. But she was thankful Travis had been there.

For the next six years, Travis had done the heavy work on the farm. He would be at the farm most days, working and playing with the children. He was always happy to do whatever she asked of him, whatever the children wanted. He knew what needed to be done, and he would make sure it was taken care of. He had been there any time she needed advice and every time she had a problem.

Travis had taken Cleve and Luke hunting and fishing with him when they were very young. Too young, she thought. And he

---

84   Philippians 1:21–26.

had taught the boys how to swim well. He told her that learning to swim well would help keep them safe around the water.

Travis had also taught the boys how to shoot and handle the guns. He had taught them how to clean and care for the guns too. They learned how to skin and process game, even before they were strong enough. And Travis had taught them how to use the big hunting knife.

He had also taught them how to ride Bess. The boys had grown under his care, and she was now happy she had let Travis do it his way.

Travis had been there to rescue her the day the tornado hit the farm too. He had worked into the night to dig her out of the collapsed barn, had taken care of her injuries, and stayed with her and the children until she could function again. He had torn down the damaged barn and had built a new barn, almost singlehandedly.

She had recited Scripture he had taught her when she needed strength. Like when he had been confronted by the gunfighter. *The Lord is my light and my salvation—whom shall I fear? The Lord is the stronghold of my life—of whom shall I be afraid? When the wicked advance against me to devour me, it is my enemies and my foes who will stumble and fall.*[85] She hadn't known if he was dead or alive that day after she heard his rifle shot, but the scripture he had taught her stayed in her heart and on her mind. She had endured until she knew he was safe.

He had been there when Luke had trouble at school and had led the family, and the town, to forgiveness. He had also shown them what forgiveness was when he had been injured, and almost died, forgiving the one who had shot him.

Her husband had been with her when the two babies had been born, and he had helped her deliver Naomi when Dr. Cooper could not be found. Mrs. Cooper had said she was coming but had not arrived until Naomi was washed and swaddled, lying at her mother's breast.

---

85 Psalm 27:1–2.

She had never had to deal with anything by herself. Now he wasn't there. She determined that she would stay strong, like he had showed her.

Travis had been strong in every situation. He had told her what had happened to him during the war and about losing his wife and sons. Then he had given up his home and his daughter. She didn't understand how he could survive all that had happened to him and still have such peace. He had told her the peace came from the Lord.

Yes, he knew the Lord, and he held to his God. She would remember Scripture and lean on God too. Like Travis had taught her. She wasn't going to fall apart but would remain faithful to her husband's God. He would become her Lord too.

She would have one purpose: to care for her family until Travis returned with Mary, now relying on Christ's faithfulness for her strength.

Cleve had made his decision the day his father left. He would take care of the farm, and he would protect his family. He would make his father proud.

Cleve was now taller than Travis, at thirteen years of age, but not as strong. He was still growing, though. Cleve had helped his father do everything on the farm and knew that he could manage it himself. His father had taught him how to hunt and shoot. He knew how to care for the gun and how to skin and process game.

And the rifle would be ready in case there was trouble.

He had learned, *The father of a righteous child has great joy; a man who fathers a wise son rejoices in him.*[86]

Scripture would still be read in the house, even with Mary gone. Cleve would see to that also.

Cleve had less than two years left in school and was hoping to find a way to continue school and become a lawyer. But right now, he would take care of the farm.

---

86   Proverbs 23:24.

All little Angus knew was that two of the most important people in his life weren't there anymore. Daddy wasn't there to hold him or to sing to him. Mary wasn't there to play with him.

Angus asked about his father and Mary often, and it usually made Mama cry. Every day Cleve would tell his little brother to stop asking.

Cleve tried to take Travis's place with Angus. He would hold Angus and play with him. He tried to rock him and sing like Travis had done. But Angus wouldn't sit still on Cleve's lap, and Cleve's voice wasn't as nice as his father's.

As the days and weeks went by, Angus asked less and less. Then he quit asking. Now Cleve wondered if he had forgotten their father.

Naomi was fussier than she had been in the past. Cleve knew it was the absence of their father's calming presence. Naomi wasn't getting as much attention either, with both her father and her older sister missing.

Cleve often watched Naomi. She was getting bigger, growing, learning new things, and her father wasn't there to see it. Cleve was saddened by this. Their father had enjoyed watching every new discovery she and Angus made.

Luke continued with his days the way he had always done—a little work, a little play, spending most of his time alone in the barn. Daddy would bring Mary back. Luke had no doubt. When he heard a rider coming, Luke would run to see if it was his father. When it wasn't, he would go back to whatever it was he was doing.

Chapter 32

Winter came, and the days were short, but the nights long and cold. Occasionally Mark would receive a telegram from Travis simply giving a location. Once it said "Ogallala." Mark told Brenda and the boys it was located in the Nebraska Territory.

The last time they heard from Travis, he had made it to the Dakotas. He was near Snow Moon Corner and was following a lead of a white girl at a Lakota settlement on the Great Sioux Reservation.

The information had come in a letter from an Indian agent. The Dakota Superintendency of Indian Affairs had received a report that a girl had come in with a Cheyenne party that was being pursued for violating treaty agreements. It was reported that the girl had been left behind when the Cheyenne moved on. The information had not been verified, but Travis thought the timing and location would be right for the band he had been chasing.

Travis was now holed up in a mud dugout just outside an Indian village near the headwaters of the Heart River. He had never felt this cold and didn't remember ever seeing this much snow, not even on his mountain.

He would be taken to a white girl being held to the north at an isolated camp of Lakota who had stopped moving to await spring. The Indian guide had told him to wait. He'd been waiting five days.

The Lakota were a dangerous people who had just lost a long war to keep their land. Only a portion of the chiefs had signed the treaty. That treaty was now being violated by the white men, making all the Lakota unhappy. This could work against Travis so he was doing everything he could to please the Indians he was with.

Discouraged and thinking of his family back in Harris, Travis sat alone, cold, and hungry. He hadn't wanted to leave his family, but he had to find Mary. He was feeling scared for them all—for his family left alone without protection, and for his daughter, kidnapped by the savage men. He prayed daily for the protection of each of his family members and for peace in his heart.

But that worried him too. He'd had peace in his heart when he had left his family in the mountains. But they had been brutally attacked and had not survived, despite his prayers. Except for Sarah, who had been injured and was now blind. Travis's heart was heavy, and he felt the heaviness in his chest as he fell asleep wrapped in an old buffalo hide he had found inside the dugout.

The wind was blowing hard, and the snow had been coming down sideways for days.

Why are you downcast, O my soul, and why are you in turmoil within me? Hope in God; for I shall again praise him, my salvation and my God.[87]

Travis woke up suddenly. Hope in God, his hope was in God. The Spirit was reminding him of his source of power.

Travis spoke out loud, "We give thanks to you, Lord God Almighty, the one who is and who was, because you have taken your great power and have begun to reign."[88]

And he began to sing praises.

Travis spent the rest of the night reciting Scripture and singing praises to his God. As the sun came up that morning, he was still reciting Scripture, "Have I not commanded you? Be strong and courageous. Do not be afraid; do not be discouraged, for the Lord your God will be with you wherever you go."[89]

Just as he finished the scripture, a large man burst in the door. During the night, it had stopped snowing outside, the wind had quit blowing. All was calm.

---

87   Psalm 42:11 (ESV).
88   Revelation 11:17.
89   Joshua 1:9.

"Come," the Indian said and walked off into the snow.

Travis jumped up, taking his blanket and rifle with him, and followed. They walked for some time, maybe two miles, in the hip deep snow. Travis followed in the path of the big man whose steps and massive size cleared a path, making it easier for Travis to move.

But it was still difficult walking in the deep snow and cold.

Travis had to move fast to keep up with the big man. He was breathing hard and shivering when they arrived at their destination. His feet and hands were burning cold.

Travis was escorted into a buffalo-hide teepee. Two Indians sat close to the fire, wrapped in animal skins. A hand was extended, indicating a spot on the cold ground for Travis to sit.

The Indians looked at Travis a moment, then the younger one spoke, "What do you seek?"

"I'm lookin' far my daughter," Travis said through chattering teeth. He had to get his body under control. The Indians would not respect weakness.

"Where was she taken?" The younger Indian was still talking.

"Kansas, near Harris." That was better, his voice didn't sound as cold.

"We have not been in Kansas."

"I was told Cheyenne brought 'er 'ere." Travis was warming up beside the fire.

The two Indians exchanged looks, and the younger one got up and left. Travis sat silently with the older man. Neither took their eyes off the other. After some time, the older man said, "You have a peaceful spirit, why do you carry a gun?"

Travis glanced down at the rifle lying across his lap. "Sometimes ya 'ave ta fight," Travis replied. This Indian spoke English too. This was good. It would be much easier to communicate one on one than through an interpreter.

The old man nodded. "You have been searching long?"

"Yes, a long time."

"But you are not afraid."

"No."

"Why are you not afraid?" the Indian asked.

Travis replied, "My God's Spirit tells me 'The Lord himself goes before you and will be with you; he will never leave you nor forsake you. Do not be afraid, do not be discouraged.'"[90]

"You walk with your 'god?'"

"Yes." Travis said. "'E 'as told me, 'Since we live by the Spirit, let us keep in step with the Spirit.'"[91]

The old Indian then asked, "Is your god a god of peace or of war?"

"Of peace," Travis replied. "Now may the God of peace, who through the blood of the eternal covenant brought back from the dead our Lord Jesus, that great Shepherd of the sheep, equip you with everything good for doing his will, and may he work in us what is pleasing to him, through Jesus Christ, to whom be glory forever and ever. Amen."[92]

"Blood brings peace?" The Indian's face showed question or was it unbelief?

"Yes, when it is freely given. 'How much more will the blood of Christ, who through the eternal Spirit, offered himself unblemished to God, cleanse our conscience from acts that lead to death, so that we may serve the living God!'"[93]

"And this man brought back from the dead?"

Travis was happy the Spirit had revived him the night before, it prepared him for this exchange with the Indian. "'For God so loved the world that he gave his one and only Son, that whoever believes in him shall not perish but have eternal life.'[94] God's Son said, 'Father, if you are willing, take this cup from me; yet not my will but yours be done.'[95] God's Son was willin' ta do what 'is father wanted, even die."

"Why would a father want his son to die?" the Indian asked.

Travis answered, "'This is how God showed his love among us: He sent his one and only Son into the world that we might

90	Deuteronomy 31:8.
91	Galatians 5:25.
92	Hebrews 13:20–21.
93	Hebrews 9:14.
94	John 3:16.
95	Luke 22:42.

live through him.'[96] 'For Christ also suffered once for sins, the righteous for the unrighteous, to bring you to God. He was put to death in the body but made alive in the Spirit.'"[97]

"This Christ became a god too?" The Indian was showing interest.

"Yes, 'e is God too. 'E said, 'I and the Father are one.'"[98]

The Indian said nothing, and the conversation stopped abruptly. They sat quietly now, looking at each other.

Over the last four months, Travis had learned about these Indians and how to negotiate with them. You only answered the questions you were asked. You did what the Indian did, and you didn't respond to aggressive moves. You stayed where they told you to stay, you kept eye contact, you didn't show fear or weakness, and you didn't talk or ask questions unless you were given permission.

Travis thought he had been there a good hour or two when the younger Indian returned with someone wrapped in a blanket. It was a girl, dressed as an Indian, but Travis couldn't see her face.

The older man asked, "Is this who you seek?" And the younger man removed the blanket roughly. Mary! It was Mary! She stood there, staring at her father, her eyes wide, but her face showed no recognition.

"Yes, this is my daughter." Travis wanted to jump up and grab her, hug her, but he needed to finish the negotiations.

"You may talk to your daughter." And both Indians left.

Travis stood up and faced Mary. "Mary? Are ya all right?" Travis asked as he put a hand softly to her face.

"Daddy?" she responded, almost at a whisper. He could see she was about to cry. But she wasn't moving. It was like she heard him but didn't see him.

He slowly reached out and took her gently in his arms to hug her. He held her and could feel the tears from her eyes as they wet his shirt. He pulled her to the ground with him, and tears began to

---

96   1 John 4:9 (NLT).
97   1 Peter 3:18.
98   John 10:30.

roll down his cheeks into his beard. He held her on his lap, like a baby, and began to softly rock and sing to her.

Finally she reached up and put her arms around his neck to hug him back. She buried her face in his neck and silently cried more.

They were still sitting there when an Indian woman came in and sat two bowls of food on the floor and backed out the opening, keeping her eyes on them both.

More wood was brought in, and the fire gave off more warmth. They were left alone, and Travis was unsure what to do, so he stayed where he was and held Mary.

The next morning, no one came with food, and no one came with wood. The fire was about to go out, and the enclosure was getting colder. Travis made the decision to go outside. This was not proper behavior, and he knew this could cause problems for himself, but the cold was now biting.

Slowly he opened the teepee flap and put his head out. The Indians were gone. There were no other teepees. During the night, the tribe had silently broken camp and left. Travis gathered wood and went back inside to put it on the fire. It was cold. He had never been so cold, but the cold didn't seem to bother Mary.

Chapter 33

At the Indian Agent's office, Travis and Mary were given an escort to the settlement of Picktown. There they stayed, waiting for the weather to improve.

Travis sent a message to Mark that simply said, "got her." When Mark received the message, he collapsed onto his chair with, "Thank God they are both safe." He felt like a burden had been lifted. He put his head in his hands, praying another, "Thank you, Lord," before he left to tell Brenda.

Travis and Mary spent their time getting to know each other again. Mary wasn't the same happy talkative girl. She was very quiet. She would nod or shake her head in answer to her father's questions but barely said anything. She would sit quietly for hours and wouldn't respond to other people. She seldom smiled. She stayed close to her father but wouldn't look into his eyes.

Her father would hold her for hours every day, letting her know that she was safe and loved. He sang to her, but sometimes he would get short of breath or start coughing.

Travis quoted scripture he knew Mary was familiar with, trying to get her to repeat it with him. "Give thanks to the Lord, 'for he is good, his love endures forever.'"[99]

But she wouldn't say anything, she wouldn't respond.

He even tried telling stories, but he didn't seem to be getting through to her. Then as he told her another story, she began to smile. She thought he looked silly.

---

99   1 Chronicles 16:34.

"There was this baby wide-mouthed frog"—and he said wide-mouthed frog opening his mouth as wide as he could—"that wanted ta know what other animals fed their babies. So the wide-mouthed frog"—opening his mouth wide again—"went ta the farm an' asked the cow." And Travis opened his mouth wide again to talk for the frog. "Mz. Cow, what do ya feed ya babies?' The cow said, 'I give my baby milk.'

"Frog went ta the horse an' asked"—Travis opened his mouth wide again to talk for the frog—"'Mare, what do ya feed ya baby?' 'I sometimes let my baby eat grass,' the horse said.

"The frog saw a barn owl an' asked"—with his mouth open wide—"'Mz. Owl, what do you feed ya baby?'

"The owl said, 'Baby wide-mouthed toad frogs.'"

And with as small a mouth as he could, Travis talked for the frog again, saying, "Don' see many a 'em round 'ere, do ya?"

Mary was smiling now, a big smile. Travis loved her smile, but it faded quickly.

Mary didn't want her father out of her sight. She would silently cry and retreat into her shell if he left her for more than a few minutes. She always looked scared when he came back.

The snow started melting, and the horses were able to get through to the next community. Travis held Mary in front of him on the horse for four days while traveling, until they reached the railroad.

The train didn't go directly to Harris; they would have to change trains a few times. The Indian agent gave Travis a choice of routes, through Lansing or Denver. Travis smiled. Denver, of course. Maybe the wait time between trains would be long enough to see Sarah for a few minutes.

At the train station, Travis sent a telegram to his son-in-law, Thomas, giving arrival day and time. As they got on the train, Mary was holding onto her father's arm; just like Sarah had done getting on the train so many years ago.

On the long ride, Travis told Mary about Sarah and Thomas. He told her everything he could think of about Sarah, except how Sarah had been blinded. He told Mary that she would get to meet her big sister and see the city in the mountains.

He told her about his own mountain and his life growing up with his grandparents, and he continued to tell her about God's faithfulness.

Travis's cough had gotten deeper and his breathing had become heavy, but his only thoughts were of getting Mary home.

*****

Thomas and Sarah were waiting at the train station when Travis stepped off the train with Mary. They came to greet him. As Sarah approached with her arms outstretched to take her father's hands, Mary recoiled. Travis took one of Sarah's hands and hugged it to his face. "I'll hug ya 'ard in a little bit, child." Then he spoke to Mary, "It's okay, this is ya sister. Don' be scared." And he put his arm around her.

Thomas leaned in to whisper to his wife, "There's a young girl with your dad. She looks scared."

Thomas and Sarah both had questions on their faces, and Travis saw it. He smiled at Thomas, and asked, "Can ya get us out a 'ere?" Thomas and Sarah hadn't known about Mary. Travis's telegram had just said:

ARRIVING 6:00 P.M. MONDAY TRAIN FROM DAKOTA STOP TRAVIS

They climbed into the carriage. Travis was trying to hold back a cough as he put his arm around Mary, drawing her to his side. As they started moving, Travis briefly explained what had happened.

"Mary was taken by Indians last fall. I followed 'em in ta the Dakota Territory." Travis took another deep breath, causing him to cough. Then he said, "An' I found 'er almost two months 'go now. It's taken us this long ta get this far. Snow is awful up there. I can't wait ta get warm."

Then he backed up and told them about his marriage and his new family.

"Me an' Mary's mama got married four years 'go. Mary 'as two brothers, Cleve an' Luke, an' then me an' Brenda 'ave two more. A boy, Angus, named after Mary's father. 'E's, gosh, three now. And Naomi, I don' know. Mary?" Travis looked at his daughter. "How old would Naomi be now?" She didn't respond so he continued, "She was just gettin' her first tooth when we left." Mary wasn't responding to anything that was being said.

Sarah was excited about her father's family. Thomas was concerned about Mary and about Travis's health. Then Sarah told Travis about his grandchildren.

There was five-year-old Joshua, two-year-old Joseph, and Sarah had just discovered she was expecting another. Mary said both of the boys were beautiful and looked just like their namesakes. Travis didn't know how it was possible for Sarah to know this, but he took her word.

Travis sat smiling, and the more Sarah talked, the bigger his smile got.

The light from the gas street lanterns was hitting Travis off and on as the carriage rolled through the dark streets. Thomas thought Travis looked tired, and he could hear his father-in-law breathing hard and wheezing. His left eye was almost closed, and Thomas wondered if he had injured it. Travis had a few coughing spells before they reached their destination, and Thomas grew more concerned.

When they arrived at the large townhouse, they were given an opportunity to wash up, then they sat down to dinner. Mary refused to eat, and Travis ate little. Travis asked for something Mary could take to the room with her. He was given a plate with bread and cheese.

Sarah showed Travis and Mary a room upstairs that Mary could sleep in. It was a large room with two long curtained windows facing a courtyard in back of the house. The windows looked out over a well-manicured yard, a bare garden plot, and a carriage house and stable. Like the rest of the house, the room was simple, with only the necessary furnishings. It was nicely decorated, and Travis could tell someone had put time into choosing what was in it. However, it didn't look like it was used very often.

Mary was given fresh nightclothes, and Sarah offered to help Mary get ready for bed. Mary pulled away from her and clung to her father.

Travis apologized and told Mary, "When ya an' ya sister, Sarah, get ta know each other better, ya'll be friends."

Travis let Mary get ready. He helped her brush her hair and braided it for her. She ate a few bites, then he tucked her into bed.

He sat down on the edge of the bed, waiting for her to go to sleep. Mary curled up and lay against her father. It took a long while for her to fall asleep. When she did, Travis went downstairs where Sarah and Thomas were waiting for him. He still had his coat on. He wasn't warm yet.

Sarah hugged her father again and sat down beside him, holding his hand. Then she asked about Mary.

Travis started talking but didn't get far when a coughing spell hit him. He found himself squeezing Sarah's hand and let go completely when he realized he was doing it. When he stopped coughing, he couldn't seem to catch his breath and was a little dizzy. His chest had begun to hurt, and he now held his arm across his chest, trying to help the pain.

Thomas got him some water and said, "Tomorrow I'm going to look at you and Mary. That cough sounds bad. Don't even think about leaving until I'm through with both of you, and I say you can go home."

Travis nodded. He was beginning to think he needed help. This problem he had breathing, and the coughing, were getting in his way.

They talked a while longer, then Thomas stood up and moved toward Travis. He had spotted Mary hiding behind the doorway. He silently pointed Travis in that direction and knelt beside his wife, talking to her quietly.

When Travis saw Mary, he stood up and started toward her. Mary ran to her father and clung to him. She was shivering but not from the cold. She was scared.

"I'll take 'er upstairs an' stay with 'er. I'll see ya in the mornin'." And he turned, moving toward the stairs, but stopped when he started coughing again. As the coughing continued, he leaned on a chair until it stopped. He straightened up, breathing heavy. Travis moved slower now. It looked to Thomas like Mary was supporting her father.

Chapter 34

The next morning, Thomas was waiting for them when they came downstairs. He escorted them into the dining room.

"After you eat breakfast, I'm going to take both of you over to the hospital where my office is. We're going to look at you two and see what we can do to help."

Just then, Sarah walked in holding little Joshua's hand. She had another woman with her, carrying Joseph. Travis's face showed the shock. Yes, they looked just like his own boys had looked. These two could have been his children at that age. Travis wanted to go to them and hold them, but Mary was clinging to his arm tightly.

He turned to her, putting his hand on her face, so she would look at him. "Mary, these are ya nephews, my gan'chil'en. Would it be okay with ya if we 'old 'em? Can I 'old one, an' ya 'old ta'ther?" Mary looked into his eyes slowly. She held his gaze, then slowly nodded. She let go of his arm but moved closer. Travis smiled approvingly and nodded.

"Joshua, come sit on Gan'pa's lap." Travis patted his leg. Sarah moved beside her father, and Travis took the five-year-old onto his lap. The other woman must have moved toward Mary too fast because when she got near, Mary pulled away, closer to her father. Travis turned to Mary, still holding Joshua.

"Mary, this is Joshua. Do ya see Joshua?" Mary turned in Travis's direction. "Would ya like ta 'old Joshua?" The boy was playing with his grandfather's beard. It was long, he hadn't trimmed it in weeks.

Mary looked at Travis but didn't respond. Travis gently slid Joshua onto Mary's lap.

"Don' drop him. Put ya 'ands on 'im just like ya use ta do Angus. That's my girl. Joshua's a big boy, ain''e? 'E's a lot bigger 'an Angus."

Travis reached out for Joseph and drew him close. The grandfather closed his eyes and laid his face against the toddler.

Travis enjoyed his grandson's touch. They didn't stay there long when he started coughing. Sarah took Joseph back as Travis struggled for breath.

The other woman left with the two boys.

"I'm going with you to the hospital. We can visit on the way. Mary, I'd like to get to know you better. When we get back home this afternoon, we can play with the children. Would you like that?" Sarah was taking her cue from Travis. She was speaking to Mary gently, carefully. Mary gave Sarah a small nod.

"She's noddin' at ya, Sarah," Travis struggled to say, smiling his crooked smile.

*****

Thomas tried to take Mary into an exam room alone, but Mary would have none of that. She wouldn't let go of her father, so Travis went in too. Sarah followed.

Thomas checked Mary out, using Travis to talk Mary into letting him touch her, and found no physical problems. He had another doctor join them, and they tried to draw Mary out of her shell, but she retreated closer to her father.

Sarah joined them and got Mary to respond some. Mary was beginning to trust her sister.

When they had done all they could with Mary, Thomas said, "Okay, Papa, let's take your shirt off."

Travis didn't move.

"Papa?" Travis loved that Thomas called him Papa, like Sarah did. "I can't take care of you unless you let me."

Travis turned to Mary. "Mary. Will ya go with Sarah? Let Sarah show ya round. I saw some pretty flowers just outside the doors." Travis stopped to cough, then continued, trying not to cough again. "Can ya go find out what kind they are? Maybe we can take some 'ome ta ya mama."

Sarah put her hand out for Mary. "Go on, Mary. Take Sarah's hand," her father told her.

Mary did as she was told, and Sarah started moving out the door with Mary in tow. When the door closed, Thomas asked, "Okay. What are you hiding from them?"

Then as Travis was unbuttoning his shirt, Thomas dismissed the question and began his exam. "Cough for me."

Travis coughed gently once. Then the next cough came without Travis trying, then another. Thomas was listening to Travis's chest. As the coughing got worse, Thomas stopped to help Travis stay in an upright position.

When Travis stopped coughing, he was breathing hard, wheezing again. His left hand was in a fist pressing against his chest as he struggled.

Thomas didn't respond to the sound or Travis's pain.

The doctor commented, "So you got shot right here." And he put two fingers on the scar on Travis's side. He pushed around in that area and onto Travis's chest and added, "And you had some broken ribs."

Thomas put a hand on Travis's back, under his open shirt, without looking but stopped when he felt the scars. He removed the shirt. "What happened? Is this what you're hiding?" Travis nodded, still trying to get air.

Thomas looked at his father-in-law's back for a moment then returned to his exam. Thomas had Travis cough more and listened to his back. He poked and prodded, and Travis coughed more.

The exam was near an end when, without warning, Mary burst into the room, running to her father. She grabbed him. Then she saw the ugly scars. Mary let go of Travis like he was poison and backed up and kept backing up until she was out the door and had backed into the wall on the other side of the hallway. She stared at her father, the scared look on her face slowly changed to that blank stare she had once had.

Travis got up and put his shirt back on, buttoning it as he approached Mary. Sarah was now in the room. Mary had pushed past her, and Sarah could tell something was wrong.

"What's wrong? What's going on?" she asked. Thomas moved to his wife and put a finger on her lips, letting her know to be quiet. Then he tapped her ear, silently telling her to listen.

Travis was in front of Mary now. He was talking quietly, moving slowly toward her. She slid down the wall until she sat in a ball on the floor, hugging her knees.

Travis lowered himself, kneeling on the floor. He touched her face, gently moving her chin up so she looked into his eyes. Then he spoke slowly, "I'm okay. It don''urt. It 'appene' long, long time 'go."

Mary didn't seem to understand, so Travis continued, "It's okay. It don''urt anymore. I'm fine."

He started pulling Mary into his arms, and she began to cry. "It's okay, it's okay," he kept repeating softly.

Travis sat down and pulled her further onto his lap. There they sat on the floor, in the hallway of the hospital, as he rocked her. Travis struggling for breath.

As her crying began to slow, Travis felt her relaxing. Mary didn't look up but kept her head against his chest and said softly, "I didn't mean for them to do it. I didn't mean for her to get hurt. I didn't know they would whip her. I didn't know, I just wanted to go home, I didn't know." She began to cry again.

Travis spoke gently to her, "I know ya didn', an' it's okay. She never blame' ya. She knew it wasn' ya fault.

"I saw 'er at Camp Sturgis. The doctor was takin' care of 'er, an' she told me"—and Travis stopped to cough, then continued, "She told me she 'ad been with ya. She told me where ta go ta find ya. She's okay now. She was goin' 'ome, back ta 'er father." Travis was talking softly to Mary but had his eyes on the wall in front of him. He was still rocking Mary. She was calming, listening.

"I'm sure she's probably sittin' on 'er father's lap right now, with 'im 'oldin' 'er in 'is arms, just like I'm 'oldin' ya."

Looking up at Thomas, Travis had tears in his eyes. His voice sounded weak. "We can go 'ome now, can't we?"

"Sure, give me a few minutes to get the carriage out front."

Chapter 35

In the carriage, Mary sat quietly beside her father, protected under his loving arm. She looked better, peaceful.

Thomas leaned forward in his seat, talking quietly to Travis. "I'd really like to keep you in the hospital, but considering Mary, we're going to treat you at home."

Travis nodded, he looked tired, beaten. He was breathing hard, and his eyes were glazed over. Thomas thought he looked like he had no strength left at all.

"You've got a severe case of bronchitis. That cold dry air in the Dakotas attacked you hard. I think we've caught it in time, though, I don't see any sign of pneumonia yet. We should be able to keep it from turning into something worse, but you're going to have to go to bed and stay there. If you don't, this could get really bad."

Travis nodded. "Okay. Whatever ya say."

*****

Mary allowed Sarah to take her to see the children while Thomas helped Travis into bed.

When they were alone, Thomas asked, "Papa, do you know who Mary was talking about when she was on your lap on the floor?"

Travis was sitting on the edge of the bed. He closed his eyes briefly and nodded. "'Nother girl that was kidnapped by the same bunch a Indians. I think what happen' was 'er an' Mary tried ta escape." He stopped to take a few breaths.

"It was Mary's idea, but ta'ther girl was whipped far it. Then the Indians left 'er there ta die. That was just north a the Nebraska

Territory. I found 'er not too long after it 'appene' an' knew I couldn' 'elp 'er. So I took 'er on ta Camp Sturgis. I carried 'er on my lap far two days ta get 'er there."

Thomas sat down beside Travis on the bed, watching his father-in-law's hands open and close as he spoke.

"The doctor looked at 'er, but there was nothin' 'e could do. She died in my arms the next mornin'. I was so close ta catchin' 'em. I was only twelve days from 'ome. But I couldn' leave that little girl there ta die by 'erself."

They sat quietly for a moment, until Travis started coughing again. Thomas gave him some water, telling him to drink a lot. Then he helped Travis finish changing into his nightclothes and put him into bed. Thomas sat on the chair across the room as Travis went to sleep.

Thomas hadn't spent much time getting to know Travis when they had first met six years earlier. They'd only had two days to prepare for the wedding, that's mostly what they talked about. Thomas had actually spent more time visiting with Mark Forester than he had with Travis. Most of what Thomas knew about his wife's father, he had learned from his wife and the marshal in Harris.

Now Thomas's thoughts were on this man lying in front of him. What had this man been through the last few months? He had followed the Indians who had abducted his stepdaughter into a hostile area alone. What had that been like? What bravery! And to have been so close to finding Mary and then stopping to take care of a dying girl.

Thomas had seen people die. He was a doctor in a large city's hospital, but to have a lonely little girl who had been hurt so brutally die in your arms. Thomas just couldn't imagine what that was like.

Then Thomas's thoughts turned to Travis's scars. His body was covered with them. Sarah had never mentioned this. Some of the scars were newer, she might not have known about them. Some of the ones on his back were older, but some were more recent. How much suffering had he been through? What had he endured?

Travis was a humble man, so gentle, and he sang so beautifully. But he had suffered so much with these injuries and losing his family and home. Yet he wasn't angry. He wasn't bitter. Nor was he crushed. The man was a fighter.

Thomas smiled. Yes, Papa was a gentle man, but he was also tough. He had to be tough to be a lawman in a rough cattle town. Thomas looked to the corner where Travis's rifle stood and to the table where his gun belt lay. Thomas nodded. "I bet he knows how to use them too," he said softly, and turned back to look at the man in the bed.

Thomas thought about what Sarah had told him about her father. How he had taken care of wounded soldiers, injured and sick neighbors, and cared for the destitute. He had cared for his family's every need alone on the mountain. Thomas thought of the story his wife had told him about how Travis had been forced to work in a bloody battlefield hospital for years, away from home, not able to communicate with his family. And how he had taken Sarah— blinded—hundreds of miles into the city looking for help, not knowing where to go or what to do—uneducated, unable to read or write.

Thomas could see that he and Sarah loved each other. How hard it must have been to make the decision to leave his daughter in Chicago.

And the money, how had he gotten the money to pay Sarah's medical bills? He couldn't have made much, uneducated. He must not have kept anything for himself, how had he survived?

Not just survived but prospered.

Scripture came to Thomas's mind, *He has shown you, O mortal, what is good. And what does the Lord require of you? To act justly and to love mercy and to walk humbly with your God.*[100]

That's how Travis had endured so much. He followed God in everything he did.

Thomas realized there weren't many men like Travis. His wife's father was a special kind of man, a man after God's own heart.

---

100   Micah 6:8.

Thomas reached over and opened a drawer. He took out a Bible and thought for a moment, trying to remember the scripture he wanted.

He turned to James 1:12 and read,

> "Blessed is the man who perseveres under trial, because when he has stood the test he will receive the crown of life, which God has promised to those who love him."

Yes, Thomas thought, this was a righteous man, and he has stood the test. Thomas prayed that he would be counted among this man's children and that he could stand strong in the faith as Travis had done.

That afternoon, Thomas put a special delivery letter on the train addressed to Mark. The letter explained that Mary and Travis had made it to Denver safely and were staying with them while Travis recovered from illness. They were in good hands. They would be home when Travis was able to travel again.

*****

Over the next couple of weeks, Travis lived his life from the bedroom. Thomas brought in a nurse to care for him.

The first few days, Travis felt worse. The doctor had said the side effect of the medicine would make him feel bad, but the medicine would help his breathing. Travis slept most of the time, but when he was awake, he would lie in bed, unmoving, and stare at the empty room. And cold, Travis was still cold all the time.

After a few days, Travis began to feel the warmth in his room, but there was no fireplace or stove. He asked Thomas about this and was told the house was modern, with all the new conveniences.

"It's steam heating," Thomas said. "There are pipes running inside the walls from a boiler in the basement to cast iron radiators in each of the rooms." Thomas pointed to the radiator against the wall.

"I'll show it to you when you feel better."

Travis liked this kind of heat, it felt good.

As he rested, and the medicine did its job, Travis began breathing easier, but he was still coughing quite a bit.

One morning, early in his recovery, he woke to the sound of his daughters giggling. They were sitting on either side of him on the bed. Sarah had scissors in her hand, and they were trimming his beard. He closed his eyes and lay there, enjoying their sweet sound, allowing them to finish. When the scissors pulled, he said, "Ouch!" Both of the girls stopped laughing and didn't move, but when Travis smiled, they began to giggle again. He listened as they left the room, and he went back to sleep, the smile still on his face.

Sarah and Thomas would come to talk with him, and the children were brought in for short periods of time. Mary slept on the bed beside her father every night.

As Travis began to improve, Thomas would allow his father-in-law out of bed for short periods of time but told him no moving around the house. He had to stay quiet in his room.

Thomas would sit with Travis often during the night, as Mary slept. They talked quietly about their families, home, jobs, life, death, and God. They got to know each other deeply. Thomas's admiration and respect for Travis grew.

When Travis told his son-in-law he was glad he had gotten sick, Thomas had reminded Travis of scripture, "And we know that in all things God works for the good of those who love him, who have been called according to his purpose."[101]

Yes, even Travis's illness had become a blessing, in more than one way. The illness had caused them to spend more time in Denver than Travis had planned. Travis had wanted to stay just long enough to change trains, focused on getting Mary home. But the sickness had kept them there longer. He had gotten to see his daughter and had gotten to know his son-in-law and his grandchildren. And Mary made great improvement under Sarah's care.

The incident at the hospital had broken through the barrier that Mary had built around herself. She was coming out of her

---

101   Romans 8:28.

shell and had forgiven herself for hurting her friend. She had accepted her father's words that it was not her fault. Travis didn't tell her that her friend had died.

Sarah and Mary became friends, just like Travis said they would. Mary began following Sarah around the house and even said a few words to her older sister in answer to questions. They laughed together, played with and cared for the children, and did their chores together.

Mary would allow Sarah to brush and braid her long hair before bed. Travis would lay in bed, watching the nightly ritual. Sarah would tuck Mary in bed, then would come to Travis and kiss him good night too.

Mary began playing quietly and talking when she was alone with the children, but would stop talking if anyone else came into the room. She was also interacting with Thomas some, but she wouldn't talk to him.

When Travis was feeling better, he came into the parlor to find Mary rocking Joseph. She was softly singing, Joseph asleep on her lap. Travis was standing in the doorway, smiling, when Mary looked up and saw him.

"Can I join ya?" he asked. Mary stopped singing and nodded her head. "I love ya singin'," he said as he sat down. "Can we sing somethin' 'gether?"

She thought for a moment and nodded again.

"Do ya remember this one?" And Travis began softly, "Oh my Lord, great in power and majesty." She was moving her mouth, but Travis wasn't hearing anything.

He continued singing. "You sit enthroned above"—her voice now sounded like a whisper—"let all creatures be glad." Yes, she was singing! "And praise Him forever."

Travis went to her and hugged her. "That was beautiful, Mary."

"Yes, it was beautiful." It was Thomas. He was home early. "Now you go back to bed, Papa. I want to listen to your chest again."

The two men went upstairs, and Thomas closed the door.

"I want your shirt off this time," the doctor said. He listened to Travis's chest and his back. Then he said, "Now tell me, what happened to your back? And your arms and your leg and your hand?" Thomas took Travis's hand and opened it to reveal the scars on the palm of his hand.

Travis pulled his hand back and closed it. "Does Sarah know 'bout my scars?"

"Yes, she figured it out when I told her what had happened with Mary and the other girl. And then, she was there and heard what happened with Mary at the hospital. And she can feel the scars on your hand, Papa. You can't hide them."

"I'm so sorry. I didn' want 'er ta know. I didn' want Mary ta know either. I guess I was tryin' ta protect 'em. There's so much evil in this world. They've both seen too much already. I didn' want ta brin' any more a it home ta 'em." He stopped for a moment and rested his head in his hands, his elbows on his knees, squeezing his forehead. "But I guess it 'ad ta come out." He looked up at Thomas. "Let Sarah know I'm okay. Jesus 'as taken care a me, an' 'e'll keep on takin' care a me."

Thomas nodded at Travis. "I know you want to protect them, but they're not children anymore. You raised Sarah right, Papa. She relies on the Lord for her strength. You don't have to worry about her. And Mary's stronger than you think she is too. She's going to be fine. It will just take time."

Travis nodded. Then he told Thomas the whole story, about being beaten while at the hospital during the war, about the surgery to repair the unhealed wounds, and about the reoccurring pain in his shoulder. They talked about Travis being shot by the twelve-year-old son of the storekeeper and about the broken ribs. They talked about the range war and the gunfighter. Then they talked about his eye.

Thomas looked at the drooping eye. He smiled. "I think I can help you with this. This tendon right here"—and he pressed on the side of Travis's eye—"it's really tight. If I cut it, then the muscles should release. It's been like that a long time, so it won't stop all the drooping, but it should help. Do you want me to? It will leave a small scar right here." And he pressed a finger against Travis's face again.

Travis smiled. Maybe Jessie would leave him alone. He nodded to his son. Yes, he knew Thomas well, and he loved him. Travis felt like Thomas was his son too.

"Okay," Thomas said, "now let's look at that shoulder."

Thomas decided massage and stretching would probably improve the pain in the shoulder, and he showed Travis how to hold his right arm out and pull it over his body using his left arm. The doctor didn't think it would take long before Travis could feel a difference, maybe just a few weeks.

Then Thomas went to the top of the stairs and shouted for Mary. Travis froze. What was he doing, yelling at her like that? Travis started to get up and put his shirt on, but Thomas came back into the room and told him to take his shirt off and sit down.

Mary came in a minute later. She didn't seem scared. She was simply answering Thomas's call. Had Travis been so disconnected during the time he had been sick that he hadn't seen the improvement she had made? She came to Travis and took his hand.

Thomas then explained to Mary what he was going to teach her and why she needed to do it. He showed her how to hold Travis's shoulder, where to put her fingers, and how to move her fingers to stretch the muscles and relieve the tension. He taught her to feel the different bones, muscles, ligaments, and tendons that connected and formed the shoulder. Then he showed her how to rub her father's shoulder to relax the muscles.

Thomas told them this was new science being taught. Dr. Cooper may have read about this, but he probably wouldn't have been able to do it if he hadn't been taught hands-on.

Travis smiled again. He would be able to show the old doctor something new.

Mary practiced and looked at Thomas for approval. He corrected what she got wrong and praised her when she got it right. Then he told her anytime she walked up behind her father, she should rub his shoulder for just a few minutes. If she did it several times a day, especially at first, that would be all that was needed to relieve his pain. He told her thank you and sent her back downstairs.

When they were alone, Thomas talked to Travis about Mary. "You're doing just what you need to do with her, Papa. She's been through something we know nothing about, and we don't know how to help. Be patient with her but encourage her to do new things. Protect her where you can, but don't smother her. I see improvement in her, but it may take years, and she'll probably never be the same girl she was before. She's been through too much. But like I told you, she's going to be fine. God has a plan for her too."

Travis smiled. Yes, that was true. It was nice to have someone around that would remind him of God's love. Then Travis asked, "Are ya tellin' me we can go 'ome?"

"In a few days. You still have a little rattle in your chest. As soon as it's gone, maybe two or three days, you can go. That cough is going to hang around for a while, but with rest, it will go away too. When you get home, I want you to take it easy for a few more weeks. Let that cough go away before you start doing much. You don't want to have a relapse."

Chapter 36

The train pulled into the station as Travis and Mary looked out the window to see their family. Mark Forester and Jake Monroe stood nearby.

Mary was nervous and held to Travis's arm. He was afraid she might repeat some of her previous behavior, so he softly told her what was going to happen, trying to keep her from being anxious. She nodded but didn't talk.

They stepped off the train, Travis carrying a banjo in his hand. It was a gift from his daughter Sarah. She had even bought him a case to protect it as he traveled home.

Brenda ran to Mary, but Mary recoiled into her father's arm. "It's okay, Mary, it's just ya mama." Then Mary stepped forward slowly and allowed her mother to hug her, but she didn't return the hug.

Then Travis addressed Brenda and the others that could hear. "She's okay, just take it slow an' gentle. She scares easy." He reached out for his wife and pulled her into his free arm and held her. She hugged him, then backed up to look at him. She smiled. Then she reached up to touch the small fresh cut beside his eye.

"I'll explain later," he whispered.

Travis was then welcomed home by his older sons, but Angus was a little shy. Travis understood, he had been gone too long, he would have to build a new relationship with the younger children.

Mark and Jake shook Travis's hand quickly as he walked past, welcoming him home.

Travis let Cleve take the lead in putting everyone in the wagon, and Travis slid onto the back with Mary, setting the banjo case beside him. Cleve looked at him questioningly.

Travis said, "Ya the man, Cleve. Ya been doin' it for months now. I'm not gonna take it 'way from ya." Cleve smiled and went to take the reins to drive his family home.

Jake and Mark came out late that afternoon to visit. Mary clung to her father at first and wouldn't talk. She kept her face buried against her father's sleeve. But it only took a few minutes for her to relax and begin smiling at them.

Mark could see that Travis was tired, but his eye wasn't drooping much. He seemed weak and coughed occasionally. Travis sat quietly as Mark and Jake held most of the conversation, but he had a smile on his face.

Mark told Travis, "We're not staying. I just wanted to put my eyes on you again and to make sure that you and Mary were all right. I'll be back out to talk in a few days."

They would let him rest and spend time alone with his family.

The next day, Travis and Mary walked the farm, looking at the fields, the barn, and the house. But Mary wouldn't go near the aspen grove.

Cleve had done well caring for the farm. When he saw that he was unable to do the work his father had done, he made the decision to let a few of the larger fields go. He concentrated his effort on the three smaller ones and the big wheat field.

The house and barn needed a little work, but Travis thought they looked good. He was home and his family had remained safe. That's what mattered.

As he and Mary continued walking, he recited scripture, "The Lord is my strength and my shield; my heart trusts in him, and he helps me. My heart leaps for joy, and with my song I praise him."[102] And Travis started singing. He smiled at Mary as he sang, and she smiled back. But she didn't join in the song.

Travis prayed another prayer of thanksgiving for the grace and mercy God had shown to them while he had been away from home. He loved his family and was thankful to be back.

---

102   Psalm 28:7.

Dr. Cooper came for a visit, and Mark came with him. Jessie talked on and on about nothing, and Travis smiled at him. Today Travis didn't mind the nonsense.

Over the next few days, there was a steady stream of visitors. Judge and Mrs. Barker, Mary's best friend, Angie, and her father, Miss Spurgeon, Mr. Smith, the preacher, and Jessie even brought his wife when he came for a second visit. Mary was shy and didn't talk, but she didn't seem as scared as she had been that first day home.

Luke tried to give Mary the book she had left under the trees, but Mary refused to take it. Mary would rock and sing softly to Naomi and play quietly with Angus. But she wasn't talking to the older boys or to her mother unless she had to, then it was only a few soft words. Travis kept reminding them to be gentle and patient.

He recited Proverbs, "Gracious words are a honeycomb, sweet to the soul and healing to the bones."[103]

Travis had to tell Luke again and again. He was repeating Colossians to Luke almost daily too, "Therefore, as God's chosen people, holy and dearly loved, clothe yourselves with compassion, kindness, humility, gentleness and patience."[104]

Luke interrupted him one day with, "But if we hope for what we do not yet have, we wait for it patiently."[105]

Travis smiled, Luke was learning, but was he applying it?

The summer ended, and Luke and Cleve went back to school. Cleve was now in his final year. Mary had missed most of her final year of school. If she would go back now, she could finish with Cleve, but she refused to go.

Travis had not begun his deputy duties again, and Mark had been out to the farm several times to ask when he was coming back to work. Travis guessed it was about time. He had not planted the larger fields this summer but had done only what Cleve had begun. After arriving home late in the season and still recovering from his illness, he just didn't see the point in working himself to death to

---

103   Proverbs 16:24.
104   Colossians 3:12.
105   Romans 8:25.

catch up. He needed that time with his family too. But now the harvest would be lean. They would need the money the deputy's job brought in.

Travis was sitting on the porch steps with a coffee cup beside him and the banjo on his lap, slowly picking at the strings. He was thinking about going into town to talk with Mark.

Mary walked up behind him, knelt down, and started rubbing his shoulder. Travis hadn't had any pain since Mary had been massaging his shoulder. He also hadn't been in any fights. Yes, he would have to go back to work, but he also needed to find a way to get Mary to talk more.

As he sat there, he began talking to her, "Thank ya, Mary. That feels good. When ya finish, would ya read ta me?"

Mary stopped rubbing his shoulder. She didn't speak.

"Mary, if ya not gonna read ta me anymore, would ya teach me 'ow?" Travis turned to look at his daughter.

"Please. I miss ya readin' the Scripture. I've counted on ya ta read it ta me far years. I know Cleve is readin' now, but well, don' ya think it's time I learn ta read far myself?"

Mary smiled. It was the first smile he had seen on her face in weeks.

"I'm gonna go in ta town far a little while. What do I need ta get far ya ta teach me? Where is ya slate?" Travis got up and stood in the door, looking into the room like the slate should be there. "Do ya know where it is?"

She nodded.

Travis added, "Do I need ta go ta the school an' borrow a book?"

Mary replied softly, "Ask Miss Spurgeon for *McGuffey's First Reader.*"

"I'll do that. Be ready when I get back. Ya is not gonna 'ave ta tell me ta do my 'omework. I'll do it, an' I won' fight ya." He smiled his crooked smile and turned to go into the house to put the banjo and cup away.

Chapter 37

Travis returned to his lawman's job. He had stayed away from town since his return. There was just no need to go, except to attend church. He hadn't seen Mark much either.

As they walked the street near dusk that first night, they talked about the town. It was growing. A cattle yard had been put in near the railway station, and the railroad was planning on adding tracks through the territory.

Zinc had been discovered nearby, and a mine had opened up, bringing hundreds of people into the area. There was a mining camp, controlled by the company, and most of the people associated with the mine stayed there.

Sometimes miners and their families would come into town, usually in groups. Miners were a rough bunch, but most were good people. They didn't cause trouble. However, they had no problem fighting with the cowboys.

Occasionally there would be trouble at the mining camp, and Mark would have to deal with the problem. The company didn't want the lawmen in their camp. Mark didn't mind staying away, provided everything was taken care of lawfully. And there lay the problem. The company wasn't exactly honest with its employees.

The town now had a newspaper, but gossip still moved faster. The newspaper, however, would clear up confusion that was brought on by the fast-moving lips.

"The town's growing," Mark said. "But the cowboys still come into town at the end of the week and get drunk. Some nights are still busier than others."

Mark had missed Travis. He was glad to have his deputy back. He was getting too old to do this job alone, especially with the growth the town had seen. He was still strong and healthy, but sometimes he was just tired. He wasn't thinking of quitting, but he wanted to slow down.

They continued talking as they walked.

The Mitchems' son, Jon, had left town while Travis was away, he was headed for an oil field in California. No, Travis had not heard that; he would miss Johnny.

Mrs. Nelson had sold her farm and had gone to live with her younger sister in Cleveland. Yes, Brenda had told Travis this.

Mr. Smith wasn't able to do much around the farm anymore, and the marshal thought he wouldn't be with them much longer.

Yes, Travis knew this too. He had been out to visit Mr. Smith several times. They had talked, Travis told Mark, and Mr. Smith was ready to join his wife. He had told Travis what he wanted done when the time came. Travis had agreed to oversee Mr. Smith's affairs.

And Dr. Cooper was still practicing medicine but was having trouble with his eyes.

That would explain it. Dr. Cooper had never said anything about the cut beside Travis's eye. The resulting scar was small, but still fresh, and a prominent mark on his deeply weathered face. Jessie had not commented on the scar either. The doctor couldn't see it; he was going blind. This saddened Travis.

*****

In early spring, they were again walking the street together. The nights were still cold, and they walked, bundled in their jackets. Mark had the collar turned up on his coat, keeping the cold air from going down his neck.

When the conversation started to drag, Travis said, "Mary's been teachin' me ta read." Mark stopped walking and gave a short laugh. "What'd you say?"

Travis smiled his crooked smile. "Ya 'eard me."

"How long has this been going on?"

"Since school started."

"Well, good for you! How's it going?" Mark started walking again, and Travis followed.

"Okay. It's easier than I thought it would be in the beginnin'."

Mark smiled. "Are you good at it yet?"

"I'm in the fifth grade," Travis said proudly and raised his chin, poking his chest out, giving a chuckle.

Then Travis changed the subject quickly, drawing attention away from himself.

"Cleve wants ta be a lawyer. I'm thinkin' 'bout lettin' 'im go live with Thomas an' Sarah next fall an' go ta school there. If I do that, I won' 'ave 'im ta 'elp me on the farm. Luke works, but 'is heart ain't in it. 'E's a good kid, we're not 'avin' any other problems with 'im, but I can't get 'im ta work steady. If I let Cleve go ta Denver, I'm gonna 'ave ta cut back at the farm."

Mark was now smiling. Travis looked at him and wondered why he would be smiling about a problem Travis was wrestling with. "What's so funny?" Travis asked.

"Well, I think you just became the answer to my prayer," the marshal replied.

"What are ya talkin' 'bout?"

Mark put his arm around Travis's shoulder as they walked on. "I'm getting old. Sometimes I just don't want to do this job anymore." Travis stopped suddenly and looked at his friend.

"Don't look at me that way." Mark laughed again. "I'm not quitting. I just don't want to work as hard. What if Cleve goes to Denver, and you cut back at the farm and raise just what your family needs? You can become my full-time deputy. The pay will be a lot better, and since you can read, you can take over some of the paperwork too. In a few years, when I'm dead and gone, you can just step into the marshal's job."

"Ya is a long way from dead an' gone, Mark." Travis turned and started walking again. He needed to think about this, pray about this. Mark talked some more, but Travis wasn't listening. Mark smiled, that's the way it was with Travis. The conversation was over.

*****

Travis had been to the mining camp that morning and served a warrant. Now he sat at the marshal's desk. He had finished going through the stack of papers Mark had left for him. There were two summonses to be issued, he'd need to go by Judge Barker's later.

The deputy wondered, "Is this all there is ta this job?" There was more sitting around during the day than he liked. There weren't any cowboys in town causing trouble. The few that he saw were actually working. Most of the activity was at the train yard, the mercantile, and the blacksmith's shop.

Travis had handled one small theft incident a few days ago and had stood in the courtroom a few hours the last two days as the judge took care of local business. Other than that, there had been nothing to do.

Another morning, Travis had stopped in and straightened up the courtroom. He was preparing for the next session which wouldn't happen until next week. Then he had walked toward the school and said hello to the children as they arrived. That activity would end soon too. School would let out in a little over a month.

With nothing else to do, Travis went outside and started walking the street.

*****

Mark and Travis were standing at the bar of the Buckskin, watching the activity. There were a few men drinking alone, one had fallen asleep at the table. Cowboys at another table were involved in a quiet card game. Two cowboys sat at the far side of the room with one of the barmaids.

It was early in the afternoon. Travis was preparing to go home for a few hours, and he was telling Mark there had been nothing to do that morning. Travis talked about the lack of activity during the day.

Mark responded with, "You get paid for what you know to do if there's trouble, not for doing it. If there's nothing to do, you get paid the same. If you shoot someone, there's no bonus. Pay is still the same." Travis grinned and rolled his eyes.

As Mark laughed out loud, the man at the far side of the poker table stood up and yelled something Travis didn't understand. They both turned to look in the man's direction as the man drew his gun and fired a couple of shots across the room.

Travis dove over the bar as a bullet splintered the wood where he had been standing. Travis looked to his left and saw two others crouching with him. To his right, he saw Mark's hand sticking motionless out past the end of the bar. Travis reached over to grab the marshal's hand to pull him to cover. But as his own hand appeared from behind the counter, the gunman shot again, hitting the edge of the brass footrail near the deputy's hand. The bullet hit with a clang and ricocheted off.

Travis pulled back. He turned around and looked at the bar mirror. There stood the shooter, in the middle of the room, facing the bar.

"Your turn, Deputy," the shooter yelled.

Travis responded with, "Put ya gun down."

Another shot rang out, and Travis heard glass break. He could see blood pooling on the floor near Mark's hand.

"Last chance," Travis yelled again.

"My gun's out, you're not that fast, Deputy."

Travis picked up a bottle, aimed, and flung it over his head backward, straight at the shooter. He rolled fast across Mark's hand and fired his rifle once, twice. The man went down on his knees behind a chair, blood soaking the front of his shirt but still holding his weapon. The gunman fired another shot. Travis felt the bullet go past, and it hit near Travis's leg as he pulled the trigger again and returned fire. The man was down now, but the gun was still in his hand.

As Travis watched, he wondered how this man was still alive with the rifle shots in him at such close range.

Travis crawled slowly out from under the table, rifle in hand, still watching the cowboy. He walked toward the shooter who was still moving. Travis looked him in the face as the cowboy slowly raised his gun toward Travis. The butt of the rifle swung and hit the man's hand. The pistol flew a few feet to the floor. Travis stepped to it and kicked it further away.

"Watch him," Travis said to the nearest man whose head was peering out from behind a column. The deputy turned toward his friend who was lying unconscious on the floor.

Before Travis could get to Mark, Jake came running to the door, looked the room over quickly, and dropped beside the marshal. Travis stopped to watch, happy someone else was caring for Mark. Travis had just shot a man. His mind and body were quickened. He needed to calm down.

"He's still alive," Jake said. He called two men by name and told them to help him take the marshal to the doctor's office. They picked the big man up, and another man joined them as they moved to the street.

Travis looked at the man he had just shot. He didn't remember seeing this man before. He wasn't a man, he was just a kid, not much older than Cleve. Now he had stopped breathing.

The deputy looked at the other men who had been at the table. He knew two of them, the other he had seen around. Travis thought he worked at the T-Bar.

Travis had the rifle in his hand and used it to point at the three men. "I wan' ta see all a ya in the marshal's office first thin''morrow mornin'. Don' make me come lookin' far ya!" And Travis turned to follow Mark to the clinic.

Chapter 38

Luke came running into the house out of breath and blurted out, "Daddy was in a shoot-out in town!"

Mary looked up from what she was doing, and that was all she heard. She ran out the door and was down the road before her mother or Luke could catch her.

"He killed the man who shot the marshal," Luke added, looking at his mother.

Mary ran past Cleve, and Cleve knew where his sister was going.

Cleve yelled at her, "He's okay! He's not hurt!" But she kept going. Cleve thought about going after her, but he had just walked all the way from town, he didn't want to go back. He'd go home and get a horse to go back into town later to get her.

Mary ran all the way into town, to Jessie's clinic. She flung the door open, out of breath, and saw her father standing in the next room. Blood was on his shirt, but he was standing up. Moving to him, she looked at his shirt, pulling it here and there to check for holes, but she didn't see any. She flung her arms around his middle to hug him, bloody shirt and all.

He returned her hug with only one arm. He hadn't taken his eyes off Jessie and was still holding the rifle in his right hand. He didn't say anything to her. He was listening to Dr. Cooper.

Jessie was looking at the marshal. "Travis, I just can't see it. I can hardly see the wound. I can't do this." Jessie held out his hand, looking at Travis. "Look at me, I'm shaking so bad I'd kill him even if I could see!"

Travis asked, "Can ya leave it there? Get the doctor in from Saline or Hayes?"

"I don't think we have that kind of time. Travis, you're going to have to do it."

"Doc, no! I can't do that!"

"You took a bullet out of him once before."

"But that was simple. This isn't. Look at that, I could kill 'im!" Travis declared.

"There's nobody else to do it. You've got to try!" Jessie was saying, "I'll help you. Come on, get over here."

Mark lay on the table as Travis stood over him. It had been too long since he had cared for a wounded man. He had never done anything this dangerous. Travis remembered helping with this type of extraction, but he couldn't remember much. Travis didn't feel like he could do this, especially to Mark. But what choice did he have?

Dr. Cooper stood on the other side of the table.

"Travis, you have to. He's going to die if you don't try. I can't see it, I've looked. My eyes just aren't good enough, and I'm shaking too much. Nobody will blame you if he dies."

"I'll blame myself," Travis said softly, but Jessie didn't hear him.

Mary stood against the wall. She had refused to leave the room. She wasn't leaving her father. She was scared, Travis could tell. But so was he. Travis wanted to ask Jessie to take her out of the room, but he needed Jessie with him.

Travis prayed softly for Mark and for himself, "Guide my 'ands, Lord, let my eyes see what I need ta see. Protect this man when I make a mistake." It was the same prayer he had prayed over hundreds, maybe thousands, of men following battle. The same prayer he had prayed over Mark when he had found him thirteen years ago. But now Mark was his friend.

Travis added, "Please, Lord, protect my friend. Don' let 'im die by my 'and." Travis looked up and saw Mary "An' take care a Mary. Don' let this scare 'er."

Then Travis took a deep breath and spoke to Jessie, "Okay, what do I need ta do? What am I lookin' at?"

Dr. Cooper began to explain to Travis what he was seeing, what he was looking for, and what to avoid. Travis worked slowly as Jessie talked. Travis's mind was running fast; he was getting anxious. It was hard to concentrate on what was before him.

"Slow down," Travis spoke softly to himself, "take it easy. Ya can do this."

Then Travis heard the Spirit speak to him, *I will instruct you and teach you in the way you should go; I will counsel you with my loving eye on you.*[106]

The deputy took a deep breath and began to relax. Yes, that was better. He was calming down. He began to remember what he had learned at the hospital. He was able to concentrate. His mind and his hands were now working together.

Travis looked, but he didn't see it. Jessie told him to cut the skin some so there was more room to pull the muscle and tendon's out of the way if he needed to, to watch for the bullet's path, and then to feel for it. Yes, there it was, but Travis couldn't reach it. There was so much blood he couldn't see clearly. He tried again. He needed more hands.

Travis looked over to Jessie, his hands shook too much. Travis didn't want to ask him to help, it would be too dangerous. Mary!

"Mary, can ya 'elp?" She took a step forward. "Come 'ere, come on, 'old this. 'Old it still, 'old it very still."

Mary did what she was told. She was doing a good job. "Now put ya finger 'ere. No, under. Now pull it back. Good. Good."

Mary was watching. She wasn't disturbed by the blood or what her father was doing to his friend.

"Don' let go, I've almost got it. There!" Travis pulled back and held the bullet in his bloody fingers. He passed the bullet to Jessie and turned back to their patient.

"Now what?"

Jessie told Travis what to do, and Mary helped. She was good at this. She followed instructions without hesitation, and she didn't seem to mind the blood. This surprised Travis.

---

106   Psalm 32:8.

When Jessie told Travis that he was finished and to step back, he kept Mary, instructing her how to clean up and prepare for what they would do next.

Later that night, Travis sat with Mark. It was the same large cushioned chair he had spent weeks in after he had been shot. Mary slept on her father's lap, her head resting on his shoulder.

Travis watched Mark sleep. He thought back to their beginning, to when he had taken the first bullet out of Mark. He had used his hunting knife that time. He hadn't known what he was doing then either. God had been good and saved Mark's life. Travis prayed God would do the same thing now.

Then he thought of the first night he had walked the streets with the marshal. He had been in Harris about two weeks and had gotten a job at the livery stable.

Mark found Travis that night behind the livery stable with a small campfire and a couple of fish. He stood there, talking, and let Travis finish his meal, then he invited Travis to see the town.

When they got to the Buckskin Saloon, Mark had bought him a drink which he had not wanted. He held the drink and took a sip every few minutes, just to be polite. Some cowboys were getting loud, and Mark was watching them.

Mark moved to take care of the disturbance but had gotten in a fight in the process. A drunk, just a few feet from Travis, had started to pull his gun, and Travis had punched him in the stomach with the butt of his rifle. That had caused everyone in the room to look his way.

Mark introduced him to the cowboys, "Boys!" Mark had said, "Meet my new deputy."

Travis chuckled. That had become a routine evening for him.

He woke Mary gently. "Mary. Mary, can you let me stand up. I need some feeling back in my legs." He laughed softly.

She stood up to let him get out of the chair. Then she sat back down, curling up, drawing her feet underneath her into the seat.

"Daddy, do you think Dr. Cooper would let me help him here in his office?" she asked softly.

Travis smiled. "I think 'e would probably love it, but we'll ask 'im in the mornin', just ta make sure."

Jessie was elated! He loved the idea of Mary helping and put her to work immediately. Dr. Cooper took her hand and led her into the exam room. "Mary, come here, let me show you this."

She went with Dr. Cooper. There was no hesitation. That crooked smile came to Travis's face. "Thank ya, Lord. She's gonna be okay, isn't she?"

Travis stayed with Mark until Jessie was finished with Mary. Then he left Mary watching their patient, and he headed to the marshal's office to meet with the three cowboys.

The newspaper ran the story "Marshal Forester Shot" on the front page. The editor felt it his duty to tell the whole story, so Travis played an important part.

Travis and the editor, Daniel Elshout, had met only a few times. They would say hello when they passed on the street but had never talked. They had not gotten to know each other.

The editor did some investigative work and gave some background information on Travis without talking to the deputy. The article told the town that this was the second gunfighter the deputy had defeated. Travis didn't know where this man got his information.

An accompanying article talked about Travis rescuing his daughter from renegade Indians. The story had also mentioned that the marshal's deputy had some medical training while in the military and had "assisted in the surgery" to remove the bullet and had helped save the marshal's life.

What was written was accurate, as far as the story went, but parts were left out. Travis didn't need or want the attention it brought.

Travis talked with Elshout, telling him that this boy that shot the marshal wasn't a gunfighter. He was just a smart aleck kid who thought he could make a name for himself. Then Travis explained the danger involved with an article like this. He, and the town, would now have the same problem they had several years ago. Travis would need to be watchful of gunmen testing their ability on him, but now he didn't have Mark to watch with him.

There had been a few encounters after Travis had killed the gunfighter a few years ago. The marshal had handled most of them, and all had been taken care of without gunplay.

The editor had said the story was accurate and good business but admitted to writing in a way that stretched the truth just a bit.

After more discussion, Daniel Elshout finally agreed to "tone it down some" next time.

Travis prayed there would not be a next time.

Chapter 39

Mary now spent her days with Dr. Cooper, and she learned fast. She was even talking to him and asking questions. Jessie told Travis that her energy "wears me out." But Travis could tell that Jessie enjoyed every minute of it.

Cleve began preparations to go to Denver. Travis had written Thomas a letter. Yes, a letter. Travis hoped Thomas could read it, his printing wasn't pretty.

Thomas was surprised when he received it.

My dear Thomas,

I take pen in hand to let you know that I have learned how to read and write. Mary taught me. She is doing good and helping me with the spelling. She has started helping Dr. Cooper at the clinic and enjoys the work.

I write to ask, Cleve wants to continue school. Would you give permission for him to live with you and Sarah and go to school there? I don't know about these things, but maybe you could help. He wants to study law.

Thomas must have written back immediately after receiving the letter from Travis. Then he put the return letter on the train special delivery. Travis received it less than three weeks after mailing his own. School was about to end; Cleve would have all summer to make plans.

Thomas's letter had said:

> Sarah and I would love to have Cleve stay with us. There is a fine school near the hospital. I'm sure he could attend there. He would need to be here before September to take the entrance tests.

As Travis read the letter to his family, Cleve jumped up shouting. This was exactly what he wanted! He jumped around the room until his father told him to settle down. He had to be told more than once.

When he was quiet, Travis continued reading.

> We are happy Mary is doing well also, and that she enjoys working with the doctor. Tell her that if she wants to come too, I can get her a position in nursing school, or if she is interested, we may train her in massage, remedial exercise, and physical education so she can help other people the same way she helped you.
>
> If she comes, make sure she teaches your wife how to massage your shoulder.

Travis looked at Mary. She had grown into such a pretty young woman. At sixteen, she wasn't a little girl anymore.

She was standing at the window, looking out to the aspen trees, smiling. Travis knew that they would lose her too, but that was okay. Travis smiled. "There is a time for everything, a season for every activity under the heavens."[107]

Cleve said, "But Mary never finished school." All eyes turned to Cleve. "Well, she didn't. Do you think that will matter?"

*****

Travis lay awake thinking and praying that night. Mary had made such progress. He didn't want her to be disappointed now.

---

107 Ecclesiastes 3:1.

He didn't want her to suffer the rest of her life because of one decision she had made.

Travis had made one decision that had changed his life and his family's forever. He had cared for the soldiers. He had taken them into his barn and then taken them to the Union camp. He had not thought about that for a long time. Now the guilt came back to his mind.

No! Travis thought, and he got out of bed and ran outside, into the field, wearing his nightclothes.

Standing in the dark, his voice resounded into the night, "No! I will not accept the guilt! I did what *my Father* told me ta do! I was followin' *my Lord's* leadin'! The blame lies with the men who murdered my family! If there was any fault with what I did, *my Father's* as long since forgiven me!"

Travis spoke angrily to the accuser, "'You belong to your father, the devil, and you want to carry out your father's desires. He was a murderer from the beginning, not holding to the truth, for there is no truth in him. When he lies, he speaks his native language, for he is a liar and the father of lies.'[108] I 'ave no guilt! My thoughts lie ta me!"

Travis looked toward heaven and raised his hands, dropping to his knees. "'(Ya took me) from the ends of the earth, from its furthest corners (ya called me. Ya "said,) 'You are my servant'; I have chosen you and have not rejected you. So do not fear, for I am with you; do not be dismayed, for I am your God. I will strengthen you and help you; I will uphold you with my righteous right hand.'[109] 'Above all else, (I will guard my) heart, for everything flows from it.'[110]

"'Whatever is true, whatever is noble, whatever is right, whatever is pure, whatever is lovely, whatever is admirable—if anything is excellent or praiseworthy (I will) think about such things.'[111]

---

108   John 8:44.
109   Isaiah 41:9–10.
110   Proverbs 4:23.
111   Philippians 4:8b.

"'For God hath not given us the spirit of fear; but of power, and of love, and of a sound mind.'"[112]

And he began singing loudly, praises to his God. The guilt had finally been removed. He was free!

The next morning, before the children arrived at school, Travis was there waiting for Ms. Spurgeon.

When she arrived, Travis talked with her about Mary and the offer of education and training that had been made for his daughter. He asked if there was any way Mary would be able to continue and finish her last year of school over the summer.

"Mr. Britt," Miss Spurgeon began, "Mary was always far ahead of the other students. She was always so smart. I was disappointed she did not return to school this year."

The teacher stared at Travis quietly for a moment. Then she continued, "I'm not generally allowed to do this, but you gave me a second chance once, and I appreciate that. So I'm going to give Mary a very unusual opportunity because her circumstances are unusual. If she comes next Monday and takes the exit exam with the other students that are finishing, and if she passes, I will award her diploma."

"She's been out a school far almost two years," Travis replied. "Do ya think she can do it?"

"I don't know, but I'm going back east to visit my family in two weeks. I won't be here this summer. This is all I can do for her." Miss Spurgeon opened the door and stepped into the school building.

Travis sat down on the steps. He gave a big sigh and started to think, chewing on his bottom lip. He was still sitting there when Cleve and Luke arrived.

They stopped to ask their father what he was doing. Travis explained and told his sons what the teacher had said. Cleve immediately offered to tutor Mary for the next five days. He told his father, "It will be a good review for me too."

Graduation day came, and Cleve received top honors. He finished first in his class of six, but his scores were far above the

---

112   2 Timothy 1:7 (KJV).

others. Mary was near the bottom, but she passed, her diploma was just as good as Cleve's was.

That summer, Cleve worked hard on the farm. He borrowed several of Judge Barker's books "to read for fun," he had said.

Mary spent all her time with Dr. Cooper, who tried to teach her everything he knew. She enjoyed her time working with the old doctor.

Mary had not spoken to Mark since her return. But she was forced to talk while caring for him. When Dr. Cooper had nothing else for Mary to do, she would read to Mark. As the days passed, Mary began to play checkers or dominos with him. Jessie even got in on a few games. The games passed the time for all of them.

When Jessie allowed Mark to go home, Mary went with him. Jessie had given her instructions, and she followed them, too closely, Mark thought. He wouldn't be able to get away with not following the doctor's instructions the way Travis had done when he had been shot. Mary watched his every move, but she was taking good care of him.

Mary began talking more at home too. She was still quiet, and everyone had to listen closely when she spoke, but she was talking. She told her mother what she was learning from Dr. Cooper, and she was even joking with her brothers some.

Mark had recovered and was now spending a few hours a day in the office, doing paperwork. The deputy still handled all the work in the evenings alone. The courtroom, warrants, arrests, and the other marshal's duties were still Travis's responsibility alone too, at least for another few weeks.

Travis had just left the courthouse and rounded the corner headed for the marshal's office. It had been a long dull morning in court, and Travis was ready for a nap.

As he passed the Buckskin, Travis glanced inside, just to see who was there, then walked on. Stepping to the street, he heard a voice. "Deputy! They say you're fast." Travis froze.

"No, not really," he replied without turning around.

"Well, that guy you shot was my friend. I'm faster than he was, and I'm going to find out if you're faster than me. Turn around."

Travis didn't move. "We don' need ta do this. Just walk 'way," Travis said as he began to take another step forward.

A shot rang out and splinters flew from the column just a foot away from Travis. He stopped again. People had scattered, but now a few faces were beginning to show in the windows and doorways.

"I said turn around."

Travis heard a click, then a familiar voice spoke behind him.

"He doesn't need to." Travis's eyes widened. It was Cleve.

"Turn around, Dad. I've got him."

Travis turned around slowly to look at the gunman. Cleve was standing behind the guy with his rifle pointed at the gunman's back. The gunman was just a kid too, not much older than Cleve. Travis took a few steps and pulled the pistol from the boy's holster. Then he took the boy by the arm, looking at Cleve.

Cleve was smart. He was standing a few feet away from the boy. Cleve still had the gun cocked and pointed at him. He had poked the boy with his rifle, letting the boy know the gun was there. Then Cleve had backed up just far enough to have room to respond if the gunman turned on him.

"Thank ya, Lord, that he didn' 'ave ta shoot this guy," Travis said softly. Then he smiled at Cleve. "Thank ya, son."

People started coming out the doors. Across the street, Daniel Elshout stood on the boardwalk in front of his newspaper's office. Travis stopped to stare at him for a moment, knowing he had seen everything and hoping he would not put Cleve's name in his newspaper. They would talk in a few minutes, as soon as Travis took this guy to the jail.

"C'mon, son," Travis said to Cleve. "The marshal will want ya statement. What are ya doin' in town anyway?"

*****

Within a few weeks, Mark was walking the streets with Travis again.

Mark told Travis how grateful he was for Mary's company during the long days of recovery, and how thankful he was that Cleve stepped in and helped when he did.

"I really enjoyed being around Mary, and I like Cleve too. I liked talking with him when he gave me his statement on what happened with that other kid. Cleve's a smart guy. I know I never tried to get to know either of them but now..."

Mark's thoughts changed. "I guess I just miss my children. It's been a long time since I've seen any of them. I've got nineteen grandchildren now. And two great-grandchildren." Mark gave a laugh. "Can you believe that, I'm a great-grandfather? Never seen any of them," Mark said sadly, and he changed subjects again.

He had done a lot of jumping around with his conversations lately. Travis thought he had probably had too much time to think while he was laid up at Jessie's.

Travis understood, it had happened to him too. He had spent too much time in his own head when he had lain in that bed. Way too much time. If he hadn't had God to talk to about his thoughts, he just didn't know what he would have done.

"And I'm sorry I didn't spend more time with you when you were shot. I just never realized how long the days are when you can't do anything or even leave that room. But we both made it through," he continued, smiling. "And I'm thankful we're both alive. Travis. Thank you for taking the bullet out. Jessie told me you didn't want to do it but...well, thanks for trying and doing it. That's twice now." Mark chuckled.

"Please don't make me do it again." Travis smiled.

"Why, don't you want to start helping Jessie and become a doctor?" Mark joked, shoving Travis a little with his elbow. "It might be safer than being a marshal."

Travis rolled his eyes and shook his head. That wasn't funny. Mark laughed and continued his rambling.

Travis had performed the marshal's job well in Mark's absence. No one thought of him as a stupid mountain man anymore. He didn't look like a mountain man anymore either. He still wore a short beard, but it was well cared for. His clothes fit well and were neat and clean.

He still spoke few words, and that was okay, no one questioned his ability or his authority. He was easily becoming one of the most respected men in town.

Chapter 40

Mark and Travis were in the marshal's office. Each had a cup of coffee in their hand, and both had their feet propped on the desk. The door opened, and a man and woman stepped in.

"Good morning. I'm looking for the deputy," the man said.

As Travis put his feet on the floor, he replied, "Can I 'elp ya?" The man looked at Travis and asked, "Your daughter was taken by Indians?"

Travis was now cautious. "Yep," he said as he stood up.

"Did you get her back?"

"Yep."

"Thank God!" The man seemed relieved. He stepped forward, extending his hand. "I'm Stephen Kane, this is my wife, Delores."

Travis shook his hand. Then Mrs. Kane stepped to Travis and put her arms around his neck, hugging him. "Thank you," she said softly. Travis looked to the marshal, a questioning look on both of their faces.

Travis turned back to face the couple.

"We're Beth's parents," the man said. His eyes were still on Travis. Travis shook his head slightly. He didn't remember a Beth.

"The girl you took to Camp Sturgis?"

Travis's face now showed recognition and surprise.

"Elizabeth," he said softly, taking Mrs. Kane back into his arms. "I'm so sorry."

Stephen Kane spoke again, "We're leaving Kansas. We're going to Nevada where our son lives, but we couldn't leave without finding you and thanking you."

"We are so grateful for what you did." Mrs. Kane had tears in her eyes. "When we found out what happened, we went to Camp Sturgis. The doctor there told us what you had done for her, how you took care of her. We just couldn't leave Kansas without finding you."

Mr. Kane asked, "How is your daughter doing?"

Travis invited the couple to get a cup of coffee, and they walked down the street to the hotel. There the Kanes talked about their Beth, and they asked about Mary again. Travis told them that his daughter was doing well now but that it had been a long hard road.

The Kanes asked if they could meet Mary. Travis hesitated, then told them, "Mary doesn't know that Beth is gone. She was so upset 'bout what 'appene'. It was the worst part of what she went through. I told Mary that Beth went ta be with 'er father.

"If she sees ya," Travis said, looking at Stephen. "If she sees ya without Beth…"

"Oh, I see. I understand," Stephen said. They sat silent for a few moments, then Stephen asked, "Is she at the doctor's now?"

Travis nodded.

"What if you take us over there, and we ask the doctor to look at the cut on my arm?" Stephen pushed his sleeve up to show Travis a bandage around his arm. "We can see her, but she doesn't have to know who we are."

Travis thought for a bit, then nodded. "Okay."

Travis started to pay for the coffee, but Mr. Kane stopped him. "No, I've got this. I'd like to buy a cup for the man that took care of Beth."

Travis nodded again. Before they went to Jessie's office, Travis took his knife and cut the bandage off Stephen's arm, reached down, got some dirt, and rubbed it on the skin next to the cut. Travis told him that there needed to be a reason to go, a clean bandage didn't need to be replaced.

At the clinic, they found Mary reading to Jessie. Jessie looked at the cut briefly and asked Mary what she thought. Travis smiled, Jessie couldn't see it, but he wouldn't admit it in front of other people.

Mary spoke softly to Jessie, telling him the cut was deep but had begun to heal. She got some water and washed the arm. Then she reached to the counter and picked up a roll of bandages and wrapped it around the man's arm. She tied it off and pulled his sleeve down over the bandage.

When she finished, Mrs. Kane thanked her for taking care of her husband and asked her about her work with the doctor.

Mary answered softly, never looking straight at Mrs. Kane.

Jessie held the conversation with Stephen Kane.

They stayed longer than Travis liked. He tried to get them to the door several times, but someone would always start talking again. Mostly it was Jessie.

When they did finally start out the door, Mary quietly said, "You look just like Beth. I'm sorry about what happened to her."

Everyone turned to look at her. "I really liked her. We could have been friends." Mary was looking at Mrs. Kane.

Delores Kane went back into the room and put her arms around Mary. "I'm so happy you were with her. I know it was hard on you, and I'm sorry it happened, but it gives me comfort to know my Beth was not alone." They held each other and cried, talking softly.

When the Kanes left, Travis stayed with Mary. Mary had a smile on her face, she seemed at peace. It had been good that Mary talked with Beth's mother. Good for both of them.

Travis asked, "Do ya want ta go 'ome?"

"No, I'm okay. I'll stay here," Mary responded softly. "I want to finish that article we were reading, and I've still got some things I need to get done today."

Travis gave his daughter a hug and turned to leave but stopped when Mary spoke again.

"Dad, her injuries were too bad, I knew she wouldn't survive." She smiled at her father. "But thanks for what you told me. It wasn't a lie, and I know that. God is her Father too, and I know she's with him."

Chapter 41

On Sunday, two weeks before the children were scheduled to leave for Denver, Judge and Mrs. Barker invited Travis and his family to their home after church. They shared a meal together.

Travis sat at the table, in the fancy dining room, throughout the meal and said very little, that crooked smile on his face. Mary sat silently beside her father, but she looked happy. The judge and Cleve held most of the conversation. Brenda and Mrs. Barker talked quietly at the other end of the table about the little children who played near their feet. Luke sat bored, and everyone could see it on his face.

As the meal came to a close, Judge Barker stood up.

"Thank you, everyone, for being here today. This is a day of celebration as these two young people begin a new chapter in their lives. Today as you are about to begin something new," he said, looking to Cleve, "I want to finish something that Travis and I began two years ago." The judge laughed. He was a jolly man who enjoyed life and showed it.

He reached behind him and picked up a piece of paper, a huge grin on his face.

"This is your adoption certificate. Cleve. Mary. Luke. Please come sign this, and you will officially—and lawfully—become the child of your father."

It wasn't necessary for them to sign the paper. Travis had already signed the legal documents. The judge had just thought it would be fun to let them be a part of the process. So he created a document for that purpose.

Cleve sat looking at the judge with his mouth open. He raised his hand and opened his mouth, like he was going to say something but didn't. A smile came to his face. He would leave for school bearing his father's name.

Mary threw her hands over her mouth, and tears came to her eyes. She then leaned over and hugged her father. She was still holding him when Luke spoke.

"Where's the pen?" Luke asked with a stoic look on his face. He stood and walked toward the judge.

Judge Barker began to laugh. "Here you are, my boy." And he handed Luke the pen and inkwell.

Travis said, "It took a while. I didn' even know I could do this when we first got married." He looked at Brenda who was smiling.

"I don't know why it took me so long, I know that Pharaoh adopted Moses, an' I know God adopts us when we accept Jesus. It just never occurred ta me that it needed ta be done legally. When I found out this was possible, I wanted it ta 'appen right then, but it wasn' God's timin'. I guess 'e wanted me ta learn more patience."

Luke interrupted with, "It is not for (us) to know times or dates the Father has set by his own authority."[113]

Everyone looked at Luke who continued without looking up from the paper he was signing. "'With the Lord a day is like a thousand years, and a thousand years are like a day.'[114]

"'For my thoughts are not your thoughts, neither are your ways my ways,' declares the Lord.'"[115]

Luke looked up and faced those that were gawking at him.

Travis smiled. "Where did this come from?"

"I've been reading the Bible," his son replied casually. The expression on his face didn't change.

Cleve corrected him, "No, I've been reading the Bible, every night after supper."

Luke sounded like he wanted to argue. "And I've been reading it in the barn." Then the look on his face calmed and he softened

---

113   Acts 1:7b.
114   2 Peter 3:8b.
115   Isaiah 55:8.

his tone. "The house is too noisy with Angus and Naomi making noise and you and Mom talking all the time."

Travis asked, "'Ow long 'as this been goin' on?"

"I don't know. Sometime during the summer after Angus was born. The preacher gave me my own Bible."

Cleve looked annoyed. "Is that what you've been doing instead of finishing your chores?"

A sheepish smile came to Luke's face, and he gave half a nod, half a shake of his head. "I've also been praying." He paused then added, "And listening to God."

Luke turned from Cleve and looked into his father's eyes.

"Daddy, God's talking to me now too. I hear him."

Travis was smiling. He let go of Mary and got up, moving toward Luke. They embraced for just a moment before Luke pushed away with, "Okay, that's enough. Cleve, get over here and sign this."

The judge gave a big belly laugh and passed the pen and document to Cleve.

*****

Later that afternoon, Travis sat on the porch steps, picking at the banjo. He was watching Cleve chase and wrestle with the little children in the yard. Mary and Brenda were inside when Luke sat down beside his father. He was now as tall as Travis. Luke wasn't a skinny little kid anymore. He looked older than his twelve years. He had filled out and was getting stout. Travis didn't know how he had gotten so strong.

"Dad, I've been talking to Pastor Rabb. We've talked a lot since you left to go get Mary. Anyway I've accepted Jesus as my Savior and my Lord. Pastor Rabb will baptize me next Sunday before the church picnic."

Travis stopped picking and smiled at his son.

Luke smiled his sheepish smile. "I want to praise God at the river, but you know I can't sing. Would you do it for me?"

The smile left Travis's face. He continued to look at Luke for a moment, then turned to look at the little children again. He gave a small sigh.

"Did the preacher tell ya ta ask me that?"

"No, sir, we didn't even talk about it."

Travis thought for a moment, and the smile returned to his face. "Yes, I'll sing praises ta God far ya."

"Thank you, Daddy." Luke put his arm around his father and gave him a squeeze. "And would you play your banjo too?"

Travis shook his head and gave a small laugh. "Ya is askin' a lot, son." Travis turned to look at Luke again. His son had an expectant look on his face. Travis could still see the little boy in him.

Travis's smile widened. "But it is a time to celebrate. I'll do it this once."

Luke's face broke into a big grin. But the grin faded. "And, Dad, I'm sorry I haven't done a good job doing my chores. I'm going to do better, I promise."

Travis smiled at his son, winked, and nodded his head. He went back to picking at the strings.

Chapter 42

Everyone at the church on Sunday morning went to the picnic at the river following the service. The preacher baptized two women and two young people before he baptized Luke. Luke had asked to be last.

The congregation had sung together before the baptism began. Travis had managed to keep the banjo hidden from most eyes until now, avoiding comments and questions. When Luke stepped into the river, Travis was standing at the edge of the water, outside of the group. He began to pick at the strings. Heads turned. When his son came up out of the water, Travis began to sing.

"Holy Spirit, come from above." Everyone was looking at Travis. Luke was the only one who moved as Travis sang. He came out of the water to stand in front of his father, a look of admiration on his face.

"And praise his name."

As Travis finished, Luke smiled and hugged his father. "Thank you, Daddy. That was beautiful."

They walked away from the water to where Brenda had a blanket spread on the ground. Travis picked up a towel and threw it over Luke's shoulders.

Families moved to their lunches. As people passed Travis, they spoke to him about how beautifully he had sung and how much they had enjoyed it. Travis responded to most with, "Thank ya, but all glory an' praise goes ta God."

This was what he had not wanted, people praising him instead of praising God. Flattery meant nothing to him. Travis wasn't interested in what people thought, he wanted to please God.

When Travis saw the preacher coming toward him, he rolled his eyes and looked away, hoping to avoid any further conversation about his singing. It didn't work.

Pastor Rabb sat down on the ground beside Travis. "Travis. Thank you for using the talent God gave you to glorify him. It was stunning, and I know God enjoyed your praise. Thank you for letting us share in your worship of him."

Travis was surprised by what was said and responded, "I don' think many people realize the song was far God an' not far them."

Pastor Rabb replied, "I know, most people think everything is about them, but it's not, and you and I know that. That's our mission, as mature Christians, to teach younger believers that there's more than just this life. 'But just as we have been approved by God to be entrusted with the gospel, so we speak, not to please man, but to please God who tests our hearts.'"[116]

Travis responded with, "If I were still trying to please people, I would not be a servant of Christ."[117]

"Yes," the preacher said, nodding his head. "It's sometimes hard to stay focused on Christ when the world is pulling us in other directions. That's why I appreciate you so much. You have raised these children to know the truth and to love God. You stand for truth with the way you live too. 'Let us not love with words or speech but with actions and in truth.'[118] You're an encouragement to me. I just wanted you to know that." And Pastor Rabb got up and moved to talk with someone else.

Everyone was enjoying the afternoon. Children played freely, and their parents visited. Travis sat against a tree, smiling, quietly picking at the banjo. People had gotten over the shock of his singing. As he continued to play, they had gotten accustomed to the music and now seemed to be ignoring him.

Travis stopped playing to listen. There was yelling upriver.

He stood and turned to see Luke dive into the water. Travis moved toward the riverbank, dropping the banjo.

---

116 1 Thessalonians 2:3 (ESV).
117 Galatians 1:10b.
118 1 John 3:18.

A woman screamed, and Brenda grabbed Naomi, not knowing what was wrong. She looked around and didn't see Angus. Wait, there he was; he was with Mary. He was safe.

Luke was swimming into the current as Cleve jumped into the water downstream from Travis. Cleve was headed toward the middle of the river, swimming against the current.

Travis looked further into the river to see a child's head and arm come out of the water, then go back under. The current was pulling the child downstream.

Everyone was watching. Luke was getting closer. Cleve was downstream, headed that way also, he might be able to intercept. There was a woman crying nearby, and another screaming in the distance. Travis didn't look to see who was making the noise. He was focused on his boys.

Another man jumped into the water. He waded out till he was waist-deep and stopped, watching Luke and Cleve.

Luke was now diving under the water. Travis started moving downstream and toward the water's edge. He would stay near his sons, if they needed help, Travis would be there. He unhooked his gun belt and left it where it fell. Cleve was now diving too.

Luke came up this time with the child in his arm. He was struggling to keep the child's head above the water. People were shouting at Cleve, pointing to Luke. Cleve responded quickly and swam to help his brother.

As the two boys brought the child near the bank, the man that was in the water moved to take the child.

"He's not breathing!" the man yelled as he turned back toward the onlookers.

Travis pushed past others to take the child. He laid him on the ground and began working to revive the lad. People gathered around to watch. The child was limp. He wasn't responding. Travis picked the child up and roughly squeezed the boy's stomach with his arm again and again and again. Water spewed from the boy's mouth as the child began to cough. Travis turned him around quickly to hug the child to his chest, then leaned back and looked into the boy's face

Travis's hand was now on the boy's head as he pulled the child close to him again.

The boy's mother ran to grab her child. She took the boy in her arms and dropped to the ground, hugging him as she cried.

Travis stood up and watched a moment, thankful the boy was alive. He looked up to see his drenched sons standing beside him, breathing hard. Reaching over to hug both of them, he said, "Let's go home."

Travis looked past his boys and saw Daniel Elshout among the people. Travis hadn't seen him earlier. He seemed to be everywhere something happened. Travis gave a sigh and shook his head. There would be another conversation tomorrow. The three moved away from the crowd.

Several patted Luke and Cleve on the shoulder as they passed by. A man slapped Luke affectionately on the back and stopped him to talk about what a strong swimmer he was, asking how Luke had learned to swim so well. Luke smiled and pointed to his father. A few more people spoke words of appreciation to both of the boys and to Travis as they continued to their wagon.

Travis laughed at Luke as he climbed into the buckboard.

"Luke, this is the second time today ya 'ave been in that water. Ya've been wet all afternoon. Is ya through playin' in it? Ya sure ya is ready ta go 'ome?"

*****

Goodbyes were said and hugs were given by all as Cleve and Mary Britt stepped onto the train headed for Denver. Travis held his two-year-old daughter, Naomi, while twelve-year-old Luke and four-year-old Angus stood beside him.

Cleve handed his rifle to Luke. Luke took it with a nod, accepting the commission Cleve had given him to protect the younger children.

"Watch out for Dad too," Cleve added as he smiled at his father.

Brenda was walking along the side of the train as it began to move, trying to get one more look at her oldest children. She would miss them, but she was proud of them.

Travis waited patiently as Brenda watched the train leave the station and move down the tracks. When his wife was ready to leave, they walked to the wagon. Travis lifted the little ones into the back to sit beside their brother. Brenda was softly crying as he helped her onto the seat. Then her husband climbed up beside her.

"We're back ta three chil'en, just like we started," Travis commented as he flipped the reins and started the horses moving. "The 'ouse is gonna be quieter without those two round."

"Not for long," replied Brenda. She took his hand and placed it on her stomach. Travis looked at his wife and smiled his crooked smile.

Luke smiled too, then put his arms around the little children and said, "Blessed is the man who fears the Lord, who greatly delights in His commands. His offspring will be mighty in the land; the generation of the upright will be blessed. Wealth and riches are in his house, and his righteousness endures forever."[119]

---

119   Psalm 112:1b–3 (ESV).

Chapter 43

The Year 1900

It had been years since Daniel Elshout had been out this far. The newspaper's business took place in town, and unless he needed information from someone in this direction, he didn't come this way.

The fields were overgrown with trees and brush. This part of the farmland hadn't been used since, well, since the incident with the Indians. Daniel had never seen crops on it. It was bare the first time he had seen it. What remained of the fall crops had been left in the field, going to waste.

Now the view toward town was hidden by the trees. The small clearing where the house stood couldn't be seen until you were close. As Daniel approached the house, he saw a small pasture with three horses on one side and a tiny garden on the other.

Looking toward the barn, Elshout saw the old man, but the man wasn't looking his way. Maybe his hearing had gotten bad, he should have heard the horse as Daniel rode up.

The man had a pitchfork in his hand and was moving hay to a stall.

This was not a conversation Daniel looked forward to, but if he was going to get what he wanted, it needed to happen. He had talked to the town's lawyer and to the sheriff. Both of them told him he had better do it soon. The old man's daughter was coming in a few weeks, and she planned on taking him home with her. The man in the barn didn't know this. Elshout would have to keep this to himself.

The newspaper man knew a lot of the story, he had talked to people in town, and he had seen some of it play out right before his eyes. He thought it was important to write this story truthfully. People needed to hear. But Elshout wanted the whole story, and he needed it straight from the man it had happened to.

He moved his horse closer to the barn and could now hear the old man softly singing. He still wasn't looking this way.

Daniel smiled as he looked at Travis. His voice was still strong, despite his age. The song was beautiful. The words were clear too. Daniel could understand every word.

Travis's pronunciation had improved over the years. He had lost a lot of the strange speech and accent that had affected his speaking years ago. He was now much easier to understand. Daniel had never been able to connect this dialect with any nationality or region. He had never known where it came from. If things went his way, he would find out soon.

"Morning, Travis," Daniel said loudly.

Travis turned to look his way, then walked to the barn door and stopped, leaning on the pitchfork.

"Mornin'."

"Can I talk to you?"

"Go 'head."

"Can we go sit on the porch?" Daniel pointed toward the house.

Travis left the pitchfork stuck in the ground where he had been standing and slowly walked toward the house, saying nothing. He dropped onto the rocking chair and stared at Elshout. Daniel looked around quickly. There was no place for him to sit, no other chairs. He backed up and sat at the top of the steps, leaning back on a porch column.

Where should he start? He decided to jump in with what the man's sons had said.

"I've talked to Luke and Cleve, and they're all for what I'm going to ask you, so don't say no yet. They think this is important. I want to write a series of articles. Stories about you, about your life." Elshout stopped to see if he was getting a reaction. Nothing. Travis hadn't moved. He was still rocking, looking directly at Daniel. His expression hadn't changed.

"I'll run them in the paper when I finish each one, and then when we're all done, I want to put them into a book. People are writing these little dime novels about outlaws and everyone is reading them. They're making these outlaws and gunfighters into heroes. That's just not right. I want to give them a real hero's story."

He stopped again to see if there was a response, ready to defend his point against opposition. Still nothing. He had expected an argument. Was Travis even listening?

He remembered, soon after he'd arrived in Harris, Marshal Forrester had told him about talking to Travis. He had said, "You could talk to Travis for hours, with him looking straight at you, and never say a word." He had been told, "You can be sitting right beside him talking, and he won't hear you, but he'll hear the baby crying at the other end of town." Marshal Forrester had laughed and said, "That's Travis."

Elshout had thought the marshal was exaggerating, but over the years, Daniel had observed this too.

Jake Monroe, the gunsmith, had recently told Daniel something similar. Travis hadn't been seen in town for quite a while, and Elshout had asked Jake about Travis.

Jake had told Daniel he saw Travis a couple times a week. They would have coffee together at the farm, but, "Don't expect Travis to talk to you. We've been having morning coffee together for years. It's just his company, I guess, it's sure not the conversation. There isn't any. I wonder if he even hears me talking."

Elshout hadn't seen Travis since last summer. He looked a lot older now. Travis had quit coming into town. He hadn't been to church since the cold weather started last winter. Elshout didn't go to church much, but he had noticed, when he was there, that Travis was missing.

He had asked the new preacher about Travis recently and had been told, "I've heard about him but never met him. He's never been to church, at least not in the six months I've been here."

Daniel thought it was sad that the preacher had never made an effort to visit Travis. Travis had been such a big part of that church in the past.

"I know we've had our differences in the past, but we worked them out, didn't we?" Daniel said. "I won't write anything you don't like. I won't put anything in the paper without your permission. You'll get to read and approve everything.

"I've already written an introduction to the series. Both Luke and Cleve have read it. They both approve. Now I want you to read it before you make up your mind. Think about it. Luke and Cleve both said they wouldn't ask you to do this, but they also said it was a good idea and that the story would be good. Cleve said he'd like to know some of the missing parts himself." Daniel grinned.

Travis was still rocking, staring at Daniel. He hadn't moved, except for the rocking. He hadn't made a sound either.

Elshout held out some pages. "This is what I have at this point. Read it, please. I'll be back out in a few days to talk to you some more."

Travis didn't take the pages, so Elshout stood up and placed them on his lap. Travis looked down and put a hand on top of them to keep them from blowing away in the wind, and kept rocking.

Travis wasn't talking, so Daniel Elshout continued, "I'll go now. Do you need anything when I come back? Anything from town?"

Travis shook his head, still looking at the papers on his lap. His expression hadn't changed. It was a sad expression but a peaceful one. He didn't look disturbed by this.

"Okay," Elshout said. "I'll see you in a couple of days." Travis nodded, and Elshout turned around to go to his horse. As he was mounting, he looked back at the porch. Travis was gone.

Daniel had a sudden feeling that he was causing the sadness he had seen in Travis. Travis was generally a happy man, but he didn't like to talk about himself, Daniel knew this. While he had been the town hero for many years, no one seemed to know anything about him before he came to town, including his sons.

Thinking about it, Elshout thought that Luke might know something, but he wasn't talking. When Daniel had first spoken to Travis's son about this project, Luke had clammed up. The only thing he said was, "Dad won't like this." Cleve had been excited about it and had pushed Luke into agreeing. And it wasn't easy to push Luke.

Daniel had watched those two since he had come to town over twenty years ago. They had both been young. He had watched them grow and mature until they left for school in Denver.

Travis and his daughter Mary had not been in Harris when he had first arrived. He learned later that Mary had been taken by Indians, and Travis had gone after her. They returned the following spring but had stayed to themselves for months after their arrival.

He had seen Cleve caring for his family while his father was away. He had continued the same way after his father's return. Daniel thought this strange, but it wasn't his concern.

Daniel had heard about Cleve, only a boy, standing boldly before the school board and speaking of a teacher's misconduct.

Daniel had seen both Cleve and Luke swim into the swift current of the river to help rescue a drowning child. And he had seen Cleve stop a young man on the street who had wanted a gunfight with Travis. Cleve was someone to watch, so was Luke.

Cleve had stood beside his brother Luke at the carnival the year their father was gone. They were both boys, but they stood with the men in a sharp-shooting competition. Elshout had reported on that contest in the newspaper.

The marshal had paid the boys' entry fee, along with his own. Almost every cowboy in the area had entered. It was a large competition, the first shooting contest in years.

Mark Forrester had come in fourth place, and Daniel, being new in town, had thought this would have been embarrassing to the marshal. But Forrester had continued to stand proudly with his missing deputy's sons as they advanced in the competition.

Cleve had gotten fifth place, which was impressive for a boy that age. But Luke, the youngest participant, had won the prize—a Winchester model lever-action rifle.

Luke had told the men he was going to give the rifle to his father when he returned. Everyone had wondered if Travis would make it back with Mary. He had been gone several months at this point, and people in town were beginning to talk. Elshout had considered that maybe the men had allowed Luke to win.

But Elshout had run into Luke not too long after that, while hunting, and they had continued their hunt together. Luke had spotted a doe a distance away and had bagged it with a clean steady shot. Daniel wouldn't have tried that shot himself because of the distance, but Luke had done it. That's when Daniel realized Luke just might be that good.

That carnival story was the only time Travis's children had their names in the newspaper, and it was only because Travis wasn't there.

When asked how he learned to shoot, the publisher had been told, "Daddy taught me." At this time, Elshout had not met Travis, but he was already impressed with stories he heard about the missing deputy.

Elshout had been there when Cleve stood before the school board a second time following the former slave's exodus from the south to Kansas. Black children were being denied acceptance to the school, and people had stood on both sides of this issue. Cleve had given a strong argument for accepting these children into the school. The board had listened, and so had the town. Cleve had used Scripture for the basis of his argument.

He had quoted James 2:8–10, "If you really keep the royal law found in Scripture, 'Love your neighbor as yourself,' you are doing right. But if you show favoritism, you sin and are convicted by the law as lawbreakers. For whoever keeps the whole law and yet stumbles at just one point is guilty of breaking all of it." He had gone on to talk well over twenty minutes using example after example of grace given by the townspeople for offenses much more grievous than what the newcomers were being accused of. Cleve had convinced the board there was no basis for these accusations. Cleve's father had accompanied his son to the meeting and had stood beside his son when opposition had gotten heated.

Cleve's words were written in the newspaper and credited to "a concerned and informed student."

Elshout could have gotten a good story from both of these kids several times, but Travis had put a stop to it.

"Ya won' put my chil'en's name in ya paper," he had said. "Tell ya story, sell ya papers, but my chil'en's name won' be in it."

Elshout had backed down. There was something in Travis's expression, in his voice, that intimidated Daniel. He didn't know what it was. It wasn't fear. Maybe it was respect. But whatever it was, he had backed down and complied with Travis's request.

Then Cleve was gone. He and his sister Mary had left town together just shy of two years after Daniel had set up his newspaper office.

It was years before Cleve came back. And except for a few weeks the summer after his mother's and sister's death, he had stayed away from Harris. When he did come home, he brought a wife, two small children, and a law degree.

He was now the town's attorney and handled a big part of the legal business in the area. There was talk he was going to run for state representative in the next election. That had not been verified. If he ran, Elshout was sure he would be elected.

Mary had returned when her mother died. She had cared for the younger children a few years, then had left for medical school back East. She hadn't come back.

Luke had hung around town for a year after he finished the eighth grade, but then, just like his older brother and sister had done, he left for school in Denver. When he came back, he knew exactly what he wanted, and he got it. He was elected sheriff, the youngest sheriff in the state.

He beat out the former sheriff by a wide margin. The man had only been in office a few years and had been appointed by the town council when the office was created.

Everyone that had been in Harris when Luke was growing up said he had the greatest sense of fair play and justice of anyone they knew. They said he would make an outstanding sheriff to work alongside his father who, at that time, was the federal marshal. They had worked well together.

People knew Luke as trustworthy and fair but demanding. He followed the law. There was no procrastination, like with the earlier sheriff, and there was no favoritism.

That had caused some problems in the beginning of Luke's tenure. Those the past sheriff had favored still expected their benefits, but it didn't happen. Luke was honest. He wasn't intimidated by anyone nor swayed by bribes. It had all worked itself out over the first few years. Now Luke had been re-elected several times without opposition.

Both of the Britt boys were well respected, and most of the people credited their good character to the way their father had raised them.

Chapter 44

Travis had finished his chores and had eaten a few bites. He now sat on the front porch. In his hands he held the story Daniel Elshout had written. Travis was nervous about reading it. He didn't want to see what had been written about him. He didn't want to relive parts of his life. He knew Elshout hadn't written about his marriage to Brenda and how happy they had been. He hadn't written about how much he loved his children. The story would intensify the violence, tragedy, and evil he had experienced.

But this evil had not won, there was peace after the violence. There was joy after the tragedy. Travis was a fighter, God had stood with him and fought for him. Together they had persevered, they had overcome. God was still with him, encouraging him.

But sometimes, God had to work hard. Travis was alone now and not able to do many of the things he had done throughout his life. Old feelings would sometimes return, and he would get discouraged. God would always rescue him from these moods, but Travis still struggled with them.

Scripture came to Travis's mind, *I have told you these things, so that in me you may have peace. In this world you will have trouble. But take heart! I have overcome the world.*[120]

"Yes, Lord. I know," Travis said. "Ya is with me, ya've always been with me. I do have peace, even with all that has happened."

The Spirit responded, *Woe to those who call evil good and good evil, who put darkness for light and light for darkness, who put bitter for sweet and sweet for bitter. Woe to those who are wise in their own eyes*

---

120   John 16:33.

and clever in their own sight! Woe to those who are heroes at drinking wine, and champions at mixing strong drink, who acquit the guilty for a bribe, and deny justice to the innocent! [121]

"I know," Travis said. "I've seen the boys that worship the gunfighters. The ones that think bein' mean is fun. I know they, and all of us, need ta learn the joy in love, not pride an' arrogance. But will this make a difference?" And he patted the papers laid under his hand, indicating the story.

For our struggle is not against flesh and blood, but against the rulers, against the authorities, against the powers of this dark world and against the spiritual forces of evil in the heavenly realms. [122]

"Ya want me ta fight this battle against evil usin' a book?" Travis asked his Lord.

God's Spirit spoke again, *For the word of God is alive and active. Sharper than any double-edged sword, it penetrates even to dividing soul and spirit, joints and marrow; it judges the thoughts and attitudes of the heart.* [123]

"Yes, I know. Ya words are written in ya book, an' ya words change the heart." Then Travis said sadly, "I'll need ya help. I can't do this by myself."

And the Spirit spoke again to Travis's heart, *Fear not, for I am with you; be not dismayed, for I am your God; I will strengthen you, I will help you, I will uphold you with my righteous right hand.* [124]

"Okay," Travis said. "I'll do what ya want. I always try ta do what you want." And he moved the paper closer to his eyes, turning it toward the setting sun, and began reading the first page.

Today I want to bring you a story of a man. A man you all know. A man who has been a part of this town for many, many years. I won't start at the beginning, and as of today, there is no end. I'll start somewhere in the

---

121 Isaiah 5:20–23.
122 Ephesians 6:12.
123 Hebrews 4:12.
124 Isaiah 41:10.

middle with a love affair and a relationship that grew out of concern, need, and Christian charity.

Well, Travis thought, that's a good place to start. He was a little surprised at what Daniel had written.

Scripture came to Travis's mind, *Discretion will protect you, and understanding will guard you.*[125]

"Thank ya, Father," he responded.

Travis went on to read about how he had cared for a widow and three young children and how he had befriended a lonely old couple. The story told of his work ethic, of holding multiple jobs, and how he had given himself to the town and made it his home.

It told of his marriage. It told of forgiveness given to a young boy who caused a near-death accident and to a teacher who made a horrible mistake. It told of a friendship begun in nowhere, Nebraska that had never died.

It told of skills and talents hidden for years, and then presented as a gift to those who needed them. And it told of the joy brought by friends and family who surrounded him following the death of a small child and a loving wife, helping him to overcome the pain.

Nowhere in the story did it give Travis's name. Or Brenda's or anyone else's. Anyone that knew him would know who the story was talking about. But reading it himself, he could distance himself from it because he never had to see their names. Travis was thankful for that.

Then it added:

> This is only part of the story. What you will read over the next several weeks will be the whole story, beginning to—no, not the end but to the future. It will be told by the soul that lived it through a life of courage, sorrow, thankfulness, tragedy, love, heartache, and joy.

125

Is there regret? If he could, would he change anything? We'll ask him.

Would he change anything? Oh, what a question! So much he would change. Or would he? If Ruth had not died, he never would have had Brenda or those seven beautiful children. But he would have had Joshua and Joseph and who knows how many other children with Ruth.

If Sarah hadn't been blinded, they would have never left the mountain. She would never have met Thomas, and he wouldn't have that brood of precious grandchildren. If Mark had not been injured, Travis would have never come to Harris. If Mary had not been taken by Indians, would she now be a doctor? Or would he have learned to read, or would he have sent Cleve to Denver? Would Cleve and Luke still be working the farm?

This was too much to think about tonight. Too much to think about anytime. Travis was tired. He wanted to sleep now, but he knew this one question would haunt his rest.

"Lord, help me!"

Chapter 45

Travis had made breakfast and was sitting on the front porch, his plate beside him on the small table. He heard horses coming, but with the overgrowth of trees around the farm, he couldn't see them yet. He reached over to pick up his plate, ate a few bites then set it down again. He wasn't hungry.

He recognized the horses before he recognized his sons. Travis smiled.

"Hi, Dad," Luke yelled before the horse came to a stop.

Travis smiled, picked up his hand and waved, and then let it flop back to the arm of the chair.

"Morning, Dad," Cleve said as he leaned over and pulled his father's hat up to kiss his father on the forehead, then replaced his hat. Travis smiled his crooked smile and reached up to straighten the hat.

Luke went inside and pulled two chairs from the table that sat nearby, passing one to Cleve.

"Dad, do you remember last year when the town tried to get approval for an electric power plant? They sent out letters but then didn't get enough of a response to move on the project. Well, they're moving forward now," Cleve said.

"The company will send someone to select the site and start construction soon. We ought to send them an offer for a piece of our land to build it on. I can probably work out a deal with them to hook us up and provide us with electricity for next to nothing. What do you think? You want to try it?"

"We'll see," Travis said. He really didn't care if he had electric lights. He'd seen them at the state capital, and he hadn't been impressed by them.

Cleve changed the subject. "Daniel said he came to visit you yesterday."

Travis nodded.

"Well, what do you think? That was a pretty good article he wrote. Don't you think so?"

Travis nodded again. "Yeah, it was nice."

"So are you going to let him do it? Are you going to talk to him?" Cleve asked.

"You know, you don't have to." Luke injected. Cleve looked at his little brother sternly. But he wasn't that little anymore. He was taller than Cleve by about six inches and much larger in frame.

Travis didn't want to talk to the newspaper publisher, but God wanted this story told. It was always a struggle until Travis took the first step and obeyed. It was still a struggle within him now. That uneasy feeling of not wanting to do something that you knew you had to do.

"I'm gonna talk ta him." Acknowledging that he would do it didn't make him feel any better. "Then you will know the truth, and the truth will set you free,"[126] he said more to himself than to the boys. "I don't want ta, but God wants me ta do it."

Luke stooped in front of his father. "Are you sure? You don't have to."

"Yeah, I do. Me an' God talked last night, an' he told me ta. Ya need ta know all a it too. How much did Sarah tell ya when ya was livin' with her?" Travis asked, looking at Cleve.

Cleve replied, "Nothing. I seldom saw her. I was at school and the library most of the time and studying. Mary spent a lot of time with her, but I tried to stay out of the way with the kids running around and all the activity. I had trouble concentrating on my studies, so I tried to stay to myself."

---

126   John 8:32.

Luke said, "We talked a little, but she never said much with the kids around, mostly we talked about what was going on there."

"Well, ya is gonna learn a lot 'bout me now, an' some a it ain't good. Other people is gonna find out too. Then ya is gonna have ta face 'em. Ya need ta know everythin', an' I don't know if I can talk 'bout some of it more than once."

Cleve looked serious. "Dad, what happened that's so bad that you can't talk about it?"

Travis's eyes moved to the floor, he couldn't look at his son. "I let Sarah's mother an' brothers die," Travis said coldly, tilting his head down more, now staring at his lap. He was chewing on his bottom lip.

"Daddy? What?" Cleve couldn't find the words.

"I left the farm. I was doin' what I thought I needed ta do. But while I was gone, they was attacked. My wife an' my two sons was killed. Sarah was in the house when they burned it down round her. I wasn't there to stop 'em. I wasn't there ta help Sarah after it happened. She hasn't always been blind, ya know. She was nine, ten maybe, when it happened." Travis looked at Luke, then at Cleve.

"I had been forced to work far the troops at the hospital. It wasn't my choice. They wouldn't let me go home. I saw things on the battlefield no one should see. I did things I can never forget. And the whole time, Sarah was at my g'an'father's, injured an' blind. I couldn't help her. I couldn't help my family. I couldn't even help myself."

Cleve sat stunned. He never realized anything like this had happened to his father. He had never thought about Sarah's mother or what might have happened to her.

Luke put a hand on his father's arm. "But it wasn't your fault."

"I know. But far years I blamed myself. I felt the guilt. It wasn't until after I got home with Mary an' y'all was all safe that I realized it wasn't my fault. But I had also abandoned Sarah in Chicago. I couldn't take care a her. I couldn't find a job. I just gave her ta this man. He was a nice man, I made sure he was a strong Christian. He had a nice family, but I just left her there an' walked 'way."

"That's not quite the way it happened," Luke said.

Cleve looked at Luke. Did he know about this?

Travis looked at Luke too. "Yes, it is. I failed her as a father. Ya ask Sarah. One day, I took her ta his house, an' I left her there an' just walked 'way. I never asked her if she wanted ta stay, I never gave her a choice. I didn't tell her I was goin' until I left. She was cryin' far me not ta go, ta take her with me. An' I left her, an' I walked 'way.

"I never went back ta see her. She found me, years later. I don't know how she did it. I don't know why she wasn't upset with me—"

Luke interrupted, "But, Dad, you were taking care of her when you left her. You couldn't support her. You did it to help her."

This was now a private conversation between Travis and Luke. Travis sat forward, facing Luke. They weren't paying any attention to Cleve.

"But how is other people gonna see it? A lot a them will see it as me abandonin' her. And I did. I can't talk ta people 'bout this. People is gonna see the good I did as me tryin' ta make up far the bad I done. Is that gonna glorify God?"

"You did nothing wrong, but even if you did, God says, 'For I forgave their wickedness and will remember their sins no more.'[127]

"God knows what you did and why you did it. You weren't being wicked, you did it out of love. But no matter what we have done, we are forgiven and justified through Christ. 'God made him who had no sin to be sin for us, so that in him we might become the righteousness of God.'[128] What you did wasn't wrong, and Sarah didn't even think about forgiving you because she knew why you did it. There was nothing to forgive."

Luke realized that his father wasn't forgiving himself. Travis knew God's mercy but not his own forgiveness.

Luke said, "'Therefore, if anyone is in Christ, he is a new creation. The old has gone, the new is here.'[129] You're not the same person you were then, you're not the same as you were yesterday.

127   Hebrews 8:12.
128   2 Corinthians 5:21.
129   2 Corinthians 5:17.

You need to forgive yourself. Everything is not your responsibility. God controls what happens, can you accept that?"

Travis sat silently for a few moments, letting this truth sink in. "But other people won't understand," Travis said softly.

"Are you trying to please other people, or are you trying to please God?" Cleve asked.

Travis sat back in his chair. "I don' know. I feel like I'm tryin' ta protect myself, but that's not what God wants, is it?" Travis felt a heaviness he hadn't felt in years. "I'm gonna need a lot of help with this."

Luke said, "'What, then, shall we say in response to these things? If God is for us, who can be against us?'[130] Let's pray about it." And he took his father's hand and closed his eyes. Cleve pulled his chair closer and took his father's other hand, bowing his head to join them.

---

130   Romans 8:31.

Chapter 46

Luke walked into the newspaper office to find Cleve already there, talking with Daniel Elshout.

Cleve was saying, "And one of us needs to be with you when you go out there. You don't need to talk with him unless one of us is with you."

Luke injected. "And if we say it's time to stop, you stop. You don't ask him anything else until we say you can. Do you understand me?"

"Okay, I understand," Daniel said innocently. "What's changed? You were all for this a few days ago." Daniel saw the change in Cleve's attitude toward the project.

"I mean it," Luke said, ignoring Daniel's question. "I know how you are. You'll slip one little why in there. Or you'll start talking about something else and just pop another question right in the middle. None of that, do you understand?"

"Yeah, I got you," Daniel said, his forehead in furrows. "Why so serious? What's the matter with him?"

"He's agreed to do this only because he thinks God wants him to. He doesn't want to do it. It's already upsetting him," Cleve said. "He's going to tell you about things that are going to upset him even more, things he might have twisted in his head. We're going to make sure he's got it straight in his mind, and then we're going to make sure the story doesn't get distorted because of the way he talks about it. It'll be the truth, and it's not going to get skewed in the process. When other people read it, it's going to be the straight facts, not your opinion or his feelings about it."

Daniel gave an apprehensive okay. Now he was concerned.

Already this wasn't going the way he had wanted it to.

"And I want to know what you're going to ask him before we get there," Luke added.

*****

Later that afternoon, Luke and Daniel rode out to see Travis. Travis was in the vegetable garden beside the house. Travis looked up long enough to see who was coming, then went back to his hoeing. They heard him softly singing as he worked.

Luke got off his horse and joined his father, taking the hoe and continuing where his father had left off. Daniel stood at the edge of the turned dirt and watched. When Luke got to the end of the row, he turned, took his father's arm, and they left the garden, headed to the porch.

Before they got to their seats, Daniel asked, "Well, Travis, what did you think of what I wrote?"

Travis sat down on the rocking chair. Daniel had no idea how old this man was. His beard was completely white. The hat seldom left his head, but you could still see some brown in the gray hair showing beneath it. The deep lines on his dark weathered face made him look older than he probably was. The cold mountain wind and the hot Kansas sun had taken their toll on him.

"It was okay. Ya can print it. But I ain't gonna answer ya last question, 'Are there any regrets?' We ain't goin' there," Travis said.

"Okay, I can take that out. Anything else?"

"No."

Elshout could tell he would have to draw the story out of Travis. He had expected this. Travis had never been a talker, except when he was protecting his children. Then he could argue with a bull and stop it from charging.

"So when can we get started?" the newspaper publisher asked.

"Whenever ya want."

"Okay. How about now?" And without waiting for an answer, Elshout asked, "Can you tell me that one event in your life that changed its direction? When did you think your life was going one way, and then it went another?"

"Whoa!" Luke said. "You didn't tell me you were going to ask that question."

"I just thought of it."

Luke attacked. "This is what I was talking about, you asking questions that come out of nowhere."

"No, Luke, it's okay," Travis said. "The one event that change' my life 'ad ta be the war. 'Fore the war, we was 'appy, We 'ad a good 'ome. I 'ad a beautiful young wife I adored, an' three small chil'en. We 'ad a good life. The farm was producin', I made good money trappin'. My g'an'father lived close by. After the war..." Travis stopped to think for a moment and shook his head.

"After the war, my 'ome was gone, my wife an' sons was dead, my daughter was blind, my g'an'father was dead too. I didn'...I wanted...I. No..." Travis stopped and took a few deep breaths as he thought about how to phrase his answer. "I couldn' take care a my daughter. I couldn't find a job. Everythin' was different."

The shock could be seen in Elshout's face. This was something he had not expected. He knew Travis had served during the war, but he thought the war would have changed Travis's ideas, his desires, not his home. This happened to the Southern soldiers. There weren't many that had losses like this in the north. He understood why this might be difficult for the old man to talk about. He was writing it all down. Hurrying, trying to get it all and not miss anything.

"Okay, let's back up. Where were you living? Tell me about your home."

"We lived on a moun'in in Virginia. Well, what's now West Virginia. My wife an' I had built a 'ouse near my g'an'parents. I grew up there, lived there my whole life."

"What about your parents?"

"Ma died when I was young. I don' know, maybe two or three. She died givin' birth. The baby was never born. Pa died a year or two later. There was a flood ever' spring when the snow melted, an' we was standin' there, watchin' the water run past, when the ground gave way under 'im. Took nearly the whole side a the mountain with it. I was a little ways over, playin' in a small runoff comin' down the hill.

"'E probably could of gotten out, but a tree fell on top a 'im, pushing 'im under. I never saw 'im come up. I was little. I didn't know what ta do. I kept lookin' far 'im 'long the side, watchin' the tree float down the river. Followin' it. I probably would 'ave fallen in if Niko 'adn' found me later that mornin'. He took me 'ome. That's when we 'came friends with 'is family."

"Okay, stop." Elshout wrote some more then asked, "Who's Niko?"

"Niko was a Tutelo Indian. He an' 'is family lived there on the moun'in too. I don' know, maybe a couple a miles from Papaw. 'E 'ad a Suwanee wife. They 'ad fourteen or so kids. I never saw 'em all. A couple a the youngest boys was close ta my age. I used ta stay with 'em some. Niko would take me inta the woods with 'em.

"I remember once, me an' Nastabon was playin' in this cave. We was way back in there, an' it was pitch-black. Ya couldn' see a thin', an' we wasn't even thinkin' 'bout findin' our way out. We could 'ear Niko callin' us, but it was echoin' off the walls. We couldn' tell where he was. He couldn' find us, an' we didn' care.

"We was probably in there far 'ours when we found a small openin' in the ceilin' a the cave. Nastabon shoved me up on 'is shoulders, an' I got a hold on the roots an' pulled myself out. Found a small tree that was down an' got it loose. Stuck the end inta the 'ole, an' Nastabon crawled out an' we went 'ome.

"We just left Niko there, lookin' far us. Like boys'll do, we didn' even think 'bout 'im. Niko spent the night in the cave, still lookin' far us. The next day, 'e came ta the farm ta tell Papaw we was missin'. I was in the barn workin'. Made Niko so mad. Papaw thought it was funny."

Elshout was having trouble keeping up. Travis was actually talking. This was unusual.

"I use ta run back an' forth between our 'ouse an' Niko's by myself. Just a little bitty thin'. Got attacked by a bobcat once, think I got to close ta her den.

"I'd only 'ad a knife far a couple a weeks, but I carried it with me ever'where. I don' know 'ow, but I managed ta kill it an' find its cubs. Took 'em ta Niko's. 'E bandaged me up, then 'e went an' got the dead cat an' skinne' it. Let us play with the cubs that day, then took 'em off that night. Wouldn' tell us what he did with 'em, but soon after, he started teachin' us 'bout the animals an' 'ow ta hunt with a knife an' a spear.

"Papaw had already taught me ta shoot, but, of course, I didn' 'ave a gun. Wasn' hardly strong enough ta pick up the long rifle. But Papaw didn' like me goin' after the animals with only a knife, so the next time 'e went inta town, 'e bought another rifle."

Travis stopped to laugh. "It was more than twice as tall as me, an' I 'ad to stand on somethin' ta get it loaded. 'Ad to prop the barrel on somethin' ta hold it up ta shoot, but I carried it anyway."

There was a break in the talking while Daniel caught up with his notes. Then he asked, "What's the first memory you have?"

Travis thought for a moment. "Ma screamin'. That sound is 'ard ta forget. I was really little. I was just runnin' round, like little kids do, an' I ran inta a tree. There was a small branch that 'ad been broken off." Travis laughed. "Pa probably broke it off ta use as a switch on me. Anyway there was a little nub sticking out, an' I ran right inta it. It went right next ta my eye."

Travis put his crooked little finger up ta his eye, indicating the spot.

"I couldn' move. I 'member Ma's scream. Ya would a thought I was dead. There was no blood, nothin'. My g'an'ma got me off an' put a bandage over it far a few days. When the bandage came off, I couldn' open my eye. One mornin', maybe two years after it 'appene', I woke up, an' it was just open. Ma died 'fore it opene', though."

Luke said, "I had forgotten about your eye. When I was little, I tried to hold my eye like you did but never could. I never did know why it was like that. Or why it got better. What happened that it quit drooping?"

Travis laughed again. "When me an' Mary stopped in Denver on the way back from the Dakotas, Thomas looked at it an' cut the tendon that was 'oldin' the muscle tight. 'Urt like the devil far, I don't know, maybe a couple of months. Then it just 'eale' itself."

"That's what that cut was. I didn't know that either," Luke said. "You hardly notice it now."

"Whose Thomas?" Elshout asked.

"My son-in-law. 'E's a really good doctor."

"And who is he married to?"

"Sarah. My oldest daughter."

Elshout nodded. "Okay, just to clarify in my mind. Your folks died, so you were raised by your grandparents. Mother's or father's parents?"

"Father's."

"What's the one thing you can say they taught you?"

"To love God. Papaw used to read the Bible ever' night an' teach at our Sunday meetin's. It was real important ta 'em to know what God wanted an' ta do it."

"Okay, what else?"

"G'an'ma taught me natural medicine an' folk healin'. Papaw taught me huntin', trappin', leather work, an' 'ow ta take care a the farm. An' music. 'E was real gifted in music."

Travis stopped to laugh again. "But 'e couldn' sing. Horrible voice. 'E tried. I always thought it was so funny when I was a kid. I thought 'e was tryin' ta be funny. When I got older, I realized 'e just couldn' sing. But 'e kept on singin' anyway."

"What did Niko teach you?"

"Shoot! Everything else. Animal behavior, trackin', weather, water an' land movement, survival, 'ow ta live off the land. He took me to the Indian camps, an' I learned from 'em too. 'E 'elped with trappin' an' shootin'. 'E knew more than Papaw did.

"Oh, an' 'ow ta hold my temper. That was a big one. The man never showed an emotion, even when 'e was mad. That time 'e got so mad at me an' Nastabon far bein' in that cave, 'e just looked at me. Said a few choice words in 'is language but never showed that 'e was upset. Ya would catch 'im smile ever' once in a while, though. The rest of us would be holdin' our sides, we'd be laughin' so 'ard. 'E'd just be standin' there with that little grin on 'is face."

Daniel smiled. "Did you know what he was saying when he was mad at you.

"I knew a few a the words. That's 'ow I knew 'e was mad. I'm glad Papaw didn't know what 'e was sayin'. 'E might not a let me go with 'im anymore."

They talked on for another couple of hours about the mountain and Travis's grandparents and his life growing up.

Then Luke said, "Okay, let's call it quits for today. Don't want to wear you out."

He rummaged through the kitchen and found something for his father to eat for supper. Then he and Daniel rode back into town.

Chapter 47

A couple of days later, Cleve came to the farm with Daniel. They had the second story written and a copy of the newspaper with the first story printed in it.

Cleve didn't seem as excited about the project as he had the first day he had talked to his father about it. Now Cleve and Daniel talked casually a few minutes about the initial response to the article while Travis listened.

Then Elshout said, "How about giving me some information about your wife and children? Where did you meet her? What was her name?"

Travis had talked about her some during their last meeting, but he had never called her by name. Travis took a few deep breaths to steady himself and tried to clear himself of emotion. He didn't know why, but he could talk about Brenda much easier than he could Ruth.

"Ruth," Travis said quickly, then took another deep breath. "I was out on the moun'in, further from 'ome than I usually went. I ran across her father's farm, an' there she was. The most beautiful thin' I ever seen. I 'ung round a while an' did some work far 'er family. Then I talked 'er father inta lettin' me marry 'er. It didn't take long.

"I wondered if 'e was just tryin' ta get rid a 'er, but I don' know why 'e would. They weren' poor. That was usually why fathers married off their daughters so they wouldn' have that mouth ta feed. But 'e was doin' good. I never understood it. But I was 'appy 'e let us get married.

"Marriage was different on the moun'in. There was no preacher or judge ta do it. I put my 'and on the Bible, an' I promised ta take care a 'er. That was it. We put 'er things in a sack an' went back ta my g'an'parent's 'ouse."

The three men sat on the front porch, talking about building the house and clearing the land for farming. Travis explained trapping and hunting and how no part of an animal went to waste.

They talked of having children and of Travis's grandparents. Travis told them about their church meetings and some of the neighbor's injuries that he had cared for. He explained how life on the mountain worked, how neighbors took care of neighbors, and about the isolation. Travis told them of his grandmother's death.

Then Elshout asked, "If you were isolated on the mountain, how did you find out the war started?"

Travis thought for a moment. "I think one a the neighbors had been inta town an' 'ear'd 'bout it."

Daniel waited, but Travis didn't say anything else. Until now Travis had talked freely following each question. Now he wasn't expounding on the subject at all. Daniel asked, "So how did you get involved?"

Daniel and Cleve were watching Travis. Cleve was now concerned, his father was staring off at the trees, chewing on the inside of his bottom lip.

"There was a battle near us. Some a the wounded soldiers ended up at our place." Travis couldn't bring himself to say that he had brought them home. "Then some gray soldiers showed up an' took their injured. They took most a our food too. It was close ta winter. The fall crops had already been harvested."

There was a break in what Travis was saying. Daniel waited, and when nothing else was said, he asked another question.

"Did you take care of the injuries?"

Travis nodded but said nothing.

"Hey, Dad?" Cleve said. "You got any coffee made?"

"No."

"Let's take a break and go make some." Cleve reached over and took his father's arm to help him out of the chair and guided him into the house.

Daniel sat on the porch alone for a few minutes, looking over his notes and adding some here and there. Then Cleve came back.

"I'm going to help you get this information from Dad. Seems like he doesn't want to talk, so there must be something coming that he doesn't want to remember. We need to be careful."

Cleve went back inside, and when he came out again, Travis was with him. He handed Daniel a cup and sat back down.

Over the next couple of hours, Cleve asked small seemingly insignificant questions, gathering pieces of information from his father. They learned about the trip to the Union camp with the injured soldiers and of his conscription into the army during battle and his inability to convince others that he wasn't a part of the troops.

They talked about battles, death, blood and disfigurement, and about Travis's many responsibilities during this time. He told of spending day after day with the doctors during surgery, followed by days of burying the dead. He talked of going into battle from sunup to sundown to bring the wounded out, then of looking for injured in the dark, hearing their moans but not being able to find them.

Travis told of an explosion that had happened near him and had caused blood to run out his ear for days. He'd lost his balance because of this and had trouble standing and walking. But he had to keep working, despite this, because so many others needed his help. He spoke of the noise he still had in that ear. How it interfered with his concentration sometimes and was a constant reminder of the battles. And he talked of caring for the wounded day after day after day.

Then Travis stopped answering questions.

Cleve said, "Okay, let's quit for now."

"No. There's somethin' I need ta tell ya," Travis said. "I just don't know 'ow ta say it."

Cleve and Daniel sat silently as they watched Travis process his thoughts. Cleve knew this wasn't going to be good.

Travis started slowly, like he was having to think about each word as he said it. "I was never accepted with the staff at the hospital or with the officers. I think they saw me as an intruder, an ignorant mountain man with no education an' no skills."

Travis wasn't looking at the others; he was looking toward the trees.

The story began to come faster, but they could still tell he was thinking about how he said things. "Like I said, I did my job good an' was probably better with the wounded than most a the others, but I didn''ave any military trainin'.

"In the beginning, I didn' know 'ow ta act or who ta talk with or who not ta approach. I think they saw that as stupid. Or maybe deliberately disrespectful. I don' know. I didn' understand 'em, an' they didn' understand me.

"I don' even think they thought I was worth...well. Sometimes with the way they treated me, the things they 'ad me doin'." Travis shook his head. He couldn't find the words to use. "I don' know.

"But there was this one doctor that wanted me with 'im whenever he was doin' surgery. That caused problems with the other hospital staff. I don't know if they was jealous or just filled with anger or scared or what. They would...well. They weren't nice when I went back ta my regular duties.

"Anyway one night I was goin' ta get a wounded soldier somethin' ta eat when this officer—the one I 'ad trouble with earlier. The one I told ya 'bout. 'E came up behind me. Never said a word until he was finished, then he said, 'That will teach ya ta stay where ya belong.'"

Travis hesitated, then added, "I just need ta show ya. That's easiest."

Travis stood up and turned with his back to them as they waited, wondering what he was doing, what he would show them. Then he dropped the shirt off his shoulders, revealing the scars.

*****

It was getting late. The sun was just going down. Daniel Elshout was a distance from the house. Travis stood at the edge of the porch with his back to Cleve, the same place he had been standing since he had stood up. He had not turned around to face the others since he had showed them the scars.

Cleve asked his father, "Do you want me to feed the livestock?"

"Thanks." Travis nodded.

When Cleve had finished, he found his father on the chair beside the cold fireplace, his open Bible on his lap, his eyes closed. Cleve took the Bible and closed it, laying it on the nearest table. Then he got a blanket, laid it across his father, and patted his father's arm.

"Dad?"

"Bye, son," Travis replied softly without opening his eyes. He was finished, he wanted to be alone. Cleve turned the lantern down low and left the house. He needed to find Luke and talk to him. Right now.

Chapter 48

Travis woke up several times during the night and had trouble going back to sleep each time. Long before morning, he had given up. Memories of the war rattled through his head. When he slept, visions of battles and wounded, dead and dying, plagued him. He didn't want to think about these things anymore.

Maybe he would go fishing. But not by himself. He needed noise, he needed activity, something to stop the voices in his head. If he could get on his horse, he'd find his grandsons and see if they wanted to go with him.

He did his morning chores and then managed to saddle his horse. He walked the horse to the edge of the steps, positioned the animal, and mounted from the third step up.

Cleve had built a home for his family at the far end of the property, closer to town. The trees and thick brush had overgrown what used to be the fields they plowed. The same fields that Travis had used as a shortcut the day Mary was taken by the Indians. There was a thin trail that Cleve's boys used when they visited their grandpa, but it was too small for a horse and rider. Travis would have to go through town to get there.

Travis arrived at the large house and yelled hello. There was no answer. He rode toward the back of the house and yelled again. Still no answer. They weren't here. One of the children would have heard him if they had been home.

He really needed those noisy active boys right now. He rode to the back of the barn. The wagon was gone. No telling where they were.

Headed back through town, Travis spotted Jake's shop. Travis stopped in front and looked at the door, wishing Jake would see him and come out. He sat there, but it didn't happen.

Travis slid off the horse and went inside. There was a young man at the table with rifle parts scattered in front of him.

"Jake 'round?" Travis asked.

"No, not yet. Can I help you with something?"

"No, just lookin' far Jake."

Travis walked back outside. Now what would he do. He could go home or go fishing alone. Normally going fishing alone would be his choice, but not today. He still wanted noise.

"Hey, Dad. Wow, you haven't been to town in a while."

It was Luke.

"Hi, son."

"Do you need something?"

"I came ta see if Cleve's boys wanted ta go fishin', but nobody's 'ome."

"Nope. I saw the whole bunch of them headed out to the Wilson's place a little while ago."

"Jake's not 'ere either. Guess I'll go 'lone." Travis untied his horse and walked him to the end of the boardwalk, positioned him, and got on. The boardwalk wasn't quite as high as his steps, but he made it without much difficulty.

"Dad. Wait. Let me get my horse. I'll go out to the farm with you."

"I'm goin' fishin'. Ya got thin's ta do. Ya don' need ta be sittin' in the middle a nowhere with an ol' man."

"No. But I can go fishing with my father," Luke replied.

They spent the morning fishing and talking about happy events of the past. Luke and Travis shared stories from their lawmen's jobs and laughed about the stupid things the cowboys did in town. They spoke lovingly of Luke's mother. They laughed, remembering joyous family events and good times with friends.

By late morning, Travis was feeling better. God was good. It hadn't taken long to get Travis over that foul mood he had been in.

His thoughts had turned to happier times. Now he was feeling the lack of sleep he had gotten the night before and was ready for a nap.

Travis struggled to get on his horse. Luke saw it and thought about going to help his father, but Luke didn't want to embarrass him. Travis had never said anything to Luke about the pain he had in his hand or his shoulder. But Luke knew. When Travis was on the saddle, he looked over and saw his son watching him. Travis turned his horse and started home.

They took their fish home and threw them in the horse trough to save for supper, and Travis went to lie down.

Cleve's boys came to see their grandpa the next morning. Uncle Luke had told them he had been looking for them, and they had come to the farm to see what he needed. They helped with the chores and played a few games of checkers. Travis got a couple of knives out and let the boys practice their whittling, something their mother didn't like them doing. The knives were too dangerous, she had said.

They all kept it a secret, she didn't need to know. But she did know. Travis had talked with Cleve and Jenny when the boys weren't around. He had assured Jenny that he would supervise and take care of them. Cleve had told his wife that he had begun using a hunting knife when he was much younger to skin animals. Jenny had finally agreed, saying, "Don't tell me when you do it, I don't want to know." She knew Travis loved his grandchildren and would take care of them.

The boys left for home, taking some vegetables from the garden with them. Travis ate the lunch the boys had brought him and settled in on the porch to read the second story Daniel Elshout had brought a few days before.

He didn't want to read it, so he sat on his rocker holding it. Then he went inside and got his Bible. He would renew his mind before he tackled the article.

He opened to where he had left off when he had closed the book that morning. As he continued reading, he came to Ephesians 4. In verse 20 he read:

That, however, is not the way of life you learned when you heard about Christ and were taught in him in accordance with the truth that is in Jesus. You were taught, with regard to your former way of life, to put off your old self, which is being corrupted by its deceitful desires; to be made new in the attitude of your minds; and to put on the new self, created to be like God in true righteousness and holiness.

Travis realized he hadn't been living in righteousness. He had let old unholy thoughts enter his mind. Deceit had crept in, and he was allowing self-pity to override joy. The old lies that he thought he had gotten rid of had returned. How had he let this happen? His attitude needed to change.

Travis prayed, "Search me, God, and know my heart, test me and know my anxious thoughts. See if there is any offensive way in me, and lead me in the way everlasting."[131]

He heard God respond. *I the Lord, search the heart and examine the mind, to reward each person according to their conduct, according to what their deeds deserve.*[132]

Travis exclaimed, "Father, no. Please! 'Have mercy on me, O God, according to your unfailing love.'[133] Don't give me what my deeds deserve, 'According to your great compassion blot out my transgressions. Wash away all my iniquity and cleanse me from my sin. For I know my transgressions, and my sins are always before me.'[134] 'Create in me a pure heart, O God, and renew a steadfast spirit within me.'"[135]

And the Spirit responded, *But when the kindness and love of God our Savior appeared, he saved us, not because of righteous things we had done, but because of his mercy. He saved us through the washing of rebirth and renewal by the Holy Spirit.*[136]

---

131   Psalm 139:23–24.
132   Jeremiah 17:10.
133   Psalm 51:2a.
134   Psalm 51:1b–3.
135   Psalm 51:10.
136   Titus 3:4–5.

"Thank ya, Lord," Travis replied. He knew his old memories were contributing to his unholy thoughts. This needed to stop.

He laid the pages Daniel had given him on the floor beside him and went back to reading his Bible, renewing his spirit. The wind blew slightly, and the pages on the porch began to flutter. Page by page, they blew to the ground.

He was still reading when three riders approached the house. They were close when he looked up to see his sons and the newspaper publisher.

"Keep me focused on you, Father. The past is the past. Strengthen me for this day," he prayed.

Cleve leaned over as he got off his horse and picked up a paper that was on the ground. He looked around and saw more blowing away. He grabbed a few more but let others go.

As he walked onto the porch, he asked his father, "Dad, did you read this?"

"No, an' I ain't gonna. Ya can read it an' make sure it says what it needs ta say. I can't. I can't continue ta revisit these memories."

Daniel asked, "But you are going to finish telling me your story?"

"I'm gonna tell ya. An' once I tell it, I'm finished with it. I'm not lookin' at it 'gain. Now what do ya want ta talk 'bout taday?"

"I thought we'd just pick up where we left off, at the end of the war. Tell me about your homecoming."

Travis sat there a few long moments, closed his Bible, and hugged it to his chest. Then he began talking.

He talked his way through Virginia and his destroyed home, through learning of his family's death and Sarah's blindness. He told of Papaw's death and their trip to Charlestown. Travis talked about his first winter home, the trip to Chicago, and searching for the doctor, about his inability to find work, and of the kindly man that took Sarah in. He talked about the depressing years of wandering, looking for work, and of his loneliness.

He'd been talking steady for hours again. His mouth was dry, and his voice was getting rough when he said, "That's it. That's all I got taday. Go 'ome." And he got up and went into the house.

The three men on the porch looked at one another. They had all been absorbed in what Travis was saying. Travis hadn't shown emotion through any of it. His sons had not remembered to care for their father's needs. They hadn't noticed his voice quivering at times or his hands holding his Bible so tightly his knuckles had turned white.

The brothers got up at the same time and followed their father into the house. But Travis wasn't there. They looked in every room. He was gone.

The backdoor was open. It was always open in good weather. Luke looked out to see his father on his knees at the edge of the trees, still hugging God's Word.

Cleve walked up behind Luke as they watched their father. They could hear Travis talking, but they were too far away to understand what he was saying. They knew he was praying.

"I got a letter from Thomas yesterday," Cleve said softly. "They'll be here next Tuesday."

"That's good. He needs somebody with him," Luke responded. "I wish I could stay, but I've got to be in town tonight. I'll see if I can work something out so I can be here for the next few nights."

"I'll stay for a while tonight and see if I can talk him into going home with me for supper," Cleve said. He was silent a moment, then added, "He's having trouble getting on and off his horse."

"I know. It's been coming for a while. Has trouble with the buckboard too," Luke said.

"What's the matter with him?"

"His hand. The one that was cut up when we were kids. It's gotten to where he can't grip anything, can't hold on. It gets stiff and swollen sometimes. He's never said, but I think it hurts him. Doesn't play his banjo anymore either. His shoulder bothers him too," Luke explained. "He's had problems with it since before he and Mom married. You remember how Mary and Mama used to rub his shoulder? I think that stopped the pain. Nobody's done it since Mary left. I don't think he can lift his arm anymore. You know how he is. He'd never let you know if he was hurting."

"I didn't know that about his hand. Didn't realize his shoulder was that bad either. He's always talked to you more than he has me," Cleve said casually. There was no malice in the comment.

"He always trusted you more," Luke said, smiling at his older brother. "But our baby brother told me about his hand years ago. He and Dad were close, living here just the two of them those last few years. I started watching Dad before he retired, and even then, I could tell he was having a problem with his shoulder. Since Reid left, I've been trying to keep an eye on him. It's hard to do, though, when I have to stay in town so much, and he never leaves the farm."

"Oh. I don't guess I think about Reid much. I never really got to know him. I was gone before he was born. He was maybe ten when I came back. He was always so quiet. He'd disappear when I came to see Dad. We didn't have much contact."

"Yeah, he had just turned two when I left, was eight when I came back. Naomi was twelve. We got to know each other only because I lived with them a few years when I first got back to Harris," Luke said. "I would have stayed, but when I got elected sheriff, I had to be in town. It was rough on Naomi having to take care of the house and Reid after Mary left."

"But Mary needed to go," Cleve stated. "The medical school had already delayed her entrance two years. They wouldn't do it again."

"I know," Luke agreed. "Daddy practically pushed her out the door, but then he couldn't afford to pay for help. He was paying for three of us to be in school, that's more than he could afford. Don't know how he did it. That left Angus, Naomi, and Reid to take care of everything at home. But Reid was so young. I didn't realize it until I came back, but they didn't have enough money. He was sending most of what he made to us."

"He sacrificed a lot for us."

"The three little kids did too," Luke said.

"Do you think Dad will go home with Sarah?" Cleve asked.

"I don't want him to. I want him here," Luke said. "But he needs somebody. Sarah would be good for him. Thomas would be too."

Chapter 49

Daniel found out that Travis's daughter was coming the next week and decided to visit Travis more often. He was afraid Travis would leave, and the story wouldn't get finished.

Neither of the brothers were available one afternoon, so Daniel decided to go alone. He knew Cleve and Luke would have something to say about it. But Daniel had watched Travis. He thought he knew when to back off and when he could push forward.

Daniel arrived at the farm alone. Travis didn't acknowledge that neither of his sons were there.

They talked about Travis finding Mark injured and about capturing the outlaw that had shot the marshal. The talked about Travis's arrival in Harris and about how he became the deputy. They talked about the years that followed, about Travis's reunion with Sarah, and about being shot by the storekeeper's son, about fights in saloons and on the street, of farm work and his marriage, and the range war. They had gotten to the time Mary had been taken by the Indians. This was just before Daniel had come to Harris. He had heard the stories and was more familiar with this part of Travis's life.

Then he asked the question, "What happened between the time you left to find Mary and when you found her?"

Travis stiffened and looked away. He had never shared any of this with anyone. Except for the few days he spent caring for the girl he had found, no one else knew what had happened. He thought briefly about lying, about skipping the events and just telling Daniel he had trouble following the Indians.

Then the Spirit corrected him, *The Lord detests lying lips, but he delights in people who are trustworthy.*[137]

Travis sat up taller in the chair. He'd tell the whole truth.

"I started out by myself, but Mark followed me. We rode tagether maybe a day an' a half, then he wanted me ta stop at one a the forts ta see if there was more information an' ta get supplies. I's livin' off the land an' followin' the trail. I was goin' where God told me ta go. I didn' want ta stop. We had an argument, only argument we ever 'ad. I left without 'im.

"I followed the Indians inta Nebraska Territory, then I lost 'em. Took me several days ta find 'em 'gain. When I did, it was just by accident. I was ridin' up on this camp, just after dark, an' I realized too late it was an Indian's camp. But I was committed by this time. I had ta talk ta 'em. Turned out it was the Indians I was lookin' far. They knew who I was. At least they knew I had been followin' 'em. One a 'em attacked an' overpowered me. I'm ashamed ta say I wasn't ready far 'em.

"As they was tyin' me up, I caught sight a Mary bein' drug 'cross the ground toward the horses. But there was nothin' I could do. Mary saw me, I could see it in 'er face. She started strugglin' more, tryin' ta get 'way. Then they hit me, an' it knocke' me out. I woke up durin' the night, an' it took me till midday ta get myself loose. Almost broke my arm twistin' it ta get it out a the ropes. I took off after 'em, but the next day I come across this girl. She was 'bout Mary's age, maybe a little younger. She had been stripped an' beaten."

Travis steeled himself once again, to take all emotion away, and continued, telling Daniel about Elizabeth and what had happened until her death three days later. Then he stopped.

When he spoke again, he said, "I can't help but think it was my fault. If I 'andn' been so clumsy ridin' straight inta their camp, they wouldn' 'ave captured me. But they 'ad changed horses an' was wearin' white man's clothes.

---

137   Proverbs 12:22.

"If I hadn' let myself get captured, Mary wouldn' a seen me get 'it, an' she might not a tried ta escape. If she 'adn' tried ta get 'way, then Elizabeth wouldn' a been beaten, an' she might still be 'live."

Travis was staring at the porch, and he had quit talking. Elshout felt he had made a terrible mistake. He never should have come without one of Travis's sons with him.

After sitting there, watching Travis stare at the floor for a while, Daniel thought he would try Cleve's trick.

He asked, "You got any coffee made?"

But he got no response from Travis. Daniel got up and went inside. He didn't see a coffeepot on the stove. He rummaged through the bare kitchen a bit and still didn't find one, but there was a half-empty cup on the table.

He looked into the front room and saw it sitting at the edge of the fireplace. He picked it up and took it back in the kitchen. There was no fire in the stove. He didn't know where the coffee was. This was pointless. He stepped back onto the porch, and Travis was still sitting the same way. He hadn't moved. Maybe he would talk some more.

"I couldn't find the coffee," Elshout said and sat back down.

"Travis?" He waited.

"Travis? Look at me." Elshout waited. "Look at me, Travis!"

Travis slowly lifted his head and looked at Daniel.

"What happened when you left Camp Sturgis?"

Travis stared at him for a long time, moving his mouth like he wanted to say something but couldn't. Then he finally said, "I...I went north." And he went back to looking at the floor. "It 'ad rained the night 'fore. The trail wouldn' a been gone by now, there was no reason to backtrack. I knew where they was 'eaded'. Elizabeth had told me. The Indians spoke perfect English. They 'ad teased the girls, tellin' 'em were they was goin' an' tellin' 'em nobody would find 'em there.

"'Bout two days out, I picked up what I thought was their trail. It wasn' the direction they 'ad told the girls they was goin', but I figured they must 'ave lied ta the girls. I followe' the trail inta the Lower Brule Reservation an' caught up with 'em.

"It was the same horses all right, but different Indians. Somewhere along the trail, they had traded horses with these guys, and I had missed it again.

"There was a couple a white girls there, but not Mary. I manage' ta negotiate their release, then I took the girls ta Fort Thompson."

Travis went on to tell of finding an isolated burned-out cabin, attacked by Indians. He had buried the family he had found there.

He talked of being followed and confronted by Indians on three separate occasions. He told of being shot at and a knife fight he had been forced into for no other reason than to prove his courage. He spoke of long discouraging days and even longer depressing nights.

He talked of the snow and the cold and his fear for Mary and his fear for his family. He talked of being alone in the freezing mud dugout. Daniel thought he even looked cold as he talked about the freezing weather. Then he suddenly stopped.

"I can't do this," he said. "God spoke ta me. He told me what ta do. He told me where ta find peace."

He hadn't looked at Elshout since he had started talking. Now he seemed to be talking to someone else.

"Ya told me my hope was in ya. Ya said I would praise ya, my Savior an' my God." Travis closed his eyes, and Daniel sat there, watching as Travis lifted his face toward the sky. Daniel continued watching as Travis's face went from taut and defeated to peaceful. The tension drained from Travis, and the color in his face brightened. That crooked smile came to Travis's face as he relaxed back into his chair.

"Travis?" Daniel said.

"I'm through. Go 'ome, Daniel." Travis took a deep breath, letting it out completely as he started rocking, enjoying the Spirit's presence and comfort.

Daniel wasn't sure what had just happened. They both sat there, not moving, except for the rocking. Travis didn't speak to him again and kept his eyes closed. After several minutes, the rocking slowed, and over time, Travis's head gently rolled to the side, then relaxed to his chest.

Was he all right? Was he asleep? Was he praying?

Elshout wasn't sure what he should do.

"Travis?" No response. "Travis? Are you okay?"

Daniel heard a horse coming and looked up to see Luke. Well, he'd have to face the consequences now.

Luke noticed his father's posture before he got off his horse. He looked at Daniel and shook his head as he jumped down and ran to his father. Luke knelt beside him and put his hand on his father's arm, softly calling him.

"Dad? Dad?"

Travis lifted his head and opened his eyes slowly. He smiled at his son and lifted his hand to pat Luke's arm. He let his hand remain on Luke and closed his eyes again, still smiling.

"Come on, Dad. Let's go in the house." As Luke helped his father out of the rocker, the Spirit moved with Travis, continuing to comfort him. Luke turned his head to Daniel and quietly but sternly said, "Don't move. I'm coming back."

Luke had reprimanded Daniel thoroughly. Daniel knew he deserved it. He left, promising not to return until he was called for.

Luke had kept Daniel's notes. He wanted to know what had disturbed his father. But after reading them over, he still wasn't sure. Maybe Daniel hadn't written it down. Was something going on with his father that he didn't know about?

His father seemed at peace, but he was too quiet. Disturbingly quiet.

Chapter 50

Luke spent Friday with Travis. They sat on the porch, drinking coffee in the early morning, Travis still enjoying God's companionship. Luke talked about his job and Cleve's kids. Then he talked about Sarah, Thomas, and their eight children.

Travis hadn't said anything all morning, but he was smiling and seemed to be paying attention to what Luke was saying. Travis hadn't seen Sarah's family in six years, not since he had accompanied Naomi to Denver. Travis's thoughts began to wander, and he felt the Spirit slowly move away. The smile left his face.

Naomi. Where was his little girl? What had happened? What had he done that had turned her away from him? He had relied on her so much to help him, and she had never complained.

Then she married suddenly and broke contact with almost everyone in the family.

Naomi had married during her second year at the university. Although she had her small wedding at the Stewart home, she had very little contact with them following the ceremony. And then she had disappeared.

The only member of the family she had any contact with now was Angus. Angus would receive a letter every so often and would relay the news to Sarah, who would relay it to the rest of the family. There was seldom a return address. But when there was, Angus would always write back. Many of his letters were returned undeliverable.

No one knew why Naomi had stopped contact with the others, not even Angus. It bothered Travis and Reid the most. Travis because he loved his little girl, and Reid because Naomi had been the one to care for him most of his life.

When Luke saw that his father wasn't paying attention or responding to him anymore, he said, "Come on, Dad. Let's get the chores done so we can go fishing."

Fishing. That would always get his father's attention.

They worked together around the farm, repaired a few things at the house, and then they went fishing.

*****

Travis had asked that Daniel come to the farm early Saturday morning. He told Luke he wanted to finish the interviews so he could stop all this foolishness and get back to his life.

Daniel had come with Cleve, and they had talked through Mary's rescue, Denver, and their return. Travis told of his illness and Mary's state of mind through the ordeal. They talked of Travis learning to read and his transition to full-time deputy, of the gunfight when Mark had been injured, the surgery that followed, and of Mary's improvement while working with Dr. Cooper. They talked of Mary and Cleve leaving for school and of Angus and Naomi growing.

There was conversation about the good years while Travis worked with Mark, of the cowboys' senseless conduct, the capture of a wanted outlaw, and of the stagecoach being robbed. Travis talked cheerfully about the birth of his two youngest children and of the babies growing. They talked at length of a gunfight in which Mark and Travis had been victorious against five members of a wanted outlaw gang.

They took a break for lunch. Travis was feeling good about the morning and enjoyed the casual conversation the others had as they ate ham and biscuits Cleve's wife had prepared. Travis had rested for a little while but had gotten up uneasy about what was coming that afternoon.

Travis had gotten used to his afternoon naps. They had started long ago, before his marriage to Brenda. The late nights at the saloons and the early morning rounds in town left little time to sleep at night. He had never stopped this habit. He still rose early and usually went to bed late, unless his shoulder was bothering him especially bad.

Then he might lie down, but there was no sleep.

Now it was time for him to talk again.

Neither Travis nor his sons were ready for this. Travis closed his eyes and said a silent prayer, asking God to stay close to him and close to his boys. Luke had been there, he had lived through it too. Travis looked at Luke.

"It was the winter of '83. The flu was bad that year. Angus 'ad gotten it, an' we 'ad isolated 'im in one a the bedrooms. Then Brenda got it. We took Naomi, Colleen, an' Reid over ta Mildred Anderson's, an' she was takin' care a 'em. Luke didn' wanna go with 'em, but the little ones needed 'im. 'E was still goin' ta school, in his last year. 'E would get things far me when 'e was in town an' leave 'em 'ere on the porch. I was stayin' 'ome, takin' care a the sick. Then Mildred thought Colleen was gettin' sick, an' she sent er 'ome with Luke. If she was sick, now Luke was exposed too, so 'e started sleepin' in the barn. I don't know if she was sick then or not. She was actin' a little strange, sleepin' more than usual. But it was a few days 'fore she started runnin' a fever.

"Then I got sick. Angus was feelin' a little better an' startin' ta be more demandin'. 'E was six, still not really old enough ta understand what was happenin' ta everybody else. 'E tried to help, but mostly 'e just got in the way. I did all I could for all a 'em, but it wasn' enough.

"Colleen was only two, an' she was really bad. I was tryin' ta care far 'er. I fell asleep on the bed beside 'er. When I woke up, I went to check on Brenda. She was gone." Travis stopped and looked at Luke.

"When I found ya mother, I was crushed. I didn' know what I would do without 'er. And I'd let 'er die 'lone. I should 'ave been there with 'er. But I'd been in the other room for 'ours." Travis stopped talking for a moment but continued picking at a loose thread on his pants.

"I called Luke an' asked 'im ta go get Mark far me. When Mark got 'ere, I told 'em both 'bout ya mom." Travis was now looking at Cleve.

"Mark stayed with Luke far a while, then went inta town ta make arrangements with the undertaker. I was on the porch with Colleen when he come back. She was wrapped up in a blanket. It was cold outside, an' I 'ad fever. I was sweatin' and shiverin' at the same time. Mark tried ta get me ta go inside an' finally said I needed ta take Colleen in 'fore she got pneumonia. But Colleen was the reason I come outside.

"I 'ad gone inside when Mark left, an' she was so hot, lyin' there, whimperin'. I knew the fever 'ad ta come down. I tried washin' her down with cold water, but I was sick too. I was so tired, and I was upset over Brenda. I'm really not sure what I did. I didn't mean ta, but I fell asleep 'gain. When I woke up, she was asleep too an' still so hot. I tried to give her some willow bark tea. I don' know how much I got down 'er. I'd been givin' it ta 'er far days, but it didn' seem to be doing anythin', so I started ta take 'er outside in the cold ta try an' get the fever down. But she started shakin'. By the time I got ta the porch, she 'ad calmed down. She got quiet, so I held 'er 'ere a little while then I looked at 'er 'gain. She was gone. She died in my arms. I couldn't bring myself to say it, I kept hopin' she'd come back ta me.

"Mark finally realized what was goin' on an' came up 'ere an' took Colleen. Laid her beside her mother. Luke 'ad been watchin' from the barn door. I'm not sure what 'appene' then. I remember Luke's face, standing there, 'lone in the yard." Travis was looking at Luke.

"Then Mark took me in the house an' took care a me an' Angus far the next few days."

When Travis stopped, Daniel turned to Luke and said, "Maybe you can fill in here."

"Mark took Colleen inside, then came back and told me she was gone too. But I had already figured that out. He sent me to get Jake. I told Jake what had happened. We went by the undertakers and came back here. Mark talked to Jake from the porch and then

Jake took me home with him. We buried Mama and Colleen two days later. Neither Mark nor Dad were there.

"Jake had sent a message to Cleve. He didn't come. He was in the middle of testing at school, and they wouldn't let him leave for an extended time. Mary quit school right there in the middle of the semester, and she and Thomas were here maybe five days later.

"Angus had recovered, and Dad was better but not well yet. Thomas said he wasn't contagious anymore, so Mary went and got Naomi and Reid and brought them home.

"Thomas took care of Dad and tried to help with the rest of us. He and Mary seemed close. He was a comfort to her. He wanted to be sympathetic and friendly with me, but I was a tough guy, I didn't need a stranger taking care of me. I wanted my father.

"But Dad was so weak from the sickness and grieved by Mama and Colleen's death. He couldn't comfort anyone except Naomi and Reid. He would hold them all the time. Naomi got so tired of it she started running from him. She didn't know Mary or Thomas, so she came to me. She and Angus kept asking for Mama, and we couldn't get them to understand that Mama wasn't coming back. She was only five, Angus six.

"Dad and Thomas would sit up at night after the rest of us were in bed. They would talk about Mama and Colleen and the rest of us kids. I would lie in bed and listen to them. That was my biggest comfort, lying in bed, listening to them. I wanted to be sitting there with them but couldn't bring myself to do it. I wanted to be able to talk with Dad like Thomas had. I didn't realize then that it was just a matter of me getting older.

"When I came back, after going to school, we had that friendship. I just needed to grow up. And I learned what a good man Thomas was while I was in Denver and living with them. We became friends too.

"But at the time, I was in my last year of school here and planning to go to Denver that summer. When it came time to go, I couldn't bring myself to leave. I think I still needed my dad. I know he needed me. So I waited another year."

Travis stopped him. "I knew ya were there. I knew ya neede' me, an' I tried. But ya 'ad turned ta Mary. Every time I tried ta talk, ya would say, 'Mary an' I talked 'bout that already.'

"But I remember one afternoon, I found ya in the barn. That was ya favorite place ta read the Bible. Ya was readin', an' I sat down with ya. Ya ignored me. Ya kept on readin'. Do ya remember the verse ya stopped on?"

"No."

"I do. That was the most comfortin' conversation I 'ad durin' that time, and it was with ya," Travis said. "Ya read it ta me. 'If we died with him, we will also live with him; if we endure, we will also reign with him. If we disown him, he will also disown us; if we are faithless, he remains faithful, for he cannot disown himself.'[138]

"We talked 'bout seein' ya mom 'gain," Travis went on. "An' ya quoted Revelation 21:4 ta me. 'He will wipe every tear from (our) eyes. There will be no more death or mourning or crying or pain, for the old order of things has passed away.'

"Ya told me that God's words were a 'ealin' balm ta a 'eart that was broken by loss."

"I remember that." Luke broke in. "We quoted scripture to each other. We got into a debate, trying to remember scripture that would be better than what the other person remembered." Luke laughed.

His father smiled. "Do ya remember which one we decided was best?"

"I think it was, 'Now is your time of grief, but I will see you again and you will rejoice, and no one will take away your joy,'"[139] Luke said.

Travis smiled and spoke again, "Then ya told me this poem ya had learned in school. I didn't understand it, but ya explained it ta me. I remember the exact words ya said, 'We don't need to be afraid of death. If ya have Jesus ya can't die, 'cause death is like sleepin'. Ya go to sleep on this side an' ya wake up in Jesus's arms.'

---

138   2 Timothy 2:11–13.

139   John 16:22b.

That meant so much ta me, knowing that ya understood an could say it so beautifully."

Cleve sat quietly the whole time they were talking. He had remained in Denver. Sarah had stayed with him. Sarah had been the one to comfort him. She had never mentioned her own mother's death, now Cleve wondered why.

But he now understood why he and Sarah had formed such a bond during that time. They had both suffered the loss of their mother at a time when they had both felt alone. Neither had received comfort from the people they wanted it from. Both were wrapped up in other things. Sarah, recovering from injuries, and him trying to concentrate on his studies.

Sarah had known his pain and what he had needed. She had tried to provide it. Cleve realized that was when he had begun to love Sarah and treat her like a sister.

He had lived with Sarah and Thomas for seven years. Cleve had attended secondary school, the university, and had done post-graduate work. His time spent in Denver had been longer than the four years he had lived with his father.

Mary and Luke had not spent that much time in Denver. They had returned to Harris and had lived with their father as an adult. Now Cleve realized he had lived with his father less than any of them, and compared to his siblings, he really didn't know his father.

Cleve began to smile, thinking of Sarah. He may not know his father, but he knew his older sister, and she would be here in just a few days.

Travis looked at Cleve, a look of compassion on his face. Travis knew his son had not gotten to grieve like he should have.

Travis hadn't either. Twice now, his wife had been buried, and he had not been there. Twice he had lost children, and his grief for them had been mingled with his grief for his wife. Twice he had wondered, could he have saved them if things had been different, if he had been home or if he had not been ill himself. Travis knew he still grieved for all of them.

Travis had hoped he would one day move past grief and guilt, but it had continued to revisit him occasionally. Now that he was old, he knew it would remain.

Scripture came to Travis's mind, *I keep my eyes always on the Lord. With him at my right hand, I will not be shaken. Therefore my heart is glad and my tongue rejoices; my body also will rest secure, because you will not abandon me to the realm of the dead, nor will you let your faithful one see decay. You make known to me the path of life; you will fill me with joy in your presence, with eternal pleasures at your right hand.*[140]

Travis also knew that he had followed God's path, and he had rejoiced in the Lord. His children had not been left orphans. He had survived the war, and the illness, to have joy in God's presence and to serve him.

Travis got up and moved toward Cleve. Cleve stood and accepted his father into his arms. It was the first real embrace they had given each other in a long time.

It was getting late in the afternoon, and Daniel felt like an intruder among the happy, grieving family.

"Why don't we call it quits, and I can come back out tomorrow after church?" he said.

Cleve turned around and half-joked with Elshout, "Are you coming to church?"

"I might, if Travis is going to be there." Daniel looked at Travis.

Travis casually said, "We'll see."

---

140   Psalm 16:8–11.

Chapter 51

Early the next morning, Luke and Travis were sitting on the front porch, drinking coffee and eating jam and biscuits.

"Do you want to go to church?" Luke asked his father.

After a long wait, Travis replied, "I know I'm wrong in not goin'. Hebrews says, 'Let us consider how we may spur one another on toward love and good deeds, not giving up meeting together, as some are in the habit of doing.'[141] I've gotten in that habit. But I just don' want people seein' me struggle. I want ta be left 'lone. I don' want their pity."

"They won't show you pity, they'll show you love. And that's your pride talking," Luke replied. "James says to 'Humble yourselves before the Lord, and he will lift you up.'[142] And Proverbs says, 'When pride comes, then comes disgrace, but with humility comes wisdom.'[143] Everybody needs help sometimes."

Luke sat silent, waiting for his father to respond. Then he added, "We can tie the horses up around back, get off and on there. Nobody will have to see."

Travis didn't say anything as he sat, silently rocking. He closed his eyes, and Luke knew he was praying. Almost an hour passed, then Travis said, "Okay, let's get the chores done so we can get ta church. If ya can get me on my horse here, I'll go."

*****

---

141 Hebrews 10:24–25a.

142 James 4:10.

143 Proverbs 11:2.

Luke had the horses saddled and was waiting for his father. How would this work? What would be easiest for his father? He finally decided if his father could get his foot in the stirrup, then Luke should be able to brace his father's left arm. If Travis's legs were strong enough, he could pull himself on over the horse.

It worked. But Luke thought if he made a slight adjustment to the tack in a few key areas, it would be much easier. He'd work on that this afternoon.

They arrived at church just as it was about to start. The preacher and just a few latecomers were on the front stoop headed in. Luke saw the preacher look over his shoulder to see the last to arrive. Then the pastor stopped and turned around to watch as the two men rode past and around the corner to the back.

Reverend Nicholas Gatte watched them from the podium as they walked past the side windows and rounded the front to come in.

Luke had been in church often. Brother Nick knew Luke and his brother Cleve, but he had never met Travis. He wasn't sure who the old man with the sheriff was, he could only assume.

The singing had started as they quietly slipped in the open doors, unnoticed by others. Luke scooched a few people down the pew so they could sit on the back row near the door. The man in front of Travis turned to see who was moving around, then shook Travis's hand, welcoming him back.

Travis was a little self-conscious about being here after his long absence, but he decided to just jump in. He began singing the well-known hymn with the rest of the congregation and was soon absorbed in the worship.

Brother Nick, as he liked to be called, began by having everyone stand for the reading of Scripture.

He was a tall sturdy robust man in his midfifties. He was more flamboyant than any preacher they had in the past. He could walk into a room and instantly take control. Everyone liked him. He had sandy-brown hair and wore wire spectacles that seemed to dance on his face.

After he preached a short sermon—really short—he gave an altar call. Then he asked everyone to sit again; he had something else to say.

"I had a memory pass through my head a few minutes ago, and I can't seem to let go of it. I think maybe God put it there, and I need to tell you about it.

"I served with the Union during the war. I was with advance troops, moving southwest through the mountains in Western Virginia to the Kanawha Valley. Southern troops near there were withdrawing, and we ran into some of them in the middle of nowhere early one morning.

"During the fight, I was injured and separated from my unit. I was only eighteen, green and inexperienced. I didn't know a thing, didn't know how to get myself out of there. Just after nightfall, this mountain man found me and got me on my feet. I could barely walk. He was much smaller than me, but he kept me on my feet and moving through the snow that was falling until he got me to his barn.

"He had a bunch of us there, both Union and Confederate. Most of us were injured, and he was taking care of us, bandaging our wounds.

"He had a wife, pretty little thing, and several children. They would come in, helping him sometimes, and bring us food. This man prayed over each of us every day, and he fed us and sang as he worked. They were the most beautiful praise songs you ever heard. And he talked to us about Jesus.

"Well, Southern troops came in a few days later and took their men and wiped these folks out of their food, but this family kept on feeding us. I don't know how.

"A couple days later, the man loaded those of us that remained into his wagon and took us over two mountains to the Union camp. I saw him after he helped us out of the wagon. He was helping other wounded soldiers that were waiting on the doctors to get to them. I lost track of him soon after, but a few days later, I saw him again.

"He had been forcibly recruited to work for the hospital. I talked to him, and he told me they had threatened to shoot him if he tried to leave. I watched him off and on for a few more days. Some of the officers and nurses were talking to him cruelly, pushing him around. Being extremely ugly to him. And there was no reason for it.

They were giving him the dirty—I mean really dirty jobs. Nobody was helping him adjust to military life.

"One night, I asked him why he was working so hard for the people that were basically holding him prisoner.

"Do you know what he told me? He wanted to please God. He wanted to please God!

"He told me he was a living sacrifice and quoted Romans 12 to me.

> In view of God's mercy, offer your bodies as a living sacrifice, holy and pleasing to God—this is your true and proper worship. Do not conform to the pattern of this world, but be transformed by the renewing of your mind. Then you will be able to test and approve what God's will is—his good, pleasing and perfect will.[144]

"He told me he wasn't working for the officers that were holding him, he was working for God and that it was God's desire that he served there. He said those injured men were precious to God, and he would do everything he could to help them. That, my friend, is a true servant of God, and he is the reason that I went into the ministry.

"He taught me, in the short time I was with him, what it meant to be Christian. I thought about him through the rest of the war and for a long time afterward. I wondered if he made it through the war and if he made it back to his mountain. I don't know why this came to my mind this morning or why I can't seem to let it go.

---

144   Romans 12:1b–2.

"But I just felt like I needed to share that with you. Let's pray, and we'll be dismissed."

When everyone bowed their heads, Travis got up and left. Luke ran after him. Travis headed for the cemetery, he would visit Brenda and Colleen before he went home. Luke followed.

Luke stood beside his father, but he was quiet. He would let his father process his thoughts without being disturbed.

Then Travis walked to where Mark was buried.

He asked Luke, "Is Daniel comin' this afternoon?"

"I think so."

Travis sighed. "Ya think we can finish up taday?"

"I don't know. Mark's death was a long time ago. That's what he'll want to talk about first, you know that."

Travis nodded his head and glanced toward the church. Most of the people had left, there were just a few that remained, visiting at the wagons.

That's what he had been waiting for, people to leave. Travis started for the horses.

Luke asked, "Dad, do you think that Brother Nick was talking about you?"

"Yeah, I do."

"Well, do you want to go talk to him?"

"Not taday. There's too much on my mind."

Travis struggled a little to get on his horse this time, even with his son's help. His shoulder had begun to hurt more.

When Luke turned around to get on his own horse, he saw the preacher watching them from the open back window of the church. Luke waved but kept moving, trying to keep up with his father, who was already rounding the corner of the building.

Chapter 52

Travis tried to take a nap when he arrived home, but he couldn't sleep. He wished Daniel would get there. He wanted to get this over with. But right now, he would stay in bed. He could avoid conversation that way. He didn't want to talk today, not even to his boys.

Cleve showed up with some lunch for everyone, but Luke had already prepared something. Travis hadn't eaten. Luke was beginning to worry. His father hadn't eaten much during the last week. Luke was glad Thomas would be here soon. He knew the doctor would notice quickly and find out why.

Travis heard Luke and Cleve talking on the porch and then heard Daniel's horse when he arrived. Well, it was time. Travis got up and headed for the front porch.

Daniel started before Travis sat down. "Tell me about Mark getting shot."

"You know what happened. You wrote the article," Travis said.

"But I want to hear it from you."

Travis's forehead furrowed more. Luke saw it. His dad was getting tired of these interviews.

"Mark was down at ta'other end a town, at the new saloon. I was sittin' on the porch a Jake's shop. I 'ear'd the gunshots an' started that direction. When I got there, Mark was kneelin' at the corner a the buildin', watchin' the street that ran between Morrison's place an' the café. I went that direction an' saw the location a the shooter an' next shot that came my way. I returned fire an' didn' hear the bullet hit wood, so it either hit somebody or the dirt.

"I went on ta the edge a Morrison's, an' there was 'nother shot. I saw the location a that one too an' shot back. Then I 'ear'd somebody runnin', so I ran after 'em. Caught up with 'em two streets over. They 'ad me pinned down, but I could tell where they was, even in the dark.

"I sent a couple of shots directly inta the spot an' must a caught one of 'em because they slumped back inta the open, then tried ta crawl back ta where they was. I shot 'gain an' hit 'im.

"I was low ta the ground, ta'ther guy had ta stand up ta fire, an' when he did, I 'it im too. One was dead, ta'ther acted like he was hurt pretty bad.

"Mark hadn' followed me, an' I ain't 'ear'd any other shots, so I knew somethin' was wrong. When I got back ta 'im, 'e was still kneelin' in the same spot. There was several men with 'im, so I sent a couple a guys ta get the other man that was wounded an' had some take Mark ta Jessie's office.

"Jessie had been gone a couple a years, but all 'is stuff was still there. Me an' Mark kept it stocked so we'd 'ave what we needed. When I looked at Mark, I knew it was bad. I 'ad somebody get Mary, an' we tried ta get the bullet out but couldn' find it. It was deep. It 'ad 'it an' chipped a bone, then changed directions.

"Somebody got the telegraph man up an' workin'. As soon as he got a response from Saline, we aske' the doctor there ta come.

"The other man had been brought in while I was 'lone with Mark. They was both conscious, but I was focused on Mark. The other guy kept yellin' at me ta do somethin' 'bout 'is injury. I looked at 'im far just a minute, he wasn't 'urt bad like 'e acted. I knew he would live, so I stayed with Mark. The guy just wouldn't shut up, though, kept yellin' an' yellin'. I finally knocked 'im out with ether, just so 'e'd shut up. Mary bandaged 'im when she got there, an' when 'e woke up, 'e thought the bullet 'ad been removed, so we let 'im think that.

"The doctor from Saline arrived the next afternoon. 'E looked at Mark and tried findin' the bullet. Finally found it lodged close to 'is 'eart. But the bullet had done other internal damage. The doctor said he didn''ave the skill ta get it out an' thought movin''im would kill 'im. So I sat there with 'im far three more days till 'e died."

"What happened to the other guy?" Cleve asked.

"The doctor took the bullet out, an' I took 'im ta jail. 'E was mad, thinkin' the bullet had already been removed. 'E caused some trouble far me, but the review board said I ain't don nothin' wrong. I 'ad never told 'im the bullet 'ad been removed. An' I wasn't a doctor anyway, so no one should 'ave thought I took it out." Travis smiled his crooked smile, knowing everyone there knew he could remove the bullet from a simple gunshot wound.

"About a week after the review, I was called ta the state capital, an' I was interviewed an' appointed marshal."

"Okay, that does tell me more," Daniel said. "Now tell me about the years that followed."

Travis talked of events around town the next few years, of a couple of gunfights and of a bank robbery and chase across the state that followed. He told of two murders and of a series of home invasions and of finding the culprits. He talked about the numerous deputies he had hired before he found a good one and of his children growing.

Mary had finished school, with Thomas's help, by correspondence. She had returned to Denver long enough to do the testing and to apply for medical school. She returned to Harris, waiting for acceptance. Travis told them she had been denied the first application. Thomas had speculated that it was because she was a woman. She had applied a second time and, with Thomas's help, had been accepted.

When the acceptance letter arrived, Reid was just four years old, and Mary applied for an extension. It was approved. The next year, she applied for another extension and again, it was approved. When Reid was six years old, she received a message stating that her letter of extension was no longer valid, and she would either be there at the designated time, or she would be removed from the waiting list. Travis had pushed her to accept, telling her that he would hire help, and she was no longer needed. Reid would start school in the fall, and she needed to start too. But when Mary left, Travis had not hired anyone.

He actually had to sell some land in order to pay for Mary's expenses and couldn't afford to hire help. In fact, he had sold land on three separate occasions to pay for the children's school. The land where the hayfield had been, the land beyond it to the north, and from the aspen grove going east, where Mary had been taken by the Indians, weren't theirs anymore.

The boys were shocked. They had not realized this. But they understood. They had both wondered how their father had afforded to pay for three children to attend secondary school in Denver, six to attend the university, one to attend law school, and another to go to medical college. They knew Thomas had helped, providing food and lodging, and they all had jobs off and on through the years, but their father had never said anything about the cost of their education or of financial difficulties.

Daniel interrupted, "Why was it so important to you that all your children continued their education?"

Travis responded, "I didn''ave any education, didn' learn ta read until Mary was almost grown. I knew what it was like ta be looked over. Ta be thought a as ignorant, stupid. That wasn't gonna happen ta my chil'en. I wanted 'em ta get as much education as they could. I knew if they studied hard far a few years an' got a education, they wouldn''ave ta struggle the rest of their life, like I did. People would respect 'em."

He went on to say that two years after Mary left, Luke had returned and was helping. Luke had discovered their lack of funds, and when he made money, he offered it to Travis. His father had refused to take any, so Luke would make purchases and bring the items home.

Luke thought he was hiding this from his father, but Travis knew. He had seen Luke at Jeb's store buying things for Naomi and had seen Angus carrying boxes home. Naomi would have a new dress, and Travis would notice but not say anything, or Angus would be wearing a new pair of boots, or Reid a new pair of pants when he was outgrowing the ones he had worn holes in. Travis knew where these came from, and he now told Luke how much he appreciated him taking care of his younger brothers and sister.

The next year, Luke had run for the office of sheriff and had been elected. He was now able to help more financially, but he wasn't living at the farm, so Angus and Naomi had the chores he had been doing added back to their workload.

Daniel stopped the story here. "Luke, why did you want to be sheriff?"

"Just following in my father's footsteps," he said, smiling. "I always wanted to be like my father, even from the time I was really little. I knew if I asked for a deputy's job, Dad would give it to me, but I didn't want people talking about Dad taking care of me or about him being crooked, hiring family.

"That happens a lot in other places. A family member is hired but isn't qualified or can't do the job. I didn't want anyone to even think that was happening here. I knew the guy that had been appointed sheriff, and I knew I could do a better job, so I just waited till the next election. I still got to work with Dad, but it was all open and fair. Nobody could say anything. Dad didn't even campaign for me or endorse me. I did it all on my own."

"You don't think people voted for you because you were his son?" Daniel asked, pointing toward Travis.

"Maybe." Luke nodded his head. "Probably. But if they did, that was on them, not me or Dad. And if they didn't like what I was doing, they could have voted me out. But they didn't."

They heard a rider coming, but Travis continued the story,

"Three years later, Angus left far school. School 'ad changed 'ere in Harris. They 'ad added grades. Angus was able ta go straight ta the university in Denver. Luke was re-elected, and the next year, Naomi left far school. Reid an' I was left 'ome 'lone."

They watched as a stranger approached the house fast. Luke stood up and walked down the steps to meet the man, taking the bridle to calm the winded horse.

"Are you Travis Britt?" the man asked. He looked to be one of the miners. "No, that would be my father," Luke said, pointing to the porch.

The rider didn't know which man he was pointing at, so he addressed them all, "We need help. My son fell. He broke his leg really bad."

Cleve asked, "Why are you coming here?"

"'Cause we can't find a doctor. A man in town said you might be able to help."

"Couldn't you find the doctor at the mining camp?"

"He's passed out drunk. And Dr. Edwards is over at Summersville. Please, it's really bad," he begged.

Dr. Edwards was the newest in a short list of physicians who had come to town. Others had left. Dr. Edwards split his time between Harris and Summersville. He never seemed to be where he was needed.

Travis stood up. "How old is he?"

"Eight."

"Was the leg twisted?"

"Sideways."

"Bone exposed?"

"No."

Travis nodded. "Get my horse."

Travis strapped on his gun belt and picked up his rifle as Luke went to saddle their horses. Cleve watched as Luke helped their father onto his mount. But Daniel didn't seem to notice Travis having a problem. The newspaper publisher was too excited. Daniel wanted to see Travis handle this. They would all go.

Arriving at the camp, they found the boy at the doctor's office, surrounded by family and concerned friends. The drunk doctor was stretched out on the bed, snoring loudly.

"Get everybody out a 'ere," Travis said. Cleve thought his father seemed irritated at something. This wasn't like his father, even in a situation like this, he had always been composed and in control of himself. What was wrong?

Travis looked at the leg and at the dirty red-faced boy.

"Get me some hot water," he told Cleve bluntly. And he began looking through the supplies the doctor had in his office.

"Brin' the boy's father 'ere."

When the man entered, Travis asked, "'Ow long 'go did this 'appen?"

He gathered information from the father and told the father to stand at the boy's head. He would watch, and Travis would tell him everything he was doing. The boy needed surgery to fix the leg, but he probably needed a better surgeon than the one asleep in the next room.

Travis found ether and showed Cleve how to administer it.

Travis stood over the boy. "Guide my 'ands, Lord, let my eyes see what I need ta see. Let my 'ands move where they need ta move. Let me feel what I need ta feel. Protect this boy. Don' let me make a mistake."

When the boy was asleep, Travis started working to straighten the leg. It didn't take long before he was having trouble. He stopped, looking at the boy, avoiding eye contact with his sons.

"Luke, I need 'elp. I can't 'old on." Travis's face showed strain.

"What do you want me to do?"

"I need ta be able ta feel the bone when it goes back inta place, but I can't hold tight enough ta pull. I'm goin' ta put my 'and 'ere an' hold the best I can. I want ya to put ya 'and just over mine. Up a little. Okay. Ya is goin' ta 'ave ta pull far me. 'Old his leg tight an' pull gently but firmly when I tell ya. Keep pullin' until I tell ya ta stop, then 'old it there. Don' let the pressure off. I'm gonna pull an' twist from 'ere, near his foot. If ya feel it twisting, just move with it, don' fight me.

"Dad," Travis said, looking at the boy's father. "I need ya ta 'old his leg 'ere"—pointing above the break—"ya is gonna keep the rest a 'is body from movin' when we pull. 'Old 'im tight."

Travis continued giving instructions, took hold of the boy's foot, and together they set the bone and splinted the leg.

Then he told the father, "I think he still needs surgery. I don' know if that will heal right without it. It doesn't feel straight, but that's the best I can do. The sooner ya get the surgery, the better it will be. An' I wouldn't let 'im do it." Travis pointed toward the drunk.

The father thanked Travis and the others several times before they left the building. It was dark. The men went to mount their horses.

As Luke moved to help his father get on his horse, he saw Travis leaning against the horse's neck with his eyes closed. Luke knew he was tired, it had been a long day, even before they came to care for this boy.

"Dad? You ready?" Luke asked.

Travis spoke quietly, without looking at his son, so only Luke could hear. "My shoulder hurts awful bad." Then he straightened up, seemed to compose himself, and raised his foot toward the stirrup.

As they rode, Daniel began asking questions and talking steadily. He was excited after seeing Travis preform this complicated task, so different from the responsibilities of the marshal's office. It would be a great addition to the story. After just a few questions, Travis quit talking, and Daniel soon realized he needed to quiet too. Luke stayed close to his father, and Cleve noticed this.

When they neared town, Daniel broke away and headed home. Travis and his sons headed toward the farm.

At the farm, Travis sat on his horse, waiting for Luke to help him. As he slid down and his feet touched the ground, his knees buckled. Luke caught him.

"I got you." Luke gave his father time to steady his legs, then said, "You ready?"

Travis nodded, and Luke helped his father up the steps and to his bed.

Cleve watched as they went into the house, then he took care of the horses. When Cleve left the barn, he found Luke in the kitchen. "What's going on?" Cleve asked.

Luke had a concerned look on his face. "Didn't you hear him? He asked for help. I think that twisting and pulling really hurt him. He actually told me he was in pain."

Chapter 53

Monday afternoon, the third part to the story came out in the weekly edition of the paper. It was the portion that contained the events during the early part of Travis's involvement in the war. The town was abuzz with talk.

Daniel took one of the earliest copies to Cleve's office but was told Cleve wouldn't be in today. Luke wasn't in his office either. Neither office knew when their bosses would be back. Daniel decided to ride out to the farm.

As Daniel neared the house, he saw two of the men on the porch get up and go inside. The third stood up and faced Daniel.

"Hey, Cleve," Daniel said as he stepped to the ground. "I've got the third story." And he held up the paper.

"Good. Let's have it," Cleve responded and held out his hand.

Daniel passed the newspaper to Cleve as he said, "Where's your dad? I want to ask him about yesterday."

"Dad's not feeling well. You won't be talking to him today." Cleve wasn't moving. He was standing at the top of the steps. Cleve's body language said, "You will not enter." Daniel couldn't get to the porch.

"Oh. I hope it's not serious. Do you think I can talk to him tomorrow?"

"I doubt it."

"Come on, Cleve. Give me a break. I've done everything you've asked." Then Daniel corrected himself. "Well, almost. But I'm following the rules now. Just a few short questions?" Daniel was getting louder.

Cleve walked toward him, put his arm around his shoulder, and guided him back to his horse. Then turned Daniel to face him and said quietly, "Leave. He's not talking today, probably not tomorrow either. I'll let you know when he's ready."

Cleve let go of Daniel, turned around, and walked back into the house. Daniel watched and started toward the house again. Luke stepped out the door this time and stood at the top of the steps. It wasn't the usual smile on his face. His brawny physique was more intimidating than Cleve's scholarly form.

Daniel turned around and got on his horse. He was still in sight of the house when he saw another rider coming. It was the preacher. They stopped and talked a few minutes, then Daniel turned his horse around and returned to the farmhouse with Brother Nick.

Luke was still standing on the porch.

"Good afternoon, Luke," the preacher said joyfully as he stopped his horse and began to dismount. "Beautiful day, isn't it?"

"Afternoon, Pastor. What can I do for you?"

"Was that your father with you yesterday?"

"Yep."

"And this story Daniel's been writing, it's about your father?"

"Uh-huh."

"Can I talk to him?"

"He's not feeling well."

"I'm sorry. Maybe a visit will help. It sometimes does." The smile left the pastor's face.

"No, not today." But as he was answering, Cleve came and spoke softly over his brother's shoulder.

Luke turned his head slightly to listen, then nodded to Cleve. Turning back to the preacher, he said, "He'll see you. Please make it short."

Luke turned around as his father came through the door. Travis sat down heavily on the rocking chair. Luke pulled a chair closer to his father, offering Brother Nick the other chair. Cleve returned with a wooden crate and sat down after shaking the pastor's hand in greeting. Daniel sat on the steps again.

Brother Nick looked at Travis and smiled. "You are the man I was talking about yesterday, correct?"

Travis nodded his head. "Probably."

"I can't believe it. After all these years, here you are. The minute I saw you, God spoke and brought you to my mind. I'm so glad to know you made it. I've been reading Daniel's columns with real interest. I mean, he's never given your name, but everyone seems to know who he is talking about. And then I read today's article, and I was a part of the story. I knew you."

He dropped to his knees in front of Travis, reaching for Travis's right hand and held it. "I am so sorry. And I ask your forgiveness for what happened. For the sins brought on by the war, for those in the Union Army, which I was a part of, that held you. For the acts of these wicked people who participated in these atrocities. James tells us to 'Confess (our) sins to each other and pray for each other so that you may be healed.'[145] You prayed for us, and it made a difference. 'The prayer of a righteous person is powerful and effective.'[146] Now I want to pray for you.

"Mr. Britt, I cannot express my sorrow for what happened because of your kindness to those of us that needed help." He bowed his head and held Travis's hand in both of his, resting his forehead on Travis's exposed fingers. Then he prayed for Travis.

But the preacher only knew part of the story. He didn't know what had happened on the mountain while Travis was away. He didn't know how Sarah was blinded or of Ruth's, Joshua's, or Joseph's deaths. He didn't know that the farm in the mountains had been destroyed. These parts of the story would come later.

Luke was watching his father. His face was stone and his breathing heavy. Luke could see the strain in his open eyes. But it was strange how, despite his pain, he had a peaceful look on his face.

When the amen came, Travis said, "Their sins were forgiven long ago and 'their sins and lawless acts I will remember no more.'[147]

---

145   James 5:16a.
146   James 5:16b.
147   Hebrews 10:17b.

Thank you for coming." He started to stand up. Luke stood quickly and took his father's arm, helping to steady him.

"Will we see you again next Sunday?" the preacher asked. "And can I visit you again, when you're feeling better?"

Travis nodded and smiled. Then the two disappeared into the house.

Cleve and Brother Nick were still sitting on the porch, talking, when Luke came back outside and sat down. Daniel had been sitting quietly, listening and watching.

"He's lying down," Luke told Cleve softly.

"I hope I didn't upset him," Brother Nick said.

"No, he has a painful shoulder that's bothering him." Luke smiled. "His doctor will be here tomorrow."

They continued to talk for several minutes, then the preacher got up to leave. As he was riding off, Daniel asked, "What was that all about?"

Luke replied, "You should have been at church yesterday, then you would know."

Daniel looked at both of the Britt boys for a moment, then went to his horse. He would catch up with Brother Nick and ask.

Chapter 54

The next afternoon, Thomas and Sarah arrived with four boys, ranging in age from eight to fourteen, and Reid. Cleve was at the station to meet them with his two oldest sons.

"You're not in the city anymore. Things work a little backward around here sometimes. The street will be filled with cowboys and cattle when the ranchers take them to the railroad, and you better stay out of the way. Other times you won't see a soul for days. Stay out of town in the evening on the weekend, it's rough then. We thought the boys might like to stay with us, if it's okay. My boys can show them the territory."

Cleve drove the wagon through town, pointing out different businesses, his own office, and the sheriff's and marshal's office. As they passed the closed doctor's office, Cleve talked of the need of a good doctor and his hope that had not been fulfilled—of Mary returning when she finished medical school.

Mary had gotten involved in a lengthy research project on the nerves with a prominent doctor at the medical school. She was now helping him while teaching basic anatomy and was finding her own place in the physiotherapy world.

Then Cleve told them of the book being written about their father.

"They're almost finished with the interviews, and Dad's going to be happy. He hasn't liked any of this, and I think it's beginning to wear on him. Reid, he's become kind of a hermit since you left. Went to church for the first time in six months last Sunday. That was an interesting day. I'll tell you about it later.

"But, Thomas, before we get there, Dad's having some serious problems with his shoulder."

As they neared the farm, Cleve changed subjects. "All this land is ours and used to be our farm. Dad and I would plow all this. He quit farming this area when I left for school, and he started working for the marshal full-time. It's grown over now. When I was a kid, you could see the town from our front porch. Now you can't see the house till you're almost on it. It really needs some work. There it is."

Luke and Travis were sitting on the porch as the wagon approached. Travis watched, recognizing Cleve's form on the seat, and assumed that was Cleve's wife, Jenny, sitting next to him. Travis's face brightened as he realized it wasn't and recognized Sarah. Then he saw both Thomas and Reid in the back with a bunch of boys.

It was a warm and affectionate welcome. Travis gave and received hugs from everyone. Then the boys took off through the trees and disappeared.

Thomas was the only one concerned. He had never lived in an area this open and wasn't used to letting his children run loose. Everyone assured him they would be fine. He was a little nervous about it but would trust their judgement.

Time passed quickly as the family talked and shared stories, catching up with goings-on with everyone.

The boys had been gone for quite a while when there was yelling in the woods, coming closer to the house. Sarah's oldest boy, William, burst through the trees, calling his father loudly, Cleve's son Ryder right on his heels.

"Father! Ed got bit by a snake!" Thomas jumped and ran, Cleve and Luke behind him.

"It was just a little water snake," Ryder said calmly.

Cleve and Luke relaxed.

"Oh," Luke said as he turned around to go back to the porch.

"Where is he?" Thomas asked William. Then he heard Ed call him.

"Father! Father!" Thomas turned around to see ten-year-old Edison emerging from the trees with the rest of his brothers. Cleve's son Dylan was missing. Ed stuck his arm out to show his father the bite mark, a little blood trickling from it.

"It was just a water snake," Ryder repeated.

Cleve asked, "Are you sure?" When his son nodded his head, Cleve turned to Thomas. "Just wash it out. It'll heal in a few days. Water snakes aren't dangerous."

"Daddy, I caught it." Cleve turned to see Dylan coming toward them, holding the snake, its body wrapped around the boy's arm.

"Is that what bit you?" Cleve asked, looking at Thomas's son.

Ed nodded, clutching his father's arm for protection.

"He's fine," Cleve told Thomas. "Stings like being stabbed by thorns, but it's not poisonous. It'll heal fast." Then he addressed his son, "Go put him back where you got him."

Thomas was still concerned, but no one else seemed to be. Sarah was almost laughing as Thomas and Ed walked up on the porch.

She said, "Go let Grandpa look at it."

The child stuck his arm out to Travis. "Hummm. Looks like it will leave a scar. Awesome!" Travis gave a wide smile. "Ya can tell ya friends ya survived a battle with a dangerous snake." He leaned in to whisper to his grandson, "Dangerous ta fish." And poked a finger in the boy's ribs, making him smile.

"You sure it's okay, Papa?" Thomas asked.

Travis nodded.

Sarah was doing all she could not to laugh, and Thomas could see it. He punched her in the arm softly. "What are you laughing at?"

"You. City boy. You said you wanted a different lifestyle. You were tired of the crowded streets and busyness. How do you like Kansas?"

"You're not exactly a country girl anymore yourself," Thomas said, sneering. "You've lived in the city most of your life. You've never been snake bit."

Now Travis was trying not to laugh, and Thomas could see it. He snarled playfully at Travis.

Sarah stood up, reached down, and pulled her skirt up, then rolled her stocking down. She turned around for everyone to see and said, "Where do you think these came from?" And she pointed to two small circular scars on the back of her knee.

"And this wasn't a water snake. I ran a fever for a week, and my leg swole up. I had to keep a poultice on it for days."

Luke and Cleve were now laughing hysterically. Reid sat quietly, smiling next to his father.

Reid had a quiet serious manner. He didn't talk much, never gave his opinion, and never wanted attention. Luke had always thought Reid's personality and mannerisms were a lot like their father's. But unlike his father, Reid never took control of a situation.

He had a similar built to their father also. He wasn't very tall and had a small frame. He was solid muscle, but you couldn't tell by looking at him. That short curly brown hair was like his father's had been in years past. But he had his mother's smile. Something their father had always loved.

Cleve's wife came with supper, and when she and Cleve went home, they took their four children and the four boys Sarah and Thomas had brought with them. Luke had left before they did, headed into town to relieve the deputy that had been working steady the last few days.

The house got still, and those that were left sat and talked quietly, like they didn't want to disturb the peace.

Thomas had been watching Travis. It had been six years since they had seen each other, Travis seemed to have aged more than twice that much. Thomas wished he knew how old the man was. He had asked, Sarah didn't know. She had told him her father probably didn't know either.

Travis had talked some but had been relatively quiet all day. He had sat on his rocker most of the afternoon and hadn't moved around. When they ate supper, Luke had brought him a plate, and Cleve's wife had taken it when he was finished. He hadn't eaten much. He looked tired.

"Papa, you look tired. You ready to call it a night?" he asked Travis.

"In a bit." Travis smiled his crooked smile. The sun hadn't even gone down yet. Travis usually stayed up well past dark.

As the three men sat alone on the porch, Travis said, "There's a rider comin'." Several moments later, Thomas heard it too. There was obviously nothing wrong with his father-in-law's hearing.

"Mr. Britt." It was the miner whose son had broken his leg. "My son's running a fever. He's getting worse. Is that supposed to happen?"

"Is it makin' him sleepy?"

"Yeah, he's been sleeping all afternoon."

"When did the fever start?"

"This morning. He woke up with it."

Travis looked at Thomas. "Can ya come with me? This boy broke his leg Sunday morning. I set it that night."

"Sure."

Travis asked Reid to hook the buckboard up and stood up slowly.

Talking to the miner again, he asked, "Did you ask the doctor about it?"

"Yeah, he got mad that you had been there, said a few words, and threw something across the room. Nobody's seen him since."

Travis went inside, put on his gun belt, and picked up his rifle. This doctor was a hothead. If he showed back up, he would see Travis as an intruder, and there might be trouble. Travis thought he had better be ready. He checked both his pistol and rifle to make sure they were fully loaded.

When Reid brought the buckboard to the front of the house, he asked, "You want me to come?"

"No, you stay here. Sarah's in a place she doesn't know, and it's going to get dark soon. Keep her company."

Thomas stood and watched as Travis struggled to climb onto the wagon. He sat there a moment, then looked over at Thomas and said, "Ya comin'?"

"Oh. Yeah." And Thomas trotted to the other side and climbed aboard. Travis flicked the reins, and they started moving.

As they rode, Travis filled in the details on the child they were going to see. When they had covered that subject completely, they sat quietly a few minutes. Then Thomas asked, "Are you having trouble with your shoulder again?"

"Yeah."

"Well, tell me what's going on."

Travis gave his explanation, then added, "When Mary left, I wasn't havin' any problems, she wasn't rubbin' it much. Just a little every few days. A couple a years after she left, it started. At first just off an' on, like it used ta, but then it was there all the time but not bad, I could deal with it. But it kept gettin' worse. I thought maybe it would stop when I quit fightin'. But it didn't get better. Since I quit being marshal, it's gotten worse."

"Anything else going on?"

"I can't grip with my left hand. Sometimes I can't move it, it gets swollen. Hurts if I bump it."

"Okay, I want to look at both of them later. You let me know if I need to drive this thing."

"When's the last time ya drove a team?"

"Uh?" Thomas thought about it. "Before medical school."

"Yeah," Travis said dismissively. "I'll handle the team."

Travis and Thomas met the father at the doctor's office of the mining camp. Thomas was stunned. He had never seen such poverty wrapped up in one place. These tiny houses were falling down and built so close together you could hardly walk between them. Families were jammed into them and overflowing. The trash and waste were dreadful. He could see it and smell it, even in the dim evening light.

When they arrived, the father was sitting on a chair on the porch, holding his son on his lap. The door to the doctor's office was locked.

Travis walked over to a window and banged on it with the butt of the rifle a few times, then pried the sash open. He climbed in, found a lantern, lit it, then walked to the window and asked the father to hand his son through. The miner climbed in after them.

Travis stuck his head out the window and again asked Thomas, "Ya comin'?"

Thomas followed.

Travis found every lantern he could and lit them all as Thomas started looking at the boy.

"Ya haven't found a doctor yet?" Travis asked the miner.

"No, Dr. Edwards hasn't come back. I left several messages for him."

Thomas said, "This boy needed surgery yesterday. Is this all the light we can get in here?" He had gotten used to the electric lights in the city. He took a lantern and began taking inventory of supplies the doctor had on hand.

Thomas sat with the boy, but there was nothing he could do for him until he could see better.

As the sun began to peek above the horizon, Thomas asked, "Papa, can you help me?"

Travis was surely tired, Thomas knew this. He was tired too. They had both been up all night. Thomas had gotten to sleep some, off and on, while watching the boy. Every time he woke up, Travis was pacing the floor, rifle in hand.

It wasn't good to do this kind of work when you were this tired, but he didn't feel there was any other choice.

Thomas began to gather what he needed. When there was enough light in the room, he began the surgery. Travis stood on the other side of the table doing what he was told. The boy's father administered ether under Travis's supervision.

Travis heard a noise on the porch, he turned to grab his gun. The drunk doctor came into the room, looking straight down the barrel of Travis's rifle.

"What are you doing in here? This is my office. Get out of here!" he demanded, and he moved toward Thomas.

Travis stepped in front. The drunk stopped, looked at Travis a moment, then pulled his arm back, and took a swing. Travis dipped and used the butt of his rifle to punch the man in the stomach. The drunk doctor doubled over onto the floor. Travis stuck the barrel of the gun to his nose.

"Ya stay out a the way," Travis demanded.

Thomas tried to ignore the commotion just a few feet from him, but it was hard to do. He hadn't been around guns since he had hunted before medical school. That had been thirty years ago.

This violent aggressive behavior was something he had never been around, and it made him nervous. He came from a quiet gentle family of ministers, doctors, and bankers. This was far from where he was comfortable.

Thomas had never seen Travis like this either. He knew his father-in-law was capable of this violent dominating behavior; he had to be able, he had been a federal marshal. But Thomas had always seen the gentle quiet man that his wife had told him about. Thomas wasn't sure how he felt about this side of Travis.

The drunk crawled across the floor and slithered onto a chair at a table. Five minutes later, he was sprawled across the table, asleep.

Chapter 55

The surgery had been completed, and the miner had carried his son out the door headed home. Thomas and Travis were in their wagon headed home too. They both sat quietly. Thomas didn't know why he felt tension between himself and Travis now, but he felt it.

The doctor thought talking might relieve some of it, so he said, "You were right to tell him the child needed surgery. There was more damage than just the bone. But you told him, why didn't he find a doctor that could do it and get it done?"

"There is no doctor. There's that drunk, an' I wouldn't trust him ta do anythin'. Dr. Edwards says he practices 'ere an' in Summerville, but 'e's never 'ere. It's close ta a day's ride if ya is used ta ridin' an' 'ave a good horse. Most people can't do it in a day. Ya 'ave ta cross the river by ferry. The ferry is out more than it works, an' ya 'ave ta wait a day or two before it's repaired. Ya never know.

"The nearest doctor ta us is Saline, and it's a 'ard day's ride 'cross open country. No water most a the year. Hayes is two 'ours by train, but ya 'ave ta catch the train in the early morning comin' this way, an' it's never on time. Sometimes it's early, and ya miss it entirely. It only runs three days a week. It's a 'ard ride cross-country too, an' the doctor there is old.

"We had two other doctors come in 'ere, but neither stayed more than a few months. They say they can make better money other places. That they don' make enough 'ere ta support their families.

"'Ad an agreement with a medical school ta send fresh doctors, right out a school, ta work far just one year. But the first two didn' last six months total. It's a rough town with too few people ta make it worth a doctor's trouble an' too many not ta 'ave a doctor. The mining company says they 'ave one, but ya saw 'im. There's not a good doctor far more than a hundred miles."

Thomas asked, "How often do you play doctor?"

"Not much anymore. Used ta do it quite a bit, but I realized when a new doctor came ta town, people was still comin' ta me. I was just 'nother reason the doctors were leavin'."

They got home, and Travis went to bed. Thomas told Reid and Sarah what had happened, then he went to bed too.

When Thomas got up a few hours later, Sarah and Reid were sitting on the porch. Thomas joined them as Reid was reading out loud to Sarah. It was the last story Daniel Elshout had written about Travis.

When he finished, they sat quietly. The article had ended with Travis still with the Union troops following a horrible defeat at Second Reams Station, in Dinwiddie County, Virginia. The siege of Petersburg continuing.

Thomas took the papers and began reading the parts he had missed.

Sarah finally said, "I didn't know about most of this. He never talked about the war. Poor Papa."

After a few minutes, Reid said, "I'm going fishing." And he left.

A short time later, Travis joined them on the porch. Sarah went to him, hugging him tightly. "Papa, I am so sorry. We read the story. You never told me about the war."

Travis interrupted her, placing a finger on her lips. "It's in the past, an' I want it ta stay there. I don' wanna talk 'bout it, can we do that?"

Sarah nodded her head.

Then Travis added, smiling, "And the Lord blessed the latter part of (my) life more than the former part.'[148] An' I 'ad six sons an four daughters. The first daughter I named Sarah." And he took her chin in his fingers, and he kissed her on the cheek. "'Nowhere

---

148   Job 41:12a.

in all the land were there found women as beautiful as (my) daughters."[149]

Sarah smiled as Travis sat down.

When Thomas finished reading, he pulled his chair closer and took Travis's left hand to examine it.

"This is arthritis. Probably caused by the injury to you hand. Bones weren't broken, so this is probably cartilage damage caused by pulling from the tendon and muscle injury. This is muscle damage right here." And Thomas pushed his thumb on Travis's hand. "This is probably a lot of the problem. There's not much we can do about this. I'm sorry."

Travis nodded. "I figured as much."

They looked up to see a rider coming. Travis smiled and stood up, walking into the yard to meet him.

"I've got her. Best one of the bunch." And the man handed Travis a rather large dirty white fur ball.

"Thanks, Cody. 'Ow many were there?"

"Six. Like I said, this is the best one. Already showing us her nerve. Brave little thing. I kept her longer than I should have, kept them all. Wanted to make sure which were good before I decided who I was going to keep. But they're all good, I'm keeping all the others. This one is already working well with the dogs on guard."

Travis again said, "Thanks. I appreciate it."

"See you later." And the man turned and rode off.

Travis walked up the steps, holding a rather hefty puppy with thick fur and bright eyes. "I asked the sheep farmer far a puppy when he 'ad one. 'Ad to wait a while, but 'ere she is."

"Puppy?" Thomas said. "If that's a puppy, you're going to have an elephant when it's grown."

Everyone laughed.

They all spent a few minutes with the dog, then Thomas said, "Okay, Papa, get back over here and let me look at that shoulder."

Thomas moved the arm as far as it would go in every direction possible. Thomas could feel the tension when he moved it. The

---

149   Job 42:15a.

doctor could see the pain in Travis's eyes, but his face was hard, his jaw set, showing no expression. Thomas put his hand inside Travis's collar and felt the warm shoulder. Then he asked Travis to move it himself.

"Well, I think this may be just another form of arthritis, but we might be able to help with this. This isn't like the arthritis in your hand, that's in the joint. This is in the tissue surrounding the joint. We're going to do the same thing we did years ago, but we're going to be more vigilant with it. It's not going to fix itself as fast either. This may take a while.

"I need you to use this arm gently, no rough stuff. Move it, don't hold it still. Massaging it regularly will help get that inflammation down. It may hurt a little bit more while we're doing it, but it should get better over time. Okay, move over this way so I can get behind you and let's get started."

*****

That afternoon, all the boys showed up at the farm. The puppy became the new plaything as they ran and romped through the barn and corral.

Later that afternoon, Reid hooked up the buckboard and they all headed to Cleve's house for supper.

Luke was the last to arrive with a somber look on his face. He was quiet through supper. Afterward he separated himself and the other men, away from the women and children.

"The doctor from the mining camp has filed charges against you, Dad, for assault, illegal entry, and practicing medicine without a license. Thomas, you have been charged with illegal entry and the theft of the supplies you used in the surgery."

"What!" Thomas didn't believe this.

Luke looked at Cleve. "He wanted to file charges against you and me too, but the marshal talked him out of it. Convinced him since the door wasn't locked, and he was there, he could have stopped us if he had wanted to."

Travis didn't change his expression, but Thomas heard him sigh. Luke added, "He's asked that the hearing be transferred to another county because of bias. No one here is going to convict, how did he put it? 'Their beloved marshal' of anything."

"This is ridiculous," Thomas said. "He can't possibly expect to win this."

"'E can," Travis said calmly. "We did enter without 'is consent, and I did 'ave a gun on 'im. 'E didn' 'ave one. We both used 'is supplies without permission."

Travis smiled his crooked smile. "But I'm free an' clear a the medical issue. There's no licensing in the state a Kansas yet."

Thomas was worried and looked at Cleve. "At least we have a good lawyer." He could already see the wheels turning in Cleve's mind.

"Okay, here's what we're going to do. We're going to figure out a way to file countercharges. Give me your reasoning for doing what you did. Each of the charges."

Cleve had been there, he had seen what happened the first night; he had been involved. But his brain was now working as an attorney, not as a defendant.

Travis said simply, "He was drunk, both times. There was an injured boy who needed immediate 'elp."

Within twenty-four hours, Cleve had gathered enough information and talked to witnesses who would make themselves available to testify. Now he had to figure out how to present his case.

He went to the courthouse and filed his countercharge, three counts of neglect and malpractice. One for not caring for the broken leg itself, one for not being available for surgery, and one for not caring for the child when he was asked about the fever. An additional charge was filed on behalf of the child's father for attempted bodily harm. He had thrown an object across the room, he could have hit the father and injured him. Cleve knew these charges were just as ridiculous as the ones the doctor had filed against Travis and Thomas. But this was his defense.

Thomas kept coming to his office, asking how it was going and wanting an explanation for every move Cleve was making. So

Cleve came up with some questions and set Thomas in front of his library of law books to research answers.

The second day into his research, Thomas came to Cleve with an article concerning what it called The Good Samaritan Law which allowed anyone to help, "with whatever means available without repercussion," another person in dire medical need. The article said this was a "universally understood moral law" and was not written in any local, state, or federal statutes. He also found state laws concerning nonincorporated communities with a population of more than one hundred.

"How many people are at that camp?" he asked Cleve.

"Over a hundred, I'm sure of that." Cleve began smiling as he and Thomas looked over the information Thomas had found. This would work.

Chapter 56

On Sunday morning, Reid loaded everyone into the wagon, and they met Cleve, his family, and Sarah's boys at the church early. Reid quietly visited with his friends as they arrived. The boys played around the church, and Cleve and Thomas wandered aimlessly through the cemetery with Travis. The women talked at the wagon as Jenny introduced people to Sarah.

Travis was avoiding talking with people and knew others would leave him alone if he was in the cemetery. As the service was about to begin, he sent Cleve and Thomas ahead of him, saying he would be along. Then he slipped into the back as the service started. Luke was standing against the back wall, like a sentry guard. This was his usual spot, and everyone expected to see him there. When the final prayer began, Travis stepped out into the aisle to leave and Luke followed.

Travis slid into the wagon, hanging his legs over the back edge. He and Luke talked about nothing of importance as the congregation began to exit the church. Several came to speak to Travis, expressing their interest in the ongoing newspaper story and their concern for the charges against him. As usual, the whole town knew.

Only one person spoke of the similarity between the most recent printed article and the pastor's story the previous week.

It was taking Sarah and Thomas a long time to get out of the church. Cleve and his wife had come out to tell Travis they were following the boys to the farm. The boys, like a small herd of cats, had taken off running down the road.

When Sarah and her husband came out, Brother Nick was with them. They walked toward the wagon.

"Mr. Britt, I just met your daughter. Is this the little girl that would follow behind you as you cared for us? Oh my. I remember you sang so beautifully for such a child. Do you still sing? Oh, I must come to talk with you more."

The preacher kept rambling with Sarah, but Travis was through. He was ready to go home. He wasn't listening when Sarah invited the pastor for lunch on Monday.

*****

Brother Nick arrived early and sat with Reid, Travis, and Thomas on the porch as they waited for the final preparations to be made. The pastor spoke excitedly of the newspaper coming out that afternoon, thinking Travis would want to see it immediately. Travis let Thomas hold most of the conversation, but the pastor kept directing comments and questions to Travis.

After they ate, Travis excused himself, took his puppy, and went to the barn. Reid followed him.

"Dad, what's wrong?"

"I can't seem ta get that mining camp off my mind. That's never been a good place ta work. The boy's father agreed ta testify against the doctor. The mine management won't like that. That miner could be in danger," Travis explained.

"Do you want me to go out there and check on him? I can say I'm just checking on the boy." Reid smiled.

"Would ya? That would ease my mind. Be careful, though, that's a rough place."

Reid, like his father, never left the house without his rifle. Reid slid his rifle into the scabbard on his saddle, waved to those on the porch, and left the farm.

Reid and Daniel Elshout passed each other on the road and stopped to talk for a few minutes. Then they rode on their separate ways.

Travis saw Daniel coming. The preacher was still here. Travis didn't want to talk anymore. He was getting annoyed with these people. The pain in his shoulder made him irritable. That was his problem and he knew that. But he couldn't stop the pain.

He thought about disappearing into the trees and staying gone till they both left, but the Spirit spoke to him, *Everyone should be quick to listen, slow to speak and slow to become angry, because human anger does not produce the righteousness that God desires.*[150]

"I'm sorry, Lord. Calm me, please. Ya want me ta go back an' just listen, don't ya?" Travis asked.

Rise up; this matter is in your hands. We will support you, so take courage and do it.[151]

"Yes, Father," Travis said sadly. "Ya want me with 'em at the 'ouse. I will obey." And he headed back to the porch.

The preacher had taken the newspaper from Daniel and was sitting down as Travis arrived on the porch. The rocking chair was empty, but Travis didn't sit. He passed the others and walked to the far edge. He grabbed a broom leaning against the wall and began mindlessly sweeping, concentrating on the cracks between the boards, like there was something stuck in that one spot.

Elshout had known Reid. Reid had done work at the newspaper, and he and Daniel had become friends. They had not seen each other since Reid left for school two years ago, and Daniel had wanted to visit with him, but Reid wasn't here now. They would have to talk another time.

Daniel also knew Travis had other children that had arrived the previous week. He had come to deliver a copy of the paper to them. Daniel had not intended for the story to be read now. He knew Travis didn't want to hear it.

Daniel had come to understand how much of Travis's past disturbed him. Travis seemed to take responsibility for things that were out of his control. Daniel didn't want to cause him any more distress.

---

150   James 1:19b–20.
151   Ezra 10:4.

Brother Nick started reading. It seemed to Travis that he thought he was doing a good deed, reading to Sarah.

Travis stood behind the preacher. Brother Nick's back was to Travis. He could see Sarah's face, and if Thomas turned his head slightly, Travis could see his face too. Daniel sat on the steps, his back also to Travis.

Brother Nick read in a loud strong voice. He seemed happy that Travis had returned and was listening with the others. Daniel had tried to interrupt and stop him, saying he was sure the family wanted to read it for themselves. But Brother Nick was a man who took control. There was no stopping him.

He read about the last few months of the war, the patients, the battles, and about Abe Lincoln and Washington, DC. He read about Travis traveling home through Virginia and about Travis's return to his daughter. His voice faltered a few times, and he didn't seem as confident as he read of the death of Travis's family and of Sarah's injury. He stopped briefly to look at Sarah and Thomas. Tears were escaping onto Brother Nick's face. His emotions had revealed themselves.

"Oh my," he commented as he looked at the newspaper again.

Then he continued reading about Charleston and Chicago. He read about finding the doctor, the music school director, and Travis's inability to find work. As he came to the last line, he stopped reading and again said, "Oh my."

Brother Nick turned around to look at Travis, who now stood with his back to them. Daniel turned to look at Travis too. He had been focused on watching Sarah and Thomas and had not turned toward Travis through the entire article. Travis wasn't moving.

Brother Nick continued, "And because he loved his daughter, he left Chicago alone and headed West."

It was quiet now. No one spoke. The only sound to be heard was a woodpecker in the trees and a couple of katydids near the porch. Thomas had moved to stand beside his wife, his hand was now pancaked between her shoulder and her hand. Sarah sat looking toward the barn.

Daniel wasn't sure how much Sarah could see, or if she knew where her father was. But he knew Travis needed her right now. Daniel softly said, "Sarah, I think your father needs you."

As Sarah got up to move toward her father, Daniel said, "Pastor, let's go." He took Brother Nick's arm and pulled him toward the horses.

As they were leaving, Brother Nick turned around to see Sarah and Travis in each other's arms, Thomas behind them with a hand on his father-in-law's shoulder.

Chapter 57

Reid rode into the mining camp and asked the first person he saw where to find the boy with the broken leg. The man shook his head and turned away, saying nothing. Reid moved on to someone else. Person after person refused to talk. He wasn't getting any information today, so he turned around and started back through town headed home.

Just past the last building, toward the edge of the trees, a man stood, half-hidden by the shadows. As Reid passed, the hidden man threw a rock he had been holding in his hand. It hit the horse, startling her and causing her to stumble. As she regained her footing, she bucked. Reid held on. He was a good rider. The man on the ground could see that. He picked up another rock and threw again. This time it hit Reid, knocking him from the horse.

Reid slowly got up, a little dazed, blood running down his neck from a cut on the jaw, just below his ear. The horse was already down the road and still running. Well, Reid thought, pressing his eyes together a moment, I'll just have to walk. He put his hand to his injured face, then brought it down to look at the blood on his hand and started walking.

A few minutes later, a wagon came up behind him fast, forcing him to leave the road. Then it stopped just in front of him. The woman holding the reins stood up, turned around, and asked, "You looking for the boy with the broken leg?"

"I was. Back at the camp."

"Get in," she said quickly. "Come on, don't take all day get in." She sounded like she was in a hurry.

Reid slid onto the back. She yelled, flicking the reins sharply and the horses picking up speed quickly. Reid wasn't ready and almost fell off the back, the wagon swaying and sliding in the dirt.

There were blankets and sacks piled in the wagon and three small children crouching together under the seat. Reid started making his way to the front to talk with the woman. But as he crawled across the blankets, he realized there was something under them. Picking up one edge, he found a booted foot. And beside it the boy's splinted and bandaged leg.

Reid threw the blanket off completely and found the boy, obviously in pain as the wagon tossed and bumped on the road, and a man unconscious and badly beaten.

Reid yelled, "Take the right fork." He would guide them home to the doctor and safety.

Reid's horse had arrived home with an open bleeding wound on her shoulder. Travis had put her in the barn and struggled to get his own horse saddled. When he went into the house for his gun belt and rifle, Thomas had confronted him with questions and arguments, trying to keep him from going after Reid alone. Trying to convince him to find Luke and let Luke handle this.

Travis had been upset when the preacher left, and Thomas knew Travis hadn't been feeling well. He wasn't ready to let his father-in-law out of his sight, especially with his guns.

But Travis knew Reid was in trouble. He knew that he could find his son faster if he did it himself, instead of going into town to get Luke. Travis felt he never should have let his quiet unassuming little boy go to the mining camp alone.

Before Travis could get past Thomas, and out the door, they heard a noisy wagon approaching. They moved outside to find the wagon sliding to a stop, Reid already yelling for Thomas.

As Travis and Thomas got to the wagon, Reid was on the ground, moving toward his father's horse. He yelled at his father,

"I'm taking your horse into town." He mounted and rode off quickly.

Thomas and Travis got the injured man and the boy inside and began caring for the man. It was the boy's father. Sarah tried to calm the woman.

****

Reid was still moving quickly as he arrived at the sheriff's office. Luke heard the horse come in fast and come to a sudden stop. He was headed outside when Reid began yelling for him. They returned to the farm to gather more information. The woman told them everything.

"Those ruffians that work for the mine boss caught James at the end of his shift, as he was coming out of the mine. They told him he didn't have a job anymore and that we had one hour to get out. Then they followed him home. They didn't give us an hour. They came right into the house and started throwing things out the door and pushing James around, wouldn't let him do anything to get us out. Then they threw him out the door and started beating on him. I don't know who that wagon belongs to. It was just sitting in front of the house, so I used it."

Thomas was now standing with them, listening.

Luke asked, "Thomas, how's he doing?"

"I don't know. He's been beaten bad. We'll just have to wait to see if he wakes up."

"And the boy?"

"He appears to be okay."

As the group stood in the yard, talking, no one noticed Reid go inside. He got his hunting rifle that Travis had put away and came onto the porch. He aimed and fired, making everyone jump. Luke and Travis both crouched and drew their weapons, ready for trouble.

"Come out of there!" Reid demanded. Two men came out of the trees. They looked unarmed.

"We don't want trouble, we're here to help. James is our friend."

"They are, they're our friends," the woman said.

Travis and Luke put their pistols away, but Reid remained vigilant, his rifle still pointing at the men.

The rest of the afternoon was a beehive of activity as Thomas continued to care for the injured man and the boy. Sarah entertained the children and cared for the man's wife. Luke and Travis gathered information from the miners.

Cleve and the deputy came to join them. Then the lawmen and Cleve left to do their jobs, taking the two miners with them.

Reid remained on guard. Travis watched him and was proud. But he'd always been proud of his youngest son. His quiet passive son now stood strong, on alert and guarded, watching for trouble. He had seen a possible threat, and he had taken action.

Scripture came to Travis's mind, "*When a strong man, fully armed, guards his own house, his possessions are safe.*"[152]

Travis smiled, then the scripture continued in his head, "*But when someone stronger attacks and overpowers him, he takes away the armor in which the man trusted and divides up his plunder.*"[153]

Reid wasn't experienced, but he sensed more trouble approaching. It would take more than Reid's watchful eye to protect those in this house from what was to come.

Travis prayed, "Keep this house safe, Lord. Protect my chil'en an' all in this house."

And the Lord spoke to him, *Have (I) not put a hedge around (you) and (your) household and everything (you) have?*[154] *The angel of the Lord encamps around those who fear him, and he delivers them.*[155]

"Thank ya, Father," Travis said. The Spirit continued, *Be alert and of sober mind. Your enemy the devil prowls around like a roaring lion, seeking someone to devour.*[156]

Travis grew more concerned, there was still trouble coming. He moved to talk to Reid, advising him on the best way to watch for trouble and warning him of the trouble the Lord had told him about.

---

152   Luke 11:21.
153   Luke 11:22.
154   Job 1:10A.
155   Psalm 34:7.
156   1 Peter 5:8.

Reid listened and nodded, then responded, "'Surely he will save you from the fowler's snare and from the deadly pestilence. He will cover you with his feathers, and under his wings you will find refuge; his faithfulness will be your shield and rampart. You will not fear the terror of the night nor the arrow that flies by day.'[157] 'A thousand may fall at your side, ten thousand at your right hand, but it will not come near you. You will only observe with your eyes and see the punishment of the wicked.'"[158]

Travis smiled at his son.

Reid had turned from his father and was looking toward the trees again. He could see three sides of the house from the porch. But Reid was concerned. The back was vulnerable.

Reid continued, "If you say, 'The lord is my refuge,' and you make the Most High your dwelling, no harm will overtake you, no disaster will come near your tent. For he will command his angels concerning you to guard you in all your ways.'[159] 'Because he loves me,' says the Lord, 'I will rescue him; I will protect him for he acknowledges my name. He will call on me, and I will answer him; I will be with him in trouble, I will deliver him and honor him. With long life I will satisfy him and show him my salvation.'"[160]

Reid smiled at his father, and his father understood. Reid would stand guard, but he was relying on God's protection, not his own abilities.

Travis walked into the house and saw Sarah sitting on the floor with the miner's children.

"Sarah, I want ya ta go stay with Jenny," he said.

"No, Papa. I'm staying here," she replied.

Travis told her, "It's too dangerous here. They're tryin' ta stop testimony at the hearin'. They're hidin' somethin', or they wouldn' be doin' this. This is gonna be a blemish on the company, an' they don' want that. They won't stop with what they have already done ta that man in there."

---

157   Psalm 91:3–5.
158   Psalm 91:7–8.
159   Psalm 91:9b–11.
160   Psalm 91:14–16.

"I'm aware of that. I'm not your baby girl anymore, Papa, even if you still want me to be. I know how evil works, how it spreads. I've seen it with my own eyes. This is not your fight alone. I will stay here. I will take care of these children. And I will pray," she said firmly.

Yes, she had seen evil work and had seen it spread. She had experienced it. His daughter was strong, both her will and her spirit.

Travis went to her and knelt beside her, kissing her cheek and pressing his face to hers. "Ya is a strong woman, an' I know that. But I'm still ya father, an' I still love ya. I'll always want ta protect ya."

Travis went to his bedroom and pulled a wooden box out from under his bed. It contained Mark's gun belt and pistol. He loaded them and took them to Thomas.

"Put these on."

"What? No. I don't know how to use that."

Travis and Thomas stood watching each other.

"Ya need it, just in case somethin' happens. Ya need ta be able ta protect ya'self, protect Sarah. I tried ta get her ta leave, but she won't."

Thomas said nothing, just kept watching Travis, or was he looking past Travis. Travis looked behind him, and Sarah was there.

"I'll take them," she said. Reaching her hand out, she found the pistol and pulled it from the holster. She felt the gun, looking at what she was able to see, opened the cylinder, checked for bullets, then closed it and heard it snap. She felt the weight of the gun in her hand and raised it with both hands, pointing it toward the empty back wall.

"I've thought about it for years," she said. "What if I had been able to get to the gun upstairs that day? What if I had been able to use it? Could I have stopped what happened? Could I have saved Mama? Or the boys? It haunts my nights.

"When I'm at home with the sleeping children, and you're at the hospital, it sometimes consumes my mind. It rips at my heart." She was talking to Thomas. "What would I do if someone attacked us? How could I protect the children? And you know, there's so much going on in Denver now, it's hardly safe anywhere. I got

Cleve to teach me years ago. And I had him buy me a couple of guns. I've got them hidden in the house. Then when Joshua and Joseph were old enough, I had Luke teach them, and he took them out and bought them guns too. And when Mae turned sixteen, I had Angus teach her. They all know where the guns are. Reid is going to start teaching Chloe when he gets back to Denver."

She stopped to wait for a response from Thomas. She knew he didn't like guns, that's why she hadn't told him. He wasn't saying anything. He was just looking at her.

Travis had never realized she had felt the guilt too. He wanted to go to her, to hug and comfort her. But it was Thomas's responsibility to do this now, he was her husband. Travis placed the gun belt in Sarah's hand, kissed her on the cheek, and left them to work this out themselves.

Chapter 58

Travis sat on the backsteps with his rifle, praying.

Reid walked the front porch, just like he had done all afternoon. He hadn't sat down. Every so often, Reid would quote Scripture. He was praying too.

The miner's children were asleep in one of the bedrooms. The injured boy, the miner, and his wife were in another.

Sarah and Thomas had talked and were continuing to talk at the table. Apparently there had been a lot that had not been said over the years. Travis was trying to leave them alone.

The sun was going down, and they had not heard from Luke. Travis didn't know if Luke had been to the mine or what was happening outside his house. So far, it had been quiet at the farm.

Evening fell and it was dark now. It had been for a while. Travis thought the dog was asleep, but without moving, she began a low growl. She was lying at Travis's feet. He reached down and patted her gently. She was such a good dog.

The Spirit spoke, *Now let us make a covenant before our God to send away all these women and their children, in accordance with the counsel of my lord and of those who fear the commands of our God.*[161]

And the Spirit continued, *He said, 'Come what may, I want to run.' So Joab said, 'Run!'*[162]

Travis got up quickly and went in the house. "Sarah," he said quietly. "Get the woman an' the chil'en. Go out the window in the back, cut through the trees quietly. Go straight through. Ya will

---

161   Ezra 10:3a.
162   2 Samuel 18:23a.

come out at Cleve's house." He picked up Mark's gun as she stood, and he put the gun belt over her shoulder.

"(God) is (your) hiding place; (He) will protect (you) from trouble and surround (you) with songs of deliverance.[163] Be quiet. Tell Cleve ta get Luke. If they ain't there, get the marshal. Send 'em here. Thomas, go back there with James an' the boy. Get all a ya on the floor. Hide."

Travis went to Reid.

"They're here," he said softly and returned to the backsteps.

The dog was now a distance away, still growling softly. She was following something, her head and body turning, crouching, moving slowly, watching whoever it was that was moving around to the side of the house.

At least they were on the other side, away from where Sarah was escaping.

Travis saw movement, and the dog began to bark. Then he saw light and smoke as whoever was in the yard fired toward the porch. There was a rifle shot. Travis's rifle was already up. He fired toward the light. There were more shots from somewhere on the other side of the house, and the dog ran out of sight.

Travis cut through the house to the porch. Reid was on the floor, his rifle pointed toward the barn. "Two of them went into the barn," Reid said. "I think there's another one next to the road."

Then they heard the dog attack and a man yell. The dog yelped, and all was quiet again. Then they saw fire inside the barn.

"I got ta get the horses," Travis said and started to get up.

"No." Reid pushed his father down. "I can move faster. This is a diversion. They want us away from the house. You can spot them better than me." And Reid rolled off the porch and started moving toward the barn, low to the ground. There was another shot, and Reid hit the ground, rolled a few times, and got up running. He made it to the barn and disappeared inside.

---

163   Psalm 32:7.

Travis saw someone at the side of the barn. As Reid sent the first horse out, the man ran behind it around the house and out of sight.

There was gunfire inside the barn. Travis saw the man moving beside the road and fired at him. He went down.

There was more gunfire in the barn.

Then Travis saw his dog. She was running for the house. She went up on the porch and through the open door, barking wildly. Travis kept low and followed her in. There stood a man in the kitchen, lantern in one hand, gun in the other. The dog was growling, circling.

The man smiled at Travis, and Travis understood. He would lose his house. If he shot the man the lantern would fall and break, catching the old dry wood on fire. Travis waited. There was more gunfire from the barn.

The man suddenly threw the lantern and fled out the door, the dog after him. Travis tried to move out of the way as the lantern hit the floor near his feet. He fired and struck his target, then moved quickly to put out the fire on his boot and pant leg where the lamp oil had splashed. He yelled at Thomas to get the man and the boy out of the house. He had to help Reid. He couldn't think of the house right now.

Travis ran back through the house and toward the barn. The backside of the barn was now engulfed in flames. The fire was moving quickly toward the front, lighting the entire area. Travis ran inside.

"Reid!" he yelled. And a shot came through the fire. Travis dropped low.

"Dad." Travis heard his son behind him. He turned around and saw Reid crouched behind a chest of tools near the door. Travis reached him and saw blood on his leg.

"We're gettin' out," Travis told him, helping him up. They slipped through the barn door, and Travis looked up into the eyes of the third man who had come around the side of the barn. Travis knew his rifle was empty. He pushed Reid away and watched.

"I'm told you were fast in your day, old man," the man said arrogantly. He holstered his gun and stood ready.

Travis dropped his rifle and prayed, "The Lord is my strength and my song, he has given me victory."[164] And Travis drew his pistol.

The flames in the barn were now licking their way out the door as Reid struggled back to where his father was lying on the ground. Travis was on his side, rocking gently back and forth, both arms encircling his chest. Reid dropped to the ground and pulled his father into his arms. Feeling the heat from the flames, Reid started sliding backward, pulling his father with him. Reid continued to pull his father back until he could go no further. He had backed up into the corral fence. Reid looked up, still holding his father, to see the barn and the home he grew up in totally engulfed in flames.

"Doggone it! That hurts!" Travis said, his jaw clenched. Reid stopped, looking at his father. "I landed on my shoulder." Reid gave a gentle laugh and relaxed, hugging his father to him.

---

164   Exodus 15:2a (NLT).

Chapter 59

The three dead men had been taken to town and were identified by the miner's wife as those who had beaten her husband. They worked for the mine boss. Everyone knew this.

They had the mine boss at the marshal's office. He was being detained on state and federal mine violations discovered while searching his office. Testimony of several miners secured these charges. A search for further evidence was ongoing at his residence and office. Other criminal and civil charges were pending, the result of Thomas's findings in the law books. The charges continued to multiply.

The mine had been shut down, at least temporarily, until investigators sifted through the records. The company, as a whole, would be under investigation.

The alcoholic doctor had disappeared. Luke and the current marshal felt they would perhaps never find him. He had embarrassed the company and brought attention to the misconduct that had taken place in management. He had probably been disposed of by now.

Without their accuser to testify, the charges against Travis and Thomas were being dismissed.

The deputy had gathered supplies from the doctor's office and taken them to Thomas, who had taken care of Reid's bullet wound and Travis's burn. Both were minor.

James, the man that was beaten, and his son, had been taken into town. They were now being cared for at Dr. Edward's office, although no one had seen the doctor yet.

James had regained consciousness and had also identified the men who had beaten him.

Daniel had arrived early in the morning, just after the gossip in town told him of the trouble at the Britt farm. He had talked with everyone. Travis could tell he was excited to have something he considered big to write about.

Travis saw Elshout coming toward him again. "Hey, Travis. I know there's a lot going on right now, but I just have a few short questions to finish the articles on you. I'll get with you tomorrow for that, if it's okay."

Travis said, "Nope, I'm through. Anythin' else ya need, ya 'ave ta get from somebody else. 'Forgetting what is behind and straining toward what is ahead, I press on toward the goal to win the prize for which God has called me heavenward in Christ Jesus.'[165] I'm not goin' back."

Daniel looked at Travis. He wasn't sure he understood what Travis was talking about. Just then, Elshout saw Thomas and excitement escaped onto his face. He'd talk to Travis's children instead. Elshout turned to catch up with the doctor.

Travis now sat on a stump, looking at what was left of his house and barn, scratching the dog's back and thanking God for keeping his family safe.

The Spirit spoke, *Every good and perfect gift is from above, coming down from the Father of the heavenly lights, who does not change like shifting shadows.*[166]

Travis saw his daughter and her husband coming toward him.

Sarah sat down on the ground beside her father and leaned on him as he put an arm around his little girl.

Thomas said, "Papa, this has got to be hard, but we think we might be able to make things a little better for you. Our purpose for coming here was to talk you into coming back to Denver and living with us."

Travis just looked at him, reached over, and patted Sarah's hand that held his arm.

---

165   Philippians 3:13b–14a.
166   James 1:17.

Thomas continued, "But after our talk yesterday, and after what happened the last few days, well, we've changed our mind. Denver is not the place for you."

Travis didn't move, his eyes remained where they were, his expression didn't change.

"We want to build a house and move here to be with you." Thomas smiled.

Travis's smile slowly grew as he closed his eyes. He took a deep breath and let it out slowly, then looked at Thomas.

"'This is the confidence we have in approaching God: that if we ask anything according to his will, he hears us.'[167] I've been praying that my children would return to me." He leaned into Sarah and hugged her, resting his head on hers. "Thank ya, Lord."

Thomas sat down, and they saw Reid limping toward them, assisted by his brother Cleve.

"How's your leg, Dad?" Reid asked. Thomas had cleaned and bandaged the burn on Travis's leg, and now Travis sat with his burned boot off and his leg outstretched. What remained of his pant leg dangled close to the ground below the bandage.

"Shoulder hurts more," he replied. "Ya okay?"

"Yeah, won't take long to heal."

Cleve said, "Dad, with everything that's been going on, I haven't had a chance to tell you. But now seems like a good time. A few nights ago, at the last town council meeting, we received the name of the company that's going to provide electricity for the town." Cleve smiled slyly. "Guess what company is building it and who the company is sending to oversee the project and eventually be the plant manager."

Travis's smile widened, and he softly asked, "Angus?"

"That's right, he'll be here in just a couple of months."

Angus had only been with the company three years. While still at the university, he had impressed the company with his senior thesis on ethical and efficient electricity and had been hired right out of college. Using his proposed model, the company had already

---

167   1 John 5:14.

seen monetary savings while expanding their factories, both in number and in production.

Then Sarah made the comment, "You know he has a girl he's serious about? Met her last year at the Christmas Eve Benefit for the orphanage. Her father is a board member."

Travis liked that Sarah was involved with his children. They had all gone to Denver for school, and all had lived with Sarah and Thomas at some point. Sarah kept in contact with all of them, except one, and had truly become their big sister.

The one child that Sarah was not in contact with was Naomi. She had never been able to get close to Naomi.

"Okay," Thomas said, always the analytical one. "We need to decide where we will build the house. And I want the office close by. Let's make sure it's in a place where we can connect to the electricity easily. And we'll just go ahead and wire the house that way to begin with. Of course, we still want the furnace heating. I want steel this time. Do they have gas in this area? Do you have telephones out here? And plumbing. I want a water closet!"

Everyone laughed. Things were going to get interesting.

One by one, the others moved away, leaving Travis alone again. But he was never truly alone. He continued his conversation with God.

Travis said, "I know 'that the Lord (my) God is God; he is the faithful God, keeping his covenant of love to a thousand generations of those who love him and keep his commandments.'" [168]

The spirit spoke to him, *Even to your old age and gray hairs I am he, I am he who sustains you. I have made you and will carry you; I will sustain you and rescue you.* [169]

---

168   Deuteronomy 7:9.
169   Isaiah 46:4.

Chapter 60

Thomas and Sarah built a house near Cleve with the doctor's office and clinic nearby. They moved to Harris with their five youngest children, leaving the three older children and Reid in their home in Denver.

Reid and two of the Stewart children were attending the university, and one was attending medical school. Chloe would return to Denver in a little over a year to attend the university. The four younger boys and Cleve's children would follow. Thomas planned to keep the townhouse for their use. He would use it also when he attended the semiannual board meeting of the hospital. An elderly couple was left to care for the townhouse and oversee the young people.

Thomas would retain ownership of the hospital in Denver, and his office in Harris would be a subclinic, giving him a steady income and easy access to supplies and equipment as he grew and improved the Harris Clinic. He wouldn't need to worry about supporting his family with his earnings in Harris.

Thomas had also contacted the home office of the mine. He and Cleve had negotiated a contract to provide medical care for the miners. Thomas didn't think the company's lawyers had read the fine print on the contract. As the mine's doctor, he would also be in charge of sanitation regulations and enforcement, along with housing safety inspection. Changes were coming, whether management knew it or not.

Angus came to town bringing his new wife. They had gotten married while Thomas and Sarah were still in Denver, making arrangements for their move to Harris. All the Stewarts had attended the wedding.

Angus and his new wife were now staying with Thomas and Sarah. Their new home, just down the road, would be completed soon.

New stables and a carriage house were being built for the entire family to use. The carriage house had a place not only for their horse-drawn carriage but for an automobile and a garage of tools and spare parts. Thomas had bought a motor carriage, and he would be able to tinker with the engine any time he wanted to. The motor carriage was being shipped and would arrive by train soon. It would be the first in Harris. Angus was talking about getting a motor car soon also.

Angus and Cleve had come to an agreement, and the construction of the power plant had begun on Britt land, at the far corner of the property, nearest to town.

Travis had stayed with Cleve until his new home was built. The small house, very similar to the place that had burned, was situated behind everyone else's. It was separated by a small field, the carriage house, stables, and pasture. It was pushed back, almost hidden in the trees. Thomas had insisted on modernization. Travis had insisted on isolation.

Cleve had plowed a field and was teaching Thomas's sons, William and Adam, to plow. Travis was teaching all of his grandsons how to farm. They had planted vegetables, and there would be enough for everyone in the family. There would also be enough, if the boys worked hard, Travis told them, to sell and make some pocket money. The boys would learn and care for the crops under Travis's watchful eye.

He was also teaching Sarah's boys how to care for and ride the horses. And he was taking all of his grandsons hunting and fishing.

Cleve and Jenny had discovered they would have another child soon, and Thomas would be there for the delivery. Jenny was happy about this. She had delivered the last two children with no doctor or midwife available. She had been attended only by a few experienced mothers in town.

Cleve had filed his Declaration of Intent to run for state representative in the upcoming election. Daniel Elshout was serving as his campaign manager.

In finishing the last article, Daniel had asked each of Travis's children, "How do you think your father was able to accomplish all he has done? How was he able to overcome the difficulties that were put before him throughout his life?"

All five of Travis's children, which included Thomas, had told the newspaper publisher that it was the presence of Jesus Christ in their father's life. Each told him how they saw God working in their father's life and how their Father God's love had brought their own father through each struggle. Each had told Elshout how their own father's love, and the love of God the Father, had influenced their lives.

Daniel had listened. Luke was the last of Travis's children that Daniel talked to. Luke had asked Daniel if he knew Jesus. They prayed together, and the newspaper man accepted Jesus as his own Lord and Savior. Cleve and Luke were now meeting with Daniel regularly, teaching him how to read his Bible and helping him understand what he was learning.

The newspaper articles had finished running in Harris and had been picked up by a newspaper at the state capital. It caused a buzz with everyone wondering, who was this Kansas marshal? Travis had been an occasional figure in Topeka and was known by many. Everyone in the state and federal offices knew his name and reputation. Near the end of the series, several people began to recognize who this story was about. Word spread, causing even more excitement as the book became available in stores.

The last article, and the last chapter of the book, told of Travis's faith in Jesus and how that faith was entwined with his daily life. It spoke of the Kansas marshal's walk of obedience to his Lord God and how God's provision had been powerfully displayed throughout his life. The article talked of Travis's prayer life, of his courage, and of how God had strengthened him when he was discouraged. It told of his faith being passed to his children, and to others, and it spoke of his hope to come.

The governor and several other federal and state officials from Topeka had come to Harris and awarded Travis the first ever State Commendation for Outstanding Achievement, given to a sworn law enforcement official. Travis had almost missed the ceremony. He and several of his grandsons had been fishing that morning, and the boys had assured their parents they would have their grandfather back in time for the ceremony. But the fish had been biting. They had all lost track of time. They had arrived home just in time for Luke and Thomas to hustle their father out the door and to the courthouse steps for the informal ceremony. The ceremony was followed by the town's street celebration in honor of their local hero. No one saw Travis slip away early. When Travis was called upon during the festivities to give an impromptu acceptance speech, he couldn't be found. The task fell to Cleve. Thomas found Travis later that night, sitting quietly in the dark, on his back porch with his dog.

The book was selling well, not just in Kansas but across the country; it was a refreshing change from the outlaw and gunfighter stories. Daniel was enjoying his new fame, now being recognized as a skilled writer.

The initial excitement and celebrity status caused by the book had ended, and things were settling down to a relaxing routine for Travis. He was thankful.

Travis's shoulder had calmed down too. There was still pain but at a level that could be tolerated. Thomas expected to see even more improvement over time. The former marshal's hand still bothered him, but without the severe shoulder pain, he was feeling much better. People had begun to see the old Travis, with his quiet smile and subtle joking, around town more often.

Travis had even begun helping Jake a few hours a day at the gun shop. Jake called Travis his "specialist in antique and older weapons." Some days Travis had work to do, but other days he did nothing but sit and drink coffee.

From his front porch, Travis could look out to the new stable and carriage house being built. He could look across the garden and open land toward his children's homes and was able to watch his grandchildren playing in the distance.

But now, Travis sat on his back porch, looking toward the trees and enjoying the late afternoon quiet. The evening shadow was long across the ground. Sitting in the back of the house, it seemed isolated. It felt more like his mountain than it did Kansas.

A back porch. That's something he didn't have at the old house. Nor indoor water, nor heat in every room. Travis had to admit he liked this. Electric lights would come soon, along with fans to cool the hot summer air. Fans, that's something he looked forward to.

As he sat on the back porch, he read the Gospel of John and the story of the prodigal son. Travis stopped to ask God to be with Naomi. She was his prodigal, and he still loved her.

God brought scripture to Travis's heart. It reassured him that Naomi would be faithful to God, and he would see his daughter again. *Start children off on the way they should go, and even when they are old they will not turn from it.* [170]

"Yes, Lord, thank you for that promise. You know where she is, and I know you are taking care of her. She will return one day, won't she?"

God spoke to him again, *Be still and know that I am God.*[171] Yes, God was God, and he was in control. Travis sat quietly, rocking, enjoying the presence and fellowship with his Lord.

Angus came through the house, calling his father, disturbing the calm.

"Dad! Hey! Dad! There you are. I've got a letter for you."

Angus handed Travis the letter. Travis opened the letter and looked to the end of the letter to see who it was from.

"Angus, it's from Naomi," Travis said excitedly. He turned around to look at his son, but Angus was gone.

Travis turned to the beginning of the letter and began to read.

---

170   Proverbs 22:6.
171   Psalm 46:10.

Dear Father,

I want to sincerely apologize for the way I have acted the last few years. I was wrong, and I ask your forgiveness.

Last month, I picked up a book that was lying on the ground. Someone had lost it. I saw that it was about a marshal in Kansas, so I took it home to read. I was shocked, to say the least, when I realized the story was about you. As I continued to read, I began missing you and realized how much you have always loved all your children, including me.

Father, I have made two horrible mistakes. One was turning from you, the other was marrying Sam. You sent me to Denver for an education, but I used it to escape what I believed was an awful homelife. I was wrong, there was nothing awful about being home with you. Awful was following Sam from city to city and never having a home of my own. Never knowing if Sam would find work or if we would eat that day.

Sam was in an accident and died a few months ago. I've been trying to make it on my own with my daughter, Ruth. I now want to ask again for your forgiveness and also ask, can Ruth and I come home? I love you and miss you.

The last letter I sent Angus told of Sam's death. Angus replied by sending me money to come home. He said that you miss me. I hope so because we're on our way back to you.

I love you,
Naomi

About the Author

Inspired by a home school project, Jean DeFreese Moore began the story of a mountain man for her granddaughter. But God had other plans for the stirring journey of Travis Britt. The story was shared with friends, and these friends encouraged her to continue sharing through publication. Finishing her fourth book, Travis's story comes to a close, but his legacy lives on through the lives of his children and grandchildren.

Moore says, "It's been a remarkable experience. God has shown me so much through the story and has been faithful to give me what was needed to tell the story of his servants to others."

Her first book, A Father's Love: Faith and Family, introduces us to Travis Britt, a simple man living in the mid-1800s. He is thrust into the Civil War and loses almost everything he holds dear. But following God, he is able to rebuild his life and leave the gift of faith to his family.

The second part of the story was inspired by a grandson who told her the story of Faith and Family needed to continue. His comment brought discussions of obedience to God and the inspiration for A Father's Love: Justice and Forgiveness. Travis's youngest son, Reid, is called by God to serve justice within a criminal organization that stretches across the Midwest.

That story continued with A Father's Love: Joyous Hope, as Travis, Reid, and the Britt family continue to follow God regardless of the trials in life. Reid teaches others that, despite disappointment and suffering, they are still able to experience God's love and joy.

The fourth book, A Father's Love: Sacrifice and Service, takes the family from a local conspiracy to the deadly Spanish flu pandemic and World War I. Travis returns to his roots, searching for something he feels is missing from his life. Instead, he finds his love for his family remains strong.

Jean DeFreese Moore received her bachelor of fine arts degree from Louisiana Tech University. She was one of many contributing artists to paint the entry hall mural at the Lincoln Parish Historical Museum housed in the Kidd-Davis House built in 1886. She also served several years as set designer for a dance academy and has taught art at a private Christian school. Most of her career was spent in Athletic Media Relations at her alma mater.

Jean is an accomplished artist. Her exhibit The Life of Jesus in Acrylic Pour was scheduled to be a part of the showing Risen: An Easter Celebration, which opened the same week COVID-19 shut down her city. The exhibit was quickly changed to an online exhibit and was viewed over 31,000 times on social media and 1,200 times in video form. The exhibit has now been shown, in full or in part, continually for over twenty-four months in four separate venues.

Moore enjoys painting landscapes, specifically mountains and trees. Most of Moore's paintings are done using the fluid pour method. Her paintings have been used on the cover of all four of her books.

Jean enjoys an active retirement as full-time grandmother to seven. Along with painting and writing, she is also involved in her church's children's ministry and active in her local Painting with Prayer group and the Community Men's Shed.